P9-DCY-786

MONSTER HUNTER MEMOIRS

GRUNGE

IN THIS SERIES by LARRY CORREIA

THE MONSTER HUNTER INTERNATIONAL SERIES:
Monster Hunter International • *Monster Hunter Vendetta* • *Monster Hunter Alpha* • *The Monster Hunters* (compilation) • *Monster Hunter Legion* • *Monster Hunter Nemesis*

MONSTER HUNTER MEMOIRS (WITH JOHN RINGO):
Grunge • *Sinners* (forthcoming)

MORE BAEN BOOKS by LARRY CORREIA

THE SAGA OF THE FORGOTTEN WARRIOR: *Son of the Black Sword*

THE GRIMNOIR CHRONICLES: *Hard Magic* • *Spellbound* • *Warbound*

WITH MIKE KUPARI: *Dead Six* • *Swords of Exodus*

MORE BAEN BOOKS by JOHN RINGO

BLACK TIDE RISING: *Under a Graveyard Sky* • *To Sail a Darkling Sea* • *Islands of Rage and Hope* • *Strands of Sorrow*

TROY RISING: *Live Free or Die* • *Citadel* • *The Hot Gate*

LEGACY OF THE ALDENATA: *A Hymn Before Battle* • *Gust Front* • *When the Devil Dances* • *Hell's Faire* • *The Hero* (with Michael Z. Williamson) • *Cally's War* (with Julie Cochrane) • *Watch on the Rhine* (with Tom Kratman) • *Sister Time* (with Julie Cochrane) • *Yellow Eyes* (with Tom Kratman) • *Honor of the Clan* (with Julie Cochrane) • *Eye of the Storm*

COUNCIL WARS: *There Will Be Dragons* • *Emerald Sea* • *Against the Tide* • *East of the Sun, West of the Moon*

INTO THE LOOKING GLASS: *Into the Looking Glass* • *Vorpal Blade* (with Travis S. Taylor) • *Manxome Foe* (with Travis S. Taylor) • *Claws that Catch* (with Travis S. Taylor)

EMPIRE OF MAN (WITH DAVID WEBER): *March Upcountry* and *March to the Sea* (collected in *Empire of Man*) • *March to the Stars* and *We Few* (collected in *Throne of Stars*)

SPECIAL CIRCUMSTANCES: *Princess of Wands* • *Queen of Wands*

PALADIN OF SHADOWS: *Ghost* • *Kildar* • *Choosers of the Slain* • *Unto the Breach* • *A Deeper Blue* • *Tiger by the Tail* (with Ryan Sear)

STANDALONE TITLES: *The Last Centurion* • *Citizens* (ed. with Brian M. Thomsen)

MONSTER HUNTER MEMOIRS

GRUNGE

Larry Correia &
John Ringo

MONSTER HUNTER MEMOIRS: GRUNGE

This is a work of fiction. All the characters and events portrayed in this book are fictional, and any resemblance to real people or incidents is purely coincidental.

A Baen Books Original

Baen Publishing Enterprises
P.O. Box 1403
Riverdale, NY 10471
www.baen.com

ISBN: 978-1-4767-8149-5

Cover art by Alan Pollack

First printing, August 2016

Distributed by Simon & Schuster
1230 Avenue of the Americas
New York, NY 10020

Library of Congress Cataloging-in-Publication Data

Names: Correia, Larry, author. | Ringo, John, 1963– author.
Title: Grunge / Larry Correia, John Ringo.
Description: Riverdale, NY : Baen, [2016] | Series: Monster hunter memoirs ; 1
Identifiers: LCCN 2016015143 | ISBN 9781476781495 (hardcover)
Subjects: LCSH: Secret societies—Fiction. | Monsters—Fiction. | Hunters—Fiction. | BISAC: FICTION / Fantasy / Urban Life. | FICTION / Fantasy / Contemporary. | FICTION / Action & Adventure. | GSAFD: Fantasy fiction.
Classification: LCC PS3603.O7723 G78 2016 | DDC 813/.6—dc23 LC record available at https://lccn.loc.gov/2016015143

10 9 8 7 6 5 4 3 2 1

Pages by Joy Freeman (www.pagesbyjoy.com)
Printed in the United States of America

As always

For Captain Tamara Long, USAF

Born: May 12, 1979

Died: March 23, 2003, Afghanistan

You fly with the angels now.

And to my wife, Miriam, for putting up with me talking about this non-stop during the birthday party she'd spent weeks organizing.

FOREWORD

A few years back a new author by the name of Larry Correia started writing with Baen. I heard about him quickly. Many of my readers were talking nonstop about his Monster Hunter International series. I sort of ignored it. I used to be a compulsive reader. These days, for various reasons, I don't read much. I don't want to steal good lines, which I've done accidentally from time to time. I find most reading less interesting than I did before becoming a full-time author. Very few people (some of the top Baen writers excepted) write well enough to keep me engaged. I can think of and write stories better than ninety percent of the published stuff out there. The last point being that the part of me that used to need to be filled with "story" is these days mostly filled with my "story." It's what I *do*. Just say I read a lot more nonfiction than fiction these days.

But I was in one of those moods and someone suggested, again, *Monster Hunter International*. Larry had kindly given me a book as a freebie so I picked it up, went "Huh, let's hope it's any good..."

And put it down the next day and went and found the other four. And binge-read for a week. (They're thick books compared to this one.) And really enjoyed myself. And liked the universe. What's not to like about big guns fighting big monsters with lots of big booms?

As the main character says in a later book: "Who *doesn't* carry a light antitank weapon in their trunk?" That's the kind of character I think we can all get our heads around.

And as is my wont, as long-term readers know, my brain went far afield. What was it like back in the eighties for Monster Hunters? What were the similarities? What were the differences? Lot less tech for one thing... Hmmm... And then I crawled into a hole of caffeine, sleep deprivation and nicotine and...

At a certain point, I *had* to write it. As with earlier "new" universes, it was an imperative need. I had other things I should write. This was screaming at me: "WRITE ME! WRITE ME!"

I had no idea if Larry or my publisher, Toni Weisskopf, would approve. Generally Toni will publish my grocery list. I make Baen a fair shekel on my weakest series. (Which, by the way, is probably the competing Special Circumstances series.) Would they be okay with it?

Toni loved the universe and was ecstatic to hear I wanted to write in it. More money! (*Ka-ching!*) More good stories! (Toni's both a professional businesswoman with a bottom line to make and a long-term fan of SF/F. She likes both.)

Larry used to be an *accountant*. This was making money for almost no work. And he had read my stuff and trusted I'd write it well. His only gripe was that I churned out two books in *less than a month* (what part of "WRITE ME! WRITE ME!" was unclear?) and now he had to make sure they were both compatible to the universe. If I kept up at this rate, which I won't, he'd be doing nothing but editing for the rest of his life! And he had miniatures to paint!

Hope you enjoy.

—John Ringo

This was all kind of a surprise to me, but when a really successful writer comes along and says, "I'd love to write something set in your world. I've already written a couple books of a spin-off series; want to publish them?" You say yes.

It is tough to let somebody else play in your sandbox, but I checked it out. Happily, *Grunge* was a good book, and I had a lot of fun reading it. But there was still a whole lot of world-building John didn't know about, and couldn't have known, because I'd not revealed it anywhere yet (and as the regular MH fans have seen,

I plan this stuff out far in advance). While reading the original manuscript, I inserted about two hundred comments about how the Monster Hunter universe worked, what had *really* happened in the past, what bits of lore would or would not fit, technical bits, and that sort of thing. He said, "why don't you just change all that?" And that's when this project turned into a collaboration.

I'm a writer, not an editor (seriously, much respect to editors, that's a tough job) and it took me longer to edit this than it took John to write it, so his idea of "almost no work" differs a little from mine. But I tried hard to change as little as possible to keep everything in line with the rest of the MHI universe and still remain true to John's original story in his original voice. Though there were a few bits that . . . well, I'll just say, my kids read these books, John. Those scenes can live on as apocrypha.

I hope you guys like it.

—Larry Correia

PROLOGUE

"Oh, that's a lot of spiders," Phil muttered as the Ma Deuce opened up.

We'd expected a lot of spiders. Given the number of missing "homeless" (you're not supposed to call them bums anymore) there had to be a major nest. Hell, we were expecting a shelob. What we hadn't expected was a tidal wave. The long, broad corridor was packed with a mass of writhing eight-limbed, eight-eyed, furry, horrible, fang-dripping, brown, couch-sized-body arachnids that covered not just the floors but the walls and the ceilings.

I opened up with my Uzi, killing as fast as I could fire and reload. I had my shotgun slung in case it got to close work, which it looked like it would, and a Barrett M82 at my feet if that became necessary.

It was nearly a hundred yards to the curve and it seemed like that wave covered the distance in an instant. Six of us were firing, seven if you counted Roy feeding rounds into the Ma Deuce, and it just was not stopping them. We really should have set up the Pig as well. They were falling off the ceilings and walls and dropping on the floor but there was just a never-ending tide of the damned things. A bunch of the wounded were shaking off the fire and the aftereffects of ethanol poisoning and clambering back to their furry feet.

"Blow the claymores!" Roy screamed as the wave passed the

last claymore position. If too many got inside the final protective line . . . Well, you don't recover from most giant spider bites. They'll just stun you with their venom, so they can take you back to their nest and drink you later. But the flesh dissolving enzyme they use to turn you into drinkable chow gets mixed into the paralytic agent. So you just dissolve slower. If you're lucky you might just lose an arm or a leg if they get you there. If you're lucky. Anywhere on the torso it's just a long, slow, agonizing process of doctors trying very hard and failing to save your life as you scream in agony and beg them to just kill you. Which they won't, the bastards.

"Not till the shelob's on the trap," Brad said, calmly.

As if he'd summoned the damned thing, the shelob came around the corner.

I knew I had to concentrate on the closing offspring but the shelob sort of caught everyone's attention. At that point as a Monster Hunter, I thought not much could shake me but I'll admit I sort of peed myself a little bit. We'd gotten all this stuff—claymores, C4, Ma Deuce, hundreds of fifty-cal rounds and a shitload of other guns and ammo—to the firing point by Jesse backing a U-Haul truck down the brick-lined, arched tunnel high and wide enough it wasn't even a real bother. We'd driven our cars down the old maintenance tunnel for the now defunct Portland cistern that was the presumed nest of the shelob and her offspring. You couldn't quite get a tractor trailer down the tunnel, but it was close.

The shelob was slithering down the tunnel with its legs squashed to either side of its elephant-sized body and sort of flattened out to fit.

It was that fricking big. All hair and spidery eyes and poison-dripping fangs long enough to use as daggers if you had the courage and could, you know, manage to kill it.

"Fuck me!" Louis screamed, redirecting all the Ma Deuce fire at the enormous arachnid.

"Blow it!" Roy screamed. "For God's sake!"

"Wait for it," Brad said, still calm. He was laying down fire with an M16 and I wondered if maybe I should have gone with that Mattel crap for once. Rifle rounds, even little 5.56 ones, would have been nice about now. "Waaait . . ."

The shelob finally slithered past the bright yellow paint on the walls that marked the trap. She was about to get a C4 enema while claymores shredded her loathsome offspring and ended the threat to Portland's underground.

We'd spent hours setting up the trap. Just back from the yellow lines on the walls was a pile of C4. C4 was one and a half times the same power as TNT. It was enough to toss a semi-truck into the air. It was going to shred the shelob, guaranteed. The firing circuit led to that pile of cataclysm, then spread out. Multiple lines of det cord led to two hundred claymore directional mines in a multipoint daisy chain. They were securely anchored to the floors and walls and many of them were angled up, anticipating our unwanted visitors on the ceiling. And it wasn't a single daisy chain. There were lines between sets, extra lines within sets. Nothing was going to stop each and every one going off. We were totally ready.

"NOW!" Brad bellowed.

"Bye bye, you arachnid prick," Phil said, hitting the contact for the electronic line on the detonator. He hit it again. "Detonation fail! Going chemical!"

All of our fire, or possibly the thousands of arachnid legs, had somehow cut the wire leading to the electronic detonator on the C4. But Phillip Jimenez was a former Army engineer and knew all about redundancy to firing circuits in combat. Besides the electrical circuit, there was a "chemical" circuit consisting of a fuse igniter which led to a short fuse, then another section of det cord. Slightly slower than electrical but sure enough guaranteed.

The fuse igniter only took a second to hit the detonator but a second was a long time with hundreds of fucking spiders headed towards your position. Not to mention big momma. By the time it hit I'd switched to my Winchester pump and was belting out 12-gauge on spiders that were getting close enough the falling ones were a hazard.

The cord detonated with a *crack* that could be heard even over our fire. But the trap failed to detonate. Again.

"Detonation fail!" Phil bellowed. Again.

"What the fuck do we do now?" Roy screamed. He'd switched to his pump, covering Louis while twitching, writhing spiders poured off the ceiling like a shit-brown waterfall.

You might be wondering how I got myself in this particular predicament.

My name (which I hate) is Oliver Chadwick Gardenier. My friends call me Chad or Iron Hand.

This is my job. I'm a Monster Hunter.

Note:

Recently my buddy Albert has been trying to organize the archives. It's a pretty big job, but he seems to like it. It would probably be easier if we didn't keep trashing the place. The other day Albert found this old stack of memoirs that had fallen behind a shelf, and judging from the dust and damage, they'd been lost there since the fire set during the Christmas party. When Albert saw that I was mentioned, he brought them to me to read.

I couldn't believe my eyes. I didn't know that Chad had written any of this down.

Reading this brought back a lot of memories.

What can I say about Chad? He was tough. You couldn't find anybody braver. But mostly he was smart to a fault, and sometimes too clever for his own good. He was cocky, but he earned it. Some of the things in these memoirs... Most of the things in here I wasn't around for, and for the rest, well, Chad could be a bit prone to exaggeration, an unreliable narrator I guess you could call it. But he really was gifted, and by that, I mean like really *gifted. The monster languages he talks about? That's legit. He's still the only person we've had who managed to learn those. The fights and some of the stunts he pulled? He really was that nuts. Now, with the ladies? I'll say we had a bit of a philosophical difference about his outlook on life and leave it at that.*

These memoirs are a great find. We can learn a lot from the Hunters that came before us, and man, Chad was involved in some crazy *stuff.*

Chad was one of the best Hunters we ever had. He's not just another silver plaque on the wall. He was my friend.

Milo Ivan Anderson
Monster Hunter International
Cazador, Alabama

CHAPTER 1

The other day I was dealing with a newbie who was telling me his tale of woe about how he got into hunting. Mother had been bitten by a zombie and rose. He had to kill her with a shotgun. My response was:

"Nothing says 'I love you' like double-aught to the face."

He looked really shocked and hurt. One of the reasons to write these memoirs is to put that, yeah, seriously cold reply in perspective. 'Cause it's true and I meant it from the heart.

I've been writing these memoirs as diaries and notes for a while so they're going to be choppy. And I'm not sure how much to write about myself. Earl says we learn about hunting from the Hunters that came before us. I've read some of those old diaries and you really don't understand the person very well. Just what happened with very little perspective.

So I'll give you as much as I've learned about hunting and hopefully whoever reads this, if anyone bothers, it'll help you out sometime. And since family shit comes into it from time to time you're going to have to learn about my fucked up family. So here goes.

My mom and dad are academics. I've met some good academics over the years. And I think that academics are important. Research really does make the world a better place. But I fucking hate my family. I really, really do. The Good Book says that you should honor your father and mother. It didn't anticipate my mother and father.

Dad's a professor of philosophy. He finally settled down to a steady gig at the University of Kansas since his alma mater, Harvard, knew better than to hire his philandering ass. I've come to the conclusion that modern philosophy is entirely devoted to coming up with new excuses for cheating on your wife. I really shouldn't bitch about my dad. God knows the apple didn't fall far from the tree there. But at least I don't try to cloak my aggressive womanizing in faux philosophy. I figure my life's bound to be short. I don't want to waste any time and I'm philosophically against leaving behind a young widow and kids who can't even know I was a hero. Hit and run is the only reasonable choice for a Monster Hunter, in my opinion.

But the excuses finally ran out around the time I was eight. When I was ten, and whining about them getting back together, Mom gave me a way-too-age-inappropriate explanation of what it was like to walk in on your husband in bed with not one but *three* coeds and the suggestion that she join in.

The divorce was around the time I was holding up a homemade sign, made by me under my mother's tutelage, reading "Give Peace a Chance!" As everyone in the Vietnam antiwar rally was chanting, "*What do we want? Peace! When do we want it? Now!*" I was chanting "*What do we want? Ice cream! When do we want it . . . ?*" I hated those rallies. Fucking unwashed hippies talking about the importance of Lenin and Marx while all I wanted was for my mom to bother fixing me a bologna sandwich. But no! What God-damned "good for you" shit was it this week?

My mother was a professor of anthropology and mythological studies. It turns out she could have been a primo source of information on monsters. I probably could have asked questions along the lines of "Okay, but how do you *kill* a lamia?" But that's getting ahead of myself.

Then there's my fucking brother, Thornton. Thornton, who had no problems with his stupid name, was the apple of my peace-loving mommy's eye. That's because the vicious prick kept his violent tendencies behind her back. My mom did not have eyes in the back of her head but I frequently had two black and blue ones. Thornton was as vicious a bully as you'd ever care to find. He was always big for his age, never tired of finding victims—me for choice—and, like Dad, always had an excuse. Mom knew damned well how disgusting the bastard was but she had that incredible ability found in so many minds like hers to simply ignore all the evidence in favor of her personal view of the world. And in her personal view of the world, Thornton Ainsley Gardenier could do no wrong. Thornton got straight As. Thornton's goal was to be an academic just like Mom and Dad. Thornton was four years older than I was and firmly believed I needed a good kidney punch every day of my existence.

You'd think I'd enjoy killing him but I really didn't.

Oliver Chadwick Gardenier, on the other hand, could do no right. Every kid at some point wants to please his mother but I gave up real young. Maybe it was trying and failing to get either parent to notice that I was being used as a punching bag by the apple of their eye on a daily basis. Maybe it was when I came home from kindergarten with a note that said I was "too advanced." I was already reading at college level and doing algebra, and was making the other kids look bad. And my parents sat me down and told me I needed to be "socially appropriate." God, Mom hated herself for that lecture in later years. I threw it in her face with every subsequent report card showing straight Cs.

Yes, I got straight Cs, with very few exceptions, all the way through school. Got any idea how hard that is? When you'd taught yourself Aramaic at the age of nine? Getting straight As is easy. All you have to do is a little studying and get all the answers right. Graduating every single paper and test, *precisely*, so as to get *exactly* a C? Especially papers. You gotta be able to read your teacher's mind to get a C on every single paper.

But I was duly centered in my social peer group. Just like mommy said I should be. Fuck you, Mom, you monster-loving bitch.

She forced me to take violin lessons. It turned out that it came naturally to me. I was a virtuoso. This would come in handy later on in life. When Mom was around, I played badly on purpose.

There are lots of books and memoirs about the poor misunderstood smart kid surrounded by dumb people. I suppose I was one of those (as an IQ test later proved) but it was really more the "poor misunderstood kid who just wants to be normal." I wanted to play football. "Too violent." I got scolded and a three-day grounding for playing cops and robbers. "How dare I support the fascist prison state?" Then there was the time I brought home papers for JROTC and managed by the tiniest of straws to fail to give my mother a stroke. It was close. God, it was sooo close. On the other hand, that attempt to kill my mother led to the best times of my life and a new family who finally understood me.

The summer when I was twelve I rode my bike five miles to a barber's on the other side of town 'cause I'd asked one kid, who was bitching about it, where he got his hair cut. The barber had been a soldier once, turned out he was airborne back in World War II, and had cut military hair for years at Fort Knox. I walked in with shiny blond hair down to my ass, still with some of my baby curls, and climbed into a chair.

"Sir, I hate to use foul language. My mother is a fucking hippy bitch. And I am sick and tired of this God-damned hippy hair. Would you please cut it *all* off? I promise not to tell."

"Son," he said, breaking out his clippers, "parents, as with children, are a cross we all must bear. But as long as she does not discover the source of your haircut, we have a deal. And it's free."

When my mother came home from another of her damned committee meetings, which meant I had to scrounge as per usual, I was waiting by the door sporting a high and tight with my formerly ass-length hair in one hand.

"Here!" I said, gleefully. "You can make a wig out of it!"

Since New Orleans I've shaved my head bald. Not that it matters to my mother anymore. We haven't spoken since Thornton's funeral nor do I ever intend to see her again.

About that time, my mom arranged for a series of psychological and learning tests through one of her "close personal friends" at the University of Kentucky. (Did I mention Mom eventually went gay?) I had become "obsessively violent" (I really wanted to play football), "sexually dangerous" (I was dating a seventh-grade cheerleader) and had "clear learning disabilities" (perfect straight-C average).

Between bouts of testing I was subjected to "therapy" which consisted primarily of ongoing militant feminists' rants about the evil male patriarchy. The tests came back that I was:

Borderline paranoid schizophrenic, check; oppositionally defiant, at least with idiots and bitches like my parents and their friends (well, except for some of my dad's "close personal friends" who even at the age of twelve I tried like hell to pick up); obsessive heterosexual (that means so straight you can use me to adjust lasers); and, oh yeah, that IQ test?

My bastard brother had crowed like mad when he'd tested as a 136 IQ and immediately joined MENSA. My parents were both high IQ academics, proud MENSA members with letters after their name and papers to their credit. I was the official family moron.

It was like that line in *The Princess Bride*.

"Have you ever heard of Aristotle? Socrates? Morons!"

Yeah. It was like that. I'd decided to just see if I was as smart as I thought I was and blasted through the test full bore.

Einstein would have gone "Whoa!"

"Figures," I said when shown the results.

"How can you have *this* IQ and get straight *Cs*?" my mom shouted at me.

"Got any idea how hard it is to get *straight* Cs?" I asked. "I mean, a *perfect* C average? You said I needed to be 'socially appropriate' in my academics all the way back in kindergarten and what's more '*appropriate*' than absolutely in the middle of the pack?"

I'd carefully kept from her that I was already reading some of her research material, even the stuff in ancient languages. I'd figured out Latin at six, Greek at seven and Aramaic by the time I was nine. By twelve I was working on Hindi and Hittite, having already mastered Coptic and hieroglyphs.

On the JROTC thing: When I started high school, I tried every gambit to get into "normal" stuff. My mother was, in general, against all competitive sports—at least if it was a "go/no-go" situation. Football? Too violent. Baseball? Supports the concept of linear thinking. (Seriously.) She was fine with soccer which was also "go/no-go." See the above about being able to justify anything that fit her world view. Soccer was European and thus good. So, I tried out for soccer. I'm naturally athletic, fast as hell and had been kicking a soccer ball around since I was a kid, since soccer was "appropriate." The coach moved me straight to varsity forward. Mom even came out for the first game. I scored both goals and she happily congratulated me for I think the first time in my life.

I quit immediately. Damned if I was going to do anything my mother *supported*. There *had* to be something wrong with it. Which there is. Soccer is for pussies.

But giving her the JROTC papers was mostly an exercise in seeing if I could really get her to stroke out. She, recognizing the gambit for what it was, tore the papers up in front of me, threw them in my face and then slapped me, not for the first time. She couldn't hit nearly as hard as Thornton, who, thank God, was safely in Stanford by that time, so I just took it, per normal, and looked at her.

"That all you got?" I asked. "You hit like a girl. And what about 'violence never settles anything'?"

Oh, I really loved when I started getting smart and knowledgeable enough to have that argument with my "peace-loving" mommy.

"What about Hitler? Was using violence against Hitler okay? What about the Viet Cong fighting the evil right-wing tyranny of the South Vietnamese government? They used all sorts of violence. Was that okay?" Later, as my reading expanded, it was "Violence seemed to settle the question of Rome versus Carthage well enough. *Cartago delenda est*, right?" Which would start a lecture on "How can you discuss Rome and Carthage in depth and get a C in Ancient History?"

Pro-tip: If you've got that teacher who hates smart kids, use all the *correct* names of pharaohs on the paper. 'Cause those kinds of teachers never know how stuff *should* be spelled. Khufu instead of Cheops. Things like that. Which are all "wrong" from their perspective. I wrote a paper in seventh grade Social Studies that I got an F on. I later turned in the same paper, word for word, with more annotations and citations, in a senior level college Egyptian History course. Got an A.

I never ever used any form of violence against my mother. I just cannot raise my hand to a lady. Not that my mother was ever much of a lady. But the reverse was not the case. Apparently violence is all good when it's getting your mad out at your "inappropriate" son. Or if you're a good commie killing evil fascists. Or if you're the Weather Underground. Et cetera.

Anything to fit the world view.

Don't get me wrong. I've found God since those days and I still have an issue with Christians and Catholics (including some priests of my experience) who think that Jesus is going to keep fags, prostitutes and people who sleep around out of Heaven. God would have before Jesus. Sure. Definitely. And the Old Testament isn't entirely to fill page count. But basing all your so-called Christianity on Prophets, Isaiah and St. Paul is cherry picking like mad. It's adjusting reality to fit your world view.

Jesus is when God started to realize he'd created something weirder than even He realized and stopped having such a mad-on at us.

I think in the old days He gave a lot of orders He didn't realize weren't ever going to be perfectly obeyed by ninety percent of humanity. Since He made us in His image, I suspect after Jesus died for our sins, the Savior reported in how seriously messed up we all were and why. I mean, puberty! Puberty for God's sake! You gave us *puberty*! And you think masturbation is *our* fault? We don't even know what it *is* the first few times! "Don't commit the sin of Onan." "What *is* the sin of Onan?" "To spill your seed upon the ground." "What if I'm laying down grass seed?" "Not that kind of seed." "What kind of seed then?" "Never mind."

After Jesus died for our sins and carried up the full download of just how messed up it was to be stuck in a human body, God must have gone "Well, Me, I guess We've gotta forgive the poor saps." These days I think you've gotta seriously mess up to get Hell. I've even got some supporting evidence.

My brother is probably in Hell and I'm sort of comfortable with that even if I'm still wrestling with how he got there. Maybe I should change my name to Cain.

Back to JROTC. I'd gotten the papers from the assistant JROTC instructor, Mr. Herman J. Brentwood. He also taught shop and, of all things, chemistry. I had his shop class (another thing to poke a sharp stick in my mother's eye, just like as a kid I used to go around jumping up and down on every crack I could find in the sidewalk) and had picked them up there.

The next day he asked me about them.

"Did you get the papers signed?" he asked as I was trying not to cut my fingers off with a jigsaw.

"No, sir," I said. I was polite just to piss off my mom. She hated it when I said "sir" and "ma'am" since they were "antiquated social constructs of the dominant patriarchy." Besides, Mr. Brentwood was one of those people you just automatically tended to say "sir" to and if you didn't you regretted it. "My mother does not approve of the military. I knew that. Truthfully, sir, I got them as much to infuriate her as to join."

"The Good Book says that you should honor your father and mother, son," Mr. Brentwood said. There might have been a Supreme Court ruling that prayer in school was banned. But that sort of statement wasn't out of place in Lexington, Kentucky, in 1977.

"Sir, with respect, you don't know my father and mother," I said, carefully. "I cut my hair when I was twelve to get back at her. It was down to my butt." I carefully did not say *ass*. "She was upset about that and thought it was great when my older brother started smoking dope. With her and her friends. She's a member of the American Communist Party, an antiwar activist at least if it's fighting commies, commies murdering people to support the downtrodden is all good. And my dad, who is a professor in Kansas, has never found a coed he wasn't willing to... engage in carnal knowledge with, sir. He's the kind of professor a cute girl can always get a good grade from for... sexual stuff, sir. Sir, I'm just counting the days until I can get out of hell."

"Any idea what you're going to do with your life, son?" Mr. Brentwood asked.

"So far, all I've got is what I'm *not* going to do with my life, sir. Which is anything that my parents approve of."

Which was how I found new parents.

My mom and I were barely on speaking terms at that point and I had already found other places to be most of the time. I had friends, and their parents were often cool with couch-crashing. But the Brentwoods' really became my new home and I finally found a mother and father I could relate to.

Mr. Brentwood looked like a straight-up stereotype. He'd joined the Marines in 1942, right after Pearl Harbor, gotten put in the infantry and proceeded to slog his way across the Pacific. When the War was over he went home, married his high school sweetheart, went to school on the GI bill and after spending some time working in the chemical industry he got a job as a teacher at Central High School and had been a fixture there ever since.

He still wore a high and tight and could still fit in his WWII uniforms.

Mrs. Martha Anne Brentwood had raised four children and had "empty nest syndrome" something fierce. From what I got from their kids, who still dropped by frequently, she'd always been the Kool-Aid mom, meaning theirs was the house all the neighborhood kids frequented. She cooked a full dinner every night. My mother considered cooking to be a relic of the evil patriarchy and also was a just *horrible* cook. My mother *not* cooking was probably the only thing she ever did to make the world a better place.

Not so Mrs. Brentwood. It was all "Southern Style," heavy on fried, but she used more original herbs and spices than the Colonel could count. After long years of inedible health food and badly cooked Indian food or some similar... fecal matter, I just seriously pigged out. (Not that good Indian food is bad food. I've gotten to be pretty serious about good ethnic food. My mother burned water.)

I miss Mrs. Brentwood's cooking. They're still around but I'm just so fricking busy these days.

Violating virtually every rule in the book, Mr. Brentwood introduced me to shooting and gunsmithing without my mom's consent or, fortunately, knowledge. He had a shop in his basement that we spent many an hour in working on molds, reloading and so on and so forth. The man is a virtual encyclopedia of guns and remains someone I call when I'm stuck on something. He introduced me to both the M1 Garand, his weapon of choice, and the Thompson, an unusable beast of a weapon in my opinion.

But he wasn't just the stereotype former Marine. One incident during the battle of Tarawa had changed his view of the world. You see, he was smart and had a flexible mind. When something violated his world view, he didn't simply dismiss it.

Given what this memoir is supposed to be about you may be thinking that's monsters. As far as I know, and I've delicately sounded him out, Mr. Brentwood has never encountered any of the stuff I now kill for a living. What he did encounter on Tarawa was a banzai attack. Not his first, but the first where he came face to face, bayonet to sword, with a Jap officer. And lost.

Fortunately, his platoon leader shot the officer in the chest with his .45 before the backstroke would have ended my future foster father's life. But it got Mr. Brentwood thinking. The platoon leader, correctly, collected the sword as a souvenir and sent it home. (His kill, his souvenir.) Later, Sergeant Brentwood managed to get his hand on one as well. And still later found someone who knew something about them. And slowly became something of an unrecognized expert on Japanese katanas.

"Anything lethal is worth paying attention to" was his reasoning.

He studied them, bought them, sold them, traded them and even had made a couple using more or less traditional techniques. In the 1950s, studying kendo was considered beyond odd, right up there with crazy. He didn't care. "Anything lethal is worth paying attention to." He learned Japanese specifically to understand bushido better. He didn't buy into all of it, and seriously hated the Japanese themselves, but he was something of an American "sword saint." He can, to this day, absolutely brutalize me at kendo and I've used kendo in real action against major monsters. I cut the head off a two-hundred-year-old Greater vampire in action. Not "Stake, chop" but "Slash, slash, slash, off with the head." (And one leg and an arm.) And that old man can *still* kick my ass.

Pro-tip: Inside a certain distance, generally about twenty feet, a blade of some sort is generally better than a gun. There are arguments for a stubby at that range. But a blade is generally better. And there's no better blade than a katana in my opinion. But they don't call me Iron Hand (圧制) for no reason.

Since I finally had a father figure who wasn't, in my opinion, bug-shit crazy, I naturally had to follow in his footsteps. When he realized that I'd learned kanji in about two months' not particularly hard study, it sort of pissed him off.

"Chad," as he called me. "Next year, you are taking my chemistry course. And if you get anything other than an A, you're never coming over for dinner again."

So next year I took high school chemistry and physics in the same semester. Perfect A in chemistry.

You guessed it. Perfect F in physics.

Gotta maintain that C average.

I mean, I *learned* the physics. I even liked it. I've applied it repeatedly over the years. Especially $F = ma$.

But gotta maintain that C average.

I dated a lot. I hardly ever studied. (Including chemistry.) I finally got permission to do track and field. That took up some time. I spent most of my evenings (and eventually nights) at the Brentwoods'. It wasn't like my mom cared. She'd repeatedly noted that she'd considered aborting me since I wasn't "planned" and in retrospect had made the wrong decision. Getting me out of her life was as much her goal as mine. Feel the love.

I mowed lawns starting from about thirteen. I got slightly better jobs working mostly in construction when I turned sixteen.

Generally day labor but it paid better than mowing lawns. I kept focusing on shop versus college prep. Through Mr. Brentwood, I got a part-time job as a mechanic when I turned seventeen and that was great. Good money and it gave me a chance to pick up a car cheap and get it fixed up the way I liked it. It was a 1976 Cutlass Supreme that was definitely a Monday car.

In those days, really bad vehicles were by hoary adage built on Mondays and Fridays. Monday 'cause all the workers were hung over and Friday 'cause all the senior people had called in sick or something and the assembly line was all fucked up.

Bottom line, *everything* was wrong with this car, which was why I got it cheap. Classic example of the height of American automotive manufacturing in the 1970s. The only thing that wasn't badly put together was the Delta 88 engine which absolutely screamed. The tranny leaked like a sieve. The rear differential sounded like a rock crusher. The shocks were shot and it was barely three years old. The headliner was already sagging. The underbody was rusting and it had supposedly been rust-proofed at the factory. The ugly green paint job was flaking off.

I put sooo much work into Honeybear it was just silly. I don't think, with the exception of the engine, at this point there is one original part. And I've rebuilt the engine twice. On the other hand, I'm still driving her.

Kendo, shooting, track and field, dating, fixing up Honeybear to better-than-new condition. There were quite a few girls in that school who were, in the parlance of the time, "easy." It was just past the Sexual Revolution into the Sexual Evolution and pre-AIDs. Good times. And, yep, had at least a short fling with most of them. That was one area where the apple did not fall far from the tree.

Sing it with me: "Those were the best days of our lives..." I'm one of those people who fucking *loved* high school. Probably the only hard part was that most of my friends, and dates, really *were* dumb as a stump. I occasionally had to hang out with the nerds just to have something resembling intelligent conversation. Which in those days meant playing the occasional D&D game.

That came in surprisingly useful later in life. I'm pretty sure that Gary Gygax knew people, if you know what I mean.

I was born December 6th, 1962. Since celebrating birthdays, or any other similar holiday, was an antiquated notion of the social construct, the first real birthday party I had was when the

Brentwoods threw one for me and my pals when I turned fifteen. On December 7th, 1980, one day after my eighteenth birthday, and the anniversary of those crafty Japs bombing Pearl Harbor, I went down to a strip mall by the old post office and entered the office of the Marine recruiter.

"Good afternoon, Staff Sergeant," I said in my most polite voice. I was wearing a good, clean, carefully creased, button-down white shirt, carefully creased black dress slacks and a high and tight. "I would like to join the Marine Corps."

There were things I knew about joining the Corps that most recruits didn't really think about. One of them was the ASVAB, the Armed Services Vocational Aptitude Battery. It is, still, one of the best vocational tests on the face of the planet. If you don't try to futz with it, it will point you in the correct direction in terms of your usefulness in the military as well as a job you're going to more or less enjoy. (In general.)

But the thing is, if I pushed it all the way, I'd end up doing signal intercept or some such shit. I wasn't interested in listening to scritches, beeps and whistles that might be a signal for the rest of my life. That's probably where I would have maximally supported the Marine force, yeah, but I was joining the Marines to kill commies... I wanted to be infantry.

So I got a perfect C.

Man, I studied for that fucker. There were books and books you could find about the ASVAB. I analyzed it, spindled it, folded it and mutilated it. I knew exactly the scores and answers that would make me perfect machine-gun fodder and just above perfect cook.

When I walked back into the recruiting office to talk to the staff sergeant, the first words out of his mouth were:

"Son. Have you ever thought about the infantry...?"

I kept from jumping for joy and shouting *"Yes! Fucking nailed it!"*

I graduated June 6th, 1981, with a vo-tech diploma. My mother didn't attend my graduation but the Brentwoods did. Mr. Brentwood drove me to the MEPS station on June 19th. I raised my right hand and swore to defend the Constitution of the United States against all enemies foreign and domestic. They didn't mention supernatural, oddly enough. I did half wonder if it gave me license to kill my mom. And I was in the Marines.

From the first night I spent at the Brentwoods', Mr. Brentwood had ensured that I understood the standards expected of me if I was going to stay at their house. I'd always been the neat freak in my parents' house. Mr. and Mrs. Brentwood just dialed it in a bit. Then there was the shooting training and generally "Marineness" of the whole existence.

Bottom line, with a couple of exceptions, I more or less ghosted boot camp.

Don't get me wrong. Marine boot camp was and is hard as shit. And the sand fleas at Parris Island have to be experienced to be understood. But...

The first day we were being introduced to the M-16 rifle I made one of my minor errors. The instructor was detailing how to fieldstrip the weapon. We were sitting cross-legged in a circle. I was paying strict attention to his guidance. Such strict attention that I didn't even notice my hands were, instinctively, stripping the weapon down as he spoke. The instructor noticed and stormed over.

"On your feet, Recruit!"

"Sir, yes, sir!" I screamed, popping to attention.

"What the hell do you think you're doing, Recruit?"

"Sir, paying strict attention to your guidance, sir!"

"Was my guidance to begin stripping your weapon, Recruit?"

"Sir, no, sir!"

"Why is your weapon stripped, Recruit?"

I looked down and sort of blanched.

"Uhhhh...*No excuse, sir! I just...No excuse, sir!"*

The instructor at that point apparently noticed that not only was the weapon stripped down to disassembly of the bolt, it was neatly laid out. And he'd probably half noticed that I had, in fact, been watching him carefully the whole time.

"You stripped it without looking, didn't you?" he asked in a much more casual voice.

"Sir..." I said, not sure what to say.

"You go to ROT-see or something, Recruit?"

"Sir, no, sir!" I said. I knew I had to say something. "My foster father was a World War II Marine, sir. Sergeant Herman J. Brentwood, sir. I just...When I had the weapon and it was stripping weapons, sir...Sir, no excuse, sir."

"Put it back together?" the drill instructor asked, again almost casually.

"Sir, yes, sir!"

"Blindfolded?"

I took a chance. "Blindfolded in a hurricane while making love to a beautiful woman, sir!"

He slowly reached into his pocket and pulled out a stopwatch.

"Take a cross-legged position, Recruit," the drill instructor said. "If you do it to time, with your eyes closed, I'll let you off on this one."

"Sir, yes, sir!"

I assembled it in half the required time and tried *never* to stand out again.

But...then there was a Marine Corps tradition.

When I joined up, I tried to get the Brentwoods as my next of kin. No such luck. I had family. I therefore *had* to list my damned mother as next of kin. Which meant in boot camp, I had to write my mother a letter once per week.

"*Dear Mother:*

"*I am here at Marine Corps boot camp in Parris Island and loving every minute of it. Today's training was on the proper method of bayoneting babies...*"

I don't know why I even bothered. A few weeks later I received the letter back with "Return to Sender."

This prompted an inquiry from the same drill instructor who had been the instructor for assembly and disassembly of the M-16. This inquiry being full-on head tilt on the nose with the brim.

"I thought your foster father was a Marine, Recruit!"

"Unofficial foster father, sir! My mother is a member of the Communist Party and used to drag me to her God-damned Vietnam War peace marches, sir! When she found out I was joining the Marines, she asked how I could become a babykiller, sir! I answered 'babies don't dodge, so it's easy,' sir!"

One of the more junior drill instructors was standing by and turned away with a coughing fit at that one.

"Do you have an unofficial foster *mother*, Recruit?" the drill instructor barked.

"Sir, yes, sir!"

"You are hereby instructed to write to your unofficial foster mother for the remainder of training!"

"Sir, yes, sir!"

I already had been writing the Brentwoods, anyway. About a week after that a large care package arrived. Homemade peanut brittle, Momma Brentwood style.

And, yes, there was enough for the whole platoon. And a smaller package specifically for the drill instructors. That one was separately sealed. I suspect it was her famous rum balls.

Other than that, I tried like hell not to stand out other than by doing everything as perfectly as possible. I had all the regular chickenshit that bothers people down pat via Mr. Brentwood's teachings. Folding socks and underwear? Got it. Biggest problem was he'd taught me the Old Guard way based on footlockers and we'd upgraded to pussy wall lockers. I could pack my greens in a seabag and have them come out like they'd been sent to the dry cleaners. Shining boots? I'd take firewatch most nights and get them to a glossy sheen. Bounce a quarter off the rack? You could bounce it to the moon. Cleaning weapons? Favorite part of the day. Waking up in a split second when the drill instructors entered the bay? Mr. Brentwood had even drilled me on that, much to Mrs. Brentwood's annoyance. (She got *seriously* tired of that garbage can being banged at 0430 every morning for the last six months of high school.)

Boot camp still sucked but that was its purpose.

And who showed up at that graduation? Mr. and Mrs. Brentwood, of course. He wearing his First Marine Division patch on his ball cap along with his campaign ribbons, four purple hearts and two Bronze Stars.

Turned out the Sergeant Major had been one of his privates in Korea.

The POST Sergeant Major.

Mr. Brentwood had never mentioned being at the Frozen Chosin. Or Inchon. Or being somebody that Chesty Puller knew by name. The Post Commander treated him like royalty.

I had a lot to live up to.

But, truthfully, there wasn't much available when I reached my permanent party. 'Cause welcome to the Cold War and the end of the "Hollow Military" period. We still were getting shit for training budget and most of our time was spent painting rocks.

I was, also, assigned to the Second Marine Division. First Battalion, Eighth Marines. (One-Eight.) No string-pulling involved. Kentucky recruits went east and that was Second Marine Division, where I became just another grunt at Lejeune.

And just as I'd set out to be the poster child for C average, I set out to be the poster child Marine. In this I was going to get an A+. I could shoot, move and communicate. I was always gung ho as shit. To the point it sort of annoyed some of my fellow grunts but fuck 'em. I was planning on being a Gunny in record time.

Want rocks painted? Multiple colors or pure white? I never whined or complained about the stupidest or most inane shit. Never volunteer? I volunteered for anything. I ruck-marched on weekends. I trained off-duty. Including expanding my repertoire of martial arts beyond kendo while still keeping that up. Although I didn't make much of a thing of it. That would have put me in the "weird" category and the last thing you want is to get that categorization.

We did a couple of floats the first year. Nothing much. Most floats were out to sea, turn around, board the amtracks and run ashore at Lejeune. Doing more cost lots of money. We did one long float over to the Med and some shore leave.

Liberty on a float is what most Marines join up to do. I wanted to go ashore at Rota as much as the next guy. I volunteered to be part of the unit that stayed aboard on the first rotation. Why? 'Cause that's hardcore, dude. You've been stuck on this boat for *weeks* and you *volunteer* to take the first duty so your shipmates can go ashore and get drunk? Somebody's got to stay on watch. You grit your teeth and say "Semper Fi, Staff Sergeant. I'll take it."

I think most of my squad sort of half hated me and half admired me. But we got along. 'Cause I was smart enough to never, ever, intellectualize and spoke pure grunt-speak at all times. And I was clear. Didn't care how much anyone bitched. "My goal in life is to make Gunny in record time for peacetime."

But that float was the beginning of something else. See, on a float, you get a lot of downtime. They train and they drill and you clean compartments but there's still more "off" time than at the barracks. There's only so much Marines can do on a boat. Which I knew, so I'd prepared. With correspondence courses.

See, promotion is in part based on academics, even for grunts. Want to be a staff sergeant? Better have some college or college-equivalent courses. The military provided, back then, correspondence courses through the University of Maryland for a pretty nominal fee. Admittedly, you don't make much as a private but I could still afford a few correspondence courses to take on the float for the off time. And since the Marine Corps supported it, you could even get more off time. "Staff Sergeant, permission to study my correspondence courses versus whatever made-up shit they were doing to keep us from going bugshit?"

And since my mother was no longer seeing my grades, I could let out the stops. By the time we got to Spain, I'd finished three courses. All I had to do was take the tests. When I did I got, yup, straight As.

As are easy. Perfect Cs are hard.

While in Rota I went to the US Embassy and arranged to take their Spanish Language Examination. Four hours later I was officially declared "Fluent in written and spoken Spanish," which counted towards promotion. I got drunk as a skunk that night. That was major promotion points.

Back stateside I figured "what the hell" and took the tests for various languages I'd picked up over the years. Some of the oral ones I failed the first time through. Written, I was found fluent in: Spanish (covered), Ancient and Modern Greek, Latin, German (three dialects including Old Schwabian), Arabic and Japanese. I couldn't find, through military or local colleges, tests in Hindi, Hittite or Hieroglyphs. It was like they hated the letter H.

Based on my gunnery sergeant's recommendation, I was made PFC ahead of curve. 'Cause I just oozed the epitome of Marine. I went to the Marine of the Month Board and smoked it, up to the MEU level where I had a case of the flu for the PT test at Post and got beat out by one point.

Then when all the numbers were crunched at wherever the Marine Corps crunches them, I went from PFC to lance then corporal so fast people were pretty sure I was homosexual and seriously blowing someone.

I was expert in every weapon in the inventory (promotion points), proven multilingual (promotion points), had sixty credit hours of college (promotion points), not a single NJP (non-judicial punishment) and basically walked the walk and talked the talk of the perfect Marine.

I was well on my way to making sergeant my first tour. When I went home on leave (to the Brentwoods, of course), Mrs. Brentwood was proud as hell. I sort of wanted to call my mom and tell her I'd gotten promoted from Babykiller to Senior Master Babykiller but refrained. I'd just sort of tried to forget I had been birthed by that woman.

Then we got shipped to Beirut.

Those of you with some intimate knowledge of Marine history might have noticed that my unit was First of the Eighth and it was the early eighties. Those of you with some knowledge of history may see where this was going at this point. For those of you who are totally clueless as to why "Marine" and "Beirut" might have some historical issues . . . look it up.

A few things about the mission. First, President Ronald Reagan was, arguably, one of the top five presidents of all time. I'm not going to argue that, just saying. My memoir, my opinion. But the mission was idiotic. Probably his one major stupid in his career as president. Why?

There is no such thing as a "peacekeeping mission" in the Middle East. Period. The Middle East has been at war, literally, since the dawn of history. The first known army in the world, as we recognize armies, was Sargon's at the beginning of written history. Sargon's conquests practically *are* our first written histories. (And, to be clear, Sargon was in the Middle East. Currently where Iraq is.)

There is no keeping the peace there. It's a myth. The only way you could keep the peace in the Middle East (and I am NOT advocating this) is kill absolutely every man, woman and child. And I do mean every single one. Kurds, Arabs, Druze, Israelis, Lebanese Christians, Iranians, Iraqis, *everybody.* Because every group over there has a case of the ass at every other group and not damned ONE of them can just talk it out.

Not advocating that. Just saying.

The mission reminded me of a saying down South. Some of you may not know what a yellowjacket nest is. Some places they're called ground hornets. When it rains in the South, which is mostly red clay, the holes they dig can become slippery. Saying goes like this:

"No matter how round and slick and invitin' it might look, don't never stick your dick in a hornet's nest."

What President Reagan did was stick Uncle Sam's dick in a hornet's nest. God, I love the man, and his current condition makes me want to weep. But that was his one truly bonehead move. Everybody's due one. I just wish it hadn't been at the expense of my brothers . . . and me.

But this is where my story really begins.

CHAPTER 2

I was having a dream. A really odd one. Generally my dreams involved a blonde on a beach who was very open-minded. In this case, I was standing on a dock on a lake. The water was a perfect blue as was the sky. There were hills on the far side and they were such a perfect green it was literally unearthly. It was, easily, the most beautiful place I'd ever seen.

I wasn't alone, either. There was a guy sitting at the end of the dock trying to get his reel to work. It was obviously snarled. Next to him, to his right, was a bucket presumably filled with bait. And another fishing pole. The guy was wearing a T-shirt and ball cap.

I went over, sat down on the end of the dock and examined him more closely. He was maybe in his fifties, long brown hair and beard. He looked sort of like the various ragheads I'd come to know and loathe (Christian or Muslim, they were all ragheads to the One-Eight and equally shitty.) But I didn't really get a "loathe" vibe from him. The ball cap was a New Orleans Saints cap.

The bait was as odd as the rest of the place. It sort of looked like bread but the smell coming from it was heavenly. I pulled out a pinch. Sniff. Yeah, smelled like honey and . . . I don't know what. Ambrosia came to mind. I couldn't resist and tried a bite.

I could literally live on that stuff the rest of my life. And that was the bait.

"What is this stuff?" I asked.

"Manna," the man said.

I put some bait on the hook, took another bite, and tossed out the line.

"You want this one, sir?" I asked. "I can get that undone."

He hadn't even taken the cover off the reel. He was never getting it fixed that way.

"I don't want to use the term 'hate' for something like this," the guy said. "It's too strong a word. But I . . . dislike and don't understand these modern things. This is not what I call fishing."

He took the rod from me and nodded thanks.

"So . . ." I said, starting to fix the line. "This is an odd dream."

"You usually dream about girls on a beach with low morals," the man said.

"Generally," I replied. I looked down into the water and it was as clear as air. I could see a school of fish, they looked like koi, below us. I really couldn't tell how big they were because it was so clear I couldn't get a feeling for distance. Below them were . . . There wasn't a bottom. Waaaay down there were what looked like clouds. And maybe more water. And . . .

"Is that . . . *Earth* down there?" I asked as something whipped past. "And was that a satellite?"

"Those things," the man said with a slightly aggrieved sigh. "The Boss says they're just temporary until humans figure out quantum tunneling. Whatever that is. Way over my pay grade."

He had what must have been one of the gentlest bites in history. More like the fish politely tugged on the line to get his attention. He carefully reeled it in and the koi simply followed the line in, no fighting. When it got to the dock, it carefully spit out the blunt hook. The man tossed it a ball of the bait and it kicked its tail and swam away.

"I'm starting to get the feeling I'm not in Kansas anymore."

"You weren't in Kansas when you died," the man said then winced. "Sorry, that came out rather abruptly."

"Uhm. Okay. Last I remember I was hitting the rack in the barracks." I looked around. There was a distinct lack of hellfire and brimstone which was good. But, honestly, fishing like this for the rest of eternity might just turn into hell 'cause I was already seriously bored. "Do I get to know what happened?"

"Truck bomb. I regret to inform you that the rest of your

platoon is, in fact, already through . . . *in process* and settling in nicely." He seemed from time to time to be listening to someone as if he was getting a radio call with the right terms.

"I guess I'm a borderline case?" I asked. "Few too many girlfriends?"

"While you're a borderline case, not for that reason."

"Honor thy father and thy mother?" I asked. "I'd be an atheist with no morals or conscience whatsoever. Like, say, my brother?"

"Not an issue," the man said.

"So . . ." I asked. "What's my problem?"

"The Boss thinks you've got some stuff to do back on earth," the man said. "And you're the right candidate to do it. So, up to you, there might be a minor miracle. To be honest, and that's sort of what we're supposed to be, you probably should ask for a straight pass to the next point. You're already in, that's not the problem. But the Boss wants you to do some stuff, first. Reason you might want to ask for this cup to pass from your lips is . . . Well, the best that's going to happen is *minor* miracle. Going back is going to seriously hurt. As in 'Did I just get shipped to Hell?' hurt. And the rest of your life is going to be no picnic, either."

"Stuff like make up with my parents?"

"Boss, no," the man said. "Your mother is a harpy, your brother is headed in the direction of purest evil and your father is a sexual predator of impressionable young women. Stay as far away from those people as you can! Stuff like on a mission, stuff."

"From G . . ." I said, then hesitated. "The Boss."

"Big Guy," the man said. "Patriarchal Beard in the Sky as your mother would put it. Yeah."

"Don't get me wrong when I ask this. Are there any benefits? 'Cause if I stay here, the benefits are obvious. And you did mention pain. I suspect that's something like every bone in my body broken in the blast."

"You already got the benefits, son," the man said. "You think those remarkable physical skills, the ease in learning, the fluency with languages, you think that was all *genetics*?"

"Point," I said. I thought about it for a moment. What would Mr. Brentwood do? Put that way, the answer was obvious. If he was told he had a mission from God, he'd face any challenge to complete it.

"Minor miracle it is," I said. "'Duty is heavier than mountains.

Death is lighter than a feather.' If it's my duty to go back, well, that's my duty."

"Then in a bit you'll wake up, briefly, under your desk," the man said. "Briefly because you'll almost immediately pass out from agony. The minor miracle will be that you were blown off your bed under your desk which the wall locker then fell on protecting at least part of your body from the cascading rubble."

"That would require a ninety-degree turn," I said, thinking about the arrangement of my barracks room.

"Thus the minor miracle."

"Okay. Since it hasn't come up, can I ask you your name, sir?"

"Just call me Pete. You ready?"

"Yes, sir," I said, putting down the rod.

"There is one last bit," Pete said. "The Boss sent a message. There will be a sign. And the sign shall be:" He paused dramatically. "Fifty-Seven."

"Does the Boss realize that the single most popular brand of ketchup on earth has a fifty-seven on every *bottle*?" I asked. "I'm supposed to look for a *separate and singular* fifty-seven?"

"That's all I've got," Pete said. "The Boss is a very busy guy. That's the real reason His messages tend to be cryptic. Ever read an e-mail from a Fortune 500 CEO? Short, blunt, to the point and nearly indecipherable. That's what I got. 'Throw him back if he will. Job to do. Sign shall be fifty-seven.' Up to you to figure it out."

"What's an e-mail?" I asked.

"Take a deep breath," Saint Peter said. "Remember to look for the sign. This is going to hurt..."

OH FUTHERMUCKER!

I choked twice in total darkness. I could taste copper and the pain went through into some special place that was impossible to experience and survive. Then I passed out.

I woke up again when the pain went through the roof. There was light and dust.

"We found one!"

I coughed again, somehow realizing I had nearly been out of air. I gasped and the pain was too much...

A helicopter. Light and shadow. The smell of jet fuel and a hot deck. Someone bent over me praying. I got clear-headed enough to try to mutter: "Don't bother. You're late."

The first clear memory was being in a darkened hospital ward with an oxygen mask on my face, a really dry mouth and so high on painkillers it would have made my mother weep with joy if I took it up as a habit. From the furniture I could see and the layout, it wasn't a hospital in the States. I couldn't really move. Part of that was I didn't want to move, 'cause I could tell there would be more pain if I did, and part of that was the more or less full body cast. All I could really see was IVs, lots of plaster and both my legs and right arm up in traction. Presumably I still had a left arm. I tried to lift it. I could see it and it was moving but not real well. I decided it was just pure weakness and not nerve damage. But it wasn't getting me a drink either way.

I hated to do it, but I let out a moan. Best I could do. I was hoping some kind soul would hear it and maybe put a straw to my lips or something.

Nada.

I passed out shortly thereafter, never having seen a soul the whole time.

The next time I woke up, the ward was bustling with doctors and nurses, several of whom were speaking Greek.

"Neró?" I whispered. It was the best I could do. *"Neró?"*

"You want some water?" one of the nurses said, noticing the whispers.

"Parakaló," I replied.

She put a straw to my lips and I gulped the water down.

"Sas efcharistó," I muttered.

"You are American, yes?" she asked, confused.

"I speak a little Greek," I said. "Where?"

"You are in the military hospital of Heraclea Airbase," she said. "You were injured in a bombing of your barracks."

"Unit?" I asked.

"I don't have any information on that," she said, unhappily. I was pretty sure that was a lie. "One of the officers will speak to you shortly."

"Again, *Sas efcharistó*," I said. "Back to sleep now..."

There had been a truck bomb. Everyone else in my platoon hadn't made it. Bought the farm. Pushin' daisies. There had been a minor miracle in my case. I'd somehow ended up shielded by my desk.

I could have rationalized the dream. The brain does funky

things with trauma. The dream could have been reconstructed memory.

That would have required me being as completely idiotic as the rest of my family.

Shortly after I'd gotten the full skinny, a chaplain came through the ward bringing aid and comfort. He already had my religion. As the biggest stick in the eye I could imagine to my mother, if she ever found out, when asked my religion in MEPS, I'd answered "Primitive Baptist." I really had no idea what Primitive Baptist meant but it sounded bad. The chaplain, an Episcopalian, tried manfully to support me in my simple faith.

"Father," I said as he was trying to figure out how to deal with a bereaved Primitive Baptist. Should he ask if there were snakes available? "Primitive Baptist was a joke. I was raised Atheist. My mother refers to me as a babykiller."

"Oh," he said. Then: "What?"

"No offense, but is there a *Catholic* priest around? And how do I officially change my religion?"

A Catholic chaplain eventually made the rounds. He was a young captain, Air Force, who was Vietnamese of all things. I'd gotten to the point that I could more than grunt and moan by that time. So we talked. He had no problem with the vision or the possibility that it was simply a pain- and trauma-induced dream. Either one worked equally well in his mind. He dismissed it being reconstructed. Based on my general knowledge, I could have created it while trapped in the rubble. Or it could have been Saint Peter.

"The real question is the matter of the sign," Father Van said, thoughtfully. "It very well might involve a bottle of ketchup. Stranger signs have happened. But I rather think it will be something else. Just leave yourself open to the sign revealing itself. You don't have to look for signs, my son. A sign from God is always rather clear."

He had the inclination, but not the time, to go through all the matters necessary to convert to the Catholic faith. He suggested, since I was shortly going to be shipped stateside, that I do so there. And possibly when I'd gotten out of the full body cast.

"Pretty hard to kneel like this, sir."

"Keep the faith, my son," Father Van said. "And that saving sense of humor."

I was eventually put on a plane and shipped halfway around the world to end up at Bethesda Naval Hospital in Washington, DC. Same place they took President Reagan. Who, without any word to the press, met the plane, talked to all of us and shook my one good hand.

He looked me right in the eye as he shook my hand with his left.

"Glad to have you back, son," the President said, solemnly. "You're a credit to the Marine Corps."

"And as soon as I'm out of these casts, I'm going to be back in action, Mr. President."

You could tell he was trying not to tear up.

The White House photographer took our picture together. I have it framed on my wall, President Reagan smiling solemnly and me grinning ear-to-ear in my full body cast. Which he even signed.

He'd made a lousy choice to proceed with that particular mission. Dick, hornet's nest. He's still one of the two greatest presidents of the twentieth century and I'm going to almost give him the edge on Eisenhower.

Then came possibly the single worst moment of my life. Including waking up in hellish pain in the rubble of the destroyed barracks.

My mother came to visit.

Picture if you will. It was an open bay ward. By the 1980s, even for enlisted, they preferred shared rooms. The bay looked as if it hadn't been used since the Vietnam War. When I mentioned that, one of the nurses admitted it hadn't been used since World War II, just updated. Slightly.

And in comes my mother. Because, as "next of kin," she'd been informed her precious son had been returned to the United States. And why don't you visit?

I guess she managed to keep her mouth shut past security. But once she was on the ward, all hell broke loose.

"Mom?" I asked. I was still in a full body cast. There was exactly zip I could do. But I knew what was coming.

"Well, it serves you right, *babykiller*," she snarled, right there in front of God and everybody. Including about four Navy nurses and a Navy doctor. "The only thing that would make it better is if you'd been killed in that justified bombing! Down with Israel! Down with the tyranny of capitalism! Down with the fascist Imperialists!"

"Mom!" I shouted. "You don't understand! You never heard I got *promoted*!"

"What?" she shrieked. "Why should I care, you fascist bastard!"

"I got promoted to Babykiller First Class, Mom!" I shouted over her. "It only took bayoneting two hundred of them! They taste like chicken! Do the whole village! Do the whole village!"

You could see the "what the fuck?" expressions on the shocked faces of the doctors and nurses. But shortly after that, security was called and my mother was permanently blacklisted from Bethesda Naval Hospital.

After she, and security and the doctors, had left, one of the other Marines looked over at me.

"Dude," he said. "You've got a seriously fucked-up mom."

"You think? What gave you your first clue?"

"Babykiller First Class?" another said. "Oh, don't make me laugh! It hurts!"

"'They taste like chicken!'" the guy all the way at the end of the ward yelled.

Laughing hurt so good.

Then, naturally, the Brentwoods came to visit. And stayed. They moved in with another Marine couple they'd known for years with a house in Alexandria. They not only visited me, they visited pretty much every Marine in the hospital. Mr. Brentwood had taken a leave of absence from the school district to make sure I was going to be okay. He spent the time he wasn't talking to me going around the hospital telling WWII stories and explaining how, yep, recovery sucked pretty much the same now as back then. Mrs. Brentwood smuggled in real food.

They almost immediately heard about the incident with my mother. Mrs. Brentwood tried very hard not to be amused.

"Oliver Chadwick Gardenier," she said, shaking her head. "That was..." She stopped, looking for the right stern words and started giggling instead.

"Serves that harridan right," Mr. Brentwood said, trying to keep a straight face.

"Oh, God, I want out of this cast," I said, chuckling. "I miss eating babies."

The casts slowly came off and tubes slowly came out. Then the fun part started: physical tyranny.

I knew there was a point to it. If there was going to be any chance I'd ever be able to be a Marine rifleman again, I had to go through it. But it was really God-awful. I stuck precisely to their regime. If they told me to lift five pounds ten times, I lifted exactly five pounds ten times. And that's where it started, five pounds, ten reps. I was so incredibly weak I simply could not believe it. And I don't care what they say, the hospital food did not help. I needed some of Momma Brentwood's chicken fried steak and gravy.

Finally I was released to go live with the Brentwoods' friends, the Shermans, and made day trips to Bethesda. Then I could really start to recover. I'd lost major poundage on rubber chicken and half a beef patty. Momma Brentwood and Mrs. Sherman took turns ensuring that I gained all that weight back fast. They competed to see who could get me to pig out more. Mrs. Sherman was Korean and that's when I started my lifelong interest in ethnic foods. Her winter kimchee was awesome and her bulgoki was nearly as good as manna.

But on another subject of food. At that time, you wouldn't guess who had the commissary contract for supplying condiments in Navy cafeterias. That's right. Heinz. Not only did every single bottle of ketchup have "57" on it, every single damned ketchup *packet* had a "57" on it! There were fricking 57s *everywhere.* It was driving me nuts!

Fifty-seven Chevy? Maybe it had to do with a '57 Chevy. I kept my eye out for cars that might have been made in 1957. Could it be part of a street address? 57th Street maybe?

At one point in therapy, I thought they were going to give me fifty-seven reps. Could this be it? *Was this the moment the sign would appear?*

But, no, they went from fifty-six to fifty-eight...

I finally gave up looking. It was just too exhausting. I also never mentioned the vision, dream, near-death experience or whatever to anyone but priests and then only under the vow of confession. I did begin the process of conversion to the Catholic Church. If I'd met a saint, I figured might as well go with the main church that believed in them. At one point, one of the priests whom I was briefing in on the situation pointed out, reluctantly but honestly, that Episcopalians were saint oriented and I could have talked to the first Episcopalian priest about it.

Eh. Catholic light. Twice the ceremony, half the guilt. I'll stick with the Holy Mother. Even if it is, occasionally, a Mother.

I never went back to the One-Eight. I'd been permanently transferred to the Detachment of Patients at Quantico. Honeybear and all my gear was transferred up. I didn't have to have a billet so, with the Sherman's permission, I moved into their basement, pulling DC BAQ which was way more than the rent they charged me, while I continued rehab. I had to show up for a formation once a week in uniform. I was always neat as a pin. Hobbling on crutches gave way to using a cane and a major limp.

My confirmation in the Catholic Church was on the same day as my medical review board. I didn't have to "stand" the review. It was on paper only. So I confirmed that I wished to be a Catholic, having already been baptized, stood first communion, first confession (that was long) and all the rest. I'd reviewed all the saints that were worth reviewing. I came to the conclusion that although I might or might not have met Saint Peter, I really wasn't into the whole martyr thing. I liked Pete, don't get me wrong. But I was a warrior at heart. Not the best approach to Christianity but it was who I was. So I finally settled on Saint Michael the Archangel. Guy who had tossed Satan's ass in the clink. Flaming sword, kicking ass. Worked for me.

Had no idea, then, how appropriate the choice would be. I've anathemized more demons than Agent Franks.

The results of the medical review board came down a week later. My right thigh bone had basically been put back together with rigger tape and baling wire. There was no way it was going to support the rigors of being a line infantryman. I would have a permanent limp and all sorts of other issues.

Like, they thought, only seventy percent use of my right arm for life. Hah. When I went in for an eval and they found my right arm stronger and more flexible than my last physical before the bombing they called it "a minor miracle." Try lots and lots of workouts. After the kappa I had to throw away all my old X-rays lest doctors completely freak out. The kappa *was* a miracle.

Anyway, Infantry was out. If I chose, at that time, to re-up for a less strenuous MOS I could continue to be a Marine. But nothing involving direct combat. No tanker, no amtrack crewman. Nada. So I started researching MOS.

The Marine MOS field 5700 referred to chemical, biological and nuclear fields. *A sign!* I knew I had the brains for it. There was a problem. My ASVAB. It wasn't that I couldn't ask to retake some tests. It was that if I suddenly went from a perfect 100 (mediocre, perfect for infantry) to the 150 minimum for some of those fields... It would be pretty clear I'd deliberately boned the first test. Which, by the way, was a "federal offense."

So they came back and offered me continuing service on reenlistment; the only fields open were cook and clerk.

Not a sign. At least not one clear enough for me to sit behind a desk and be a REMF for the next seventeen years.

At 1537 hours, June 12th, 1984, pretty close to three years after my enlistment, I put most of my worldly belongings in the trunk of Honeybear, went to the final out-process station at Quantico and was formally retired (medical) from the Marine Corps with thirty percent disability.

Mr. Brentwood's words at our first real meeting came back to me.

"Do you have any idea what you want to do with your life, son?"

Not a clue. I was just hoping for a sign.

CHAPTER 3

There's a straightforward way to get from the DC area to Lexington. Get on I-66 and put the hammer down. There's a dogleg on I-79 and another on I-81 and then you're on I-64 and Lexington-bound. Most of the time you're in the hills of West Virginia. Not in my opinion the prettiest state in the world but not bad. Girls tend to be really good looking (when they're young, they age fast) and it's got decent scenery. Roadsides are trashy and the whole place has a slightly grimy industrial feel even in the country. But a decent drive.

In this case, with nothing better to do, I decided to take a more "direct" route. At least on paper. This involved lots more time on West Virginia Highway 55 (US 33). (I'd checked, there was no noticeable "Highway 57." Note the word "noticeable.")

I left town right from the out-process station and just started driving. It was afternoon and the sun was in my eyes as I headed west. DC traffic was miserable. I decided to stop and spend a little time on happy hour. Not the best choice in the world considering I was still on a light Tylenol 3 prescription—which the docs had said was more or less permanent—but I threw in some food and kept the drinking light. At 1830(ish) I left the bar and grill on the outskirts of DC and tried again. Traffic was lighter. I hooked up with Highway 55 and started wending my way through the hills of West Virginia.

The sun was beginning to fade and was very much in my eyes, when I hit the outskirts of a small town called Elkins. I was coming down into the valley when a moose jumped out in front of my car.

At least, that was what my brain said it had to be. It was the single largest whitetail deer I'd ever seen in my life. And after jumping into the road, it just stood there, looking at me, as if daring me to hit it. "Go ahead. Make my day. I'll take us both out!" Kamikaze deer.

The drinks had, thank God, worn off a bit and I hit Honeybear's brakes as hard as I could, swerving to the right to avoid the massive ungulate. I slid off the road (American muscle cars have about zero real control) and into a road sign. The deer snorted as if to say "Pussy!" and ran off.

I took a few deep breaths, adrenaline pumping, limbs shaking, muscles bunched up to really remind me how banged up I still was, and peeked at the front of my car to assess the damage. I'd barely tapped the road sign.

Which read: COUNTY 5/7.

Under it was taped a homemade sign.

"Primitive Baptist Tent Revival! Come one, come all! Isaiah 26:19!"

I couldn't help it. I just sat there and laughed and laughed for about five minutes, nonstop. Every time I thought I had it under control, I'd stop and look at those fucking signs and start again.

God's signs tend to be obvious.

"Okay," I finally wheezed. "Got the message, Pete. But, seriously, a tent revival?"

I put Honeybear back in gear and took the left fork.

I passed through a wooded area by a pretty stream, then into some fields. On the far side of the fields was another wooded area. Just inside the second wooded area I spotted another badly made sign pointing to another left. Sure enough, it also read "Tent Revival." As I approached the turn, Honeybear just shut off.

"I said, I got it already," I muttered as Honeybear coasted to a stop right in front of the gravel road. The road went up a slight slope, then over a hill. The tent revival itself was out of view.

I cranked the engine but to no avail. After a bit I could smell she was flooded. Could be anything but I was guessing something in the electrical system. Clearly "The Boss" wished me to humbly walk to this event. Well, limp. Maybe the preacher was supposed to lay on hands or something. Nice part was, the question of "did I just dream that?" was answered. God wants me to limp up that damned road, who am I to argue?

I got out, pulled out my military issue cane, and prepared to limp up the somewhat steep, very uneven road. As I did, a U-Haul van pulled over the hill, drove down to the road and, without stopping or even looking for traffic, made a right-hand turn back the way I'd come and drove away. The driver had brown hair and as he made the turn gave me the oddest look.

The reason I say "the oddest look" is that it was one of those looks you rarely see in a lifetime. It wasn't curiosity as to why a guy with a cane was standing by his car. It wasn't wondering "Should I stop?" The best I can do is say it looked the way a farmer might look at a hen that was off her lay. It was a really cold, very . . . detached look. As if I wasn't important enough to bother about.

That was when I noticed the screaming. I'd never been to a tent revival but I'd heard about them. There was supposed to be a lot of shouting, not really the way I felt was proper to worship God. I realize this is personal taste and has zero to do with what's necessary or "right." The terms are Apollonian versus Bacchanalian. The latter term, despite referencing Bacchus, Greek God of Wine, was not an insult. It was about whether you considered quiet contemplation on the mysteries of God (Apollonian) to be the proper way to worship versus jumping around and screaming "Hallelujah!" at the top of your lungs (Bacchanalian). Both had their place I supposed. I just preferred quiet contemplation.

But I wasn't hearing much "Hallelujah!" or "Preach it, Brother!" or "Amen!"

This sounded more like screams of terror.

As I was quietly contemplating this development, two young women appeared over the crest of the hill, running like the devil was behind them. They weren't screaming. They were reserving their breath for putting distance between themselves and whatever was going on over the hill.

"Run!" the one in the lead shouted as they reached the road. She was blonde, in her teens, a touch short, nice bod, definitely top-heavy, dressed conservatively in a simple top, long skirt and no makeup but I got the feeling she normally preferred shorts and a tube top.

I looked down at my cane then back up.

"Possibly," I replied, calmly. "But not far these days. What's happening?"

"Zombies!" the trailing one shouted, headed for Honeybear. *"Git in the car! Git in the car!"* She was a brunette, a bit heftier than her companion. I'm pretty sure she was the remora of the twosome.

I considered the implications of her words as the two girls reached me and frantically bailed into Honeybear, then over the seat and into the back.

"Is it working?" the blonde shouted.

"No," I said, leaning into the car. "Shortest version possible, please."

"Travelling preacher," the blonde said. "He was talking about how in Isaiah it said the dead will walk. We were outside but we could hear it. Then there was a bunch of screaming. Then everybody come running out, screaming. Then the zombies come out the tent. And none of the cars would start except the preacher's! And he just drove off! And... Shit! Behind you!"

I turned and, sure enough, there was a zombie shambling down the hill. Or at least what looked like a zombie. Its head was flopping as if it was broken and it looked vaguely like it was probably a corpse from a vehicular accident. There were other broken bones and the face was smashed up. It was also naked which wasn't the way it usually was in movies. I realized, from the still attached toe tag, that that was probably because it had been a medical cadaver or from a morgue.

It was having some problems with the slope, occasionally tripping and falling only to rise again. Which gave me just enough time to adjust. I'd seen enough in Beirut to realize that, yep, this guy, based on the neck angle, was definitely dead. Dead as a post. Should have been pushing daisies. But he wasn't.

I walked to my trunk, opened it and started rooting around as the zombie closed.

You'd think, what with growing up always wanting to own a gun and my tutelage by Mr. Brentwood, that I'd have a big gun collection. That would have been the case had I not been a Marine private. You see, Marine privates don't make very much money. Not enough to amass a huge gun collection. So the only firearms I possessed were a 1911 that Mr. Brentwood had given me for my eighteenth birthday and a .30-06 hunting rifle. While in the Corps, I had picked up a .22 conversion kit for the .45 to save money on ammo. Which was how it was currently configured. In a soft case. In one of my civvy bags. Without a magazine in the well. You never knew when you'd run across some state trooper with a hard-on for guns. I did, however, have several loaded magazines and a bunch of spare .22 ammo.

It was one of those moments when the words "Don't panic" run through your head. I had to do a series of steps in a defined order, quickly but not so quickly as to fail any of the steps. Open the trunk. Open the civvy bag. Open the soft case. Retrieve the weapon. Open the bag with the magazines. Insert one magazine in the well of the weapon. Rack the slide. Take a two-handed grip. Look around the open trunk lid...

Fire one round into the forehead of the zombie at nearly point-blank range.

There was no time to ensure that this wasn't some elaborate joke. But I really wasn't bothered. I'd seen the signs. I'd thought God wanted me to attend a tent revival. Maybe another message would be there. The message, pretty clearly, was "Save people from zombies, my son."

Listening, God.

I learned, later, that zombies tend to be somewhat harder to kill than it is portrayed in the movies. You have to scramble a lot of their brains to get them to drop.

Pro-tip: A .22 rimfire has barely enough power to penetrate a skull at anything other than short range. Once the bullet penetrates it doesn't bounce around inside like a ping pong ball. It just pokes a hole. If it fragments, it pokes smaller holes in different directions; but poke enough holes in a zombie's brain and a .22 will do.

However, at the current time I had only five magazines of ten rounds of .22 LR and a box with another two hundred. If I took the time to reconvert to .45, not hard or long, I had an additional three magazines, unloaded. And a .30-06 buried with, if I recalled correctly, seven rounds.

The zombie fell onto the trunk lid and shut it as it slid down the side of Honeybear. Fortunately, I'd dropped the keys back in my pocket. I opened the trunk back up, pulled out the rest of my mags as well as the box of .22 and walked back to the driver's side door.

"I'll just be a moment, ladies," I shouted through the windows. "Lock the doors. Be right back."

I then proceeded to trot up the road in the direction of the screaming, weapon pointed down in a two-handed grip. I was going zombie hunting.

It's amazing how adrenaline can make you completely forget you're a cripple.

As I crested the hill, I was confronted by another small field. There were a number of cars scattered around—parking in neat lines is a sissified city thing or for Germans—and a large white tent. The undead were mostly gathered around the cars, bashing at the windows, trying to get at the occupants. All of the undead were as naked as the one I'd already shot, and they'd clearly suffered a variety of deaths. Some were apparently unscathed. Some had broken limbs or necks as with the one down on the road. Most had toe tags.

As I watched, one of the windows shattered and a woman was dragged out, screaming. At least a half dozen of the undead descended on her and started ripping her apart. I could see there were more occupants in the car and they were bound to be dragged out next.

"This is gonna be interesting," I muttered, trotting forward.

I had exactly two advantages in the situation: I had a firearm, which meant slightly more range than arm's length, and I had the cars. The zombies could clearly reach a fair turn of speed in a straight line. They had a harder time with any sort of maneuvering. Which meant I had to get into and onto the cars and use them to break up the mass. The nearby woods might help as well, assuming that I could outrun the zombies from the cars to the woods. Given my current condition, I wasn't positive I was more nimble than the zombies.

I put that out of my mind and approached the group which was feasting on the woman. She looked like she was probably a mother. She'd been on the passenger side. I could vaguely see kids in the backseat, huddled on the far side. I wasn't sure where the dad had gone.

I popped one of the undead in the back of the skull. Zulu down. Shift, pop. Zulu down. Shift, pop. Zulu down.

Now I had their attention.

If I thought about it, I knew I would fail. So I didn't think about it. I simply leapt onto the trunk of the next car over and ran across the roof. There were more Zulus around the cars, but with moving meat, their attention was shifting. Arms waved at me from almost every direction as I popped Zulus in the fading light. One thing I'd already determined was that getting this over before full dark was sort of a necessity. Fighting these things in the dark wasn't something I relished.

As the zombies concentrated on getting to me from the driver's side and back, I made a leap to the next car's hood. Again, I just assumed it was going to work. I ignored the fact I had a femur made of baling wire and spit and that four months before I had been in traction. I ignored the fact that doctors told me I'd never walk again without a pronounced limp. I, in fact, forgot about all of it in the rush of combat.

Two more leaps and I'd partially broken contact and the Zulus had to maneuver around a couple of cars to get to me. As the first group approached, I took careful, aimed fire and popped skulls. Some of the rounds bounced off. Some of them missed. I waited until the leaders of the group reached the car, backed up onto the roof, checking six, and popped them as they tried to climb up. Again, point-blank range. Pop. Zulu down. Pop. Zulu down.

I'd reloaded, twice, carefully placing the empty mags in my right pocket where my ammo was, and realized that at this rate I was going to run out of loaded magazines before I ran out of Zulus. I dropped off the car, dodged around another to confuse the zombies and darted through the crowd of vehicles looking for . . . a look is the best way I can describe it.

I found it behind the wheel of a new-model Cadillac. A man with short cropped hair going gray, a stiff back and a look of concentrated fury.

"Can you reload these, please, sir?" I asked, holding up my spent magazines and a boxful of .22 ammunition.

"Sure will, son," the man said, cracking his window. "Who knew I'd need my guns at a revival!"

"You're a gift from God, young man," the woman said. His wife, also going gray, good-looking for an older lady, looked just as competent and just as angry.

"You have *no idea*, ma'am," I replied.

The Zulus were closing so I slid up onto the hood and then

up to the roof. I knew it was damaging the paint of the well-cared-for vehicle. I also knew the occupants would understand.

More zombies down and it was time to play tag again.

By the time I got back around to the Caddy, the wife just stuck her hand out the window with my refilled mags. I reloaded, handed her my expended and, with most of the Zulus still trying to get to me through the maze of cars, all my remaining .22 ammo.

By my third pass I took just one of the magazines she offered, reloaded, and in the last bit of light, fired three careful rounds into the heads of the last three zombies.

Zombie apocalypse averted. God, fifty-three (once the count had been established) bad guys... too many.

And then the cops finally arrived. And it started to get complicated.

I let Mr. Anderson, the gentleman whose Cadillac I had put boot prints all over, do most of the talking. He was one of the local attorneys and knew all the cops involved. The sheriff arrived and closed the scene down. Wounded were evacuated. People thanked me and called me a gift from God. I told them to thank God, not me. I was just his instrument. This sounded like humility and went over well. I did not get into the whole "there will be a sign" thing. I was questioned by the police. I showed them my discharge papers, ink still fresh. Tow trucks arrived. All the vehicles had somehow been disabled. Mine got added to the group to be towed.

Then the FBI arrived by Bell Jet Ranger.

I'm not sure when (or if) this will be read and how it works in your time. But in those days, the supernatural was super-secret squirrel stuff. FBI Monster Control Bureau should have been renamed the "intimidate witnesses, make up lies and kill anyone who breathes a word" bureau. Later, I was to find out why, and it made sense to an extent. At the time, it was a pain in the ass.

The lead agent was a tall, slender, good-looking guy named Showalter. He was trailed by a gigantic brute named Franks. Franks had pretty much the same expression on his face as the guy who had driven off in the U-Haul. Like everyone he met was a hen that was off her lay and probably needed to be chopped in the neck and put in a pot.

I really would not have been surprised if the guy actually

had bayoneted babies. And eaten them spitted over a fire on his bayonet. If they weren't raw.

I went full-up Marine-perfect. I had the sneaking suspicion I was in deeper shit than when I'd woken up under my desk.

"You're the shooter," Showalter said.

"Yes, sir!" I barked, standing at parade rest. I sort of expected congratulations from them but something told me the best I was going to get was "we're going to let you leave alive."

"And you just happened to be driving by?" Showalter asked.

"Sir, yes, sir!"

"That doesn't quite hold water, kid," Showalter said. "Try it again."

"Sir, upon medical retirement from the United States Marine Corps due to wounds suffered in the bombing in Beirut, I elected to drive back to my home of record in Lexington, Kentucky, sir!" I barked. "I elected to use side roads as I was attempting to determine what future I might choose given that my prior plans had been to be a career Marine, sir! The time driving gave me time to think, sir! My experiences in the bombing of the barracks in Beirut had led me to consider the world of religion and faith, sir! I have recently converted to Catholicism, sir, having been raised as an atheist, sir! When I saw the sign for the revival, having never attended one, I elected to take the turn, sir!

"My vehicle was disabled at the base of the hill, sir! Two young women ran down the hill seeking aid, sir! They reported zombies, sir! I observed one subject following them which met the parameters for an undead subject, sir! I retrieved my PW from my trunk where it had been carefully stored, readied my PW and terminated the threat, sir! I determined that said subject was, in fact, something resembling a classic movie zombie, sir! I determined that more people required aid, sir! I rendered aid, sir, fulfilling my oath of enlistment to protect against all enemies foreign and domestic, sir! Am I in trouble for terminating the Zulus, sir?"

"Zulus?" Showalter asked.

"Zombies, sir," I said. "Your pardon, sir."

"Still not buying it, kid."

"Sir, God's hand does sometimes work in mysterious ways," I said, shrugging. "Sir, that is the truth of the matter, sir."

I could tell they didn't believe me. Then there was a voice in my head. Like a real honest-to-God voice. Not Pete's. Somebody else's. It sounded like he'd spent time as a Marine drill instructor. The voice barked four words. Nothing more but I knew I was supposed to repeat them. There was also an image to go with the words. For some reason, I looked at Franks.

"One. Drop. Of. Blood," I said, looking him square in the eye. Which was, frankly, tougher than physical therapy. "One drop of blood on the tip of a sword."

Franks looked puzzled for a moment, then frowned harder. "We're done here."

"Reason?" Showalter asked, surprised.

Franks thought about that for a moment, slowly masticating gum. Apparently he was really the one in charge.

"Classified. This one's not the threat."

"Okay, then," Showalter said, clearly frustrated. He turned back to me. "What are you leaving out?"

Based on Franks' response, I knew the right answer to give.

"Sir, with due respect, that is classified above your level," I replied. "You do not have access to that compartment, sir."

"Does this compartment at least have a name," Showalter asked, "so I can determine if the compartment exists?"

I thought about that for a moment. A Marine infantry private does not normally get a top secret clearance but I knew something about the way they were set up. Besides compartmentalization, there were different "blocks" or levels of security clearance. The highest was "Block Eight." Most Presidents don't get Block Eight clearance. You had to be really, really trusted to get Block Eight clearance. And Eight is as high as it goes.

"The compartment is Block Ten, sir," I replied.

"There *is* no Block Ten, Gardenier!" Showalter snapped. "Now I know you're lying to me!"

"Agent Franks?" I asked.

He just grunted. I didn't know who Franks thought I really answered to, but he let it go.

"Sir," I said, relenting slightly. "I was not involved with the individual who let these zombies loose. You have my solemn word on that as a Marine. I truly was just driving home and truly did choose to drive back roads as a way to think about what I was going to do with the rest of my life, sir. All of that is completely and literally true, sir, on my honor as a Marine, sir. The sole and only slight falsehood was my reason for taking the turn on this road, sir. And the reason for that, sir, is classified above your level, sir. It is classified above the President's level, sir."

"I happen to know that President Reagan is Block Eight," Showalter said.

"So you have to wonder what could possibly be higher, sir," I said. "I can safely say, it is not anything in league with evil, sir."

"So," Showalter said, taking a breath. "For reasons classified above my level, according to both you *and* Agent Franks, you made the turn. *Fine*. Your car died. Caught in the mystic spell. I can accept that, although the timing is incredibly suspicious. Two girls came running for help, with which they agree. You responded. You're a recently discharged Marine. I can see that.

"Care to tell me how someone who was just discharged for wounds received in combat that left him *crippled* and using a *cane* ran around 'Like some sort of super-ninja' according to witnesses, jumping from car to car, dodging zombies and popping them in the head?"

I almost replied, based on the last bit of his question, "I invoked the awesome power of *Little Bunny Foo Foo!*" but I refrained.

"Adrenaline? Right now, sir, all I want to do is take some painkillers, lie down and get off my damned leg, sir. Then? I just did it, sir. You do what you have to do, sir, and worry about the rest later, sir."

"And I can believe as much or as little of that as I like," Showalter said. He reached into a pocket and pulled out a lancet and a vial. "Hold out your hand."

I extended my hand to him and he lanced a finger and squeezed a drop of blood into the vial.

"Don't leave town until you are given permission. The easiest way for you to have suddenly developed super abilities instead of being thirty percent disabled is if you are, yourself, a supernatural entity. This test will determine that. If you are not, I'll accept that the turn was taken for reasons 'above my clearance level' and that the rest was just training and adrenaline.

"This incident never happened. The existence of zombies or anything else supernatural is highly classified. Don't bother to blather about rights. There are none where this is concerned. If you ever discuss this incident with any person not properly cleared, you're lucky if you just end up in an insane asylum for the rest of your life. If you make too much trouble, Agent Franks or someone similar will shoot you in the head. Do I make myself perfectly clear?"

"Yes, sir!" I barked. "I do understand classified, sir."

As Showalter was finishing, the sheriff walked over and cleared his throat. "Special Agent, the Hunter team is here," he said.

"Not those bozos," Showalter snarled. "The incident is over. Why did you even call them?"

"I'd like to make sure that the area is completely cleared, sir," the sheriff said. He clearly was not happy doing "diffident."

"Fine," Showalter snapped. "But tell them no interaction with the witnesses."

"Do you have the cover story yet?" the sheriff asked. "There's press asking questions."

"The tent caught on fire," Showalter said. "Seven dead, six injured. Most of the injured aren't expected to make it."

"I'll pass that on," the sheriff said, drifting back into the night.

"Gardenier," Showalter said, turning back to me, "don't talk about this. Ever."

"Got that, sir," I said.

"And don't leave town until cleared."

Finally dismissed by the Feds, I stood there alone in the dark at parade rest. The problem was... adrenaline had carried me through the fight. But now I was just locked up. I was not looking forward to the walk back to my car. I hurt from head to toe. I'd just used a lot of muscles I hadn't used in a long time and the ones I had been using had been severely overtaxed. My right femur felt like someone had driven a stake into it. All the other, many, pins and staples and plates in my body were sending their own notes of sorrow and agony.

I thought about it for what seemed like a long time, then muttered "Fuck it" and just lay down in the grass. It was a warm night. There were some bothersome mosquitoes but nothing compared to the sand fleas at Parris Island, and the patch I'd been standing on was relatively free of blood and zombie gook.

Lying down with no support hurt, but once I was horizontal it was like a wave of euphoria hit as all the pressure came off the various bits. Somebody had apparently cut the field before the disastrous tent revival. The grass was short and in the immediate area still had a fresh-cut smell that almost overwhelmed the smell of death.

At that point I could start to think about the immediate future. I had to get my car fixed. All I really needed to do was figure out what was wrong and I could probably fix it myself if it didn't require complicated tools. All the cars had been shut down by something—magic?—so most of the damage should probably be the same. Once some other mechanic figured it out, I could probably fix it.

You might be wondering about my easy acceptance of what had just happened. I've met, over the years, thousands of survivors of these sorts of things and plenty of Hunters whose first experience of the supernatural was just as "out of the blue."

I was raised by parents who firmly believed that while the supernatural, including any reference to a deity, might be anthropologically interesting, all those crazy stories from those superstitious idiots dating from the dawn of time were absolutely and unquestionably impossible.

First, I'd already determined that just about anything my parents believed was probably idiotic. So rebelling by believing in the supernatural, including God, was an easy step for me.

Second, I'd had a conversation with a saint while dead. While this had been a questionable item prior to today, the literal sign that had led me here was pretty damned obvious. Thus, I was pre-prepared to handle this with relatively little disbelief. I also learned, early, to just take life as it's thrown at you and do the best you can with the hand you're dealt. Which meant, at that moment, considering the hand and figuring out how to deal with it.

The Feds had told me to not leave town. So I needed a place to stay. Before the bombing, I'd have just planned on staying in the car. Front seat was comfortable enough. Slept in it (and more than slept) plenty of times. But that was before I had pins and plates through half my body. I'd sort of gotten used to having a bed. Frankly, where I was at the moment was more comfortable than the car. I slapped a mosquito. Except for the occasional bug. So... could I find some kind person to get me some Off...?

"Think we got one over here," a voice said.

"If you shoot me, it will *seriously* piss me off," I replied.

Lights approached in the dark and were shined on me. They were kind enough to mostly keep them out of my face.

"Any particular reason you're lying on the ground after a zombie attack?" a voice said, sounding mildly amused.

"I'm beat to hell? I feel like pounded meat? I just got out of Bethesda? My cane was with my car which got towed? I'm not sure I could have walked back to my car and I don't even know if this town has a hotel? It's a warm night and the grass is soft?"

"You're the guy who killed all the zombies?" the voice asked.

"I can neither confirm nor deny."

"We already got the story, kid," the voice said. "What do you mean you just got out of Bethesda?"

"I was in the bombing in Beirut," I said, pulling back my T-shirt sleeve. The surgery on my upper right humerus was an easily viewable scar. "I fucking got discharged, thirty percent disabled, today. As in . . ." I looked at my watch. Amazingly, it was still only a bit past 2230. ". . . about seven hours ago. After six months of traction and physical tyranny."

"And you bagged fifty-three shamblers with a .22-converted 1911?" the voice asked.

"And stole our PUFF bounty," another voice said, a bit more aggrieved.

"I can neither confirm nor deny," I said, then paused. "What bounty?"

"Feds pay us to kill stuff like this," the first voice said. "We drove all the way from Hazelton just to find out they were already dead. Again."

"Waste of fricking time and gas," the aggrieved voice said.

"Tell you what, we'll file the paperwork for a share," the first voice said. "On your behalf. But our company gets twenty percent."

"Done," I said, too tired to argue. Then thought about it. "On one condition."

"Which is?"

"Give me a hand up and a ride to a motel?"

"Hell, kid, I'll do that and give you a business card. We're always hiring."

And that was how I was introduced to Monster Hunter International.

CHAPTER 4

"What's your name, kid?" the "boss" asked as two of the Monster Hunters helped me to my feet.

"Oliver Chadwick Gardenier, sir," I answered. "All of which I hate. Call me Chad."

"Carlos Alhambra," the man said. "Team lead for Monster Hunter International."

Carlos was probably late thirties, Hispanic, a little taller than me, and physically fit. He had a beard, long hair, and the chicks probably dug him.

"Pleasure to make your acquaintance, sir," I said, limping in the general direction of the road.

"You really are banged up, aren't you?" one of the other Hunters asked, taking an arm to help me walk.

"I've got more metal in me than the Terminator. But apparently God called me to fight monsters so I'm just going to have to figure out how to get in good enough shape."

"God called you?" one of the others asked. It wasn't an incredulous question. It sounded as if they were perfectly comfortable with the comment.

So I told them the general outline of my vision while "dead" in the rubble of the barracks. None of them seemed to have an issue with it.

"Appreciate it if you didn't mention it to the FBI," I said as

I finished. We'd reached their vehicle by then. "I told the lead agent the reason I turned at the fork was classified above his level. Franks backed me up."

"Wait, wait," Carlos said, his voice for the first time indicating he thought I had to be lying. "*Franks* backed you up? *Agent* Franks?"

"Yes, sir," I said. "Please allow me to avoid answering why. I think that's probably classified even higher. Something I said in the interview seemed to really throw him."

"All the rest I get," the guy holding my arm said. "I'm not into the God stuff but you do this job long enough and you see things that sort of erase doubt. But something throwing Franks? That'll be a cold day in Hell."

"Every day in Hell is cold," I said. The vehicle was a jacked-up '73 Ford Bronco and I looked at the climb in with trepidation. "Any chance I could get some help getting in?"

The Iron Inn in Elkins had no more rooms available but Carlos agreed to share his.

"I'd taken one of them for myself by right of age and rank," he said. "Two beds. You can have the other one."

"Thank you, sir," I said, dumping my bag on the floor.

We'd stopped by the garage to pick up my overnight bag and cane. The owner of the shop was busy as hell with over a dozen cars suddenly dropped in his lap but he'd already deduced that the problem on most of them was the coil was burnt out. Given I wasn't one of his regular customers, I could tell that I was well down the list of cars he was planning on fixing. I asked him if he would just order the part if I did most of the work myself and he agreed.

From there it was back to the motel where the team dropped off all their gear. And then dinner at the Western Steer Family Steakhouse.

When we'd gotten our trays and a table, the questions started.

"You're using a cane but you took out fifty-three shamblers?" The questioner was Edward Malone, the guy who had complained about losing the PUFF bounty. Brown hair and eyes, broad shoulders with the vague look of a weight lifter. Not a pure muscle head but someone who pushed a lot of weights.

"All I can say is 'adrenaline,'" I said as the waitress brought our orders. I took a sip of sweet tea and dug into the sirloin steak I'd ordered. I'd already had a light meal but the exertion had given me an appetite. "When those two girls came running to the car, it's like I forgot I was hurt and just did it."

"Want to start from the beginning?" Carlos said.

So I did, backing up to the accident and going through till the FBI questioning.

"After they were done, I just didn't want to go try to find my car. So I lay down in the grass. Which was where you found me. And when we're done eating, I'm probably going to have to get some help getting out of this seat. Or maybe not."

I pulled out a pill bottle and popped a couple of Tylenol 3s.

"Prescription," I said, shrugging. "More or less a permanent one according to the doctors."

"If you really think God's called you to this, Chad, you're going to have to hope He'll cure you as well." That was Franklin Moore. He was the guy who'd helped me to the Bronco and helped me in. Black, medium build, late twenties. "This job is pretty damned physical if you know what I mean."

"Really damned physical," Malone said, flexing his bicep.

"I can do it," I said. "I will do it. Would I want to as a career right now? No. I need to get back in shape. But that's just a matter of time and effort. I'll put in the time and effort."

"Good attitude," Carlos said, putting mashed potatoes on his steak and eating the bite combined.

"Can I ask some questions?" I asked.

"Shoot."

"The PUFF bounty? How's that work?"

"Perpetual Unearthly Forces Fund. Set up by the Federal Government under Theodore Roosevelt to encourage hunting of supernatural entities. Monster Hunter International, our company, has been around since 1895 and it is, not blowing smoke, the premier company in the world. We've got contracts with various state, local and even Federal agencies to send teams to deal with supernatural events when they have them. For example, this is in Randolph County. We've got the contract with the sheriff's office here. When there's a supernatural event, they call us and we have a defined period to have a team here."

"Which we always make," Malone said. "Even if the situation is already dealt with," he added, still clearly unhappy.

"Sorry," I said. "I suppose I could have let everyone get eaten so you could collect the PUFF," I added with a grin.

"Nah, man," Malone said, shaking his head. "It's all good. Just a long drive and we didn't get to kill anything."

"There's always tomorrow," Carlos said. "And the day after and the day after that. This job? There's busy times and slow times but there's *always* work. Take World War II. Just about every red-blooded male in America signed up to go fight Tojo and Hitler. But it was known that when they were defeated, they'd all go home. There was an end point.

"Join the Marines," he added, gesturing at me. "You might figure you're doing one tour or make a career. But at a certain point, you get out. This job? This war has been going on since pre-history and will be going on long after we all bite it, even if it's from old age. Assuming you last long—and the casualty rate, let me warn you, is *high*—at some point you have to decide when you've run with the big dogs long enough. I'm about at that point."

"You keep saying you're going to retire," Malone said. "Cold day in Hell, again."

"Real problem is where to retire to," Carlos said. "When I was young, the answer was 'a tropical island.' Deal with one luska and that starts to look less attractive."

"Luska?" I asked. "Wait. Carib legend. Half shark, half squid, all nasty."

"How'd you know that?" Malone asked, warily.

"My much hated mother is a professor of anthropology," I said. "I've been exposed to a lot of legends over time. I used to dig into her books when she wasn't looking, for that matter."

"Much hated?" Franklin asked.

"I'd try to explain," I said. "Let's just say that this apple got windblown very far from that tree and is glad. Can I get back to bounty? Take what just happened. How much for a zombie?"

"Shamblers aren't much," Carlos said. "About two grand."

"Two thousand dollars, less twenty percent, seems like pretty good money for the time spent," I said. "Didn't take more than twenty minutes, I'd guess. Even with the associated pain."

"Dude," Malone said, shaking his head. "Apiece. Two grand apiece."

"Each?" I sort of squeaked.

"Each," Carlos said. "You're looking at making eighty grand plus off of this incident."

"Now you know why I'm sort of grumpy about losing the PUFF," Malone said, "but like the boss said, there's always tomorrow."

"The way it works with the company is everybody gets a bimonthly check," Carlos said. "Team leads get a bit more than the regular shooters. The check is based on how the company is doing overall that month plus bonuses for any actions you've been involved in during that month."

"If a zombie, which you can take out with a .22, is worth two grand," I said, "how much is some of the other stuff worth?"

"Werewolves range from about ten grand up to about a hundred," Franklin said. "Depends on how old they are, mostly. New ones that haven't had many kills are the ten. Hundred are very rare old ones that have been killing for a long time. Vampires range from around the same as zombies for the new ones up to a few million for Master vamps."

"But nobody hardly ever sees Masters, they're so rare," Carlos said. "And if you go in against a Master with a team of twenty and every heavy weapon in the arsenal, figure you might have five survivors and might actually kill the vamp. Masters are virtually indestructible. But, again, super rare."

"And there's different kinds of zombies," Malone said. "Shamblers like you faced. Fast zombies are scarce, harder to kill and thus worth more. Ghouls, wights—which are seriously bad news—weird Asian zombies..."

"Pretty much anything you've ever read in a horror story or seen in a movie probably exists," Franklin said. "I'm pretty sure the FBI leaks stories to the movie and TV industry to make the real a myth, you know what I mean?"

"*Halloween*?" I asked. "The movie," I added to be clear.

"Revenant," Carlos answered. "Type of zombie. Unlike most, it has some sentience. Very strong, quick, intelligent and violent. PUFF depends on how old and how powerful. The worst type of revenants are liches, which are..."

"Undead wizards," I said, shaking my head. "Lovecraft?"

"Old Ones," Franklin said. "Great Old Ones, almost never. But they've got lots of servants, things left over from when they were around and followers that cause problems."

"And necromancy, all the undead stuff, probably is one of their powers," Carlos said.

"I don't suppose there are any books to study up?" I asked.

"Not with all of this being classified," Carlos said. "But if you can get back in shape and decide to join the company, there's training on it."

"I'm definitely going to get back in shape," I said. My head hadn't really been in the game on that up to now. Why go through the agony of getting all my muscles back in trim when I was probably going to be stuck behind a desk the rest of my life? Now I had a reason.

Christ, it was going to suck.

The rest of your life is going to be no picnic.

Got it, Pete.

The upside to Detroit's general lack of care in engineering and construction of vehicles is that part availability is, necessarily, high. Coils for a 1976 Cutlass Supreme are generally not hard to find.

Unless, that is, suddenly, in the middle of nowhere West Virginia, thirty vehicles, most of them American made, suddenly needed a new coil.

It would be at least three days before the shop got my part. I found that out when the Hunter team kindly dropped me at the garage on their way out of town. I'd given them all the information they needed to file the PUFF paperwork for me including my home of record, the Brentwoods'. Carlos told me it would be a few weeks to a month to get it all processed. That was fine. I wasn't sure I'd ever really see the money and wasn't sure what to do with eighty grand anyway.

In the meantime, I was standing in a garage bay with nothing to do.

"I'm pretty handy with a wrench," I told the owner, who was also the main mechanic. "And putting in coils isn't exactly hard work," I added, gesturing with my cane. "Want some help? I work cheap."

"Definitely," the man said.

His name was Bryant Sutton, owner and chief cook and bottle washer of Sutton's Auto Body and Repair, the premier auto repair shop in the town of Elkins. In his upper thirties, he'd worked in NASCAR for seven years before getting out and opening up his own place. Unlike most small town mechanics, the then-new electronic fuel injection systems and nascent computerized controls in engines didn't throw him. Me, I preferred the old stuff but I could fumble my way around EFI and E prompts.

But coils really weren't a big deal and I handled that while Mr. Sutton and his assistant mechanic Bert Henderson handled all the other "regular" repair jobs he had.

As I'd finish a car, I'd call the customer and tell them it was ready to pick up. One by one, survivors from the zombie attack would come in to pick up their repaired vehicle. To say the least, they were all surprised to find their savior now fixing their cars. They were even more surprised to see the cane. I got quite a few invitations to dinner.

Shortly after lunchtime a young lady came walking in. The face was vaguely familiar but the blond hair and chest, now barely covered by an overstretched tube top, was what clicked.

"I know you," I said, grinning.

"It's you!" the girl said, running over and giving me a very well-padded hug. "Oh, my God! I heard what you did! You're our savior!"

"Jesus Christ is the savior," I said, smiling. "I just happened to follow His directions."

"How did you do all that with..." She seemed embarrassed to point out the cane.

"Adrenaline?" I said. "God's hand? I dunno. Just seemed the thing to do at the time."

"He used to be a Marine," Sutton said. "Hi, Christy."

"Hi, Mr. Sutton," Christy said.

"I'm still a Marine," I said. "Just medically retired. Once a Marine, always a Marine. Christy what?" I asked.

"Russell," Christy said. "I'm here to pick up my parents' car. Steve Russell."

"Ford pickup," I said. "All fixed."

"You want to cash it out?" Sutton asked.

"Will do, sir."

"How long are you going to be in town?" Christy asked as I was ringing up the repair.

"My car is down the list," I said. "And the local warehouse is out of parts. So, couple of days?"

"What are you doing for dinner?"

"I've had a bunch of invitations, but I wouldn't turn one down from you," I said with a grin.

"I think my mom and dad would be fine with that," Christy said, turning shy.

"Did you . . . lose anybody?"

"We didn't," Christy said, sadly. "My friend Amy—her mom *and* dad were killed."

"The brunette?" I asked.

"Yes. Her dad got caught in the tent and her mom was dragged out of their car. We had run, but her brother and sister were in the car. They saw the whole thing."

"Gray Chevy Caprice?" I asked.

"Yes," Christy said, frowning.

"Yeah," I said. That explained why only the woman was in that car. "Saw that."

"It must have been terrible," Christy said, tearing up. "The whole thing was just so . . . crazy. You know, I never really believed before? I'd go to church and get dragged to things like revivals but . . . I never really *believed*."

"Getting attacked by zombies is what some people would call a come-to-Jesus moment," I said. "I was raised atheist. Some stuff that happened when I got injured was my religious moment. But I was still a bit on the fence until this. Now? No real major questions anymore."

"I'm not sure how I feel about it, yet," Christy said, shrugging. "I'm sort of worried about it, really."

"Why?" I asked. "Thirty-two fifty, by the way."

"I'm kinda worried some of the stuff I've done . . ." She handed over two twenties, shrugged, then looked down at how she was dressed and crossed her arms over her chest. "I didn't even think about it when I was getting dressed, but . . ."

"Jesus doesn't care about how you dress," I said, making change. "Trust me on that one. I'm not going to go all preacher on you, but most of the stuff that's preached doesn't really *get* Jesus. It's not that God thinks you *should* just sleep around or whatever or dress sexy. It's just not as important as other things. And it's a matter of how you do it. I've had a number of girlfriends. I'm not going to change that even though, yeah, I know God exists and created some of those rules for a reason. But mostly it's about how you treat other people. Do you make their lives better or worse? I think God would have more problems with a flaming bitch, you know, the 'mean girl' at school who was a total prude, than a lady who has had a 'close personal friend' or two but always treats other people with kindness and decency.

As long as having a 'close personal friend' or two doesn't ruin your view of yourself. Make any sense?"

"I guess," Christy said. "And don't get the impression I'm a slut or anything. I'm not."

"I didn't think you were," I said, hoping against hope that she was. It had been a while, what with the deployment and getting all blowed up, since I'd gotten laid. "Just don't sweat the little stuff about God and Jesus. Jesus is the savior. The only time Jesus ever got angry at people was at the Pharisees that were keeping people out of the temple who couldn't pay. Put it this way, the guy who released those zombies? Totally going to Hell when his time comes. The people who died from them? Your friend's mom and dad? Already in Heaven. Virtually guaranteed. They'd have to have done some pretty terrible stuff to get denied. I guarantee that nothing you've done in your life, or ever will do, is going to keep you from Heaven. Absent, you know, learning how to raise zombies and using them to kill a bunch of folks. You're not a secret serial killer or anything, are you?"

"No," she said, shaking her head and smiling just a little.

"There's that smile," I said, grinning. "The truth is, the lucky ones are the ones that died. They're, truly, in a better place. Seen the edges of it. It's nice. I keep thinking I should have stayed."

"When did you see Heaven?" she asked, doubtfully. I could tell she was starting to question my sanity.

"Think all this came from tripping on stairs, honey?" I asked, holding my arms out with the cane in my hand. "Double-check on the dinner invite and I'll tell you then. For now, got to fix people's cars." I handed her the receipt and the keys.

"Okay," she said. "I'll call."

"Please," I said. "I'd like to see you again."

"I'd like to see you again, too," she said, shyly.

God, please let her be a slut. I know that's a very *bad thing to pray for, but...*

A gentleman does not kiss and tell. But... wow. That girl could suck the chrome off a bumper. Not to mention she could shake daddy's little money maker harder than Stevie Nicks...

The next day I got introduced to the mayor and met Sheriff Yates again. I was offered a position as a deputy if I went through an accredited academy as well as, quietly, given the "keys to the city." Everyone had gotten the word that what happened "never happened." It was a small town. Everybody knew the outline even if some of them had a hard time believing it.

There was no news on the identity of the mysterious "travelling preacher." The identities he'd given were false. The sheriff was pretty sure even if the FBI caught up with him they'd never hear about it.

I met Mr. Anderson again, the man whose Cadillac I'd badly scuffed up. I apologized for that and he told me to quit being silly. Former Army tanker. He asked me why I'd chosen him to hand my magazines and I told him he looked as if he had his act together. I was offered several jobs by businessmen in town, both those who had been at the revival and their friends.

I attended two funerals, one a joint one for Amy's parents. Christy asked me to go with her. More pats on the back from people. Amy's brother and sister were pretty well catatonic through the whole thing. Both bodies had been cremated by order of the FBI.

Christy spent the whole night. I'd told her I wasn't staying and she said she understood but I could tell she didn't. I told her God had given me a sign that I had a job to do and I couldn't exactly do it in Elkins. I could tell she wanted me to ask her to go with me.

I didn't tell her the parts had come in for my car that day. After she dropped me off at the garage, I said goodbye to Mr. Sutton, drove back to the hotel in my repaired Honeybear, checked out and left town without saying goodbye or leaving a forwarding address.

Just slip out the back, Jack.
Make a new plan, Stan.
Just turn in the key, Lee.
And set yourself free.

Carlos hadn't had to mention the casualty rates to hunting. More than once, the shamblers had nearly caught me, and I'd seen what would happen to me if they did. There was no way I was going to leave behind a young widow or put kids in a position of being hostages to fortune. Not down the road I was taking. Not everybody agrees. The Shacklefords have been fighting monsters, and breeding, for generations.

Personally, I think they're nuts.

Or maybe I'm just a philandering ass like my dad.

CHAPTER 5

I didn't move in on the Brentwoods. I spent a few days there recuperating from Elkins and the drive, then found a furnished studio apartment. I spent a bit of my discharge pay getting a gym membership and proceeded to pound my body like a piece of cheap meat.

I was determined to become a Monster Hunter. God had called me to that, clearly, and who was I to argue? But I knew it was going to be nearly as physical, if not as physical, as being a Marine infantryman. I was going to have to get back to the point I could shoot, move and communicate.

I got a cashier's check from Monster Hunter International for eighty-four thousand, eight hundred dollars. I'd already set up an accountant and discussed the tax ramifications with him. I didn't tell him what the money was from; I said it was a consulting gig. He clearly thought it was illegal money, but as long as I was following the laws, it was all good.

The amount of tax you had to pay, even in 1984, on eighty-five thousand dollars for a single male was a nasty shock. On his advice I invested some of it. I didn't think I'd live long enough for anything to mature, but if I did, having a nest-egg would be nice. He helped me figure out a budget plan that I've stuck to ever since. I put some to charity and blocked out a bunch of the rest. I told him that part of my business expenses was going to be guns and other equipment. Again, he was pretty sure he was dealing with some sort of organized crime, maybe a contract assassin based on the guns, but I was at least doing it properly.

Slowly, I started building a weapons inventory. I'd gotten my pistol back from the sheriff—it had been briefly held as evidence—but that was just the start. I had plenty of money to live on, a small check each month from Uncle Sam that barely covered my rent, and nothing but time on my hands.

I spent the time doing several things.

I paid for a class at a local community college. That meant I could use any of the local college libraries including the local seminaries. So I began studying, essentially, my mother's field of expertise—anthropology and mythology—assiduously.

I went to the gym every day and pounded my repairs. I didn't just use the weights and treadmills. I took a yoga class. I knew that everything was going to need to be stretched out.

I signed up for several martial arts courses. At first I was nearly useless at all of them, even kendo. But slowly, as the repairs started to align and the muscles came back, I got better. I didn't only study kendo as a weapons form. There was a jujitsu class that included a double blade fighting style. Jujitsu and wah lum kung fu occupied much of my time. They also helped me find new muscles to stretch.

Pro-tip: A lot of what Hunters do involves wrist strength. Firing weapons, using blades, et cetera. One excellent physical training method for this is used by several martial arts forms. Take a wooden stick, such as is used in stick fighting. Tie a rope to it, tightly. Suspend from the rope a weight. How much depends on how strong you are and your grip and wrist strength. Hold the stick slightly outwards from your body and rotate it to raise the weight. Lather, rinse, repeat.

By the time I felt I was in shape enough to go to the MHI classes, I was doing fifty reps of fifty pounds a set. When you've got to cut off a bunch of vamp heads or you have to cut one off that's particularly strong, especially if the vamp isn't staked at the time, you'll thank me.

And if you ever have to face down the Wild Hunt with a dead-man's switch attached to two hundred claymores in your left hand, you'll thank me more.

Reading about fitness in general, I ran across a statement by, of all people, football star Herschel Walker, who strongly recommended taking ballet.

After thinking about it, I signed up for a ballet class. That turned out to be a twofer. First, it really is a great way, even better than yoga, to work on stretching and balance.

Second, I was the only male. I was also one of two males in my yoga class and by far and away the cuter one.

Did not have a lack-of-nookie issue during my retraining period. Also strenuously avoided getting anything resembling a girlfriend. I seriously considered only dating married women but that seemed like it would really impede on the God front so I declined those invitations. Twice, ladies tried to move in on me by cautiously marking territory. Neither one liked it when I courteously handed them back their toothbrushes and clothes they'd left at the apartment.

On the God front: I didn't go to church every Sunday but I hit it about every third and frequently went to confession. After delicately bringing up the subject, just using the term "PUFF," I found a monsignor as a Father confessor who was "read in" on the supernatural.

Father O'Connell also looked like a stereotype. He was heavy set, florid, with balding blond hair, pale blue eyes, a permanently sunburned complexion and was, in general, the archetype for every Irish-Catholic priest you'd ever see. He was also one of the smartest human beings I'd ever met and deeply knowledgeable of the Catholic Church's long and frequently complex battle against the forces of evil on God's earth.

He didn't think much of my philandering ways. I learned to say the rosary as a constant mantra any time I wasn't otherwise occupied. I never told him, ever, that it was a great way to keep from . . . well, there were times, even when involved with a lady, you could say prayers. Although I felt it was truly blasphemous to say the Hail Mary at such times, so I stuck to the Our Father.

The rest of the time I became a regular at several local ranges and gun stores. After I started getting in better shape, I even took to competitive shooting. I was okay at shotgun but long guns and pistol were my preference. One of the weapons I picked up was the then-new Uzi carbine in .45. It had a hell of a kick to it but thinking about what I was potentially going to be facing, it seemed like a great choice.

I applied for a Federal Firearms License. I was now officially an arms dealer. Then I jumped through the extra hoops to become a manufacturer so that I could legally make my own machine guns. You could still register new ones back then. I wanted to name my company Evil Arms Dealers, Incorporated, but was dissuaded.

The first thing I did was convert that Uzi to full auto. Using the lathe in Mr. Brentwood's basement shop, I cut the barrel down. Then I built a suppressor that screwed right onto the Uzi's locking nut. It's just a tube with baffles inside, not rocket science. I now had a fully automatic .45 submachine gun with a silencer that was not too shabby. The Uzi had tended to mangle the .45 ammo when I first got it. After looking at the problem, and bringing Mr. Brentwood in for his expertise, a little work with a Dremel tool fixed the problem. Once I smoothed and polished everything, it never jammed on me again.

I didn't get it all perfect the first time. I'd started working on it pretty shortly after getting back to Lexington. There was a good bit of trial and error, but by the time I was ready to go sign up with MHI, it was good to go. Reliable, and a serious monster killer.

That Uzi wasn't the only weapon I picked up. I really had to remind myself that one big PUFF bounty shouldn't all be spent in one place. But... it was GUNS! I'd wanted to own guns since I was a little kid. I really felt like a kid in a candy store with more money in my pocket than I'd ever dreamed I'd have and the free right as an adult American to buy any damned weapon I pleased.

I picked up a Garand that needed some work and fixed it right up. An M14 seemed like a no-brainer. I picked up an Armalite to have something in 5.56. Then an FN-FAL as a backup to the M14. An MP5 just 'cause I wanted one. I wished, badly, that H&K would make a decent weapon in .45 but no joy. I know a lot of people in the industry don't like H&K 'cause their customer service sucks and you can't get parts. That's just a German thing. The reason you can't get parts is they hardly ever break. Also a German thing. Which is why I like H&K. I picked up two custom 1911 .45s and a couple of .357s, a Colt Python six-inch and a Smith & Wesson snubby.

The other major purchase I made was of some really good

blades. I'd talked with the MHI guys after dinner and one point that was made was that often the best way to kill a monster was by cutting off its head. They had various implements they recommended. I kept my mouth shut because I already had opinions on the matter and wasn't going to just voice them with such an experienced bunch. But the truth, in my opinion, and I hold it to this day, is if you want to cut something's head off, you can't go wrong with a really good katana.

The difference is steel. The steel of most mono-metal blades is designed so it can be sharpened down to micrometric thickness. A katana's blade will sharpen down to very low micrometers or even high nanometers and still retain strength. The secret is in the folding and, assuming equal skill on the smith, the more folds is generally the better.

Another reason I didn't voice the opinion was I'd already had the same argument with my jujitsu teacher. Not specifically on the subject of the supernatural and cutting off the heads of vampires, but generally on how Japanese blades were not as good as most people made them out to be and that you really needed to use a heavy blade like the cane-cutting blades that were a feature of jujitsu and . . . blah-blah.

Fortunately, I had an in-house expert in the field and cash burning a hole in my pocket. Through Mr. Brentwood's connections I was able to secure what is described as a "three-soul" blade. The term means that it should have the ability to cut through three necks in one well practiced stroke.

I didn't tell him I was planning on using it to actually cut off heads. But other than blades with defined historical significance, the cost of a katana generally depends upon its quality and sharpness.

The three-soul blade, Mo No Ken or Sword of Mourning, cost more than a pretty nice new car. I carried it for years. It was well worth the money. It took the spine of a Greater vampire to finally damage it enough I had to retire it. And it still went through that hardened spine like most blades go through a human's.

This is the story of the blade called Sword of Mourning.

The maker, Makoto Kimura, was a swordsmith in the Emperor's court. His son was the apple of his eye. All of Kimura's other family had died. His wife had died in childbirth of their second child. So Ashio was all he had left. Then Ashio took a fever and even the doctors of the Court and the finest Shinto priests could do nothing. His beloved son and heir died.

Kimura, stricken by grief, threw himself into his work. He tried blank of metal after blank of metal but none were to his satisfaction. The master swordsmith of the court was angry with him for he seemed to be simply malingering. Swords needed to be made and all Kimura could do was throw the finest steel blanks aside as if they were trash.

Finally, he found the blanks of steel that were to his satisfaction and began the folding and reforging process.

He folded and folded and folded that steel, throwing all his grief and hurt and mourning into his work. Day and night he worked, his tears the only water used to quench the blade.

He worked for a year and finally was finished. He had created what he knew was the finest blade he would ever create in his life. Done, he committed seppuku that he might be reunited with his family.

This is the story of Sword of Mourning.

When we had it in hand, around the time I contacted MHI and was getting ready to leave Lexington, I spent the money to buy two live pigs and invited my jujitsu class along with others (some from kendo, friends I'd met shooting, couple of friends from high school) to a barbeque out at a friend's place near Elizabethtown. Part of a good-ole-fashion pig roast back then was you got the whole pig, cleaned it before dawn, then roasted it all day long. People would show up later with various dishes and in the evening, you'd rip into the barbequed pig. Good tradition.

My jujitsu instructor and anyone else who wanted (which was about fifty people including the Brentwoods) showed up before dawn for the demonstration. Both of the pigs were tied down by their snouts. Contest: Who could take off the head easiest and quickest, me with a katana or my jujitsu instructor with a cane-cutting blade?

It only took him two blows, give the guy credit. One went through the spine and most of the way through the neck. The pig dropped and the second took the head all the way off.

My pig literally stood for a moment—one guy got video—before its head slid off neatly and it dropped to the ground. People said at first they thought I'd just missed.

They both tasted the same, great, it was a good day of drinking and hanging out and arguing about better fighting forms, but...

Pro-tip: If you're going to be cutting off a lot of heads, get a really good katana.

I also picked up a very good wakizashi and a few other sharp things including two kukris: a standard and a Ganga Ram long blade.

In December I called MHI and talked to a woman with a just beautiful voice named Susan Shackleford. I was dying to meet her in person just to find out if her looks matched her voice. They did. Susan was probably the most beautiful woman I ever met and, like most guys who met her, I fell in love at first sight. If there was no other reason for me to never get married, it was the fact that, alas, she was already married to the heir apparent. Even worse . . . Well, that's a story for another day.

The day we lost Susan, my heart got ripped out and stomped flat. She was the only woman I'd ever met I was willing to give up my lecherous ways for. I'll love that woman to the day I die. The worst part is, it still feels like my fault.

Enough. She'd heard about Elkins, and Carlos had already suggested me. I assured her I was in good enough shape to get through the training and was scheduled for the next class in January.

January 5th, 1985, I showed up at the MHI compound in Cazador.

I figure that most of the people reading this have been through MHI training so I'll skip most of that. This intro has run long and I want to get to the real stuff: the Hunts.

I'll cover a few things, mostly the people, just for the history involved.

At the time, the president of MHI was Raymond Shackleford III. In his mid-fifties, he was, in his opinion anyway, in the prime of his hunting years. Tall, wiry, with slightly graying black hair and a grip like an industrial press. The guy was a monster himself, I swear. Tough as fricking nails. I'd thought drill instructors were tough till I met Ray III. He was missing his right eye from a ghoul that got too close but it didn't slow him down any. Guy hated being stuck in the office which was a frequent problem. He was also a walking encyclopedia of monsters, how to kill most efficiently.

"Don't mess around. Find the quickest, safest, most efficient way to dispatch the monster and do the job. Kill monsters, get paid, don't mess around. You're more likely to live to enjoy the money."

Dude could also seriously party. He drank me under the

table one time in New Orleans and that takes some doing. You'll be running into him from time to time in these memoirs. You knew when the boss was going to show. When the shit had hit the fan and there seemed to be no stopping it, there'd be Ray III.

The operations officer was a guy named Earl Harbinger. Average-looking, but he swaggered like James Cagney in a mob movie. The swagger was deserved. Earl was a living legend in the monster killing field. He always wore this beat-up old leather bomber jacket and, usually, jeans. Primary weapon was a Thompson. I'd considered a Thompson when I was hunting around for a good .45 subgun. But I'd fired one with Mr. Brentwood back in the day and knew they were a beast to keep on target. Earl would fire it one-handed and nail the eye of a gnat. It took me some time to figure out how any human could do something like that.

You might know the answer to that or not. Not up to me to say. Sort of becomes obvious in the New Orleans memoirs when he was never around when we needed him. Don't want to blow Earl's cover though.

Then there was Raymond Shackleford IV. Tall, like his father, but much broader and heavier bodied. Strikingly good-looking guy, like a male model. We mostly talked in the gym and the guy could pump more iron than Arnold Schwarzenegger. Another guy who was a walking encyclopedia of monsters. He also probably knew more about their genesis and the deep dark arts that created many of them than his dad. Guy was spectacularly smart and that was by my standards. He understood the monsters in a way I never quite got although a few of his lessons I've used over the years.

Ray IV is a tragic character on the order of Hamlet. Lately I've been trying to get him out of his funk over losing Susan, but there doesn't seem to be anything to do. He barely talks to his kids, much less me.

But back then were the good times. Ray was around most of the time I was going through training and always around to help a newbie. I didn't really need much help; I'd been pretrained in weapons and soaked up the monster information like a sponge. I'd even gotten back into good enough shape the PT didn't bother me. But he never minded having his brain picked and he'd quiz me on advanced stuff while we were working out. Best workout buddy I've ever had. I hear he's been getting better lately.

Then there was Susan. Ah, Susan. Tall enough that the couple of times I got a hug in regular clothing, I had to be careful where I put my face. Long legs, tight body, face like an angel except for a couple of minor scars that somehow just added to the look. Woman should have tried out for the Olympic shooting team. Especially long-range. And she was one hell of a hand at kung fu. She'd studied Dragon, initially, which I sort of considered a show art. But she'd moved into wah lum later and we occasionally sparred. I won't say she could kick my ass, but it was close.

They had one child, Julie, when I got there and another, Ray V, was born that year. Since then they've had a third, Nate, who's the spitting image of his mom so far. I've gotten to watch those kids grow up and it's been a real pleasure. Much as I was smitten by Susan, they were the best, the strongest couple I've ever met. I've tried very hard to pine from afar. I just hope someday I might meet someone as great as Susan who thinks I'm good enough to lasso.

Those people made up most of MHI's main team, the one that wears the smiley face demon patch. There were two more, Dwayne Myers, not my favorite person in the world at this point, and A. Martin Hood. Marty was a goofy kid, English and sort of doughy looking, but a great hunter. He was killed later in a "training accident" at the compound. Something about it caused Dwayne to leave the company; never got the straight story on that. Dwayne, of all damned things, joined MCB—Monster Control Bureau, the same outfit Agent Franks worked for. And he has been a pain in the ass to the company ever since. I met him again in New Orleans and... Well, getting ahead of myself again.

But the guy I hung around the most in those days was a really young guy named Milo Anderson. I sort of avoided Milo at first. The kid looked like a hippy: scraggly pink beard and long unruly hair, ugly green socks and sandals, everybody said he was smart as a whip and I sort of had a feeling of "Oh, God, what's a member of my family doing in MHI?" Boy, was I ever wrong.

Milo had joined MHI when he was fifteen after the rest of his large Mormon family was killed by a monster. The chief armorer of MHI at the time was a Marco Moss, a semiretired Hunter with one prosthetic arm and a disposition like a rhino with a hornache. Milo was his designated lackey and the guy to go to if you really needed something. ('Cause if you asked Marco he'd mostly just growl.) Milo also spent time on the Happy Face team, but most of his time you'd find him in the cavernous MHI workshop figuring out new and better ways to create mayhem. And whenever I was in town you'd generally find me cackling alongside.

The first time I really interacted with Milo was the range day when we were told to bring any personal firearms we thought we were going to use in monster hunting. I saw that at the time, and it was confirmed later, as a way to weed out people who thought a chrome-plated weapon was somehow more powerful or something.

I brought my primary 1911, the same one I'd used in Elkins, my M14 and the Uzi. I'd left most of my stuff at the Brentwoods'.

When I opened up the hard case with the Uzi in it, Milo came wandering over wearing his usual cargo shorts (it was January), green socks and Birkenstocks. Seriously. Hippy German tourist outfit.

"*What* is *that*?" Milo asked. I got the feeling at the time he didn't like me much, either. I think we both had a chip on our shoulders. We got over that fast.

Ray IV was on the line as well and they both regarded the Uzi with caution.

"Forty-five-caliber Uzi carbine reconfigured for full-auto fire. Dedicated hard-lock silencer. OEG scope. Maglite locks under the silencer with two other latch points for other items if need be. Three-position firing switch. It's calibrated to six hundred fifty rounds per minute. About the most I can handle on full-auto with .45."

"Who did the work?" Ray asked, holding out his hand.

"I did, sir," I said, handing it to him. "I've been studying gunsmithing since I was a teen and have an FFL."

"The Uzi mangles .45 ammo," Milo said, dubiously. "Feeding problems?"

"Nope. It's all about getting the internals polished right and the extractor tuned. Hang on."

I took the weapon back, broke it down on the table and showed them where Mr. Brentwood and I had modified the bolt.

"Okay," Milo said. "This I gotta see."

Ten minutes later he was grinning ear to ear. So was Ray IV.

"This thing totally rocks!" Milo crowed, putting another magazine of .45 into a target. I was impressed that some hippy teenager could put them all into a grouping the size of his palm at fifty yards.

"Milo," Ray IV said. "Tell Marco I want one of these."

I'd impressed the heir apparent.

That evening, after training, Milo stopped by the trainee barracks.

"Chad," he said. "Come on."

"Where we going?" I asked. I'd gotten over my initial skepticism a bit with Milo but we weren't exactly bosom buddies.

"Something you wanna see," was all he said.

Where we went was the workshops, an area normally off limits to the trainees.

I immediately fell in love. Mr. Brentwood's shop had everything you absolutely needed for doing gunsmithing and general design and maintenance. The MHI workshops had everything you would need, want or desire. It was like stepping back into heaven. That was when Milo and I became buddies and have remained buddies ever since. Over the years, not only have we spent many a happy hour in one workshop or another, I've covered his back and he's covered mine. Milo is the brother I never had.

They already had two Uzi .45s in the armory but they'd mostly been wall hangers. I showed Mr. Moss the fix I'd done on mine, which occasioned an incredibly rare smile, and we set out to do the same on the two they had. Over the next couple of weeks, working in the evening mostly, we configured both of them with the same system I'd designed. All three were put through reliability tests and passed them flawlessly. And by the time we'd finished those two, we had all the jigs, tools and dies necessary to, if not churn them out, then reconfigure any Uzi .45 easily.

At the time, the only silver ammo MHI had available was in .45 and .308. Having a usable (unlike the Thompson) .45 subgun was a real boost. Too often teams had had to choose between using long rifles in tight spaces against monsters that could only be stopped by silver, or a .45 pistol. I think probably the main contribution I made to MHI was the Iron Hand Uzi. It probably saved the lives of more MHI members than anything I ever did personally.

If an Iron Hand has ever saved your life, you're welcome.

The other main memory of Milo in training was "stake and chop" training. You know what I mean. Medical cadavers. One of a pair of trainees drives a stake into the cadaver's heart and the other cuts off the head.

When we were told that was the next day's exercise, I raised my hand when asked for questions.

"Can we use anything to cut off the head?" I asked.

"Anything you can see carrying on a mission." The trainer for that day was another retired Hunter named Justin Moody. He was the main trainer for "Introduction to Common Monsters."

"Roger," I said.

The next day I turned up with Sword of Mourning.

"You really think you're going to carry that with you, Chad?" Milo asked.

"I've been bothered by not having it every day in training, Milo," I said, grinning. "This isn't a sword. This is my brother."

"I thought you hated your brother," Milo said.

"You know what I mean."

My partner at that point was Sidney Marshall. I haven't really gotten into my training buddies 'cause I seemed to always be paired with the guys who didn't make the grade. Standards were tough back then. There were plenty of recruits and although there was the usual high loss rate, MHI had a pretty full roster of employees. We lost about two-thirds of our trainees over the course of the training.

I'd gone through Marine Corps boot camp. I didn't really find it that hard.

But Sidney had accepted the "stake" part. He really didn't like getting covered in blood as the stake went into the heart.

Suck it up. This job, I figured we'd spend most of our time covered in blood. My main thought on the training was that using an old-fashioned wooden mallet and hickory stake was inefficient, and I immediately started thinking about better ways to get the job done. Really, the stakes were for when you've already shot them a bunch.

When it got to the chop portion, I waited till everyone else was done. Most of them had struggled with various types of cutlery. I wasn't planning on struggling.

"Just one request, Milo," I said. "Can I move the neck down off the metal table? I really don't want to hammer Mourning into the metal. It might damage the table."

"Sure," Milo said, arms folded and eyes narrowed. I could tell he thought I was so much *bushidoshit*. "That's a much harder way to cut the neck, Chad."

"Got it."

I grabbed the cadaver, an elderly gentleman that looked like he'd died of either stroke or heart failure, and dragged him till his head was dangling off the end of the table. Then I placed my hand on Sword of Mourning, drew and sliced in one continuous motion.

His head hit the floor and rolled. It wasn't a nice thing to do to the poor fellow but there you go. One decapitated corpse. The cut was within a fraction of an inch of the table.

I flicked the sword to clear most of the blood, pulled out a silk cloth, wiped it down and sheathed it without really looking or thinking about it.

"Jesus," Sidney said.

"And that's called balling the jack," I said.

Just a couple of days before graduation, I was pumping iron in the gym, late lunch with Ray IV. It had become a regular thing. No big deal.

"Chad," Ray said. "Team leads will be coming in to pick up newbies at graduation. What would you think about joining the Cazador team?"

I was sort of stunned. Generally to get on the premier MHI team you had to spend time somewhere else. They were sort of MHI's SWAT. The team you called when you knew the shit was about to hit the fan. They also did most of the overseas work and who doesn't want to travel? Then there was the fact that since they were always busy, the PUFF bonuses were outstanding.

The flip side was, they also were a primary team in Alabama and the southeast in general.

One thing I forgot to mention. Ever since I went through Parris Island in summer, I have hated heat. I mean, I just truly hate the fuck out of it. I'd rather do a mission in the Antarctic in winter than the Southeastern United States in summer. Much less places like Colombia or Panama where the Happy Face team frequents.

I wasn't sure how to explain that I was massively honored and awed to be asked, but just really didn't want to sweat my ass off in armor in fucking Colombia. I decided to go for truth.

"I'm incredibly honored, sir," I said. I'd gotten to where I tended to just call him Ray so he knew something was up. "I really am."

"But?" Ray asked, sitting up from the bench press.

"I just hate heat, Ray," I said, shrugging uncomfortably. "I really, really do. I went to Parris Island in the summer and, ever since, I do absolutely *everything* I can to avoid ninety degree temperatures and one hundred percent humidity. Hell, if I'd gotten in shape in the summer, I'd have waited to join until at least late autumn to avoid the heat here."

"So working mostly in the Southeast and South America is not your idea of fun?" Ray said, grinning. "Got it. Where *would* you like to go?"

"Seattle?" I asked. "I hear the team up there is short and I'm sure they could use a good shooter. Maybe Illinois? Somewhere, sorry, Yankee."

"The Nelsons run the Seattle team now. They took over when Dorcas Peabody transferred," Ray said, lying back down to pump some more iron. "Good people, good Hunters and they run a good team. But I'll warn you they tend to pick your brain. They'll probably want to write a paper on your relationship with your family."

"Paper?" I asked. "Oh, Jesus, not *academics*! I take it back! I want on Happy Face!"

"Too late," Ray said, grinning. "Like I said, good people. They're both psychiatrists but they don't push it. Too much. I think they'll be good for you. But it will be up to them. If not, we'll find you a good spot. And the offer remains open. Assuming you survive the newbie portion—and Nelson's people take fewer losses than most teams—you'll end up on it eventually. You've got the gift."

"God has given me many gifts, Ray. And for every gift, God gives you challenges to balance them out."

I wish I could convince him to listen to me on that one. Losing Susan was just one of those challenges God gives us. I don't think Ray had ever really been challenged before losing her. Now he's just . . . He'll come back to us. I know he will. Susan may be gone but we'll get Ray back eventually. But since I was on the mission where we lost Susan, he's not really speaking to me at the moment.

Two days later was graduation and we got to meet the team leads. I put on my most charming smile and buttonholed Dr. Lucius Nelson in the mess.

"Dr. Nelson," I said, holding out my hand. "Oliver Chadwick Gardenier, Doctor. I go by Chad. Pleasure to meet you."

"From what I've heard, not so much," Dr. Nelson said, smiling and shaking my hand. He was the "affable and chubby" type of academic. I knew right away I was in trouble.

"Psychologically and physically abusive upbringing. Counteracademia and counseling syndrome. I loved the damned near perfect straight Cs you got in high school. That had to be tough. You go through women like a fire hose as a way to strike back at your psychologically abusive mother, not to mention your main role model growing up, your father, is a satyriast. And you found God through a near-death experience. I could write an entire book about you."

"If picking my brain gets me on your team, Doctor, I'll do it," I said, gritting my teeth.

"You also have a relentless desire to prove yourself since you had one hundred percent negative reinforcement as a child," Dr. Nelson said, "which manifests itself in obsessive attention to training and preparation, augmented by your time in the Marines and with your foster father, the former Marine. Which are all good things. Assuming some other team lead doesn't shanghai you, you're hired. We need a head-banger who can—how did Ray put it?—'Nail a rat's balls at a hundred yards on full auto.'"

"He exaggerates, Doctor," I said, trying not to grin. "Semi-auto, maybe."

"What's this I hear about a modified Uzi . . . ?"

Not the sort of academics I grew up with. Mostly. The Doctors Nelson did have the tendency to lecture and were a bit more "squishy liberal" than most of MHI. But mostly that was due to their real caring for people, especially survivors. They were always furious at the way MCB treated survivors of supernatural events.

On the other hand, they could also talk about guns and killing monsters all day long and a couple of their bloodier stories they told with positive relish.

March 28th, 1985, I packed my bags, said a fond farewell to the MHI compound (which had started to be roasting, I was glad to be getting out of 'Bama) and headed for Lexington. I had "stuff" there I wanted to pick up and it might be a while, or never, before I saw the Brentwoods again.

But I was now a full-fledged Monster Hunter, proudly wearing my Flaming Warthog patch. It was a good day.

CHAPTER 6

The Brentwoods were, thank God, comfortable with my cover story. I'd told them that I'd gotten a job offer from a security firm that handled Federal security "issues" and that the rest was classified, the offer contingent on getting back into good enough shape to pass the training program. So when I visited, they didn't ask many questions. I told them about some of the friends I'd made, Milo mostly, and some of the funnier stories that didn't involve monster-related issues. I really wanted to tell them the truth, but two things held me back. The first was that they'd think I was crazy. The second was that, if they got over that, they'd think I was crazy to do the job.

Mrs. Brentwood sensed that the job carried risks. As sort of my adopted mom, she wasn't really happy about that, especially given how she'd almost lost me in Beirut. On the other hand, as WWII generation and the wife of a Marine, she also knew about sacrifice.

So she buttonholed me as I was doing dishes after dinner.

"Chad," she said, laying her hand on my arm. "Just tell me that what you're doing is important."

"Ma'am," I replied. "It's more important than anything I'd ever have done as a Marine. There's issues that need fixing and my company fixes those issues. And, yes, you might have to attend my funeral. I'm sorry about that. But it is really something important enough to put my life on the line. Other than that..." I shrugged.

"I'll have to trust you on that," she said, giving me a hug. "We'll miss you. Again."

"You'll find some other kid who needs a real home," I replied, smiling. "There's plenty of us out there."

I'd gotten a U-Haul hitch attached to Honeybear and it was necessary for all the stuff the Brentwoods had been holding for me. Civilian clothes, my uniforms (which, with the exception of the dress blues, were perfectly useful for monster hunting), guns, blades, books, the custom MHI armor, it all added up. I put a good lock on it and hoped it wouldn't get broken into on my trip.

I ignored my mother completely. Any lingering doubts about that had been put to rest in Bethesda. On the other hand...

I cordially detested my dad for all the reasons any decent human being would. On the other hand, any trip down that particular memory lane was pretty much bound to involve hot coeds. I'd more than once knocked off one of my father's hangers-around. It was worth stopping by Kansas on my way to Seattle.

"So you went from being a Marine babykiller to being in some top-secret clandestine babykiller group," Dad said when I trotted out the cover story. But he said it with a grin. Over the years Dad's full-on liberal hard-on for violence and the military had mellowed. I think he even sort of respected me for being a Marine, which was bizarre. "From a bombing to black helicopters. Your mother must love that."

"I haven't spoken to Mom since she came to visit me in the hospital. So I dunno."

"Your mother actually bothered to visit you in the hospital?" he said, surprised. "Wasn't there some subcommittee meeting she had to chair or protest march or something?"

I told him the story. When I got to the part about telling her I'd been promoted to "babykiller first class," he burst out laughing.

"God, I wish I could have seen her face."

We were drinking some very good single malt scotch and he took a deep gulp. He'd started to develop the red nose of a heavy drinker and the formerly toned body was starting to get a bit rotund.

"It wasn't worth it. There weren't just military doctors and nurses. There were other parents visiting. That really hurt them at a time they didn't need to be hurt. Just like Mom. I seriously would have killed her with my bare hands if I hadn't been in traction."

"I've never told you this," he said, uncomfortably. "But . . . I was really proud of you when you joined the Marines. I wish you'd put that unquestionably fine mind to work more but . . . that took guts. More guts than anyone in the rest of your family. Including me."

"You look into the abyss and the abyss looks back," I said, shrugging. "Then you punch the abyss in the face."

"I love you, son," he said when he got done laughing. "You're the only one in the family that's worth a shit. When I heard about the bomb going off . . . that really ripped my heart out. I was going to visit but . . . In retrospect, I'm glad I didn't. I could imagine what their reaction would be to your liberal academic *dad* turning up after that."

"All's well that ends well," I said. "And to again quote the German: What doesn't kill us . . ."

"When you said you were dropping by I made some calls," he replied. "There's a couple of cheerleaders who seriously cannot tell the difference between Can and Kant. And if they can't get at least a C they're going to lose their cheerleading scholarship. One of them's a huge fan of Marines . . ."

My dad's a philandering, using, man-whore. But sometimes I've just got to love him.

Seattle's MHI office was actually in an industrial park in Renton. It was convenient to SeaTac and near I-5 for when we had to head to points outside the Seattle area. Which was most of the time.

I'd gotten a hotel, found a secure, air-conditioned storage locker for my stuff and generally gotten my feet on the ground, including a recon of the objective to ensure I knew where it was, before I checked in. The office was attached to a small warehouse and the only sign it was the headquarters of a premier monster hunting organization was a small sign that just read MHI in letters about six inches high. Discreet, thy name is Monster Hunting. There were also several security cameras covering the parking lot and front door.

The front door was a steel security door with a buzzer and one of the new push-button combination locks. Since nobody had given me the combination, I buzzed the door at 0900, the appointed time and the appointed place. Uniform was jeans, T-shirt and waterproof windbreaker both to conceal the 1911 and for the drizzle.

"I take it you're Chad," a woman's voice said from the speaker. "Come on in."

There was a receptionist's desk inside the door with a couple of chairs for visitors but no receptionist and no visitors. Just another code-locked door and a fair amount of dust. That door buzzed as I reached it and I noted the not terribly discreet cameras covering the entry.

Inside was a hallway and the other Dr. Nelson. Blonde and slender, Dr. Joan Nelson, looked like anything but a Monster Hunter. In fact, she looked a good bit like one of the cheerleaders that had made my stay in Kansas so pleasant, if quite a bit older. I reminded myself that *a*, she was my team lead and *b*, I didn't come on to married women. Despite that, my greeting was perhaps a touch too warm.

"Why Dr. Nelson," I said, taking her hand, "what a pleasure it is to make your acquaintance."

"You really are a lounge lizard, aren't you," she said, laughing and shaking her head.

"I'm sorry," I replied, throwing my hands out. "Put me around a beautiful woman and I go automatically into mode!"

"I'll forgive you for the compliment. Most of the team is out checking on a report of a werewolf. Turned out it was just a bear attack but the local authorities called us in just in case. They're on their way back. Let me show you around in the meantime, but keep your hands to yourself."

"I always take no for an answer," I said, definitely. "I just prefer yes. And I really don't go for married women. That's a line I try very hard not to cross. I'm still an outrageous flirt."

"Well, you won't be crossing it with me, young man," Dr. Nelson said. "I know your type. That's not an insult; it's just I'm fairly well insulated against it. But feel free to flirt all you'd like. It's a nice endorphin stimulator."

I got shown around the offices and warehouse. The warehouse contained not only the armory, including the team crew-served weapons, but also a small but well-packed explosives bunker as well as machine tools for gunsmithing.

"We don't have an in-house gunsmith at this time," Joan said. "I understand it's one of your gifts."

"One of them," I said, looking at the shop. It wasn't even up to Mr. Brentwood's level. "Any chance I can build on this? I'll get the stuff out of my own PUFF money assuming we've got the work."

"Feel free," she said. "If it's staying here, the company will buy it if it's within budget. We haven't been using that budget lately because, well, there wasn't anyone to use it. If you can, go for it."

"Anything that needs doing now?"

"We just sent the guns that needed repair out to our usual shop," Joan said. "Maybe later."

About that time there was a honk from outside and, after a check of the security cameras, I got to open the door for the team vans and meet most of the rest of the team. They were a decidedly mixed bunch.

Besides the Doctors Nelson there was an assistant team lead, Bradford Todd.

Brad was a tall, lanky Oklahoman in his early thirties with long brown hair, a neatly trimmed goatee and two gold teeth. Slow of speech and fairly reticent at the best of times, he just got more calm the worse things got. Not that he was slow in combat. He could rumble with the best of them. His back story involved a shaman in a land dispute with his family. Shaman lost.

Timmy Burgess was the newest guy on the team after me. He was from California and sported the whole California Surfer Dude thing: long brown hair he usually kept in a braid, fluffy beard, and in all but the coldest weather he was always wearing a Hawaiian shirt and cargo shorts. He'd run into some sort of sea monster at a beach party and managed to torch it with a homemade Molotov cocktail.

We lost Timmy later, but that's another story.

Louis Wagner was a rarity in the Northwest: he was black. The Northwest, at least at that time, had something like less than one percent African American population. He hailed from Chicago and still had that Chicago accent. A colony of giant centipedes had ended up breeding in an office building where he was the night janitor. Fortunately, he knew two things: centipedes don't care for pure ammonia and where to get a bunch. His main comment was that "Hunting pays a lot better than being a janitor."

Louis generally teamed up with Phillip Jimenez. Phil didn't look particularly Hispanic. He had paler skin than I do and that's saying something. A former Army engineer, he'd gotten out and gotten a job with a construction company. While digging out a trench, he'd hit what turned out to be a long-buried vampire's coffin. Unfortunately it was at night. Fortunately, he realized what it was and, without hesitating, cut it in half with the blade of the excavator.

His specialty on the team was all our explosives stuff. I made a mental note right there and then to make friends. I like explosives as much as guns, just hadn't had nearly as much experience with them at that point.

Jesse Mason was from Colorado. He'd grown up hunting and was our primary long-range shooter and tracker. His preferred weapon was a 700 BDL in .30-06. I noted that I had a Garand in storage as well as my own BDL on which I'd done some tooling. We agreed we needed to check things out on a range. I could tell there was going to be some competiveness there. That was cool. I knew he'd smoke me at long range. I'd wait till we encountered monsters to demonstrate at short.

The general way we rolled was we'd keep our basic gear at our homes or, if it was secure, in our car trunk. Those days we had a pager, big clunky thing, and one of the then-very-new car phones. Unfortunately, the range on the car phone was more or less Greater Seattle Area. Get outside that and you lost coverage. Coverage was better on the pager but not much. When there was a call-out, we got a page. Unless we were definitely "off," we were on call 24/7. Mostly we got two days off a week when it wasn't busy. But if a team got called, you had to go on call even if it was your day off. So you figured you were more or less always on call.

If there wasn't a big rush or if it was something planned in advance, we'd meet up at the office and load into the team vans. But I was warned that I'd probably be using my own car for a lot of calls. No biggie; one benefit of Honeybear was a big trunk.

Jesse got detailed to show me where to get a car phone. He road in his car, I rode in mine.

The RadioShack on 167 was our designated electronics store. While they did the install on the car phone, Jesse and I grabbed an early lunch. He suggested a nearby sushi place. Not knowing what sushi was, I agreed. You'd think with all the time I spent doing kendo and what with learning Japanese, I'd have known what sushi was. But in the early eighties in Kentucky, nobody, and I mean *nobody*, ate raw fish. All I knew was it was a Japanese restaurant.

"So, where you staying?" he asked. The restaurant had some tables but mostly it was a bar.

"Right now I'm in a residence hotel by the airport," I said, reading the menu. "Wait, this is *raw fish*?"

"I thought you were all into Japanese stuff," Jesse said, grinning at my discomfort.

"Kendo, sure," I said. I didn't tell him I spoke it. "But you don't find this sort of stuff in Kentucky. Or Lejeune for that matter."

"Welcome to Seattle," he said, still grinning. He did the order in really broken Japanese.

"With friend murder tuna tire," was what he said. "Ox foot much please."

"What is 'ox foot'?" I asked. In English. I held my hand up for the server to wait.

"Ox foot? What do you mean?"

I repeated what he'd said, verbatim.

"I said lots of wasabi."

"My unintelligible friend meant to say 'Lots of wasabi,'" I said in fluent Japanese. "My own humble experience does not include sushi or its accompaniments. What would you suggest, sir?"

"Ah, you speak Japanese?" the server said. "But you do not know sushi?"

"I am from a landlocked area. No sushi on the menu. I am looking forward to trying it. Do you know where I can find a good udon? I very much like udon."

"We do good udon. You want udon?"

"Yes, please. And I will try the yellowfin tuna roll. Is this a good roll?"

"The yellowfin is very fresh. Very good. But for you, you try it tataki."

"I am your servant in this."

"You speak Japanese," Jesse said as the server left.

"Japanese, German, Spanish, sort of a long list. Aramaic..."

"I thought you were all, 'Oorah, Marine! Bang head!'" Jesse said. "Oorah! Oorah! Gung ho!"

"I am. And I speak nine languages and read about four more. My parents are liberal academics and were antiwar protesters. I inherited the IQ but rebelled by becoming everything they, or at least my mom, hates. They were all about 'be yourself' and 'follow your own path' unless it meant owning guns and being a babykiller. Mom's description. My dad turns out to be okay with it except he'd like me to get a Ph.D. at some point. Not going to happen. I'd rather use my brains to kill monsters. I also play a very mean violin."

"I guess that sort of makes sense," Jesse said.

"You're not academic background, are you?"

"Country boy. Born and raised in a little town called Yuma, population thirty-five hundred. Down on the plains, not the mountains. Everybody thinks Colorado's nothing but mountains. Most of it looks more like Kansas."

"I drove through that bit on the way up here. Does look like West Kansas, that's for sure. What the hell kind of supernatural event did you run into out there?"

"Werewolf," he said. "I was hunting with my dad. Thought we were looking at the world's biggest wolf. Would have been a really nice trophy. Did not like it when Dad put a .30-06 round through it longways. Also didn't seem to faze it. We nailed it maybe a dozen times before it was on us. Dad didn't make it. I ended up braining it with my rifle and in desperation I managed to cut its head off. That stopped it."

"Sorry to hear about your dad."

"It was five years ago," Jesse said, shrugging. "I'm over it."

"Right."

"Okay, let's just say I do this for some reason other than the pay," Jesse said, frowning. "You?"

"Truly weird story. I had a... vision, something, when I was in the rubble of the barracks..."

"Rubble of the barracks?"

"You didn't get that I'm one of the survivors of the bombing of the Marine barracks in Beirut?"

"That had not been passed on, no," Jesse said. "Really?"

"Really and truly. But I had a meeting with someone who might or might not have been Saint Peter. I got the option of going to heaven or going back. God had something he wanted me to do so I took the duty option. There was also this cryptic

'There shall be a sign' prophecy. After I got out of rehab, during which I was always looking for the sign, I was driving back to Kentucky when, well, I saw the sign."

"What was the sign?"

"Fifty-seven."

"As in *Heinz*?" he asked, laughing.

"That was what was driving me nuts for months, yes," I said, grinning. "Turned out it was a county road in West Virginia. Five slash seven. Deer jumped out as I was driving home in W-V, I swerved, tapped the sign for it. There was another sign for a church revival. After I got done laughing, I took the turn just to see if that was what God was talking about. I thought he wanted me to go to the revival. Turns out the preacher was a necromancer who was going around attacking, well, 'religious' folks with zombies. So by the time I got there, the zombie outbreak was going well. I stopped it. I took the whole thing as being a sign God wanted me to fight monsters. Don't know why. I'm not otherwise terribly special. But here I am."

"So you're on a mission from God," Jesse said, wagging his head back and forth. "I guess that makes you pretty religious."

"I was raised atheist. I've converted to Catholicism since but, no, I'm not really what you'd call 'religious.' I've got a serious issue with temptations of the flesh. Girls tend to find me attractive and vice versa. So I'm no saint. I doubt I'll ever be able to turn an undead. On the other hand, I figure that as long as you're not a real ass about it, it matters less than most religious people think. Given that hunting is one of those 'live fast, die young' jobs . . . I think I'll gather all the rosebuds I can while I may."

"Ah," Jesse said, "I may finally have a wingman."

"Only if you're willing to settle for the remora, man," I said.

The udon was great. When the tataki arrived, I refused to do the "nibble at it" thing and took one of the thin strips of tuna covered in ginger and popped it in my mouth.

"Oh, my God," I said, chewing carefully. "I am in love."

The server was watching and smiled and nodded.

"Of all of the great exports of the Land of the Rising Sun, this must be among the greatest," I said, then took another bite.

I ended up sampling a number of dishes and loved all of them. I had to ask Mr. Brentwood the next time I called why he'd never introduced me to sushi. Of course, I later had sushi in Lexington and swore afterwards never to have any unless I was within two hours' drive from a port. Gah!

While we were sitting there, two Japanese girls came in and sat next to Jesse. After listening to them for a bit I introduced myself. They had been talking about anime and I explained that I was a voice actor who occasionally did fill-in on anime and Jesse was my agent. I did that part in English so he'd know what role to play.

Jesse tried not to show his amusement as I went about charming them. One of them, Yuki, was a foreign student at the University of Washington. Chiyo was visiting. They had stopped in for lunch on the way from SeaTac.

They didn't believe me at first when I said I did anime voice work. As part of what you could get in terms of Japanese culture in the 1980s in Lexington, I'd watched quite a bit of anime. And one particular voice actor had a very similar voice. So I quoted one of his most famous lines to them in the same voice. I humbly admitted that I was just a fill-in for the more famous voice actor and was rarely credited, but voice actors in Japan are given the sort of godlike status of movie stars in the United States. They'd met a real voice actor! And he was a cute gaijin who spoke Japanese! I even composed a haiku in honor of Chiyo's arrival.

I got Yuki's phone number and a suggestion on another bento place in the University District.

"Christ, you really are smooth, aren't you?" Jesse said as they left.

"Getting frequently laid as a bachelor is a matter of proper approach and seizing every opportunity," I opined. "Meeting girls is not the issue. Convincing them you're not going to put a ring on their finger without being an absolute and complete ass is the issue."

After three hours hanging out in the bento house, we went back to find out if my phone had, in fact, been installed. It had. I picked up my pager, went back to the office and was officially on call with the Flaming Warthogs.

Which really pissed Yuki off when it beeped at one in the morning. Chiyo wasn't really happy either since she and Jesse were in Yuki's guest room…

CHAPTER 7

"It was a *bear* attack," Jesse said, yawning and lifting a crate of ammo into the van.

The Flaming Warthogs were not particularly happy to get *another* call from the King County sheriff about *another* "bear attack" in Skykomish. They'd driven half the way out there yesterday morning only to be told by the MCB that the death was a confirmed bear attack. The claw marks and tooth marks were definitely bear and the body had not shown signs of lycanthrope enzymes. Bear attack.

"Just because it was mauled by a bear doesn't mean it was a bear," Lucius said as we continued to load the van. "The bear they darted had human remains in its stomach. But it was a black bear. Those don't usually attack humans. And they've had another attack. Two dead. So . . . possible lycanthrope."

"Not the full moon," Jesse argued.

"Give it up, Jesse," I said. I was just as unhappy about the development as he was but when it's time to hunt, it's time to hunt. I won't say Chiyo and Yuki could wait or anything. They'd more or less given me the high sign that read "Don't come back." "We're going to Skykomish. Wherever the hell Skykomish is."

"Skykomish makes Yuma look like the big city," Jesse said. "Pretty area, though."

I'd give a description of the trip to Skykomish were it not

for one thing. I learned in the Marines to sleep when you can. And given that I hadn't been to sleep yet, but had earned nature's tranquilizer the best way... I passed out about the time the van hit the side street and woke up when Timmy shook my shoulder in Skykomish.

"We there already?" I asked blearily.

Based on the blue lights from county and state police cars, the answer was yes.

The night was partially overcast with intermittent drizzle and rain. When we got out of the van, it was drizzle. Along the way it went to rain, then back to drizzle, rain, drizzle, clear sky, rain, drizzle and so on and so forth.

Working in Washington State guaranteed that you were going to get wet and spend a lot of time wet and cold. I was fine with wet and cold. Better than sweating your ass off in the heat. When I was later transferred to New Orleans; I finally found my inner bitch and complained about the weather unmercifully.

While Dr. Nelson talked to the cops, I considered my load-out. I really wanted to try out the Uzi in action but the conditions mitigated against it. Subguns were for close terrain, interior or really close brush. While the forest might be a bit close, it technically was open terrain. That said long rifle. So I broke out the M14. This was before the days of ready access to all sorts of high-speed night-vision so the best I had was a pair of issue binocular NVGs. They weighed a ton back then.

To go on top of my issue body armor, I'd rigged vests depending on what weapon I was carrying. That way I could make the decision on site and not have to change a bunch of stuff. One vest was pre-loaded for "open country combat, M14." Nine magazines for the 14, two WP grenades, two frag grenades. Frags can get you in trouble inside but are the cat's pajamas in brush or forest. All the vests contained 1911 mags with silver ammo, a first aid kit, flashlights, two one-quart canteens and two small tactical knives. There was a point to attach a holster and I'd picked up one of the then-new Aussie SAS "tactical" thigh holsters, what is now called a "drop" holster. That held my 1911 with two magazines on the holster. In addition I had a daypack, what would later be called an assault ruck when everybody started using them. This was just a brown L.L. Bean book bag that I'd done some configuring on. The main configuration being a place to lash my katana on the left side.

Put on my armor, throw on the chosen vest, attach my primary weapon with a two-point sling, throw on the backpack and I was ready to rumble.

I noticed that I was the only one putting on a helmet.

"No helmet?" I asked. I'd already decided I wasn't a big fan of the MHI issue helmet. I liked the new Army Kevlar helmet. The way it dropped down over the ear gave nearly as much protection to the head as the issue MHI helmets and it could stop light rounds that were bouncers. The "light" MHI helmets probably wouldn't, and you couldn't get a good cheek-to-shoulder weld on your weapon.

"Cuts down on your hearing," Jesse said. "And werewolves don't generally go for the head at first. And it's a pain in the ass with the radios."

In those days our radios were full over-the-ear cans with a throat mike. The system did not fit under my helmet very well. On the other hand, it didn't fit under the issue ones very well, either.

"I think I'll keep the brain bucket."

I had to configure my load-out in the pack but that didn't take long. One hundred rounds of .308 in box, three more loaded mags, two more frags and two more WP grenades, two water bottles, more first aid and some pogie bait. I tended towards peanut M&Ms and Snickers bars. It wasn't great for long duration but it was a good sugar boost. I threw in one MRE for the heck of it.

Then I found some bushes and pissed.

Pro-tip: This was something Mr. Brentwood told me the first time I went home after boot camp and was later reinforced by a gunny I got friendly with who had combat experience in Vietnam. If you know you're going into combat, take a piss and take a dump. If you don't, you're probably going to do it in combat. The body dumps waste in stress situations to get them out of the gut and reduce all sorts of problems. Natural human reaction.

If you don't want to embarrass yourself, do it beforehand.

The site of the suspected lycanthrope attack was up Beckler Road right by a bridge on Beckler Creek. After rigging up, we got back in the vans and followed a sheriff's car up to the attack site.

The attack was a horror movie classic. A young local couple, Jody Valdez, fifteen, and Cory Drake, seventeen, had found the perfect place to make out—or based on the state of their clothing, much of which was on the back floor of the 1972 Buick Skylark and untorn, possibly more. The window of the backseat was shattered. They were more or less splashed all over the interior and exterior of the car. There wasn't much left of either of them.

"This wasn't a bear," Lieutenant Paulding said. The lieutenant was one of King County's designated "this never happened" people. I had to wonder over the years how one got promoted when the cases you worked "never happened."

"This, I have to agree, was not a bear," Dr. Nelson said. He looked mildly incongruous kitted out like a commando with his spectacles perched on his nose. He examined the scratches on the door and pulled out a tape measure. "Claw sizes and shape are all wrong. And based on their degree of decomposition and time of attack, there's too much meat taken. Bears don't eat people this fast or thoroughly."

One of the rookie cops pulled in to control the scene had to walk away and puke at that comment.

"Jesse," Lucius said. "Tracks."

"Yes, sir," Jesse said, starting to work out from the attack.

"Chad, cover him."

I had approximately zero experience at that point in tracking so I just kept my eyes out and ears open, which was hard with the radio headset. There was a dial you could dial up the ambient sound and I turned it up until Jesse said something and I got a squealing feedback.

"Ouch." I turned it down. "What you say?"

"I said I got blood trail," Jesse said. "Headed across the bridge. And, no, turning it up doesn't help. Get Dr. Nelson."

The team crossed the bridge, then down off the road, following Jesse. Once down off the road, the brush closed in and I wondered if the M14 had been the best call. The night was surprisingly still. I'd expected more sounds of insect life. I didn't know if that was normal for these woods or not but I wasn't going to ask.

On the other side of the river there was a small floodplain. That was where the brush was thickest. Our lights barely penetrated and I was expecting a massive werewolf to come crashing through the brush at any moment.

"Loosen up, Chad," Dr. Nelson said. I don't know how he even knew I was tense. "The wolf's going to hear us long before we hear it. Trying to creep up on it never works."

"Yes, sir," I said, rotating my shoulders and telling myself to loosen up. Didn't work. The zombies I'd started with had been right there and easy to target. They weren't superimproved predators where I was on their home ground. I was not a happy camper.

The trail went up a slight slope which got progressively steeper. Pretty soon we were having to help each other up the slope. Then it turned sideways across the slope, down again and hit a small trail.

"Firebreak?" I asked, looking around.

"Yeah," Jesse said, carefully considering the tracks. "And I think it's headed back towards town."

"That wouldn't be good," Dr. Nelson said.

The tracks continued down the fortunately unused firebreak until they hit US 2. We were back down on the floodplain again and it took them a bit to find where the lycanthrope had gone. He finally found a track across the road, down by the river and a slip mark on the bank of the river itself.

We crossed the river, getting quite wet and cold in the process. The rain had the river up. Not flooding but it was swift. We formed a human chain to cross it.

On the far side of the river was another paved road and the tracks ended there. There was no sign of recent breaks or activity across the road or for a hundred yards on either side of where the lycanthrope had reached the road. Either it had gotten better at covering its tracks or it had followed the paved road to avoid them.

"Okay, who is this guy and where did he go?" Dr. Nelson asked, rhetorically.

"We need more information," Jesse said. "Any missing hikers in the area? Houses up this road? Recent arrivals?"

"Agreed," Lucius said. "And preferably a ride back to the van."

There were deputies and state troopers all over the area at this point. We found one on the road and Louis got a ride back to the van. When he returned, he was accompanied by our favorite people, Monster Control Bureau.

I tuned the resultant acrimonious discussion out. MCB had called the previous attack on a hiker "Not lycanthrope related." MHI had been paged on the way in and told to stand down. If they'd continued on and gotten a track, then the two kids might still be alive.

MCB, of course, could care less about that. Like most MCB agents, the New Orleans branch in my time being an exception, they were more focused on shutting down speculation and giving Hunters a hard time. I know MCB thinks it can handle all this better than Hunters, but I've seen, at this point, the confidential GAO reports. They can't. They cost too much and it's much harder to cover up FBI and police casualties than "contractors." If the FBI started to sustain our casualty rates, the cat would get out of the bag quick. The only way for them to keep those casualties down would be to use three or four times as many agents on each case and since, man per man, Hunters also cost one-third the cost of agents . . . Start doing the math. And that doesn't even get to effectiveness. New York proved that using "mercenary" Hunters was a much better choice than cops who are paid by the hour and primarily want to make sure they just go home in one piece.

End ranting pro Hunter argument.

We needed more intel to have any chance of tracking down this werewolf before it killed again. If it hadn't already. The MCB, again, could care less. We weren't going to get anything from them; so after the usual useless back and forth; we made contact with Lieutenant Paulding.

Lieutenant Paulding had already been doing the groundwork. The cover so far was "definitely not a serial killer." But the usual questions had been asked. Any new people in town?

Skykomish had once upon a time been a tiny but bustling metropolis of far more than the current two hundred or so residents. That had been back when it was a major railway stop before Stevens Pass and when the area had been heavy into timber and mining. The combination of the changes in the railroads, environmentalists killing any chance of cutting timber and the mines closing had reduced it to a fraction of its size. These days it was mostly a gateway to the local national forest. There were some survivalist types—*"Hello!"*—that lived up in the hills but no new ones. Other than tourists passing through, no new people. Could it be one of the tourists or hikers?

"Doesn't make sense," Timmy opined. "Why go all the way out here to attack people? I mean, if you're from a metropolitan area, more targets there. And it's not as if it just turned. Isn't the full moon. It has to know what it's doing."

"Might have come out here to get away from people," Louis said. "It realized what it was, came out here to go live in the woods as a wolf and found out it's a lot harder to hunt deer than people?"

"Possible," Lucius said. "Transforming takes energy. If it was stuck in wolf form, it might have had to eat to change back."

"Start looking for really skinny hikers?" Jesse said.

"After two people you'd think it could put on some weight," I said.

"You'd be surprised."

"Okay, if we go with that," I said. "Guy goes out to the woods to live as nature and a bite from a werewolf intended him to be. Decent and reasonable thing to do. Try to keep away from people and just eat deer. Say he's from the city with no real knowledge of the woods. Maybe he brings some food with him but it runs out quick. Finds that deer can smell him a mile off and run real fast. So he starts hunting people whether his human side wants him to or not. Starvation is a strong incentive. Now he's probably changed back, right? He'll go to his camp, collect his belongings and then what?"

"Head back to the city?" Louis said.

"I'd probably head to the nearest restaurant," I said. "Where I can pay to pig out. Assuming he's got any cash."

"We'll change back into regular gear," Dr. Nelson said. "Get rooms at the local hotel. If we don't get him today, we're going to be here for a while. And stake out all the local restaurants. Especially at breakfast. Look for someone disheveled that's eating like he hasn't eaten in weeks. Best chance we've got."

"MCB will freak the hell out if we have to do a takedown in public," Jesse pointed out.

"We'll try to get him out of public," Dr. Nelson said. "And use a silencer if it comes to that."

There was exactly one restaurant in the immediate area which was part of the one hotel in the immediate area: the Cascadia Inn. It was just past dawn when we pulled up and I, personally, was ready to eat a horse. Unfortunately, the café didn't open until nine A.M. Also, several of the rooms were already being used by the Federal Government so we were stuck with two: a double twin and a "family bunk room" consisting of a queen and two bunk beds. And they wouldn't have any rooms available until after noon.

We'd put away all the heavy gear and I'd thrown on a windbreaker to conceal my .45. While waiting for the rooms or the café to open up, I sat on the front steps and watched the world go by. The weather had changed to the classic "early morning rain" of the marching cadence. With the sun starting to come up and peek through the cloud cover, I could finally get a look around. I could see why people would move here. It was the quintessential small town, like nothing had changed in decades. And it was a beautiful setting. The tree-clad mountains surrounding the town were green with spring growth. Truly a beautiful and peaceful setting for horror. The recent attacks had been the first thing of significance to happen in years and you could tell they'd really put a damper on the local community. The few people walking around were hunched and looked fearful. That wasn't right.

As I was sitting there, minding my own damned business, a hiker came walking down the railroad tracks. He was about six two with a bushy but recent beard and hair that was growing out from what had been a fairly short cut at one point. He had on new boots that looked as if they'd come from some catalog store and the backpack he was carrying looked fairly new as well. The jeans and flannel shirt he was wearing were sized for someone much heavier. Right length, but the jeans were held on with a rope and were clearly eight or nine sizes too large. This had once been a big, robust—fat, really—guy, who had recently lost at least a hundred pounds. Fast.

"Oh, you have *got* to be shitting me," I muttered as he walked over towards the hotel. He looked both ways before crossing the street. As he got closer I could tell he'd recently washed down. His hair was still wet and his face was washed but he looked as if he'd been living rough otherwise. "Café doesn't open till nine."

"Damn," the man said, looking at the sign. "I've been out camping for the last two weeks. I could really use a good meal."

"Looks like you've lost some weight, though," I suggested.

"Yeah," the man said, looking a little nervous. "Hiking's a good diet plan."

"Surprised you've got the guts for it, what with the bear attacks and all."

By then Louis had come out on the porch and was eyeing the newcomer.

"Bear attacks?" the man asked.

"Two of them," Louis said. "One last night and one the day before. The first one got a hiker; the second one got a couple of local kids."

"I... hadn't heard about that." He didn't seem worried about it. More ashamed.

"The kids were fifteen and seventeen," I said. "Just a couple of high school kids parking. Real shame."

"Yeah," the man said, his head hanging low. "Sounds like it."

"I bet you could murder a steak about now, couldn't you?" Louis said.

The man looked up and seemed to realize he was the center of both of our attention.

"I'm fine. Just... waiting for the restaurant to open."

"Transforming really takes it out of you, doesn't it?" Louis asked. "I hear it hurts, too. Not as much as getting torn apart, though."

The man's eyes narrowed.

"I'll just go looking for another restaurant..."

"Don't think so," Louis said. "Now, we can do this here in front of God and everybody or we can slip around back to continue the discussion. Your choice."

"Look," the man said, his eyes turning an odd shade of gold. "I don't want any trouble."

"Oh, it's not going to be any trouble," Louis said.

As the werewolf started to transform, I rolled back off the steps and came to my feet with my .45 in a two-handed grip. He'd managed to tag me with his growing fingernails but just barely. Ripped the hell out of my windbreaker.

If you're new to this business and have never seen a werewolf transform, it's ugly and, yeah, it's gotta hurt. You can hear bones cracking as they lengthen and bend to the new form. The jaw deforms outwards, teeth pop into place.

With newer werewolves it also takes a bit. Like a minute or more. And this guy was clearly fairly new at it. He should have controlled the transformation and attacked in human form. Human form werewolves are nearly as strong and just as durable. They still regenerate like nobody's business.

By trying to transform, it gave us the opportunity to fill it full of silver without being in any real danger.

Louis had backed up the porch and engaged while I was

avoiding the slash from the hiker/werewolf. By the time I came up and opened fire, it was already down. Werewolves are tough until they run into silver. Even then they're tough but eight rounds of .45 pretty much do the trick.

The good part was we didn't disturb the morning calm with gunfire. We were both using silencers.

The problem being that people were just getting up and heading to work and there was, for Skykomish, a fair amount of traffic on the road. As I pushed the body to make sure it wasn't going to get up again, a school bus drove past. The kids were all looking out the window and could clearly see that some guy had just been gunned down for, apparently, no reason at all. Most of them that weren't looking at the body were looking at Louis. I'm sure for some of them it was their first look at a black man and the conditions couldn't have been worse.

"I'll go get a tablecloth or something," I said, putting away the pistol. "You get to explain what just happened."

"I think the MCB guys are already upstairs asleep," Louis said. "Go bang on their door after you get the tablecloth."

And that was how I killed my first werewolf.

The management of the historic Cascadia Inn politely asked us to leave as soon as possible what with us murdering a potential customer on their front step. I suggested hydrogen peroxide as a good way to get the stain out of the walkway. As soon as the MCB had confirmed werewolf and we took samples, we were back on the road, headed home.

I slept like a baby the whole way.

Pro-tip: Werewolves gotta eat. Werewolves gotta eat lots. When you're hunting a werewolf, stake out potential food sources if that's the best you can do. And since they transform, stake out restaurants if it makes sense.

For the Skykomish Werewolf, hunger killed the beast.

CHAPTER 8

Two months later I'd settled into a steady, for a Hunter, routine. Unless I had a late night, and those were frequent what with the nature of the job and my obsessive skirt-chasing, my alarm would go off at 0430. One hour of painful stretching—my wounds were still there and I'd been adding a few new ones—and I was ready to go running.

I'd moved into a ground-floor apartment in the University District. Given my dislike for academia in general that might sound counterintuitive. But I liked the energy of the area and the one thing to be said for any university area was an abundance of pretty girls, many of whom were open-minded. It also had a slew of great hole-in-the-wall restaurants, many of which were open late or even twenty-four hours. Given my irregular schedule it was the right area to live, in my opinion. And my irregular schedule wasn't really out of place. People didn't ask too many questions. There were always people moving in and out of the area. All good reasons. But, mostly, it was the coeds.

So after stretching I'd go running. Given my job, I had a rational paranoia about being out in the dark jogging. I never wore a Walkman running. I wanted my ears free. And I'd rig up to run.

Socks, running shoes, pants appropriate to the weather, but even in winter Seattle rarely gets very cold, so generally shorts.

T-shirt. Chainmail shirt snugged over a low profile vest. Utility belt with my sidearm, spare magazines, ASP baton, mini-mag, pager and a pouch for ID, keys and some cash. University of Washington windbreaker or hoodie.

Even in winter the ensemble got hot. On the other hand, be it a supernatural entity or a mugger, anyone attacking me was in for a brief and nasty shock. Which happened three times during my tenure in Seattle. Two muggers and one werewolf. But that's another story.

Generally I'd do a light jog over to Ravenna Park, then speed up through there. There were some bums living in the park, but they generally didn't bother me. I'd do a fast run through the park, then head back on a different route. I always tried to vary my route. Just another paranoid thing. Never establish a really fixed routine.

I'd stop at a diner most mornings for breakfast after the run, get bacon and eggs with all the trimmings, then walk back to my apartment. Again, not every morning but it was one of my regular stops.

Shit, shower, shave, then it was off to yoga class. Monster hunting often involves having to move through three dimensions very fast and fluidly. I don't care how big and muscle bound you are, things like yoga and ballet are useful. That's the pro-tip. For a casual bachelor pro-tip: there are no better places to meet women than yoga and ballet. There's always a steady turnover and if they've got time for yoga and ballet classes, they've got time to spend in *la danse d'amour.*

After yoga, it was hit the gym for weight conditioning until lunch. Lunch was at any number of small restaurants in the U District. There were lots and they were constantly going in and out of business. Eventually I ended up going to one bento place at lunch every day but, again, later story.

After lunch it was either back to the gym or over to the University to hit up their stacks. I'd paid for another local course, one day a week again, which gave me access to the UW library. They had a surprisingly large occult and anthropology section. For giggles, I eventually collected and read all of my mother's papers through that source.

It sort of made me conflicted. One thing I realized was that my mom was at least as smart as I was. That was a bummer. The other thing I gathered, reading between the lines, was that she was probably as read in on the real existence of the supernatural as I was. Something about the way she wrote about it just told me she knew these things were real. Her paper on Indonesian water demons made me seriously wonder if she'd not only met one but talked to one or more. The real problem with all her papers was a complete lack of covering their weaknesses. Her paper on kappa, for example, had no notations about their various weaknesses. Fortunately, when I encountered one, I'd read other papers that did document them. Which is why I have a complete femur these days.

Most of the stuff couldn't be checked out but the nearby University Bookstore had another huge collection and I had the money to buy. We hadn't been super busy but the paychecks were good, way in excess of what I was spending on general lifestyle, and I poured a bunch of that into books. At some point I was going to have to either get a bigger apartment or a house just to keep up with the book collection. I also visited the various used bookstores in the area and picked up some really interesting stuff there.

At least two afternoons a week I went to the office, if we weren't otherwise occupied, and worked on guns in the workshop. I didn't ask for everything I'd need, want or desire at once. I built up slowly. I started with getting all the regular spares that the various team guns would need—springs, firing pins, spare bolts and barrels—then built from there. The Nelsons weren't gun nuts so they were happy to farm that responsibility off on me.

Last but certainly not least, one day a week, all things being equal, I'd go to the range. I'd pick a specific firearm for that day—pistol, shotgun, subgun, long arm—and practice pretty much all day.

Sometimes I'd end there late, but generally, all things being sane, I'd leave around five and head back to the University District. Some evenings there were ongoing jujitsu classes. Most, though, were spent on my other calling.

Another pro-tip for the philandering bastard: Weekends are for meeting women, weekdays are for cashing in the investment. Most evenings I'd spend either on a date or just staying in with one or another lady with whom I'd developed a mature and deep friendship. The District also had a slew of delivery places.

Name the cuisine, you could generally get it delivered. And I was learning, among all the rest, to cook for myself. And cook well, unlike my mother.

So I'm at the office fixing one of Louis' guns that had gotten knocked out of his hand by a ghoul when the telephone rings. The other reason to hang at the office was somebody had to answer the phones. If I wasn't working on guns, I'd have had to hang out at least one day a week, anyway.

Back to the story. Telephone rings.

"MHI, this is Chad speaking. How may I help you, sir or ma'am?"

You can take the boy out of the Marines but you can't take the Marines out of the boy.

"This is Wesley Williamson, chief of security for Microtel," a man's voice answered. "We have a supernatural issue at our offices."

"Are you one of our contract companies, sir?" I asked. We'd generally roll for anybody who called but contract companies got first dibs. Main team was out on a call already but for a company with a contract, we'd roll the secondary team, i.e., everybody who should have the day off.

"Contract number 418-851," Mr. Williamson replied.

"What is the nature of your emergency, sir?"

"We've had a demon outbreak in Quality Control. We think we have it confined to the QC section but we need them cleared out."

He sounded perfectly calm about having demons in the building as if this was a regular occurrence.

"We'll roll a team right away, sir. Should have a full team there in no more than a couple of hours, probably less. I'll call you when we're on the way."

"Looking forward to the call," he replied and hung up.

The phone already was set up to beep any number of team members. I beeped all the secondary team except myself and called Doc Lu.

"Doc, we got a call from Microtel?" The radiophone's reception wasn't great and I was mostly getting pops and hisses. "Demon outbreak in QC? They said they had a contract."

"Not again," Dr. Nelson—Lucius—said with a sigh. "Better bring some holy water and the pressurized sprayer. God knows what sort it is this time, but they mostly respond to holy water."

"Will do, sir," I said as the phone started to ring.

It was Brad and I told him the same thing. His response was mostly cursing.

"I'll call everyone and just tell them to bring their cars. You bring the van. Bring two five-gallon cans of holy water with you. You speak Latin, right?"

"Yeah," I said.

"That may come in handy. Get the big Latin Bible out of the library. Make sure you bring a shotgun. Meet us there."

By the time I arrived at the Microtel campus in Redmond, most of the rest of the team was there. Timmy was conspicuously absent. He tended to be. The guy had gotten a new girlfriend and she didn't like whatever she was doing interrupted by his beeper. It wasn't even like it was getting laid. Mostly they seemed to go clothes shopping. The girl was clearly only interested in his PUFF money but you couldn't tell him that.

So we had Brad, Jesse and myself.

Brad was already talking to a guy in a polo shirt and jeans I took to be Mr. Williamson. Total time from the call to the arrival of the van was forty-three minutes which wasn't bad in my opinion.

Brad walked back over trailed by Williamson. Williamson was tall and buff. Definitely pumped weights. He walked with that robotic walk you see in a lot of former spec ops.

"Chad, since you haven't met, Mr. Wesley Williamson, one of our regular customers," Brad said. "So . . . Looks like a small demonic outbreak in QC. Again. Jesse, take the holy water and keep them off of us. Chad and I will handle the shotguns. Once we've got them banged up enough, cover in holy water and do the banishment rite. Some indication they breathe fire."

"How many people in the area?" I asked. "Survivors?"

"Not important," Williamson said. "It's just Quality Control. We sealed the doors and called you."

I thought about that reply for a second.

"Did you used to work for MCB?" I asked.

"Yes, I did," Williamson said. "Does it matter? Is this getting the job done?"

"Any particular reason for the breakout?" Jesse asked. "It might give us a better idea what we're dealing with this time."

"Dev was using a modified you-nix daemon in are experimental gooey," was what he replied, phonetically. I speak nine languages and I didn't understand a word. "I keep *reminding* them to use spell check. Apparently they didn't and the daemon summoning caused a manifestation. Demon, daemon, you get the problem."

"Wait," I said. "You use daemons, Greek spirits of translation, in your *software*?"

"You don't really think all this stuff works on ones and zeroes, do you? Microtel lobbied for a special dispensation from the MCB so they could do R&D involving some really low-level extradimensional forces," Brad said. "Okay, as long as it's not like the last time, we can probably handle it. Let's rig up."

The Microtel campus was a group of beautiful buildings set in a parklike area in Redmond. All glass and chrome, surrounded by tree-covered mountains, working in the offices must have been a real treat.

The Quality Control department was deep in the bowels of a secondary building. We had to go down three flights of stairs. Even if we'd use one under the circumstances there was no elevator. Between the flickering fluorescent lights on the landings, half of which were out, and a strange smell that was half chemical, half decomposition, it was a creepy and eerie place before we even got to the demons.

"I guess that's the demon smell?" I asked. New guy and all. "And they're futzing with the lighting?"

"Nah," Jesse said. "I used to have a buddy who worked here. This is what it's always like."

"He get a new job?" I asked as we got to the door at the bottom. It was built like a bank-vault door.

"Some sort of transdimensional portal opened up while he was testing a new piece of software. He sank halfway into the floor before it closed. Horrible way to go."

"Microtel QC has the highest death rate of any job in the nation," Brad said. "Not that you're going to find that in any open report. Between the supernatural outbreaks, suicides..."

"That one accountant who killed ten coworkers with a letter opener..." Jesse added.

Brad keyed in the code for the door and it opened with a long, eerie creak.

"Well, that'll tell 'em we're here," Jesse said.

There was a secondary door after that one, a setup called a "mantrap." You couldn't open the second one until the first one closed. In addition, it had an electronic locking bar across it on our side. It had been locked from this side to prevent anything, or anyone, from getting out. Probably by remote.

On the wall of the mantrap was a motivational poster of piles of seeds. There was a large pile of what must have been tiny mixed seeds, that looked nearly identical, and two smaller piles of them separated.

The caption read: "At Microtel, Quality Control is our number one concern."

There was a small window looking into the far room. There was a smeared red handprint on the window and splatters of blood.

We all crowded into what was for all intents and purposes an airlock, closed the outer door and opened the inner. Another long creak.

As the door opened there was a scuttling sound like large spiders and a cackle of unearthly laughter. We'd found our targets.

Microtel QC's offices were a large room absolutely packed with computers and monitors. There were no cubicles, just battered and broken chairs in a dozen different styles. Most of them looked like dining room chairs that had been picked up secondhand, and four banks of tables consisting of raw plywood on trestles that ran from end to end of the long room. The computers were packed cheek by jowl into the room so that the occupants must have had to sit shoulder to shoulder to use them. The tables were packed closely enough you could have barely gotten out of your chair.

There had been several dozen people in the room. Now they were splashed in every direction. Heads and limbs were everywhere. Ripped-apart torsos littered the floor and tables, guts stretched around the room like a cat's cradle. It looked like a bomb had gone off.

The air was close and thick between the smell of blood and shit and the awful chemical/ decomposition reek. The blood on the malfunctioning fluorescent lights cast the room in a red glow. Every single monitor was showing a weird flickering blue screen covered in cryptic eldritch codes. The combination of the malefic colors created a sickening, lambent purple that gnawed at the very soul.

"Looks pretty much like the last time I was here," Brad said, thoughtfully.

"Oh, God," Jesse said, breathing shakily. "Not the blue screen of death. Not that again."

There was another scuttling noise and something darted from one table to the next.

"Target!" I yelled, firing a round of buckshot at the creature.

There was a screech as the silver buckshot tagged the creature but didn't stop it. It darted out of sight.

"What the hell is it this time?" Jesse asked.

"Probably something we're going to have to update the PUFF table again. You know you can never know what's going to emerge from the blue screen of death."

As Brad said that, it happened. A creature began pulling itself out of one of the monitors. First two green-clawed hands appeared. Then bat ears. Then, between the bat ears and on top of the skull, four large multifaceted purple eyes. A mouth surrounded by tentacles. Hairs that writhed like snakes. A body like a twisted, four-armed baboon.

It hissed at us then stuck two of its four thumbs into its bat ears and waggled its fingers and spare thumbs at us, cackling in a mad, high tone.

"Cridex!" It squealed at us. "Gamification! Apness! Apness! APNESS!"

"Eat holy water!" Jesse yelled.

As the holy water hit the creature, it began to smoke and let out a long scream.

"CAPTCHA! BizDee! BizDee! NewPig!" it wailed.

I shot it in the face with the shotgun. One of the purple eyes deflated and released a gray smoke. The screen shattered and it was caught in the middle, its body sticking half out like Jesse's late friend, continually screeching a profane eldritch tongue. I blasted it two more times and it finally whimpered into silence.

"Ray-boot," it whimpered as it died. "Ray-boot, by-ossse..."

The body deliquesced into a foul gray-green ichor and dripped down the now-smashed computer monitor.

"Okay, good," Brad said. "These aren't so tough. Better than that slime demon that crawled out the last time. I thought we'd never kill that thing."

I reloaded, turned on the Maglite taped to my Winchester 1200 and squatted down to flash the light under the tables. There were more intestines stretched around underneath like some crazed gut-web. I saw another of the things scuttling and fired at it. Between the chairs, the trestles and the guts, most of the pellets ricocheted away.

"Watch your fire," Brad said, considering the room. "Let's just turn the tables over. Jesse, get ready to soak them."

"On it."

Brad gestured at the first table and squatted to cover me. With a heave the table turned over, computers and monitors hitting the floor in an electronics cascade.

Jesse splashed it. There was a screech from one of the demons, then a couple of shotgun blasts.

"That's two," Brad said.

As I went to the next table, one of the demons scuttled out and dove into a screen. I could see it emerge further down the way as if instantly transporting through the screen.

"That's new," Brad said, thoughtfully. "And it's going to be a problem. I think the first thing we're going to have to do is shoot all the monitors."

"Works for me," I said, hefting my Winchester.

For the next few minutes as Jesse covered us with the sprayer, Brad and I carefully targeted and blasted every single blue screen of death in the big room. It seemed like an awful waste of silver ammo, but given it was the blue screen of death you could never be too sure.

"I wonder how these things react to fire?" I asked.

"Toss a Willie P and let's find out."

I threw a white phosphorus grenade towards the end of the room and was rewarded with shrieks. Two of the demons jumped up on a far table, batting at the phosphorus covering their blasphemous green pelts. Brad and I both opened up on them and turned them into demon offal.

Suddenly one charged out from under a table, screaming a terrible eldritch war cry.

"KATMAI! KATMAI! KATMAI!" it gibbered, its claws raised and squamous face tentacles writhing.

Jesse hit it in the face with holy water and I followed up with two rounds of buckshot. The thing popped like a balloon and covered us in ichor.

Another jumped on a table and leapt through the air at me. "Pee-bee-yahb! Jee-Cur! Jee-Cur!"

It was too close to shoot. I let go of the Winchester and Sword of Mourning flashed through the air, slicing the fetid beast in twain. The rent-asunder upper half still landed on me and face tentacles writhed on my chest as the beast's remaining claw scrabbled at my combat vest.

"Dee-ban..." it croaked at me, its hideous breath whistling in my face. Its gibbous eyes were mere inches from my own. "Deee..."

It finally, mercifully, died and deliquesced. Ichor dripped down the front of my combat suit.

"Guess that sword really does have a purpose," Brad commented.

"Christ, these things don't half stink, do they?" I said.

I flicked the sword to remove the ichor, then pulled a white silk cloth from a pocket on my vest and wiped it down. The blade cleaned, I removed another silk cloth from a small pouch on the left rear of my vest and carefully reanointed the sword in oil blessed by rabbis at the Wailing Wall in Jerusalem. There must have been faint remaining traces of the demon's ichor on the blade since the holy oil hissed slightly as I oiled the sword. Last, I resheathed it and hefted my Winchester.

"Takes forever to get that shit out of your gear," Jesse said.

It took about an hour of careful clearance to get the last of the demons. They were neither big nor tough but they were wily and very nimble. Between the guts everywhere, the packed chairs and tables and the unholy lighting, it was just a bug hunt. Other than the one that had landed on me, the closest shave we had was one that managed to add another scar to Brad's face.

The last demon was cornered in the back of the room by herding it with squirts of holy water. It tried to hide under a table from our fire but Brad and I just kept pouring 12-gauge into the area until it died.

By the time we were done we were all covered in ichor, blood and less recognizable remnants of the poor souls in the QC department. We did one more sweep, turning over tables, stumbling on chair legs and sliding in guts, until we were sure the large room was completely clear of the blue-screen demons.

"I'm starting to get the Gut Crawl in training," I said as we went back out through the mantrap. "I'm glad we don't have to clean this up. Cleaning our gear is going to be bad enough."

We'd taken samples of each of the demons' ichor remains, as

well as Polaroids of partial demons that hadn't deliquesced yet, to turn in for the PUFF—whatever the PUFF on this one might be.

"Microtel has a forensics cleaning company on contract as well," Brad said. "By tomorrow this will look like it never happened and HR will have the place full of ignorant demon fodder again."

"How often does this happen?" I asked.

"Oh, every few months they have something," Jesse said. "Definitely our number one client."

I swore then and there to never buy Microtel stock. There was no way that fucked-up company was ever going to last.

In retrospect . . . bad call financially. Spiritually, probably the right decision.

We got the PUFF report a few months later. The entities were categorized as imps. Based on the casualties and our report on their toughness, they were worth eight grand apiece. Twenty-six times eight, not bad for a couple hours' work.

It was not the last time I visited Microtel. They really were our best customer.

They still suck.

CHAPTER 9

Pro-tip: Trolls aren't as dumb as you think.

Trolls are a lot like my brother. They're big, mean, nasty, extremely violent and also very smart. They are aware of human literature: to be exact, at least that literature that relates to trolls.

And they do *not* appreciate billy goat jokes.

I was in the University Library, nose deep in a book on Japanese mythology, when my pager went off. I checked the LED readout and it was a 911 call. And it's off on another hunt.

I had a five-minute walk to my apartment where my car was parked. The apartment complex had fenced parking so I'd taken the chance on leaving my stuff in the car trunk. I picked up my radiophone and called the office.

"This is Chad."

"We got a call from Spokane," Lucius said. "Sounds like trolls. Meet at the office. We'll take the van."

"On my way." I was hoping this was a real call. We'd had our fair share of false alarms, and the last good PUFF bounty we'd gotten was for the blue-screen demons at Microtel. Hunters can sometimes go months between bounties, which was why the company did the profit-sharing thing, to keep us from wandering off to find normal jobs.

Drive to the office, move my bags and cases to the van. Draw straws for who was driving. I got a long straw, picked a seat towards the back.

Normally, that would be the point where I'd pass out. This time I decided to stay awake and enjoy the ride.

I really love the Northwest. I don't like the politics but the girls are hot, the food is good and the scenery is first rate.

We took the 405 to 90 and headed up, up, up into the Cascades. The scenery was really gorgeous the whole way. Towering, tree-covered mountains, occasional glimpses of Mount Rainier. The day was overcast, it was the Pacific Northwest after all, but for a change it wasn't raining. Really nice day.

Once you pass Keechelus Lake, the environment starts to slowly dry out. When you get to Cle Elum, it changes abruptly and you're on the dry side of the range. It seems like one moment you're in temperate rain forest and the next you're in a desert.

The back side of the range, though, is heavily farmed with lots of irrigation courtesy of all the rain and snow in the mountains. By Ellensburg, it's like the only green you see is irrigated fields. Everything else is dry, sere and brown. Even the trees feel stunted compared to the soaring furs just an hour back in the mountains.

Past Moses Lake even the irrigation gives out and you might as well be driving in Wyoming. You've suddenly gone from green-clad, soaring mountains to brown, arid plains. It's a really odd transition.

By Spokane the green is starting to return. The Coeur D'Alene mountains beyond Spokane, if not the Cascades, are still green and fertile. The bit in the middle, though, is unsettling.

Spokane is a low, sprawling city. It has a few tall office buildings, but mostly they're five or six stories, max, and the majority are just a couple. With plenty of room, it just sprawls rather than going up like Seattle or New York. And while the green is starting to return, it's mostly still arid. Yards are watered but everywhere else is about as dry as Salt Lake. Abandoned lots run to tough, arid grasses and weeds. I even saw a few tumbleweeds.

The troll problem was located in a construction area. An old building was being torn down to make way for, you guessed it, a parking deck. Apparently there'd been a nest of trolls in the basement of the structure for who knows how long. The old building had housed various businesses over the years. There were rumors for years it was "haunted" and stuff, and people sometimes mysteriously vanished.

It would be nice to give some general tips to the public.

Things like: If you've got a persistent petty theft problem and employees occasionally just up and disappear, you might want to check your basement for trolls.

Just saying.

The demolition crew had gotten the upper floors demolished and were working on the lower when two of them disappeared into a hole. The foreman, figuring they were malingering, went in to find them. And disappeared. At that point the cops were called. Two officers went into the hole, there was a sound of gunshots and screaming and . . . we got called. One of the workers had gotten a glimpse of something big, gray-green and rubbery. Ergo: trolls. Hopefully.

We pulled into the construction area and started clambering out. Two guys in suits immediately buttonholed Dr. Nelson—Joan—and started haranguing her. I tuned it out as usual and just started suiting up.

"I thought trolls hid under bridges," I said to Phil.

"They used to in the old days"—he was checking his incendiary ordnance—"because bridges were good shelter and they could steal stuff from passersby. These days, you find them everywhere but mostly underground."

"They aren't turned to stone by sunlight but they're somewhat photosensitive," I said, recalling my training. "Tough, strong, regenerate like mad. Fire's the best choice."

"Yup," Louis said, pulling out the flamethrower. "Kill them with fire! It's the only way to be sure."

"No flamethrowers," Dr. Nelson said, her face pinched. "Minimal use of incendiaries."

"What?" Phil said, frowning. "They're trolls. Trolls, fire."

"The event has so far been 'maintained,'" Dr. Nelson said, starting to strip down to her underclothes to put on her gear. "MCB said they don't want any fires, flames or explosions bringing attention to the incident."

"So let *them* go in there with nothing but small arms!" Phil said. "I've got a ten-pound thermite satchel charge all ready to go!"

I loved how Phil's mind worked.

"Maybe we should just send Chad in there with his sword?" Louis asked. "That will keep the incident sort of quiet."

"I'm up for that."

"You've never actually fought trolls, Chad," Dr. Nelson said, exasperated. "Bring the flamethrower over to the entrance and definitely bring the satchel charges. I told them we'd try to be discreet but I'm not taking casualties just to satisfy the MCB. I did point out that there was, at least, going to be a good bit of gunfire. They asked if we could use only silenced weapons and I told them to stuff it."

I switched out my frag grenades for a couple of thermite instead. Two WP, two thermite. That would hopefully do the trick.

"Any sort of a count?" Brad asked.

Up to that point, Brad hadn't said anything at all. Just kept getting his gear ready.

"Not a good one," Dr. Nelson said. "At least two but could be any number from there up."

I drew Mo No Ken and carefully oiled the blade again. I was pretty sure she'd go through a troll's neck like butter. Of course, that didn't kill them. The only way you could kill them was burning. Wasn't sure what we were going to do about that.

The construction company had blueprints of the building. The stairs that the various victims had descended went to a basement. There were two more subbasements on the blueprints and the foreman warned that, given the age of the building and how often it had been renovated, the blueprints were, at best, a guideline.

The sun had set on the drive over, not that it would matter down below. The area around the pit was lit by Klieg lights, which was just going to impede our night vision when we descended.

We carried all the spare gear over to the hole. As we did, one of the MCB guys came striding over with fury writ on his face.

"We said no flamethrowers!" he snapped, angrily.

"It's a backup," Dr. Nelson snapped back. "We're going to have to burn them somehow and at some point. That's the only way to kill trolls. And if there are more than two, we're going to have to use incendiaries. Trolls don't die for anything but fire."

"And no explosives!" he said, ignoring her and pointing at the satchel charges Phil was carrying. The satchel charges were claymore bags wrapped thoroughly in rigger tape.

"They're not explosives," Phil said. "They're thermite."

"Just let us do our job and you go . . . intimidate a witness or something," Dr. Nelson said, wearily. The Nelsons disliked the MCB even more than most Hunters did. "We'll keep this as discreet as we can."

Based on the crowd gathered outside the chain-link fence, that wasn't going to be terribly discreet. The MCB agent went over to try and scare them off.

As Dr. Nelson started to lead the way, I said, "I've got point." I held up the Uzi. "Better for this sort of work." Dr. Nelson was carrying an FN FAL, which would be difficult to use in tight conditions.

"Very well," Joan said. "Just don't get yourself killed. And no grandstanding with your sword."

I really should have listened to her on that point. We turned on our flashlights on and descended into the musty darkness. The blueprints showed the basements to be a maze. This was going to be fun.

As I reached the base of the stairs, I swung the Uzi around, checking the shadows for trolls. The base of the stairs was an open room. The room was mostly filled with debris from the demolition above. Dust, brick ranging from bits to whole blocks, some broken two-by-fours. There were two entries, one forward, one to the left. Both of them had doors that were smashed open and lying on the floor. The damage looked to be old. On the right wall was an old, framed photograph of what was probably Spokane in the 1950s. It didn't look to have changed much.

I looked over my shoulder at the good doctor and gestured left and forward.

She pointed left. Left it was.

Left was a corridor that ended at a right turn. It had rooms off of it at intervals. Some of them had smashed open doors, others were open. We cleared each cautiously. Louis, at the trail position, carefully sprayed paint on the walls indicating the best way out, a simple sideways V pointed towards the exit.

We slowly cleared the entire basement. Some of the rooms were filled with the debris of years of businesses coming and going from the building above. Others were swept clean. In one, we found what looked to be a partial human carcass. We marked it on the map for later. Seriously, how bad does a business have to be to notice it was losing employees in the basement?

Then I thought about Microtel. Whoever it was probably just got terminated for failing to show up the next day.

In many areas the dust had been scuffed by something large. In one spot there was a clear footprint. Dr. Nelson pointed it out to me and mouthed: "Troll."

So now I knew what a troll print looked like.

The stairs we'd taken down only led to this level. The next two levels down shared a stairwell that was catty-corner from the one we'd used. Getting back to the air was going to be a bitch if we had to run.

Dr. Nelson obviously had thought of the same thing.

"Louis, Brad, head back to the top and get the spare gear," Joan said. "We'll cache it here before we head down."

"Will do," Brad said.

The stairs down were open, not a closed stairwell like modern buildings. I peeked over the side and spit into the darkness.

"Be nice to just throw a bunch of incendiaries into this place and torch it," I said. The construction internally seemed to be mostly wood.

"If we have to use fire, it's going to be bad, anyway," Joan said. "We'll be trapped belowground with fire all around us. That's not a good position to be in."

"Plus it's hard to collect the PUFF when all the evidence is burned up," Phil said. "The last time we had to get a PUFF adjuster."

I took off my helmet and donned my protective mask. It wouldn't give me oxygen in the event of a fire but it would screen out the smoke and was rated to reduce the air temperature.

"What's a PUFF adjuster?" I asked, my voice muffled.

"Somebody you never want to deal with," Joan said, pulling out her own mask.

"Think MCB is bad?" Phil said, donning his. "PUFF adjusters are worse than shoggoths."

"They can be a tad intimidating," Joan said.

Phil and Louis finally turned up with the spare gear, took one look at us wearing our masks and donned theirs.

"Ready?" Dr. Nelson asked.

I rotated my neck. The drive had left me horribly bound up. I wanted to just stretch for about thirty minutes to get the kinks out.

"As I'll ever be," I said.

I took the stairs sideways, shining the light downward, looking for any threats. Nothing.

The next level down was much like the first—a maze of twisty passages all alike. There were three directions to go: right, left and an office forward. The door was half wood, with a frosted glass window on it that read QUALITY CONTROL DEPARTMENT. Surprisingly, it was undamaged.

Dr. Nelson gestured at the door and I tried the knob. Locked. I slammed my foot into the door and the ancient, rusty latch gave way. Then the door slammed back into my face and I was nose to nose with my first troll.

The thing was about six-eight, gray-green, skeletally thin and looked like a mass of rubber tubes all bound together. It swiped at me before I could dodge and knocked me sideways so hard I flew ten feet down the passageway. I managed to turn in midair, thanks to copious limbering exercises and martial arts training, and skidded instead of slamming. Before I'd even stopped, I was firing.

The whole team was pouring fire into the troll but it wasn't stopping. The troll hit Dr. Nelson and she flew the other way, slamming into a wall and falling in a heap.

I stopped firing as the troll raked Phil's armor and tore the front open like it was paper. I came back to my feet in a roll and drew Mo No Ken.

"*Assei!*" I screamed, charging forward and slashing at the troll's left arm.

It came off with an audible *Pop* and dropped to the floor.

"MY ARM!" the troll bellowed, looking down at the twitching limb. "FILTHY HUMAN!"

"Sorry," I said, taking a high stance. "Did that get your goat?"

"NOT MAKE BILLY GOAT JOKE!" The troll leapt at me, swiping with its one good arm.

I didn't so much cut as hold Mo No Ken out, simply lean back and slide it downwards. The troll's arm went right through the sword, about halfway up its forearm. The hand continued due to momentum and landed on my chest. It even managed to hold on and started finger-walking up towards my neck.

The troll's momentum carried it towards me so I stepped to the side and let it go past, then cut downward into the back of its right leg, taking out the tendons. As its damaged leg went out from under it, it dropped its head down to my height and I took it off with one more swipe of the sword.

Unfortunately, all the various bits were still twitching and moving. The body was trying trollfully to writhe its way to the head to reattach, the arm on the floor was flopping towards the body and both the missing limbs were regrowing as I watched. Then the one finger walking up my armor got to my throat and started strangling me. I pulled it off and tossed it down the corridor.

"He seemed a little gruff," I said as Louis helped Dr. Nelson to her feet. She was favoring her right arm which had taken the majority of the impact.

"They really don't like billy goat jokes, Chad," Brad said. He was working on Phil's injuries. The troll's long talons had slashed his chest but the cuts looked superficial. His armor was in tatters, though.

"I noticed," I said, wiping down Mo No Ken. "But he really didn't seem all that tough."

"That was a little one," Dr. Nelson said. "And we're still going to have to burn it."

I pulled out a thermite grenade with my left hand and held it up.

"It'll burn right through the body and into the next subbasement," Phil said. "And probably start one hell of a fire down here."

"We'll drag the pieces up to the top," Dr. Nelson said. "Separately. Louis and Chad on the gear. Brad and I will tote and help Phil back upstairs."

"I can keep going," Phil said. "It's only a flesh wound."

I'd pulled the hand off my gear and now kicked it to keep it from reconnecting to the body.

"Doctor, with due respect, carrying the torso all that way will take more than two of you," I said. "I don't think trolls will futz with a flamethrower."

"We'll all go."

We did carry the flamethrower back but left some of the satchel charges with some booby traps. If the trolls messed with those, they'd probably do our work for us.

Phil stayed up top on Dr. Nelson's insistence. We found a metal trash barrel the local bums had been using to stay warm, and dumped our troll parts in it. That kept the MCB happy.

The problem with all of us going back up was that trolls might have infiltrated back up to the first level. We did a quick sweep, didn't find anything, and headed down again.

With the exception of the one troll, we didn't find anything on the next level down. That left the lowest level.

Before we went down, we changed batteries in all our flashlights, got a drink of water and generally prepared. We still didn't know how many trolls we were dealing with or how big and nasty they might be.

The third level down was a shambles. Not only doors but walls had been knocked down. Debris was strewn everywhere and stuff had been piled all over the place. There was stationery, some of it dating back to the 1950s, boxes of pens, broken chairs, ancient typewriters and every other accoutrement of office life. It looked like an office-supply warehouse scrap yard.

As we swept towards the northwest corner, we started to hear the rumbling sounds of trolls and their constant bickering. It was in Trollish, which none of us spoke, but bickering was bickering.

"Gurgle mugga robomp!" "Bluck glog, glog, gloga, mop!" "BURRA, BURRA, MOP!"

There were at least three voices coming from behind a door marked PERSONNEL. When whatever corporation owned this building terminated someone, they were apparently serious.

We'd passed out Phil's satchel charges and I took my hand off my weapon long enough to tap mine and look at the good doctor. She shook her head and pointed to a pile of paper. If we used fire, this place was going up like a napalm strike and we were fifty feet away from the stairs through a maze.

I let the Uzi retract, quietly drew Mo No Ken and kicked in the door.

"Good morning, ladies," I said. "My name is Chad and I'm here representing the Billy Goats Gruff Monster Hunting Corporation."

I needn't have bothered with the door. They came through the fricking *walls*.

Five minutes later I was lying against a wall coughing blood. My right humerus was broken, again, along with some ribs; the forearm was torn open to the bone; I was missing two teeth and had a slash mark across my cheek that was going to leave one hell of a scar; and my armor looked like it had been put through a blender. Even my helmet had deep score marks in it. All four of us were at least injured but I'd taken the brunt.

Trolls *really* don't like billy goat jokes. And the one upstairs had been the baby.

On the other hand, bits and pieces of troll were scattered in every direction. A few of them were steaming. We'd gotten to the point of throwing some thermite grenades towards the end.

"You guys are going to have to tote this time," I grunted.

"You had to make a billy goat joke, didn't you?" Brad said, stumbling over to me.

"I think I've learned my lesson on that one."

Pro-tip: Even with a +3 Sword of Sharpness, taking on trolls hand-to-hand is a losing proposition. And never, ever, make billy goat jokes. You will rue the day.

CHAPTER 10

The humerus turned out to be a major problem.

Like my femur, it had been shattered in the bombing. The actual break there was at the upper end of the humerus, just below the tuberculum majus, the bulbous bit on the top. It had been put back together with lots of screws and a plate.

When the troll hit me and broke the bone, again, it was lower. But the torsional forces rebroke the original break and splintered it up to the tuberculum majus. What I had on the upper bit of my humerus was, at this point, more pulp than bone.

The doctors in Spokane gave me most of that when they patched me up. There were lots of X-rays and serious big words that they thought I wouldn't understand. Doctors in Seattle confirmed it and stroked their chins as to what to do about it. I insisted that I needed a working arm to do my job. They weren't too sure how to accomplish that.

Finally I asked about complete replacement. That took some more chin-stroking but in the end that was the conclusion. Most of it my insurance wouldn't cover, but the PUFF bounty on six trolls was just sitting there.

Two weeks after the fight in Spokane, I went into the University of Washington Medical Center at 0600. I woke up at 1627 in recovery with a titanium carbide artificial bone that went from my shoulder (part of which had been replaced) to my elbow (most of which had been replaced).

Two weeks later I was out of the soft cast and it was back to physical therapy all over again.

There were things I really liked about the University District. I've discussed them. And there was a fair turnover of people, so in general my philandering ways didn't come back to haunt me. Seattle is a big place but the UD is more like a small town in a big place. And that has its complications.

This leads up to the point that when I went into the physical therapy center and was introduced to my therapist . . . I'd met her before. Briefly. She was one of those ladies who was fortunately a heavy sleeper. Unfortunately, she now knew my name, address, phone number and had my recently repaired arm in her pretty little hands.

"So," she said, flexing my recently rebuilt arm. "Your name's really Oliver."

"No," I said, wincing. "It's Oliver Chadwick Gardenier. I hate all of it but I go by Chad."

"And I take it you're not really a stockbroker. I mean, when I saw the scars I'd wondered about that."

"I'm not really a stockbroker. I really was a Marine. I really was in the Beirut bombing. What I do now is classified."

"And I can believe as much or as little of that as I'd like," she said, straightening out my arm to the point of . . .

"I think that's far enough," I gasped. Oh, this was *not* going to be good.

"But here I get to decide what's *enough*," she said, maliciously. "The phone number you gave me was for a Korean grocery."

"Sorry," I gasped. Oh, the pain!

"There is no company called Heimlich, Heimlich and Purge."

"Sorry!" I whimpered.

"And I lost nearly four hundred dollars on that 'hot stock tip' you gave me."

"How was I to know pet rocks would go out of style!" This was God's punishment on me. I knew it was. Hot pokers would be preferable.

"Seriously, Chad," she said, frowning and letting up on the pressure, "you seemed like a nice guy."

"Seriously"—I sneaked a look at her nametag—"Wanda. Those X-rays you saw are the result of what I *really* do for a living. These fresh cuts on my face? Those stitches on my arm? That's what I look like after a more-or-less normal day at the office. So, yeah, I'm a dog. I'm a lousy lounge lizard who picks up nice girls, has some fun and then hopefully never sees them again. 'Cause the last thing I want to do is drag some poor woman into this life. Okay? So it's love 'em and leave 'em. Because that way, if you don't even know who I really am or where I really live or what I really do, you don't feel constrained to attend my funeral. Which will be closed casket or probably just an urn with my ashes in it to cry over.

"So, sorry about sneaking out on you in the morning and leaving your door unlocked. It was, trust me, for the best. You want the money back? I'm good for the money. But what you don't want to do is get involved with somebody in my line of work."

"You work for the mob or something?" she asked.

"I'm a contractor that derives his income mostly from the Federal Government. So, no. And I'll repeat 'classified' as in 'secret.' Which is as honest as you're going to get from me."

Four hundred bucks was not the most I've ever paid for booty but it was totally worth it.

There'd been some question about whether I could return to duty or would have to retire. I'd pointed out to the Doctors Nelson that I'd shrugged off the Beirut bombing to become a Hunter. They took the point. Medical retirements were probably the most common way people left MHI. The company was kind enough to leave me on base salary—no bonuses, obviously—during my surgery, convalescence and retraining period. It took four long months for me to get back to reasonable shape for monster hunting. I still wasn't one hundred percent but I was getting there.

Since I was out of action for a while, again, and the company was still keeping me on salary waiting to see if I could fully recover, I took a vacation.

Pro-tip: Be careful about how hardcore you are about recovery and getting back on the line. All the good Hunters want to get back to killing monsters and making money. Much of the stuff that we do is fairly mundane, for monster hunting, and you can get complacent about that. But occasionally you run into an operation or an action, right out the blue, that pushes you up to the point where really it should have involved Force Recon or Delta or something. Don't think you can just wrap the fucker and shake it off.

Stay in shape, stay in focus and when you're injured, work to get back to top form before you hit the frontline. The distance between life and death in this work is usually measured in millimeters and microseconds. One pulled muscle can mean the end of your career and we take enough casualties as it is.

That's a way of saying "Plan to take most of your vacations while you're in physical therapy or still popping painkillers."

Wanda, the cute little physical therapist, had some vacation coming up. Pointing out that this was not an intro to my life, I asked her if she'd ever been to England. She hadn't and was more than willing to go with me, doubling as my ongoing physical terrorist. The Doctors Nelson had a friend with the Van Helsing Institute and they were more than happy to welcome a visiting injured American Hunter.

Dr. William Rigby, vice chairman of the Van Helsing Institute, was a wild-haired, bushy-eyebrowed, standard English academic. Just like the Doctors Nelson appeared to be perfect examples of the American psychological industry. He looked a bit like a short, wiry version of Albert Einstein without the nose. He was still filled with shrapnel from his time as a Marine commando and Special Operations Executive member in World War II, and he chain-smoked Gauloise cigarettes, a habit he'd picked up in France while working with the Maquis. He had, in the intervening years, been everywhere and killed everything. Now he was semiretired and managed the day-to-day operations of the various Van Helsing facilities, including their archives, which were, let me tell you, extensive.

Van Helsing did some stuff that I frankly thought was smarter than MHI. For one thing, they had a visiting scholarship program with Oxford that was supported by the British Government. They had the same cantankerous relationship with BSS and MI4 as the US Hunters, but they had a much better relationship with supernatural affiliated academics. Not all of them were monster rights advocates.

Dr. Rigby provided a nice, young, female tour guide to keep Wanda occupied during the day while I dug into their archives and eventually some of the secure vaults at Oxford. What a freaking treasure trove. Oxford had been studying monsters since before the split in 1209. According to the "official" histories, Oxford and Cambridge separated due to "disputes with townsfolk."

The true story was that some of the academics had delved a bit too deep into trying to use various unearthly powers. This caused a major breakout of demons, similar to what had happened in Microtel. The pro-demon faction, if you will, was driven out while the anti-monster faction helped the local clerics run down and destroy the demonic infestation. Thereafter, one of Oxford's cares, later made secret, was to "make This world of God's Creation safe from the Unseen and unholy." The pro-demon faction founded Cambridge University, which was why the British pro-monster advocates still infest the place.

I started to put some things together about then. Growing up, my mother would always talk Oxford down and frequently went to events at Cambridge.

Hmmm...

Bottom line, Oxford's secure vaults held a lot of monster lore. Much of it was collected from all over the world during the colonial period and if there had been a monster outbreak, anywhere, any time, there was probably a paper by the Royal Society for the Study of the Supernatural about it.

The academics there were quite polite to a visiting Hunter who had been injured fighting trolls. Polite and just a tad condescending. Then I started to correct some of their literature on Japanese monsters I'd been studying as well as delving into some of the many monster language books they had. I have a pretty much eidetic memory, even after all the bangs to the head, so the first thing I did was dig into Trollish—Trul-ska' technically—to translate what the trolls had been arguing about when we found them. Naturally, it was an argument about how to prepare the humans they'd caught wandering in their territory for tea. By some immersion in Trul-ska' with one of the doctors of linguistics, I was pretty much fluent in a week. It wasn't a tough language, only consisting of a total of about nine hundred words, many of which were situationally adjustable.

I was offered a scholarship on the spot.

Before I left, once my arm was starting to work properly, I wrote up a formal paper on the blue-screen demons and Microtel's ongoing issues with them as an example of Ekaratai, as they termed them, and with the warning that as the computer industry advanced, this would be an ongoing problem that, given the power of computers, would probably worsen.

There's a reason I still use a typewriter besides being an old fogey. I deal with enough crazy-ass shit in my life. I don't need a demon crawling out of my screen.

The scholars had divided the supernatural up into various classifications, or factions. First you had your angels and devils, in the religious sense obviously, because even the staunchest atheist had to admit there was something out there, and sometimes it even helped us. Hello. The religious scholars chalked these groups up to a Creator, and the opposition to his plan as the Fallen. Beyond that, it all degenerated into arguments, like any topic involving religion.

Then there was another faction of ancient beings known as the Old Ones, which was a vast and diverse bunch of things, most of them really nasty and, as far as we could tell, in conflict with each other. They ranged in size from killable to godlike. Some said they were the remnant of a separate plan that the Creator had dropped as, well, a mistake. Others thought they were truly alien. All those academics agreed that the Old Ones were bad news.

There were references in the papers to something called "reality stones" or "ward stones" that could turn away or even destroy the greater Old Ones. I never had the time, then, to track those down. Some of these devices were created by Sir Isaac Newton. The British were understandably proud of that. But researches later had always proved fruitless despite more or less having his complete design. Something was simply missing. He might have left out a key ingredient, he was a bit of an ass that way according to some contemporary reports, or something universal might have changed since his time. Others had been created by earlier alchemists going back to the Greeks and Romans at least. Many of those had been expended over the years. It was believed that the Antikythera Device—which I had to look up—was an early ward stone despite being completely different in appearance and manner to those of Isaac Newton. Certain relics of the early Christians had been proven to have similar powers, at least in the hands of a believer.

Our best guess was that it was the Old Ones, or at least one faction, who provided the powers that raised undead. Ward stones were sovereign against undead as was the "Power of the Lord Our God" wielded by a "truly Holy Believer" of any faith. One of the Royal Society papers detailed an eyewitness account of a Hindu mystic using the power of Brahma to drive back a vampire and "return three Wights of Great Power to their Eternal Rest."

One group the Van Helsing Institute had collected a lot of information on was the Fey and I think I found that part the most fascinating of all. The Fey were found in various forms throughout the world and it was more or less a catch-all for anything otherworldly, but not related to the Old Ones. Fey ranged from Buddhist *garuda* demons to Grand Fey like Faerie Queens and Baba Yaga, all with a complex social structure and a caste system. They were mysterious, powerful, and much of the Institute's information was basically educated guesswork. They believed Fey to be exiles from another universe, although the ones who did occasionally communicate with us insisted they were here before humans. But then again, Fey were notorious for being lying tricksters. Aspects of their magic indicated that they might be from an alternate reality where physics was slightly different from this reality's. Or, possibly, they had a better handle on quantum physics. I read papers and got into discussions on both sides.

Bottom line, the Fey didn't seem interested in taking over our world so much as messing with it and trying, in general, to avoid direct conflict with the dominant sentient life-form: humans. Fey lived in and around humans in various guises, including cast-off races who had long ago been their servants. It was widely believed that elves and orcs fell into that category, and maybe even gnomes, though now they had mostly resorted to lives of crime. Then there were the powerful Grand Fey courts, some of which overlapped semi-openly with human royalty and nobility at odd times in history. One Faerie Queen in Austria had maintained a continuous Court in Vienna in the days of Johann Strauss, whom she had boosted to prominence after he won a Harper's Challenge.

Last, there were groups that fell outside the major factions. Werewolves were one of them. The supernatural etymology of werewolves was unclear. Large regions, even continents, would have one alpha werewolf which generally formed the pack culture of that region. When the alpha was aggressive, werewolves would be aggressive. When its personal philosophy was to get along with man, werewolves would do so, by and large. I thought about the

Skykomish Werewolf. We'd finally found out he'd been a software engineer who'd been bitten. He'd tried to avoid hunting humans and simply failed. Pretty obviously, whoever the alpha was for the Northwest was "pro-human."

This group also included the broad "yeti" category. Yeti included all similar groups including Sasquatch, swamp-apes or Letiche, Ebu Gogo and others. These were generally grouped into the "mammal cryptids." Some of them were believed to be extinct.

Interested in the Sasquatch, given where I worked, I dove into that subject. They were elusive so there was very little factual information on them. However, there was a partial dictionary of the Yeti language, which was probably related. It was mostly from secondary references that I was able to find a few details about the Sasquatch and one paper that had a few terms believed to be Sasquatch such as "hello," "friend," "water." There was no single word for "food" in Yeti. Like Yupik, Yeti and Sasquatch were affixially polysynthetic languages. Short explanation of that is if you had some basic cognates, you could make up any word you wanted by stringing cognates together and the listener has to guess what you mean. That's sort of the explanation.

Bottom line, if I ever encountered a Sasquatch, I might be able to at least get them to try to talk to me.

The other thing I ran across, due to a conversation with Dr. Rigby over scotch, was gnolls. They are scavengers and garbage collectors. Horribly smelly things, their main defense is their stench, they are generally nonthreatening and harmless. They live to collect garbage and anything that's decaying. They generally live in sewers in big cities for this reason and frequently can be found hiding near landfills and so on.

The Van Helsing organization had sometimes tried to use gnolls as confidential informants, because, despite their own stench, they had a very keen sense of smell and taste. They lived in more or less perpetual darkness and both found collections of wonderful decay and avoided potential predators by seeing the world through smell. Since everything eventually ends up tainting the sewers of big cities, they always knew where the monsters were at, if for no other reason than to avoid them.

The problem was that very few humans had ever been able to successfully communicate with them, but I was really good with languages. There was a complete dictionary of local Gnoll dialects at Oxford. It might not work for gnolls in the US but I was determined to try to make contact with them even if I had to use a gas mask.

I could have spent the rest of my life in those archives. There really was the soul of an academic hiding in this broken body. But I picked up a lot of really good tips for dealing with monsters I figured I'd never encounter.

Wanda went back to the States after two weeks, her maximum vacation, totally satisfied. I'd been immersed in the archives most of the time but she had a great time and that was what mattered. She left my physical therapy in the hands of a new terrorist, Gregory. Obviously, I had nothing for Gregory. The reverse was not true. Gregory found me terribly handsome.

Obsessive heterosexuality can be a pain sometimes.

Once I was past therapy and back to physical training, I bid a reluctant farewell to Oxford and the Van Helsing Institute, caught a plane back to the States and got my game face back on. I'd had enough of studying monsters, time to get back to killing them.

Shortly after I got back to Seattle, my job turned personal.

CHAPTER 11

There was a bento place I really liked right around the corner from my apartment: Saury. Saury is a type of fish mostly found around Japan, related to flying fish. They didn't actually serve saury but in general their sushi was to die for, their udon was so authentic you'd think you were eating it in Shibuya and I liked the atmosphere. It was the kind of place where if you didn't speak Japanese you felt out of place. In general, gaijin need not apply. On the other hand, I knew most of the servers and the owner by name. They called me Assei.

Police had found one of the servers, Kiyoshi, dead behind the restaurant. The body had been spotted by a bum who was dumpster diving instead of the workers there or we might never have been called. The reason we were called was obvious when we arrived. His body was nothing but skin and bones.

And I mean that literally: Skin, hair and bones were all that was left. There were a couple of big, nasty entrance wounds on his stomach with the area around them discolored. Other than that, and an expression of sheer terror noticeable even with all his face muscles melted away, there were no evident wounds.

I was the first one to respond, since I'd been home at the time of the call, and I was shaking my head wondering what got him when Brad showed up.

"This is a new one on me," I said, straightening up. The

coroners and homicide dicks were being held back by one of King County's finest and MCB.

"Spider," Brad said, immediately.

"Except, right here?" I asked, looking around the alleyway. "That doesn't make sense. Don't they usually drag them off to a lair? Not to mention no silk."

"That is unusual," he said.

I went through a list of all the spiderlike creatures I could think of. Unfortunately, every single mythology has spider monsters. Many of them, though, were so similar they were probably the same species in different areas with different names.

"Anansi kama," I said, thoughtfully. "African. Sort of a were-spider. Turns into a spider during certain days related to the stars. It attacks its victims in the open." I stopped and looked at the dead server again and it clicked. "Jorogumo," I said.

"Speaking Japanese again?" Brad asked.

"Jorogumo, or sometimes they call them Tsuchigumo, is a Japanese creature," I said. "Shapeshifter. She can assume the form of a beautiful woman. But even then the victim is supposed to be bound in silk."

"Have you gotten anything from the management?" Brad asked the King County investigator.

"He went out to take out the trash and didn't come back," the deputy said. "It was slow, they didn't really miss him. Then we got the call. We found out about it before they did. No enemies that they know of. They weren't real forthcoming but you know those Oriental types."

"Yeah," I said, shaking my head. "Damn slopes with their secrets and inscrutable faces."

"They're all over the place these days," the deputy said, disgustedly.

"You can bag him," I said to the jackass. "We're not going to get anything else from this."

By that time Dr. Lucius Nelson had shown up. I waved him off as he was entering the crime scene.

"Jorogumo," I said, walking over to the tape.

One of MCB's finest was standing by and shook his head.

"No way," the guy said, looking dyspeptic. "There hasn't been a documented Jorogumo in the United States in years. It's just a giant spider. Probably a nest around here somewhere."

"Jorogumo," I repeated. "Giant spiders stun their prey, then take them to a nest to drink."

"And Jorogumo lure men into a bedchamber for the same purpose," Dr. Nelson said.

"Which is why this wasn't just a random attack. He was left there on purpose."

"What purpose?" the MCB guy asked.

"That I haven't figured out," I said, "but when I do, you'll be the last to know."

"You better watch your ass, wiseguy," the Fed said. "You go off half-cocked and we'll come down on you like a ton of bricks."

"Are you entirely incapable of speaking without using metaphor?"

"What are you thinking?" Dr. Nelson asked, taking a bite out of a tuna roll.

Saury hadn't even closed for the murder. Give the Japanese work ethic, if nothing else. The servers were, to most gaijin, totally bland and unaffected. I could tell they were all on pins and needles.

"Mostly questions," I said. "Why him? Why there? That was a message. The problem with messages is, you have to have a context. Right now, I don't have any context. But they're scared. Very scared."

There was a back window in Saury. At one point, when I was examining the corpse, I'd seen a brief flash of someone looking out. So now my favorite noodle joint knew I was somehow involved in that business. They might just think I was an undercover cop. Given what I'd picked up about Japanese monster hunting, though, they probably knew I was Monsuta Hanta. Depending on where they sat on the subject, I might get a free meal or fugu in my wasabi. Could go either way.

"I think it was a hit," I said.

"Like a mob hit?" Dr. Nelson said. "Believe it or not, there's never as much organized crime activity as it appears. A lot of what is blamed on the mob in certain places are covers for monster activity. Las Vegas and New York especially."

"But this was a hit."

"Why some random waiter?" Dr. Nelson said. "Or was he masquerading as a random waiter?"

"Kiyoshi? He was from Miyagi Prefecture. He was a foreign

student at the university studying math. We used to chat about second-order variables, so just say he really knew his math. That and violin. I even had him over to the apartment to do some duets and jamming. His mother's name was Kocho, his father's was Kazumi. He was an only child. His parents are going to be devastated. And they weren't the target. His dad is a salaryman and his mom is a homemaker. No target there."

There was an argument going on in the back. I could see it through the pass-through. The owner, Naoki, was in a heated discussion with his manager, Hyousuke. Most gaijin wouldn't even recognize it as an argument—they looked as if they were having a polite conversation—but it was. I couldn't lip-read Japanese that well but I caught the name "Isao." It might be a name and it might be a title. It translated as "Laudable Man" and was one of the titles used by the yakuza, equivalent to "Don" or maybe "Capo" in the mafia.

Yakuza were Japanese organized crime. Mafia in other words. They didn't like to be referred to that way since yakuza roots went back further than Mafia. They'd been doing organized crime when Europe was still in the Dark Ages.

"Do yakuza in Japan ever use the supernatural for leverage?" I asked Dr. Nelson.

"Oh, gods, no," Dr. Nelson said. "I attended a seminar in Japan two years ago about Japanese monster hunting techniques and that subject came up. The Japanese yakuza are dead set against anything supernatural. They have contracts with Japanese Monster Hunters to handle it for them."

"Refresh my memory from training. What is the penalty for using the supernatural in commission of a crime? In this case, murder."

"Conspiracy to use the supernatural in a murder is the same as necromancy," Dr. Nelson said. "Automatic death penalty. No rights, no appeal. But you'd better be able to prove it if you're going to file for the PUFF. I assume you're talking about a human. What are you thinking?"

"I think...I need to see a man about a horse..."

Lieutenant Paulding's office was buried in the basement of the King County Sheriff's Office. And he didn't seem real happy to see me for some reason.

"How's the arm?" he asked.

"I'm slowly being turned into a T-800," I replied.

"You don't have the height to be Schwarzenegger," he said. "What's up?"

"I need some information on organized crime. You know about the guy behind the bento place?"

"MCB is saying giant spiders," Paulding said. "We quietly put out the warning to sewer maintenance. They're usually the first people who go missing with those."

"Too many stray cats and dogs in the University District for there to be giant spiders," I said, ticking off on my fingers. "They always stun their prey and take them back to a lair. No silk at all in the area. They tend to drip the stuff from time to time, if nothing else. Not giant spiders."

"I heard you're saying Jorogumo," Paulding said, leaning back, "which makes even less sense. Those things are rare as shit. Maybe extinct."

"In the US. I think it's a recent immigrant."

"So you're thinking org crime is using a Jorogumo as a hit... thing?" he said, rubbing his chin. "That would be bad."

"It's the only thing that makes sense. Kiyoshi was left there as a message. I'd say that the message was: Pay up or else. So... what do you know about Seattle's org crime?"

"Not much," Paulding admitted. "My beat's complicated enough. Guy you want to talk to is Lieutenant Snyder with Seattle PD. He's the head of their OrgCrime unit."

"I doubt he'd talk to me without a reference."

"I'll give him a call."

"Whatever this is, I do not want to know..."

Lieutenant Kenneth Snyder, Seattle Police Department, was a heavyset, balding older guy wearing a cheap brown suit who looked as if he'd been serious beefcake when he was younger. Now, if you didn't pay attention, he looked like a worn-out beat cop. If you didn't pay attention. 'Cause the guy had really sharp eyes.

He also had a much nicer office than Lieutenant Paulding.

"I just need to know if there's been any major changes lately in the yakuza ranks," I said. "Notably, the Laudable Man if there is one. The Japanese term is Isao."

"I know about Isao," Snyder said. "Having said I don't want to know, why?"

"You heard about the body behind the bento place in UD?"

"Yeah, he died of natural causes," Snyder said, making a grimace. "Twenty-three-year-old in perfect health dropped dead of a congenital heart defect. And somehow lost most of his body weight at the same time. Like I said, I don't want to know details. You ask too many questions about that stuff either your career is finished or you end up having a congenital heart condition."

"I think it was a message. To the owners of Saury and in general to Japanese businesses in Seattle. I don't see Naoki-sama as the type to buck the yakuza, so I'd say it was a general message. They picked a low-level unimportant guy to off in a very nasty way to send the message. The only reason to send a general message is if there's been some general change. So has there?"

"Nice deduction," the lieutenant said, sliding his chair over to a file cabinet and rummaging for a second. After a bit he pulled out a file, slid back over and tossed it on the desk. "That does not leave this room and I never showed it to you."

Enter Arata Inoue, newly promoted Isao to Seattle of the Agama-kai yakuza clan. The Agama-kai, according to the background brief in the folder, had the Northwestern US sewed up. They had an agreement with the Nakamura-ka clan that split the West Coast around Klamath Falls. Not that they penetrated much outside of major cities with large Asian populations. They focused their efforts primarily on strong-arming Japanese small- to medium-sized businesses, prostitution and gambling, again focused on the Japanese. They had some gaijin clients and prostitutes but other Asians, especially Chinese, were managed by the Tongs. They had an agreement with the Mongols for areas outside the cities. They sometimes used the biker gangs for strong-arm work.

Arata Inoue had a long rap sheet in Japan. He'd started off as a street peddler of drugs, moved into strong-arm work when he got a little older, pimped, suspected of murdering several rivals, the usual sort of thing. He'd moved up the ranks of the yakuza fairly fast. It was a meritocratic group and he had, in their eyes, great merit. He was a bit less suave and cultured than the usual upper ranks of the yakuza but he was starting to show signs of fitting in. He'd recently started to paint, for example. There was a copy of one of his paintings of a lotus blossom. I was doing a better job in the second grade.

Lots of tattoos. Lots and lots of tattoos.

In the last few years he'd been repeatedly seen in the company of a girlfriend who was suspected of being one of his paid assassins. There was a picture of the girlfriend wearing a business suit. Cute girl.

If she was a girl. I had my doubts.

The number two man in Seattle was Michael Oshiro. As might be gleaned from his first name, Michael, while being pure ethnic Japanese, was born in the United States. The yakuza grand masters did not trust States-born Japanese to run major operations. They just were a bit too gaijin. Michael would otherwise have been the replacement for the previous Isao. Michael, while never having been convicted of a crime, had been investigated for everything from human trafficking to money laundering and had a degree in economics from Princeton, my mommy's alma mater.

He had to be a bit put out by being supplanted by some thuggish, illiterate street pimp from Yokohama. And knowing the yakuza, as soon as the boss had his feet firmly on the ground and his finger on every pulse, Michael was likely to end up sucked as dry as a mummy.

Last comment was that the new Isao had been putting the fear of God into Japanese businesses in the Seattle and Portland areas. Something had them kicking out dough like there was no tomorrow. But even the best confidential informants had clammed up on what was up.

"I need copies of the pictures. Just those. Especially the girlfriend."

"Do I even want to know?" Snyder said.

"Not in a million years."

I was back in my usual spot in Saury, munching on a tuna roll, when she walked in the door.

She was the perfect picture of a beautiful Japanese girl. Small feet, small nose, wide eyes, narrow hips that showed she was a virgin. She was wearing a miniskirt and blouse that weren't quite a schoolgirl outfit but very close.

She'd apparently put in a take-out order because as soon as she got to the register Naoki-sama himself handed over a bag that was presumably filled with bento boxes. She smiled and said something to him. He gave her the best smile he could summon up under the circumstances.

As she left, I stood up and followed her out.

Either I or one of the other members of the team had been sitting in Saury for the last week. And most of the rest of the team were outside in the van waiting. As I exited the noodle shop, they started to unload. The Jorogumo, if that was what she was, had turned in the opposite direction. That was okay. Jesse and Phil were sitting in Jesse's car up that way. They got out and started walking towards her as I came up from behind. They were ostentatiously looking at a picture in Jesse's hand.

The Jorogumo spotted them—they were being obvious—and turned into the alleyway next to Saury. I sped up and trotted around the corner, hand going under my windbreaker. As I turned the corner, I drew my 1911 and started screwing the silencer on it. The Jorogumo was running now. I didn't even bother to tell her to stop. I just shot her through the spine.

If she was actually a human, that was going to cause issues.

She dropped the bag and started limping, a pretty sure sign that I was dealing with a supernatural creature. The shot had gone squarely through her lumbar vertebrae. She shouldn't have been able to walk at all. The bag spilled cash all over the alleyway and the stuff splurting from the wound wasn't blood. It was a thick, green ichor.

I trotted after her, firing several more rounds, until the Jorogumo was on the ground.

I reloaded as I approached, the rest of the team closing in on my position. The Jorogumo rolled over on her back and looked up at me with wide, helpless, pretty anime eyes.

"Please, help me," she said, holding out her hand.

"Change," I said, pointing the silenced pistol at her head.

Some people were gathering at the end of the alleyway, wondering what all the men with guns were doing. Someone screamed when they saw the wounded girl on the ground and started shouting for the police.

"I don't know what you mean," the Jorogumo said.

"A human female with seven rounds of .45 in her would be dead. Change."

The thing hissed at me then rippled. It wasn't the change of a werewolf, there was no writhing or bones cracking, it was just dropping the illusion. Suddenly I was looking at a five-foot-tall green spider.

"You sent a message," I said in Japanese, focusing carefully on its neural center at the top of the abdomen. "Now we're sending one back."

I pumped it full of rounds until it stopped twitching.

"That's for Kiyoshi," I said, reloading. "He was my friend."

"You had to do it right here in front of God and everybody?" the MCB agent asked. It was the same agent who had dismissed the idea of the killer being a Jorogumo.

"Jorogumo," I said, pointing at the body.

Jorogumo are naturally spider things and whatever they look like before they're killed, they revert to spider things in death. There was no need for a blood analysis. Jorogumo.

"Kiyoshi was a message from the new yakuza Isao," I said.

"The what?" the MCB agent said.

"Try to work with me here. Yakuza, Japanese org crime..."

"I know what yakuza are," the agent snapped.

"Isao, Laudable Man, big boss for a territory. There's a new one in town the last few months. Arata Inoue. Like the senator. No relation—I hope. He's been proving who's boss. And he was using a Jorogumo to do it."

"That's a pretty serious accusation," his partner put in.

"Are you guys seriously going to start trotting out rights of the accused at *this* point?" I asked, pointing to the body and the bag of currency. "You really think the Jorogumo picked up a bag of cash from Naoki-sama 'cause he liked her outfit?"

"She could have been shaking him down herself," Agent One said.

"In which case, she would have been afoul of the yakuza. Try to work with this thing called logic for a second. Last but not least," I continued, pulling out the pictures.

"Don't ask where these came from and I won't have to lie. This is a picture of Inoue," I said, flipping through the pictures I'd gotten from Snyder. "This is a picture of Inoue with his girlfriend. That's the picture of the girlfriend we used to spot *this* Jorogumo. She kept the same guise so they'd know who to hand the bento box to. Cogito ergo sum, Inoue has been hanging out for the last few years with a Jorogumo. The Japanese businesses lately have been terrified of something going on with the yakuza. Japanese are in general terrified of the supernatural.

They know damned well it exists. The reason they're terrified is this Jorogumo at our feet.

"Arata Inoue killed Kiyoshi Moto using the Jorogumo which means he's in violation of Federal Unearthly Code 68.158.6 Alpha. Sentence is death, no appeal. And there's a PUFF line item."

"If so, we'll take it from here," Agent One said.

"The hell you will," I replied. "Again, PUFF line item. You guys just do cleanup."

"You're not going to get into a firefight with the yakuza on my watch," Agent One said. "We'll turn this over to OrgCrime."

"You can't," Dr. Nelson said as he wandered over from the crime scene. "What are you going to tell them? That a mystical Japanese spider-woman was being used as a hitperson by the yakuza?"

The agent for just a moment had the same look on his face as when I'd handed my mom the JROTC paperwork.

Stroke, stroke, stroke . . . !

"Special Agent," I said, placatingly, "we'll keep this discreet. We'll keep this quiet. We'll get the job done. No more problems for you."

"Try not to do it right off a crowded street at lunchtime next time," Agent Two said.

"Guaranteed."

"So you want to kill a yakuza boss?" Dr. Joan said, taking off her glasses and rubbing her face.

"Whack, terminate with prejudice, however you'd like to put it," I said. "The PUFF on a Jorogumo is fifty grand. Sixty for the human who had her in employ. The real problem is we have to not just kill him, but kill him in a certain way."

"That doesn't follow," Dr. Lucius said. "What do you mean?"

"It's cultural," I said with a sigh. "If we just mow him down on a street corner, besides pissing off the MCB, it will piss off the yakuza. We have to communicate, to them, very directly. It is, among other things, a matter of territories. From the yakuza standpoint, territory is not about land, it's about spheres of influence. The Tong are the org crime for the Chinese. In this area, biker gangs and drug gangs handle the gaijin like us. The yakuza are the OrgCrime for the Japanese.

"But our sphere of influence is the supernatural. From their cultural perspective, MHI aren't cops. We're ronin, a mob vaguely affiliated with the government, with a specific sphere of influence. What we have to say to them, in terms they understand, is that not only did Arata Inoue break *their* regulations against use of the supernatural, but he intruded on *our* sphere of influence. So we can't just blow him up when his car starts. We're going to have to secure him and kill him in a most Japanese fashion."

"Kidnap him and, what, make him commit hari-kari?" Jesse asked.

"The correct term is seppuku. And, no, just cut his head off. All the way, by the way. Make it roll on the floor."

"As opposed to part of the way?" Dr. Lucius asked.

"As opposed to partway. When an individual commits seppuku, they are wound tight in a sheet so they won't sprawl and a second stands by with a sword. After they have disemboweled themselves with a properly prepared tanto, the second cuts their head down to the skin of the lower neck. Done properly, the head simply drops into their lap, still attached to their body. To cut a head off cleanly, to make it roll, is an insulting way to die."

"Isn't that adding insult to injury?" Dr. Joan asked. "Killing him in an insulting way?"

"Yes," I said, "but by intruding on our turf, their guy insulted *us*. We have to insult him back or we're just punks in their eyes. It would be an insult to them if he hadn't started it. As it is, it's simply an insult to him."

"You're sure you understand the cultural implications?" Dr. Lucius asked.

"Perfectly," I said, hoping I understood the cultural implications. The alternative was picking a fight with the yakuza. We had enough enemies. "The tough part is going to be capturing him rather than killing him."

"He's probably got bodyguards," Louis said.

"Breaks of the game. From the POV of the yakuza, that's understandable. From the POV of the local authorities, this is never going to happen 'cause it's an MCB matter. Main thing we want to avoid, from a pure moral perspective, is innocent bystanders."

The Doctors Nelson exchanged a glance. They were great with hunting monsters, but people were a different matter.

"This is one PUFF bounty I'm going to have to run past Earl first," Lucius said.

✧ ✧ ✧

Arata Inoue generally had very good habits for a gangster. His home and offices were well guarded and he always travelled with at least one bodyguard and a driver. He generally varied his routine. The exception to that was Friday night. Friday night he always visited his favorite underground club. The club was so extremely Japanese, gaijin need not apply. He entered through the back. There were guards at the back and he had a bodyguard and given his background, Inoue wasn't going to be a slouch. But that was the weak point.

The sole issue was that he didn't arrive at a regular time. He'd generally leave his offices around 2000 to go the club. But the times varied from 1700 to 2300. If he left "early" on Friday, 1700, he generally went somewhere for dinner before going to the club.

We set a watch on his office and waited. The club was in the Salmon Bay warehouse district. From the exterior, it looked like nothing but a warehouse. The cars parked around it should have been a clue as to its real nature. According to the OrgCrime file I'd read, they knew it was a center for prostitution and gambling but they'd never had enough probable cause for a search warrant.

We're MHI. Our probable cause had just been cremated and the ashes buried in potter's field. Well, most of it.

"You sure you're up to this?" Dr. Joan asked for the umpteenth time.

"Oh, yeah." There would be at least two guaranteed shooters and the boss. My target was the bodyguard. Louis had the driver. Jesse would watch one door and Phil the other. Brad was cradling an M-79 loaded with a beanbag round. He'd used the grenade launcher in Vietnam and was a sure hand with it. Dr. Joan was backup shooter and getaway driver.

Each of us had a secondary target. Louis, for example, was also packing an M-79 although his was slung. The trail car, which wasn't trailing the gangster but headed our way by another route, had Doc Lucius and Timmy packing more heat. If worse came to worse and we couldn't do "discreet," we would have to bail. We couldn't endanger bystanders and, legally, if they're not PUFF applicable, our private company just can't go around shooting people.

"Just try to make sure he doesn't make it through the door," Dr. Joan said as the signal flashed. The target was entering the basket. She started the van. "And try not to get killed yourselves."

The timing was tricky. We had to get there as he was exiting the car. If he was well out of the car, he'd be into the club like a shot and we couldn't go after him. Civilian casualties would be guaranteed. If we got there when he was still in the car, the car would drive away and we'd be in a car chase trying to follow a souped-up Acura in a Ford Econoline.

Our timing was good enough. He was out of the car but stopped well away from the door to the club when we rolled up. The van doors opened, we rushed out, and all hell broke loose.

The bodyguard, who was standing behind his boss covering his back, got nailed in the teeth with a beanbag. Inoue pulled out a Sig and fired twice, missing me with both shots. Say what you will about the yakuza, they don't spend nearly enough time on the range.

I shot him in the kneecap as Brad came around the vehicle. Another beanbag round and the local yakuza Laudable Man was tagged and bagged.

The snatch and grab was over in seconds. We were gone before the first person came running out of the club. A couple of shots were fired in our direction but we were history.

On the way out I called a certain number.

"Hello?"

The voice was pure American. No wonder the yakuza bosses didn't trust this guy.

"We have a matter to discuss," I said in Japanese. "Be at warehouse nineteen in the Mason Industries Park in three hours. Come alone."

"Who is this?" Michael Oshiro asked.

"I think that will become obvious in just a moment," I said in English with a slight southern accent, "when your phone starts ringing off the hook."

When Michael Oshiro, wearing a very nice suit, arrived alone at warehouse nineteen, he was met by two people in ski masks who politely led him into the warehouse.

The Mason Industries Park had been in receivership for years. Mason Industries had declared bankruptcy in large part because of the Environmental Protection Agency having conniption fits over all the toxic waste scattered around the property. Given that it was a Superfund site which had never gotten the funding for cleanup, it was going to sit there for a long time.

In the middle of the warehouse, Arata Inoue was kneeling under a Coleman lantern. His hands and feet were secured with plastic handcuffs and rigger tape was over his mouth. The guy had a mouth on him.

I was standing next to him, wearing a suit about as nice as Mr. Oshiro's, with Sword of Mourning sheathed in my hand. No ski mask. This had been my idea, and I was the one who was supposed to understand the cultural issues, so Earl had said this was my party. It turned out my boss was surprisingly familiar with Japanese organized crime.

"Good morning, Mr. Oshiro," I said in Japanese. "Please come in. We mean you no harm."

I emphasized the "you."

"There will be repercussions for this insult," Mr. Oshiro said, politely.

"The insult is already given." I'd managed to get MCB to let me keep the head of the Jorogumo. I removed it from a box at my feet and held it up. "This is an insult to both my clan and the clan of Agama-kai. The Old Fathers perhaps are slightly unknowledgeable in certain areas. There may be a belief that in the United States, with our silly laws and our rights and loopholes that indulge the needs of the guilty, certain actions are acceptable."

There was a whistle and Arata's head rolled across the floor. There was a massive spray of arterial blood as he sprawled in an ungainly heap.

"There are areas of concern," I said, flicking Mo No Ken to clear it. "Your area of concern is taking money from businesses for no good reason. Smacking around whores. Offering loans to the desperate for interest that will make them your slaves. We do not care about those. Those are minor issues. Our area of concern is preventing the likes of this"—I held up the head of the Jorogumo—"from spreading across the earth like the lava of Mount Fuji.

"This," I said, shaking the head so hard remaining ichor splattered on my suit, "was an insult to *my* clan. To bring this *here*? To kill with it on *our* territory? No. However, this insult was made not by the Fathers of the Land of the Rising Sun but by this worthless one," I said, toeing Arata's corpse. "The insult is expiated."

"The Fathers may disagree," Oshiro said.

"Then they can *bring it*," I said in English. "We're better armed, better trained and if you *really* want to get busy, we can bring the *entire* God-damned MHI down on your heads. Your organization fucking used the supernatural to commit a crime. That puts you all on the PUFF list and means *every single member* has a price on his head.

"The last motherfucking group the yakuza want to piss off is Monster Hunter International. My boss said your Fathers have worked with him before. They'll know. Agama-kai has already pissed us off once. Don't double down."

I dropped the head of the spider-woman on the body of the dead yakuza boss, picked up his head by the hair and walked out.

We needed something for the PUFF confirm.

CHAPTER 12

One thing I haven't covered, so far, is vampires. I liked a lot of "stuff" about working in Seattle. But like the movie later said: "The one thing I can't stomach is all the damn vampires."

Forget Santa Clara (where I worked, briefly, later), Seattle is one of the vampire capitals of the world. It's the weather, isn't it? If the cloud and rain cover is thick enough, a really strong vampire can be out briefly during the day.

They also can pass better. You see someone deathly pale in Mexico City or Phoenix and your immediate thought, if you're a Hunter, is "Vampire." In Seattle it's "Goth" or, hell, "long term resident."

Next to Microtel, vampires were our number one call-out. They should rename it Fang City.

I've got to back up on vamp details to explain the general consonant of how they turned up in Seattle so frequently.

The PUFF table listed, then, four categories of vamps. Now it's five, and since I had a hand in that, I'll go with the five set. The five categories now are Standard, Higher, Major, Greater and Master. The addition was "Major." And this chapter is about why.

Standard vampires are those turned by lower-level vampires by "bite, die, turn" who are very "new." Basically they're angry, hungry, usually confused, psychotic, strong, fast zombies.

Higher vamps have gotten past the zombie stage. They're not

much tougher, but they're thinking more clearly, like what they were like when they were still alive, but with an evil predatory twist. Higher can be downright clever. Both of these kinds are fairly easy to kill during local daylight. They're usually asleep during the day. They can be roused, but at best they act like someone on sleeping pills or who just cannot wake up without the first cup of coffee.

Major are stronger and faster than Higher vampires but the main difference is that they tend to be alert during the day. They cannot handle even weak daylight, as Greater and Master vampires can, but they are, trust me, a right handful underground during the day. These are clever enough that they generally got some daylight guardians of some sort. They also begin to have the ability to use telepathy and hypnotic dominance of humans and other sentient and nonsentient beings.

Greater vampires are immensely strong and fast, like blurringly fast and throw-you-half-a-football-field strong. They can walk in daytime as long as they are not in direct sunlight. That will still set them on fire. They can take a bit of low albedo sunlight but generally have to stay in heavy shadow. They're old enough they've generally developed a strong resistance to pain and can drink holy water if they have to. It still causes a hissing and burning reaction.

The higher they get, the more they seem to abuse the laws of physics. How do vampires get stronger? Nobody really knows. Most Hunters guess it is a matter of age, or the stronger the creator, the stronger the creation. Personally, I agree with the scholars at Oxford and think it must be a matter of how much blood they've drunk and lives they've consumed. One professor estimated that to reach Master level, they'd have to have killed about fifty thousand people.

Fifty. Thousand. People.

Now, Masters are slaughter machines. Fortunately, they're super-rare. And I'm glad.

Masters have been reported to have a huge number of abilities. Like werewolves, they transform, although it's almost instantaneous. More like dropping an illusion. They can take the form of a bat-demonlike being. Bipedal with massive talons on hands and feet. Thin but supremely strong, flip a tank, and so fast that the "sound of a thousand bats" thing is any clothing rippling in the wind as they move. You can't see them when they move according to the reports.

If you ever have to face a Master vamp, my suggestion is calling in a B-52 strike.

I'm totally serious.

But with that out of the way, I can talk about Seattle and vampires.

From what we know, smart vampires, Higher and above, get along even less well with each other than humans. A very powerful vampire can generally dominate weaker ones by force of personality. It appears two vamps of similar ability are always looking at each other as a potential lunch if nothing else. They can, apparently, still fall into something resembling love. So you can have pairs that are lovers. Het, homo, bi, whatever. And, yes, they do still have sex apparently, although they cannot produce offspring. But, generally, they don't get along real well and are very territorial and controlling.

So you're a newbie vampire who has been turned by some vamp in, say, New York, and you've drunk enough souls you're getting your headspace and timing back. Suddenly you're working for the ultimate toxic boss. If you step out of line, you're liable to get drunk by your boss for your troubles. You think about it and decide to take off. You want someplace that's got food and preferably not a lot of sunlight...

And you move to Seattle. Which seems *perfect*.

There you set about starting your own little coven of vampires and you're not going to make the same mistakes as that asshole in New York. You're going to do it *right*...

Every few months some homeless would start disappearing somewhere in our region—Tacoma, Greater Seattle, et cetera—and we'd be on another vampire hunt. And about half the leaders would have a New Jersey accent, I swear. It was like the NYC area was churning the damned things out. I later found out there was a reason for that.

Most of you have probably been on at least one vamp hunt. The vampires usually have a clutch of human captives they're feeding on, generally kept in a pit or a locked room, always in total darkness since the vamps see fine in that. Pretty unpleasant is an understatement. Always remember to bring rope and, if it's not too far of a walk, some sort of ladder, as well as the usual forced-entry tools like a Halligan and axe (generally referred to as "irons").

They're generally somewhere belowground. If you've got homeless missing in a particular area, look in basements of abandoned factories, disused subway tunnel areas, that sort of thing. Generally best to do that during daylight hours 'cause you never know what level of vampire the master or mistress is going to be.

This gets to my main vampire story, the pro-tip of which I've just covered.

Pro-tip: Just because you're dealing with a vampire that seems like it has to be a newbie, it might not be. Even old vampires make mistakes. Especially if love is involved.

We were missing students from the UD. Male and female but mostly female. There must be a serial killer on the loose! It wasn't just UD. Women and some men, all college age, had gone missing from the general area. Mostly they'd been at bars and met someone and left to go, you know, hang out, talk about Heidegger . . . Photos of them indicated they were white or Asian and, notably, all were fairly attractive.

Serial Killer in the University District!

It was something we'd seen before. New vampires who had just gotten their sentience back tend to get all into the Vampire Mystique. They were powerful immortals! Human chicks loved to have their blood sucked! The worst were the occasional former nerds who suddenly had a taste of power and dominance. They were strong! They were powerful! They were immortal!

Just 'cause you don't senesce, doesn't make you immortal. Having your head cut off is still going to kill you.

Smart vampires are careful and feed only on people nobody notices or cares about, i.e.,bums, runaways. They don't live in big palaces. (Saw that later in Eastern Europe after the Fall.) They stay on the edges and feed on the edges . . . because there are a lot more of us than them and we are very good at killing them.

We looked at this one and made a snap decision that turned out to be wr—wron—incorrect.

"New sentient vamp," Louis said, looking at the request sheet from the King County Sheriff's Office.

"Early Higher," Phil said. "Probably a nerd. Look at the pictures of the victims. He's practically picking them on whether they've got modeling and pageant background."

"There any empty mansions with a basement in the area?" Brad asked.

"Not that I know of," I said. "We could ask a real estate agent."

So Louis and I put on our best clothes and engaged a high-end real estate agent. I had just sold a successful start-up in Portland that used an advanced algorithm to speed up daemon translation processing based on "my Ph.D. in Coptic linguistics" and was "semi-retired." My scars were due to a "BASE jumping accident." I wore a tailored polo shirt and khakis. Louis was my "partner" and wore a tailored suit. I never knew Louis was such a fashion horse. He looked like a member of Jesse Jackson's entourage. We practically held hands.

There weren't many high-end mansions available near the university. I "just loved the energy of an intellectual district." True. The agent was probably wondering why we were so jumpy every time we checked out the basement. The basements were important for "Louis' wine collection." Louis was a wine connoisseur. Also, I was surprised to learn, true. He had picked up a sommelier certificate from the French Wine Institute while recovering one time. "Contract sommelier" is a great cover if for no other reason than most people don't know what it is but assume that since it's French it must be sophisticated.

No vamps in mansions, though. And kids were still disappearing.

That sent us back to our usual tramping around in sewers and abandoned factories and warehouses.

I preferred the mansions.

Brad was the expert there. Over the ten years he'd been on the Seattle team, he'd gathered so good a base of knowledge on abandoned commercial real estate that he really needed to just retire and go into that field. Another pro-tip: Spend some time working in the commercial real estate field during recovery periods. You're going to need to know every abandoned shithole in your territory.

And where Jesse was the designated tracker when we hit the woods, Brad was the one that could find the scuff mark that said "Monster" in all the other crap in an abandoned factory.

Seattle had been building for a long time. And like most cities in earthquake and flood zones (most of them) had been built on destruction. You would not believe how many old homes, factories and warehouses there were *under* the current homes, factories and warehouses.

But no matter how we looked, we could not find this bastard. And kids just kept disappearing.

Finally, I broached the subject of gnolls.

"We've got some," Dr. Joan said, her nose wrinkling. "We leave them alone, they leave us alone."

"They're harmless," Phil said. "What do you want with gnolls?"

"Van Helsing sometimes uses them as informants in London," I said. "Have you ever talked to them?"

"They don't or won't speak English," Dr. Lucius said. "We've run into them but, as Joan said, we just leave them alone and vice versa."

"Anybody got any contacts with the local trash company?"

Nobody did. Neither did Paulding.

Snyder did, though. And when I called he admitted that he owed me a favor. Michael Oshiro was, apparently, while a serious bad person, easier to work around than Inoue. Inoue had been bringing in loads of heroin and expanding that market. Oshiro was just providing, not pushing. Overall, better with Oshiro. And while he didn't have specifics, he'd heard that a "gaijin had sent Inoue's remains to the Fathers" in Japan as a message. So Seattle and even FBI OrgCrime liked me.

Very odd.

He put me in touch with a friend in the garbage business. Which was how I found myself sitting outside a rainwater outlet, by an immense pile of garbage, in the dark, wearing my gas mask, at around midnight on a rainy night. Not that there were many clear ones in Seattle.

The guy from the garbage company had been hesitant at first. They didn't want to get in trouble for illegal dumping. But he acceded to my request.

"Why from the fish market?" he asked.

"I need it as nasty and stinky as possible," I said. "Preferably the oldest and stinkiest garbage they've got."

"It's pretty nasty when it's fresh. But okay."

I sat still. I knew the gnolls knew I was there. But that huge, beautiful pile of stinky, rotting, nasty fish was just too tempting. Finally one, then another, then another, then a mass of the little creatures came creeping out of the outlet, all of them chittering in their high, guttural language.

What they looked like was . . . variable. They literally covered themselves in various sorts of debris as camouflage. Many a sewer worker has walked right past a gnoll and never seen them. They just look like another pile of garbage. A few, clearing blockages, have accidentally pushed one and gotten the shock of their life when a pile of garbage stood up and ran away.

Their basic body is a thin humanoid with a fairly human face. Bit like a ghoul's, somewhat twisted and deformed. Possibly more like an australopithecus. But you rarely can get a good look for all the junk hanging on them. They don't wear clothes, but the garbage pretty much covers everything up.

I just sat there and listened, comparing the language to the ones I'd studied in England. I was surprised that it was a variant of German Gnoll as opposed to English Gnoll. I hadn't studied that as carefully. It took me a while to get some basic vowels and nouns. And I couldn't for the life of me remember the German Gnoll word for vampires.

The gnolls were diving into the garbage with relish, the pile covered in them.

"Stinky fish!" was the main comment. One word. Basically "Urgkh!" in a high, excited tone.

"Herring!" a special favorite, especially rotten. "Ghlackt!" Choked up from the back of your throat like clearing a loogie. Sort of like Hebrew or Arabic "ch." "Lechayim!" That sort of "ch." I finally got "suck," basically the noise itself, "sluckt." And blood: "Thchut!" So I sort of had "blood-suck." "Find." "Need." "Love" or at least "good."

It took a few hours and I was nowhere near fluent. But the sun was going to be coming up soon, and the garbage pile was quickly dwindling.

"Need help, I," I said in broken Gnoll.

The gnolls all froze, then several scuttled back into the sewer.

"Friend am. Talk, speak, King. Good, good, talk."

I was probably saying something entirely different but they got the picture.

"Gnoll speak?" one of them said, creeping closer.

"English Gnoll speak," I said. "Gnoll speak here not good. Good food bring."

"Good rotten food," the gnoll said. One word, again. "Urgkh!"

"Much urgkh!" I said. "More urgkh bring. Need help."

"What help need?"

Getting across that I was looking for some vampires was tough. But it got across. I learned one of their words for vampire. They had several. I didn't understand them all. I wished later I had. They had their own categorizations for vampires and if I'd understood it better then, well...

I promised that if I could find the vampires I was looking for, I'd bring them more stinky garbage. That was exciting. The problem being the opening was nowhere near the University District and their understanding of the Seattle Underground was based on words, most of which I didn't understand yet, that were based on smells and taste. Some of them I never did understand. Humans don't have their senses. A werewolf would understand Gnoll better, but the two groups avoided each other assiduously.

I had obtained a basic map of the Seattle sewer system that had a route from the outlet to the UD. I asked if I could lead one of their number to the place I needed. One of them, a young "searcher," was assigned.

His name was basically unpronounceable. "Yechtzumblrogeckt" is as close as I can get. I called him Todd. He was fine with that.

Just before dawn, Todd and I set off through the sewers. I'd come prepared with a pair of waders, bunker gear and spare filters for my gas mask. We'd started off by Gas Works Park on Lake Union. I led Todd through the sewers for hours. The route was nowhere near direct. We had to go all the way up by Woodland Park Zoo to get over to the UD.

I would ask him names as I'd get to areas I knew. Wallingford was "house people shit" and some words based on area to delineate it from other areas that were "house people shit," basically any suburb. This was "suburb between the north water and the south water away from the highway to the east and near some docks to the south." That was surprisingly few words and some of them were polysynthetic. I also picked up more American Gnoll. That was to come in useful as hell during my entire career.

Pro-tip: If you've got any fluency in languages, try to learn Gnoll. You can order my brief dictionary of colloquial American Gnoll through Oxford University Press if you have the clearance. Seriously useful contacts. But be prepared to take a lot of showers and buy lemons.

Several times he told me we had to detour to avoid something.

I knew very few of the words but it was clear there were more monsters in the underground than we'd realized. We got lost a couple of times but I would point in the general direction I thought we needed to go and eventually we found the correct route. We finally got to the University District near dark, which was "young people eating many types of food with good shits." Also "smells like young people (teen) urine."

When we got to the designated exit point, I told him I'd meet him there at dawn the next day. Then we'd find the vampires. He knew which ones I was talking about but couldn't explain it on a map. We'd find them tomorrow.

City works was holding open the manhole in an alleyway near my apartment and had been there all day. They didn't know why and, when I came lumbering out, wanted to know why an unauthorized person was allowed in the sewer system and where the hell I'd been. It was clear I'd been down there for a while. I was covered in shit. I told them it was classified and that they'd be back here tomorrow. Get over it.

I debriefed Dr. Lucius, briefly, and we agreed the full team would meet up, here, tomorrow before dawn.

Then I got out of the gear, went home and took a long shower. Then another one. It was no use. I was just going to stink for a long time. I'm not even sure it was purely the sewer. I think it was spending all day in the presence of Todd the Gnoll.

"Todd says there are about ten human women and a few vampires. He said there are other things, about four, but I don't know what the words mean," I said to the assembled team. We were kitted up in full vamp gear as the city works people got the manhole open again. "Not vamps but some sort of undead would be my guess. He can't tell exactly where they are. But he can get us close."

"Todd?" Timmy said, yawning.

"His real name is..." and I let out the series of grunts and clicks that was Todd's name. "So I call him Todd. He's good with that. He calls me Blupurckht!gagafump! Which basically translates as 'brings-smelly-fish-garbage-not-evil-male-human.' His name means 'finder-of-big-smelly-rotten-fish-meat-garbage-shit-pile.'"

"Gotta love those gnolls," Louis said, laughing.

"They know Seattle like the back of your hand," I argued.

"And from some of the spots he avoided, there's stuff under there we never realized. I think he's going to be a really good, if smelly, contact."

"Hole's open," the foreman said walking over. "I don't know what is going on here, but we are *not* liable for any injury you may sustain while in those tunnels. I don't see why the hell untrained people are being allowed down there and I do *not* want to know why you're armed like a damned commando team."

"You really don't," Dr. Joan said, smiling.

Lieutenant Snyder knew the FBI Special Agent in Charge of the University District Serial Killer Task Force. The SAC knew damned well that it was an MCB operation and that they were just cover. It was one of the crosses that Violent Crimes had to bear. They generally got public credit when a "serial killer" was apprehended or "died during arrest." That was the good part. The bad part was they got less credit in real serial killer cases 'cause the important people in-the-know assumed that it was all supernatural and gave MCB credit where it wasn't due.

And most of the time the people who took down the actual monsters were hunters who got no credit at all.

But the SAC had made the arrangements for the city works support. I don't know if MCB was involved or not. But any tip that might lead to the "apprehension" of the UD Serial Killer was a good thing from the POV of the SAC.

And we were prepared to do just that.

Right at dawn there was a chittering from the hole. Todd was back.

We clambered down into the hole and I made contact with Todd. After a bit of back and forth, we started off.

The walk wasn't far but it also wasn't as useful as I'd hoped. Todd just led us to an outflow pipe.

"There," he said. "Many blood-suck. One..." Unknown word. "Ten human female-child. Very sick human female-child. Four..." Did not have that word and could not figure it out.

"They're wherever that outflow is coming from," I said.

"We need that foreman," Dr. Lucius said. "Honey..."

"I'll go get him," Dr. Joan said, smiling through her gas mask.

"Thank you, Todd," I said. There was no word for "thank you" so I used the Chinese "good-good." "Stinky garbage, same place, tomorrow night. Much stinky garbage."

"Stinky garbage good," Todd said.

"You can go," I said. "Thank you."

Todd scuttled off under his pile of refuse and disappeared.

"If I get taken out," I said, "somebody owes his clan two truckloads of the stinkiest garbage they can get. Long-dead fish by preference. Drop it at the same place."

"We'll take care of it," Dr. Lucius said.

The foreman finally showed up bearing a bunch of charts.

"That one?" he said, not even looking at the paper. "What do you want with the library?"

"Library?" Dr. Joan said. "Which one?"

"The University Library," the foreman said as if talking to a not particularly bright child. "That's the outflow for the University Library."

"You've got to be kidding," Jesse said. "It can't be."

"Listen, cowboy, I know this area like the back of my hand," the guy said, angrily. "That is the outflow for the University of Washington Odegaard Student Library."

The vamps were in the library I spent half my time in off duty.

Son of a bitch.

"We're going to need to talk to MCB on this one," Louis said. "We're not going to be able to just stroll into the library kitted up."

"Maybe not," I said. "We could bypass them and talk to the SAC."

"Either way, we're out of the sewers for now," Dr. Lucius said. "And we need to hurry. We're burning daylight."

The Special Agent in Charge of the UD Serial Killer Task Force was Supervisory Special Agent Robert McCormick. Forty-five, with balding brown hair, he was not the happiest camper when I turned up wearing a polo shirt and khakis but still smelling like a sewer. But he agreed to meet.

"Special Agent," I said, shaking his hand. "Sorry about the smell. We were looking in the sewers. This is my team lead, Dr. Lucius Nelson."

"Doctor," the SSA said, shaking his hand. "Thank you for your support in searching for the missing students."

"Which we've found," Dr. Nelson said, "through a Confidential Informant."

"CIs never help in serial killer cases, Doctor," the SSA said, making a grimace.

"We have special CIs. We've definitely found the students. But . . . you're aware this is not, actually, a Violent Crimes case, Special Agent. It's MCB."

"I was hoping it wasn't," he said, making another grimace. "You're sure?"

"Absolutely sure," I said.

"I'm not read in on exactly what MCB does and I don't want to be," he said, frowning. "I *know* it. *Everybody* in Violent Crimes *knows* it. I just don't officially. And if it's MCB, why are you talking to me?"

"The relationship between our organizations and MCB is . . . fraught," Dr. Nelson said. "Contentious would be another word. In this case, we need official help to end this scourge. Because the serial killers were clever enough to use a location that is virtually inaccessible, at least during the day."

"Where?"

"They're somewhere in the University Library," I said.

"You have to be kidding," the SSA said with a snort, "or your CI is nuts."

"Our CI is . . . very good. He's more of a tracker. An extremely accurate one. You know/don't know what MCB does. He's that sort of tracker. And he led us to the Library.

"Problem being, we have to get in there and . . . manage the issue without it becoming a major incident. And you can't use HRT or anything similar. MCB could, possibly, bring in a strike team. But getting one of those is pulling hens' teeth. The killers will probably kill again, tonight. If the killers find out we've located them, they'll move. If you use your usual surveillance, they'll detect it and either kill your agents or move. We have to hit them now. During daylight. And fast. And we have to carry in a great deal of gear. Thus the issue."

"You don't have to know a single thing about what's actually going on," Dr. Nelson said. "Just get us in and let us do our job."

"Any suggestions?" the SSA asked. "MCB is the one with all the good lies up its sleeve."

"We call in a bomb threat," I said. "VC verifies that it's a credible threat and rolls a team in to check it out. We go in as the 'bomb threat team.' You hold the perimeter and keep people out. We'll try to keep the rest of it discreet. Possibly a 'bomb' goes off in the basement. Then we tell MCB."

"If MCB thinks I'm poaching on their turf, they can get really nasty."

"How many more undead kids do you want?" Dr. Nelson said. "Sorry, make that *dead*, of course. Vampires don't exist."

"Let me get this straight," the SSA said, rubbing his face. "You, Doctor, are actually a *vampire hunter*?"

"You know what MCB stands for, right?" I asked.

"So why doesn't MCB handle this stuff?" the SSA asked.

"Monsters don't, officially, exist," Dr. Nelson said. "There are a variety of secret treaties on the subject. There are reasons. I won't get into them because they are complicated. Private companies are paid to deal with them. MCB does cover-up almost purely and things that are bigger than a minor vampire outbreak. This is the . . ." He thought about it.

"Third vampire group we've dealt with this year," I added usefully. "Seattle is vampire central. The serial killer hitting homeless in downtown last year? Vampires."

"Shit," the SSA said. "I wondered why that just dried up."

"We used your analysis to track them down, sir," I said. "But in this case, they've been smart. We can't go strolling into the library wearing full fighting gear."

"And you're sure they're in the library?" he asked, again.

"Pretty sure," I said. "We had a gnoll tracker track them down. He pointed out the outflow pipe. Ten hostages, a few vampires and four 'other' things. Not sure what."

"Gnoll?"

"Harmless sewer dwellers. No threat. We pay them in garbage for tips. Incredible sense of smell. They call the UD 'place where young people shit lots of interesting food.' So, we good on the bomb threat?"

"No," the SSA said, "and yes. It's a good plan. Where's your team?"

"Waiting in our van," Dr. Nelson said. "Let us get kitted up, send them the threat, evacuate the library, get us in and let us handle this."

"You said hostages."

"We'll get as many out alive as we can," Dr. Nelson said. "Won't know how many we get until it's done. But we usually get them all. Then the MCB threatens them with jail time and psychiatric time and/or death if they talk."

"Things I don't want to know," the SSA said, shaking his head. "We'll need to get your team into one of our vans. Any issue?"

"We'll bring ours into the garage and switch there," Dr. Nelson said. "If you're good for that."

"We're good. MCB is going to flip. Fuck them. They're a bunch of black-ops prima donnas anyway."

"Glad we have some agreement on that subject," Dr. Nelson said, grinning.

"The building is clear," the Special Agent who was "handling" us said. "And we're backed up to a back door. You have the plans?"

"Got them, thank you, young man," Dr. Joan said, dimpling. "We'll take it from here."

We unloaded and piled through the door before too many people saw us.

The upper floors of OUL were an open plan rectangle with multiple stairs on every side. It was also well lit by large windows. There was no way the vamps were up there.

However, the basements, which were mostly off limits to students, were more complex. There were engineering spaces, archives and support tunnels that stretched through the University and even to other buildings. They were going to be somewhere in that complex maze.

As a "bomb detection unit" we'd been handed keys to all the doors. And we went through the basements checking room after room. With very little luck.

The door was small and unmarked. It looked like it led to a janitor's closet. It wasn't even marked on the blueprints.

However, beyond was an unlit brick-lined tunnel.

"This looks promising," Dr. Lucius said, shining a flashlight into the tunnel.

The tunnel went about sixty feet and bent to the right. The left side of the tunnel was crowded with piping.

We entered with Brad in the lead. I was on trail. The order was Brad, Lucius, Louis, Phil, Joan, Jesse, Timmy and myself. Jesse and I had Uzis, Brad was carrying an AR-15, Lucius, Louis, Timmy and Joan were toting shotguns and Phil was carrying an MP5 SPD. We all were carrying stakes, hammers and flammables as well as big knives. I had Mourning in her sheath on my left side.

We got down to the dog-leg and went around the corner. About another hundred feet down there was a heavy steel security door. Based on where the door had been and the direction, we were basically passing along the northwest side of the library.

As Brad approached the security door, there was a crash. I'd been checking our six since they could come up behind us. I turned and the corridor was filled with wights.

For those fortunate enough to have never encountered wights, I'll give you a quick rundown. They're zombies on steroids. Fast, strong, agile, violent as hell, red glaring eyes, pointed snaggle teeth. Their touch is paralyzing.

I now knew what "iggleurpGRAH!" meant.

The wights went straight to paralysis on the team. Lucius, Louis, Phil, Joan and Jesse were down before they even knew what had hit them. The wights had been embedded in the brick walls as a sort of mobile booby trap.

Brad and I had both turned as soon as we heard the crash. Brad was laying down fire with his AR-15 but the wights were in the middle of us and firing was problematic. He was as likely to hit me or Timmy as the wights.

Timmy was firing as well and the proof of that was when he missed a wight at point-blank range and hit Brad instead.

Brad would have brought that to his attention in a negative way but the wight grabbed Timmy by the neck, causing him to go immediately limp.

This left me looking at the super-charged undead. I let go of my nearly useless Uzi and drew Sword of Mourning. But then a wight had paralyzed our injured team lead, and I was the last team member standing. All four wights turned their attention on me.

There is a filk popular with some groups in the D&D movement. It's sung to the tune of "Norwegian Wood" by the Beatles.

I once had a sword, or shall I say it once had me?
Oh what a sword, a beautiful sword, it was plus three!
Its ego was twelve, a fact of which I wasn't aware.
I wanted to leave and the sword oh it just didn't care!

I walked through the halls, biding my time, nothing to find.
Then, I turned a corner, and then I said, "Oh, no. Undead."

The thirty-two wights saw me coming and started to laugh!
I just closed my eyes as my sword started hewing a path!

And, when I awoke, I was alone, my sword had flown.
Now, I use a club, isn't it good...
No Ego Wood!

I swear, Sword of Mourning had an ego. Because it more or less leapt into my hand and started hewing a path.

The first wight took a swipe at me and I took its hand off at the wrist, then cut down to the leg in a coup de main, same move I'd used on the trolls. Followed through, then up, reversed, and its head was on the floor.

"Assei!" I shouted, charging the next three.

I swear I just closed my eyes and Sword of Mourning cleared a path. What I did, though, was switch from dual-hand kendo style fighting to saber. My left hand was on my hip, my right arm was extended and the wights were having to come through a wall of Japanese folded steel to get to me.

They didn't stand a chance. Arms and hands scattered in a drift on the floor followed by heads and legs.

When it was done, the wights were still alive but scattered in pieces among my fellows. I couldn't exactly torch them there. I spitted their heads with Mo No Ken and carried them further down the tunnel, around the corner. Then I collected the hands as well. They'd been touching and reparalyzing my teammates.

I came back around the corner and was confronted by a "woman of indeterminate age." Best I can say. European looking, well dressed and clearly furious.

"Those are expensive, you know," she said in a cultured voice. The accent was Latin derivative. It was mild and could have been French, Spanish, or Italian. "I hope you weren't planning on destroying them."

"I am well paid to do so, madam. They, like you, are a scourge on the Creator's Earth."

"Oh, you Hunters are so single-minded," she said, shaking her head.

"Would you prefer to discuss philosophy, madam?"

"No," she said. "I'd prefer to rip your throat out."

"Bring it," I said, going to high stance. "Bitch."

She hissed and charged me. Jesus, she was fast.

In that moment, I understood the description of Master vampires vanishing. She didn't vanish, she just crossed the intervening fifty-foot distance nearly faster than I could strike down from a high stance.

Nearly.

By luck as much as anything, Mo No Ken went through one of her outstretched arms. I had struck as if she were in front of me and that was fortunate. Her left arm flopped to the floor.

Her right arm struck me like a sledgehammer and tossed me into the wall so hard the air was driven from my lungs by the impact.

I swung again but she was just *gone*. Bent over Timmy, charging up with a little snack.

I sprung forward but as she stood, she hit me, again, this time in the stomach. The air flew out of my lungs again and I landed twenty feet down the corridor.

I hit and rolled, popping back to one knee like a jack-in-the-box, and swung instinctively.

It wasn't a good strike. It was well off the sweet spot of the katana. But I could feel the crunch as the sword went through hardened bone.

Mo No Ken went through both her legs, just above the knees.

"And that's why they call me *Iron Hand*, bitch."

She crashed into me with her right hand latched onto my harness. I threw up my right arm to protect my throat and she tore into my right forearm, ripping straight through my armor, trying to get to my vulnerable throat. It might be protected by a throat guard but she was going to go through it like light cloth.

Which was when Dr. Joan managed to crawl over and jam a stake right through the vampire's ribs. The vampire shuddered for a moment, then her fingers slowly slid off my harness and she slumped to the floor. Her mouth was still working and she was still moving slightly. She scrabbled at the hole the stake had made, trying weakly to remove it, but the stake was messing her up as badly as the wights' touch had my teammates.

Dr. Joan got to her feet with that wobbly "I'm trying to shake off paralysis" walk, partially supporting herself on the wall.

"Are you okay?" she asked. She didn't mean was I unhurt. She meant was I hurt worse than it looked.

"You get really tired of physical rehab in this job," I said, pulling out a bandage. "Shit, she was strong."

"Old one," Dr. Joan said, putting on the bandage and tying it tight. It was bloodsoaked within a second.

"Why the hell would an old one like that be so obvious?" I asked.

"Good question," Dr. Lucius said. "And good job getting her."

"Just as soon as I can stand up, I get the head," I said. Mo No Ken was still in my lap.

"You sure you're up to it?" Dr. Joan asked.

"I can take that bitch's head off left-handed."

Which I did.

There were a few more vampires, just as the gnoll had said. Most of them were on the floor in the usual weak new vamp huddle. There were, however, two beautifully inlaid coffins. In the occupied one was a just-gorgeous young man, like some sort of Raphael painting.

He deliquesced just like the others when we took his head off.

Most of the survivors were too traumatized to talk, the ones who'd been there longer anyway. But after we got them out of the room they'd been held in, the Doctors Nelson were able to coax the whole story out of some of them.

You know how sometimes a rich old lady will get involved with a younger man 'cause he makes her feel young again? And she'll start doing all sorts of crazy things to please him? Go skydiving, learn SCUBA, that sort of thing?

Yeah, it was like that.

The female vampire was old. Probably a couple of centuries. She had met and turned the beautiful young man, Stewart, sometime in the last decade. Somewhere in England. He was the one that was all into the Vampire Mystique and had convinced her to concentrate on beautiful college students instead of nasty, stinky bums.

Their lair was well hidden and they'd apparently hit several other towns before coming to Seattle. If it hadn't been for the gnolls, we never would have found them. They'd have moved on and kept doing the same thing. She wasn't stupid enough to stick around after raising a furor, that was for sure.

I kind of felt sorry for the old bloodsucker.

It was beauty killed this beast.

CHAPTER 13

Technically, I was still on rehabilitative leave. At least, that was the reason the Doctors Nelson gave for letting me have the weekend of the full moon off. If they'd been honest, I think it had more to do with me taking on what was now officially classified as a Major vampire with a sword.

But it was giving me more time to dial in my muscles and balance. And the PUFF on that old biddy could have kept me in coeds and sushi for a year. I wasn't sweating it.

The team might have been, though, because lately lycanthrope activity had been high. It seems like ever since the Skykomish Werewolf, more and more of the damned things had been popping up. These were all first-full-moon types. No great shakes, still a little confused by it all, making newbie mistakes. The problem being, no two of them on investigation had the same back story. They all seemed to be getting bit different ways. Just one of those random upticks.

But it meant the team had been busy every full moon while I'd been doing physical therapy, physical training and banging any girl I could get to hold still for five minutes. It was getting a little boring.

I was considering this as I started out on my morning run to Ravenna Park. The winter morning was crisp and cool since a cold front had just moved through. It was surprisingly dry for Seattle. The full moon was settling to the east, gilding the light frost on the trees, and as far as I knew, there hadn't been a call-out for a lycanthrope. So far, so good. Maybe the uptick had died off.

I sped up as I crossed Ravenna Avenue, heading into the park. With the cool weather, there should be a minimum of bums' activity.

As I crossed Ravenna I noted, distantly, a group of blue lights over by 54th Street. I put it out of my mind. Not my concern.

I passed the playground, heading deeper into the park, starting to push it. I really needed a good hill at this point but that would have to wait till I got back to the apartment.

I was flying along, good marathon pace, barely breathing hard, totally in the moment when the howl erupted.

"Oh, you have got to be shitting me," I muttered. "Not again."

But the howl was distinct. There was a werewolf in Ravenna Park. And here I was in light gear with a measly 1911.

I slowed to a walk, calming my breathing, gave it about two hundred feet walking then stopped, drew my 1911 and sniffed the air. Human senses were nothing compared to a werewolf but sometimes, with the new ones, you could pick up their scent.

The howl had come from near the sulfur spring. I walked in that direction, weapon in a two-handed grip, occasionally stopping to sniff. About halfway there, I smelled it at the same time as I heard the crunch of frosted leaves underfoot. From behind me.

I spun in place as the werewolf broke cover, rushing at me and growling gutturally.

There wasn't much light and exactly zero time to think. I fired three rounds and dodged to the side. Its claws scored my right arm which dropped, useless. I managed to hold onto the weapon and switched to left, turning again and bringing the weapon around in a one-handed grip.

The werewolf was on its side, panting, whining and trying to lick the wounds on its foreleg and chest. I didn't bother to close, just put the last four rounds into the body. My right arm was up to a reload and, as soon as I was reloaded, I closed till I had a solid bead on the head.

Werewolves don't turn back to human form after you kill them like in the movies. It is more like they're so tough that even mortally injured, they turn back before they expire. It started to crackle and re-form into a terribly skinny guy in his twenties with a scraggly beard and long hair. He looked like any ten students you'd see in the UD on any given day. I shot him twice in the head.

My right arm was bleeding copiously. After safeing and holstering, I pulled off all my gear until I got to the T-shirt, pulled that off, ignoring the cold, and wrapped it around my arm. Then all my gear had to go back on. Doing all that with, effectively, one hand was a pain in the arm. Then I thought about what to do.

"Fuck it."

Somebody was bound to have heard the shots, but given that Seattle PD was probably carefully *not* looking for a werewolf in the area, God knew when there'd be a response.

As I was contemplating my next move, my pager went off: 911. Wonder what *that* call was for? Werewolf? There wolf. There castle.

Shock makes you think funny things.

Finally I went back to trotting. I trotted back the way I'd come, crossed 54th Street and headed for the lights. The blue lights that is.

They had police tape up—then a new item—and a bunch of officers making sure that no one who wasn't authorized entered the scene. Which appeared to be a single family home. Although in this area it was probably a six-college-student home.

"I'm looking for Lieutenant Paulding," I said, holding up my arm. "And are there any paramedics around?"

Paulding appeared as I was having my arm rebandaged by a clucking female paramedic. Cute one, too.

"Jeez, you guys are fast," Paulding said. "I just called Dr. Nelson."

"Yeah, well your perp is over by the sulfur springs. *That's* how fast we are."

"You already got him?" Paulding said.

"More like he nearly got me. Do I look like I was on a hunt? I was out for my morning run."

"How'd you get it?" he asked.

I pulled up the windbreaker I'd refused to take off for the paramedic.

"You run armed?" he asked, surprised.

"You don't?" I said. "With all the stuff you know is running around this place?"

"Point."

"Hell, I'm wearing Second Chance and chainmail," I said. "Better safe than sorry."

About that time Dr. Joan pulled up, got out of her Honda and rubbed sleep out of her eyes.

"Chad?" she said, when directed over to the ambulance. "Are you okay?"

"Just a scratch."

"He needs to go to the hospital," the paramedic said. "He needs stitches."

"I'm sure you could stitch me right up," I said, batting my baby-blue eyes. "I've got all the gear at my place."

"You are *relentless*," Dr. Joan said, chuckling. "What happened?"

"Eighty-six two-four," I said, using the short PUFF code for a juvenile werewolf. "Encountered on my morning run. I was planning on making a strong pitch today that I was physically back in condition to return to work. On second thought, maybe a couple more weeks."

"I'll call off the dogs," Joan said, shaking her head.

"Seriously, when do you get off shift?" I asked the paramedic. "Want to catch breakfast? I make a killer eggs Benedict..."

I decided to move Becca-Anne onto my "keep this one around" list. Not only could she do really great stitches, a useful skill in this job, she banged like a screen door in a hurricane...

The arm was about healed and I'd decided to take a chance and return to Saury.

I'd been avoiding my favorite bento place for very good reason. Just because I was willing to take on the yakuza over its use of the supernatural in organized crime, didn't mean I was particularly courting fugu poison in my wasabi. Steering clear of Saury was just good sense. But I was seriously jonesing for udon and a salmon roll. And nobody did salmon roll as good as Saury.

So there I was, back in my regular spot. Let's just say I was sampling everything very carefully. Touch to the lips, wait to see if there was any negative reaction, then take a bite.

"That is really unnecessary," Michael Oshiro said as he sat down next to me. "If we were going to have you assassinated, we wouldn't be that obvious."

"Paranoia is a survival trait in both our professions," I replied. I took a careful taste of the saki.

He barked out an order to the server who scurried away like he'd met the devil himself.

I took a look over at his hands and grunted.

"I'd have thought at least one knuckle," I said.

When a yakuza failed in some manner, the traditional punishment was to cut one of his fingers, usually starting at the pinkie, down a knuckle. Some unlucky yakuza were missing most of a few fingers. Michael, surprisingly enough, was only missing the tip of his little finger. And that was old.

"If they had disagreed with your sentiment on the matter, it would have been my head, not my finger," Oshiro said. "As it turns out, they were slightly less pleased about his use of the supernatural than you were. Instead of losing a finger or my head, I got a promotion."

"I guess that means you owe me a favor."

"You did put me in *jeopardy* of losing my head," Oshiro said. "And I made the case we shouldn't put fugu in your wasabi. I think we're even."

"Then we're even," I said. "But."

"But?" Oshiro said. "I was just here to say 'We're even. Never cross my path again.'"

"The thing about spheres of influence holds. The Old Fathers in Japan use various Hunter groups to handle supernatural issues for them. Who do you use?"

"We don't, really," Michael said, frowning. "It doesn't usually come up. Except with gnomes."

"Put it this way. You've got ears all over the Japanese society here. You've even got contacts into the Tongs. Not snitches, but information transfers."

"Agreed."

"We pay for information related to PUFF-applicable entities. And we're all about ignoring ethnic origin. Five percent of the PUFF when it's cleared. If you'd clued me in on the Jorogumo, that would have been twenty-five hundred bucks. Probably more than you make out of this place in a week."

"Month," Michael corrected.

"I'm not looking for where the Mongols have a stash or the Tongs are running a numbers operation," I said, "but we've both got a vested interest in keeping the supernatural under control."

"It's a reasonable thought," Oshiro said. "Information transfer?"

I gestured around.

"I come here to eat frequently. Going to that club every Friday was Arata's one flaw. This one is mine. I really like their udon."

"Payment?"

"When the PUFF comes through, I'll add the tip as a tip. Put it on the Amex Gold. For us, it's a perfectly legitimate business expense."

"Hmmm," he said, thoughtfully. "I can see the attraction. Let me ask you a question."

"Shoot," I said. "Not literally."

"Heh," Oshiro said. "Why would someone buy virgins, other than the obvious, to my businesses, reasons?"

"Male or female or both?"

"Female virgins postpubescent or pubescent."

"Gah," I said. "Dozens of rites use those. Most necromantic. Serious hoodoo if you know what I mean. Raising major Old One entities. Raising strong undead. Messages and sacrifices to the Old Ones. Using their skin for thaumaturgic writings. Nothing good. Why?"

"We recently were made aware of a business opportunity in that area," Oshiro said. "Selling them for prostitution? Certainly. Pornography? Of course. But selling them where bodies might turn up? Or for supernatural purposes? If authorities become aware of that, the heat goes on very quickly. Assuming they are for, as you put it, necromantic purposes, is that your area of expertise?"

"Arata was legally terminated under a classified Federal code. Ignorance of the law is no excuse even if the law is classified. The same code covers human sacrifice for supernatural purposes as well. Same penalty I might add. Gladly apply it in a case like this. Got a name and address?"

"Stop by the next few days," Oshiro said. "Something might come up. And don't worry about the wasabi." He slid the ginger sauce out of reach. "Wasabi would be obvious."

I was eating at Saury—carefully, mind you—minding my own damned business, when Naoki-sama handed me an origami bird.

"A gift for you, Assei-sama," Naoki said, bowing deeply. "In thanks. For Kiyoshi."

"Wakarimasu," I replied. I didn't bother to open it.

I finished my meal, paid the bill, and walked out. I waited to get home to open up the origami. No name but an address. If I recalled the address correctly, it was in the Sodo warehouse district.

Worth checking out.

✧ ✧ ✧

"We owe Oshiro five percent of the PUFF if it's legit," I said.

"But we don't know what 'it' is," Dr. Lucius said.

For a change, both he and Joan were in town at the same time. The meeting included the entire team. Even Timmy had decided to show up.

"Just that they're in the market for virgins," I said. "If it was, from his perspective, legitimate—selling them to perverts to be broken in, using them in abusive porn films—he'd never have given me the tip. He'd have just rounded up some Thai girls and sold them on. Since he's tossing it to us, he must be pretty sure it's supernatural."

"I never like going into a situation without a clue what the possible entity might be," Dr. Joan said. "The constant disturbances at Microtel and other software companies are quite enough danger. This sounds like something much more ominous. We need to investigate before we act."

"We'll put in surveillance," Dr. Lucius said. "Very cautious, very long range surveillance. See what activity we can spot and try to determine what the threat might be."

"I've developed a few contacts," I said. "I'll see if any of them have anything on this facility."

"Phil, Jesse, up for a little recon?" Dr. Joan asked.

"I'll break out the surveillance gear," Phil said.

"I'll break out the rain gear," Jesse added. "Thanks, Chad. While we're lying on a roof in a puddle, you have fun making time with your contacts."

Becca-Anne was a switch hitter. She had a close personal friend, Cary, who worked at the King County Courthouse and had access to confidential police files. Fortunately, both of them considered boys to be fun but not something serious. Bi-leaning lesbos were some of my favorite people.

According to Cary, the warehouse was already suspected of being involved in transportation for immoral purposes, what's starting to be called "human trafficking." But these were only some rumors from fairly low-level confidential informants.

The warehouse was owned by South Seas Imports and Exports, which led to a PO box and a fairly obvious shell company. The organization, to the extent there was one, was very small and very close. It apparently paid money to the Mongols for "protection" and even the CIs in the Mongols weren't sure what was going on there. If girls went in, they never seemed to come out. Which was not a good sign.

Mongols didn't sell girls to them, but they'd been asked about it. The CIs said they'd be up for doing the deal but they had a real lack of virgins available. The people picking up the protection money were never invited beyond the offices in front. The one CI who had had contact with the people in the front office reported that they had a "really creepy vibe, man. Like fucking weird."

Trucks with containers occasionally arrived, went in, dropped the containers and left. They didn't unload at a loading dock. Where the trucks came from was a mystery. Large delivery vans went in and out from time to time. Material transported: unknown.

Jesse and Phil's surveillance turned up pretty much the same thing. There were no windows worth bouncing a laser off of and no way to see into the building. They didn't even see trucks arriving, although one delivery van had come and gone. Most of the activity seemed to take place at night, except the arrivals and departures. Those were during the day.

The one thing they did come up with was grainy video of some of the employees.

"How the cops checking this place out missed it, I have no idea," Jesse said, pointing at the video. The person in the video had a very odd gait. As if they were having to think about each movement of their legs and arms. Color close-up shots of the individual from a 1000 mm lens showed that their eyes were extremely bloodshot and they had exactly zero expression.

"Revenant," Dr. Lucius said. "That tears it. But from Chad's reports, we're looking at at least ten 'employees.' And the 'manager' has never been seen by anyone."

"This is an organized group of undead," Dr. Joan said. "That spells necromancer in big, bold letters."

"That spells powerful necromancer," Brad said. "I really think we need to call in some big guns on this one."

"We've got LAWs and a Ma Deuce," I said. "How much bigger do we need?"

"Happy Face," Brad said.

✧ ✧ ✧

Earl Harbinger came back from his drive-by of the warehouse with his jaw set and an expression I never wanted to see directed at me.

He wasn't the only one who was a bit perturbed. Papa Shackleford—Ray III—had decided he had time to come along on the jaunt and had read me the riot act over nearly getting MHI in a war with the Japanese mob. The only reason he didn't fire me was because Earl had a sore spot for the yakuza, and I'd asked his permission first. When Earl came back, though, that was set aside.

"The place stinks of undead," Earl said, pacing back and forth in the conference room. He was smoking like a chimney, much to the discomfort of Joan and Lucius. They didn't say anything but I knew they hated cigarette smoke. "About a dozen human females in bad condition—any of you should be able to smell the crap bucket from the street—and lots of blood. At least six revenants, a bunch of wights and what smells a lot like a lich."

"And you got that . . . how, sir?" Timmy asked.

I knew better than to open my mouth. If Earl said it was a lich, then it was a lich.

"None of your concern, young man," Papa Shackleford snapped.

It wasn't just Papa Shackleford and Earl. They'd brought a good part of the clan. My old buddy Milo was along as well as Ray IV and Dwayne Myers. Susan was nesting in Cazador, much to my chagrin.

"It's some sort of necromantic factory," Earl continued, chain-lighting another cigarette. "I don't know enough about that stuff to figure out a factory for what, but they must have been producing something with all those virgins they've been getting."

"It's said to summon a shoggoth, in the most traditional way, requires the souls of five innocents sold to the Old Ones." Ray IV said. "There's supposed to be rites where shedding innocent blood is how they make wights. We got a rumor that someone was offering wights for sale in California. This is possibly where they are being produced."

"Whether it is or not, it's done, now," Papa Shackleford said, definitely. "Among other things, depending on how old that lich is, that's upwards of a million dollars in PUFF. That warehouse is going down."

"Permission to speak, sir?" I asked.

"You're not in the Marines anymore, Chad," Earl said, snorting. "But my bosses are all in a really foul mood. The small item I'd like to bring up is the hostages. I know MCB could care less about hostages, but I rather do. And if we bring as much firepower as this sounds like it needs, they're going to be caught in a major cross-fire."

"Chad's got a point," Milo said, uncomfortably.

"I couldn't tell where they were located," Earl said. "Just that they're there."

"We'll do our best to keep the girls safe, but I'm not going to talk about omelets and eggs," Papa Shackleford said. "If we lose these hostages, we're still going to be saving the lives of all the other poor young women who aren't being used as sacrifices."

"If it's a factory, we probably have to move fast if we're going to have any chance of saving them," Dr. Lucius pointed out.

"In terms of the threat," Ray IV said. "The first task has to be to take out the lich. They're damned tough to kill."

"Their powers vary greatly. Touch could be instant death," Dr. Joan said. "The sky is the limit with them. Whatever magic it practices, it'll probably be fearsome. Only way to kill it is to utterly destroy the device that has replaced its heart. Phil, we'll probably need those thermite satchels."

"On it," Phil said.

"I've got something that might help," Milo suggested.

"Contact range is suicide with a lich," Dr. Joan said.

"Not if it doesn't have any hands," I said. "Or arms. As for spell-casting, I suspect most people go for the neck and cut the head off. Undead like liches can continue to speak that way. If you cut the head off at the mouth . . . a little harder."

We hit the warehouse with a full-court press. Most of team Happy Face was hitting the main roll-up doors while Flaming Warthogs were hitting the offices. Milo had been attached to our team since we had the job of lich suppression.

We'd gotten blueprints of the warehouse but according to them, there wasn't much to it. The offices were tacked on in the front. The warehouse was a large open rectangle. Some I-beam posts to hold up the roof. No construction internally had, officially, been done. What was inside was anyone's guess at this point. Doing an approach to slide in an optical probe or get up to the few small, high windows had been ruled out. Wights had pretty good senses and would smell or hear any such approach. We'd try to find and secure the hostages before we burned the whole place down. Hard, fast and make it up as you went along when we get in was pretty much the plan.

"Revenant. Cut off the head. Fire," Timmy muttered nervously, checking his FN again. He'd been avoiding about half the call-outs lately. I was starting to think he really wasn't as into monster hunting as he'd thought. His girlfriend excuse had turned out to be a little white lie. "Ghouls..."

"Cut off the head, fire," I said. "Wights, paralytic touch. Cut off the head, fire. Lich. Death touch. Burn the heart."

"With fire!" Milo cackled, tapping the sawed-off shotgun holstered over his shoulder.

We'd damn near killed ourselves before the op even started, making those damned magnesium slugs. Magnesium catches on fire if you look at it wrong. And it will just keep burning. They wouldn't penetrate much, but with the chemicals Milo had sealed into the hollow cavity of the slug, they were supposed to ignite on impact and burn at about three thousand degrees. Milling it is a special art neither of us had ever attempted. We'd gotten the fire put out, eventually, but I was going to need a new lathe. And possibly new eyeballs.

Every one of us was loaded down with every sort of incendiary device we had in the warehouse or Phil, Milo and I could gin up. We had thermite grenades, white phosphorus grenades, thermite satchel charges, flamethrowers and for the pièce de résistance a five gallon bucket of napalm with a ten-second fuse and small Comp B blasting charge.

It was gonna be a hot time in the old town tonight.

The van slowed and Louis opened the door. Showtime.

Phil exited, ran to the office door and slapped on a breaching charge. We lined up behind him along the wall and crunched.

The breacher charge went off with a loud *CRACK!* and Phil led the way in with his pump up and aiming. There were two blasts and a sort of *Worragh!* sound. There'd been a revenant in the offices.

The rest of us followed him in and started laying down fire. The revenant—sort of a fast, smart zombie—was dancing to the

Tombstone Shuffle as rounds bounced him all over the room. But it wasn't killing him, just slowing him down.

Milo called "Check fire!" and stepped forward with his shotgun, placed it on the stumbling revenant's chest and fired. It penetrated the revenant's black heart and burst into bright, white flames.

The revenant let out another *Worragh!* as it desperately batted the flames pouring from its chest then stumbled to its knees and down.

"Clear," Doc Lucius called. "Reload! Keep moving!"

I cut off its head as I passed.

There was a thunderous explosion as the main doors were breached by the much larger charge Happy Face was using. Just as it went off, the main door between the offices and the warehouse opened and a wight charged in.

Again, the entire team opened fire at once, blasting the undead with silver. It barely slowed it down but it did slow. This one, people were keeping their distance from. The wight's paralyzing touch was renowned among Hunters. In a bad way.

As everyone ran down their magazines, I called, "Check fire!"

Sword of Mourning swept out as the wight recovered its balance and charged. This time I came from low, outside, sweeping up to take off the right hand then down to take out the leg. The sword went through the undead's thigh like air. One more sweep and the head hit the floor and rolled over to Timmy.

"Keep moving!" Dr. Joan called.

We could hear a continuous rattle of fire from the warehouse proper and we needed to get in there to support Happy Face. As we hit the door, there was a dull *thump* and a blast of heat.

What greeted our eyes when we got into the warehouse was a maelstrom. There was an orange shipping container on the far side of the large warehouse. Near the center of the warehouse was a dais that was clearly some sort of altar. Happy Face was attacking from the main roll-up doors on the right. Most of the attention of the occupants was focused in that direction.

There were more undead than I thought I'd ever see in my life. Earl Harbinger was cranking out .45 ammo like it was past due date. Rays IV and III were at the doors, blazing away with, respectively an FN FAL and a Garand. Ray III rolled old school and I got a new appreciation for the power of .30-06. Dwayne Myers was working back and forth with a flamethrower.

What they faced was about twenty mixed undead and a lich which was in the midst of performing a sacrifice. The lich looked about like any other desiccated dead guy. The girl bound to the table looked to be about sixteen, Caucasian and obviously scared to death.

I wasn't sure what he was planning on summoning, but it wouldn't be good.

"Spread out," Dr. Joan said. "Phil, right, flamethrower. Try to miss the sacrifice! Timmy, cover fire from here. Milo, Chad, you're up."

Pulling my shotgun around, I sprang up the stairs and moved about ten meters left. Milo stopped about five meters out.

The pair of magnesium slugs caught the lich as it was beginning to strike downward with the sacrificial blade. They made a terrible flash as they ignited. The blast snapped the hostage's head to the side, hard. Hopefully she would be okay but I'd give an even bet she just developed permanent hearing loss in her right ear.

The lich, on the other hand, burst into flames and tumbled down the stairs.

I looked at Milo who was looking at me and we both grinned ear to ear and began cackling madly.

"Oorah!"

"Get some!" Milo shouted back.

We were running right into the cone of fire of the Happy Face team but the fire was slacking off anyway. The Doctors Nelson and Phil had dispensed with firearms and were happily throwing WP and thermite grenades into the crowd of undead while Louis and Brad engaged with flamethrowers. Timmy was taking the occasional potshot but was mostly just hunkered down. The Happy Face team had more or less paused to let Dwayne do most of the work. Fire is an excellent weapon against more than just trolls.

The problem of the lich remained. By the time Milo and I got to the dais, it had regained its feet. It immediately grabbed a necklace around its throat and waved a hand at the Happy Face team which was closer.

The fire from Dwayne's flamethrower turned back and to the side, catching Papa Shackleford in its cone.

The oldest Shackleford jumped back immediately, but his right side was covered in fire. Stop, drop and roll only goes so far. He'd had a thermite grenade in his right hand and that popped and began to glow. He dropped it but the damage was done.

Bad things were happening on the Happy Face team.

In the meantime, we'd attained the dais, and as the flaming lich prepared to cast another spell, we angled our weapons again and fired.

The near simultaneous blasts again pounded the lich, driving it into the container like it was being struck by the hammer of the gods. We didn't bother to celebrate this time, we just opened fire.

By that time, Dwayne, Louis and Brad had moved up on our right. The extremely banged-up lich got to its feet again just in time to receive a faceful of napalm from three different sources. Dwayne's ran out quickly—he'd been using it for longer than the rest—but Louis and Brad kept on cooking.

The lich was trying to run away from the fire. It ran left, then right, then straight at the two flamethrowers. It was clearly trying to activate a spell but, with the flamethrowers pounding it from the outside and our slugs burning its insides, it wasn't getting very far. On the other hand, they didn't seem to be killing it, either.

It didn't seem to be able to see. It might be able to regenerate eyeballs but it was covered in napalm. That generally cut down on that sort of thing.

Remembering what had happened to Papa Shackleford, I looked over towards the main doors. Earl was just getting done covering Papa in foam from an industrial fire extinguisher. But he didn't look real good and his right hand was burnt to a crisp.

As first Louis', then Brad's flamethrower ran out of juice, I drew Sword of Mourning.

"I'll take the arms and head," I said. "You jam the juice."

"Got it," Milo said, grimly. He'd seen what had happened to the Boss as well.

The lich was still aflame, napalm takes a while to burn out, but it was starting to get its bearings and that couldn't happen. Before the last flames were out, we'd run it down, on the far side of the building from the main doors. It was trying to mouth words, a spell, screams of agony, it didn't really matter. We were going to finish it.

I darted forward and swept Mo No Ken across. The lich had

its hands up in what is called the "final defense position." Any person who has ever seen a human burned by fire knows the position. The hands and arms curl up and inward towards the face. Mo No Ken cut through both hands at the wrists and they dropped to the floor. There was some question about whether the entire body of a lich had a "death touch" effect but I wasn't taking any chances.

The lich turned away, trying to run, and Mo No Ken swept back, cutting through its crisped head at the jawline. Any ability it might have had to cast spells was now gone. It also definitely could not see. The upper part of the head was on the floor and had landed eyes down.

Milo stepped forward, placed the shotgun against the crippled lich's back and fired. The magnesium began to flare white. But the lich was still up and moving.

I repeated the blow with my own shotgun, keeping Sword of Mourning up and to the side ready to strike. I fired two rounds, keeping them as close to the lich's heart as I could get.

Still wasn't down. And it was spinning around, trying to hit us and trying to find its hands.

"Hell with this," I said, slashing downwards. One leg out and it was on the ground, writhing.

"Sure as hell takes a lot to kill these things," Earl said as he came over, looking down at the writhing lich.

"How's the Boss?" I asked.

"Ray's rushing him to the hospital. He's tough. He'll live"—Earl was really pissed—"but I think he's going to lose that hand."

"They do wonders with prosthetics these days. You know I've got a titanium humerus, right?"

Milo was reloaded and punched more magnesium slugs into the lich's back. All that did was cause it to roll over.

"I got this," I said. I took Mo No Ken and slashed downwards; once, twice, three times and the sternum was separated from the ribs.

The magnesium slugs were in there, burning away. But the heart was still black and glistening and pumping.

"Hold on for a second," Earl ordered.

He pulled out a thermite grenade and carefully, avoiding the thrashing arms, leaned over and jammed it into the cavity the sternum had exposed. There was an unearthly howling noise as the thermite tried to burn its way through the lich's recalcitrant heart. Finally there was a nasty *blurch* sound, a wave of the most vile smoke imaginable and a scream like a thousand souls trapped in hell.

The Seattle Lich was truly dead.

The body immediately began to deliquesce and in moments there was nothing but an ugly pile of greenish-black goo.

The virgin sacrifice had survived, although for the first twenty minutes or so we had to shout at her to make ourselves intelligible. She was definitely going to have some permanent hearing loss.

There were more hostages in the container. They'd been nearly cooked, four were wounded and the container was punctured with about seven thousand bullet holes but amazingly none of them had been killed in the cross-fire.

The mystery of how they were disposing of the bodies was also solved. Ghouls ate them, bones and all.

All of the girls were from the United States. They'd been kidnapped from various towns and cities in the Midwest and West. In many cases, their families had been slaughtered while sleeping peacefully in their beds. Others had been ferreted out in the middle of the night, snatched off the street, etc. More girls had been kidnapped than those in the container. The ones that didn't meet the requirements, virgins, had been taken elsewhere. There appeared to be some sort of organized conspiracy and, given some of the descriptions of entities the girls had encountered, it involved multiple types of undead.

How very good.

Papa Shackleford had been, amazingly enough, our only serious casualty. The burns on his face were bad, and the hand was effectively gone, but he'd survived and would live to fight another day.

The MCB showed up right on time, complaining vociferously about how we'd caused a major incident without any warning and what bad people we were. Screw the fact that we'd stopped a wight production factory. Forget the fact that we'd rescued fifteen young women. We'd caused them extra paperwork and they were going to have to intimidate more witnesses.

One reason I'm never going to be a team lead: I'd have to deal with the MCB at every incident.

✧ ✧ ✧

About two weeks after the incident, I was pumping weights in the gym when I got a page. The number was unfamiliar, a DC area code, but I called it anyway.

"Chad Gardenier. You called?"

"Mr. Gardenier, this is Assistant Deputy Director Wilson. How are you?"

"Just fine, sir," I said. What did those MCB assholes want *now*? And an ADD? Just how much trouble was I in?

"I was just calling to thank you for your assistance," the ADD said. "We'd been tracking a series of mysterious serial killings and kidnappings across the US for the last two years. The . . . incident you were involved in, that I'm given to understand by your boss you broke, is the first real lead we've had. So my sincere thanks."

"Anything I can do to serve my country, sir. Any clue where the bottom is at?"

"We're still questioning the witnesses. Over the screaming objections of MCB I might add. But it's given us some leads."

"I take it, if it leads back to something you know, that you have to call MCB. Your regular agents do not want to take on the . . . individuals involved in this ring."

"We got that message loud and clear," Wilson said. "And I don't want to be involved in anything that MCB is involved in. But kidnapping and serial murder fall under Violent Crime. So until the MCB actually learns to do, you know, *investigations*, it's on us."

I had to kind of chuckle at that. Apparently the rest of the "regular" FBI liked MCB about as much as we did.

"Well, if you do track it down and would consider outsourcing, I know a company that handles that particular issue," I said, grinning.

"I doubt that would work out, but it's a thought. However it works out, thanks again. And if you turn up any more leads, please call."

"Any time."

Will wonders never cease. I've got a contact who's a yakuza boss, another who's an SSA, and I just got an "atta boy" from the freaking FBI.

Something bad was going to happen. Something real bad.

Right afterwards I got a page from the office. Microtel had called again. Something big, green and slimy was in QC.

My world righted immediately.

Three weeks later I walked into Saury and ordered my usual udon and salmon roll.

When I paid the tab, I put under "tip" $67,525. I'd checked that the company Gold Card would handle it.

Oshiro was going to be one very happy camper. He wasn't the only one.

I forgot one detail.

About a week after the Happy Face team left, I got a call from Earl.

"Something's been bugging me," Earl said.

I wondered what I'd done now.

"Yes, sir?" I asked.

"All you martial arts types have all these weird screams," Earl said.

"They're called *kiai*."

"Yeah. Whatever. Only one I really remember is 'Ichiki banzai' and that one tends to stick in your head."

That made me seriously wonder how old Earl was. He looked about forty.

"You screamed one when you were taking the lich's head off," he said. "Wasn't the normal sort of sound. Sounded more like a battle cry."

"Assei. It's my nickname from back when I was first studying kendo. Silly background story. Doesn't matter."

"Does it *mean* anything?" he asked.

"Yes."

"Don't make me reach through this phone," Earl growled.

"It means Iron Hand. There's other cultural meanings in Japanese. Sort of 'swordsman' or 'in your face swordsman.' I've always been very aggressive in kendo. Doesn't work out sometimes against really good swordsmen. It was sort of an insult by my instructor. One who charges in without regard is one way to translate it. One who strikes before he thinks."

"Got it," Earl said. "Iron Hand."

And he hung up.

The next time he had anything to bring up about me, minor matter, he just referred to me as Iron Hand. Which was how my old insulting nickname from junior kendo got hung on me in MHI.

I'll take it. "In your face" works for me.

CHAPTER 14

There was a werewolf in the Okanogan-Wenatchee National Forest, hereafter Okano. We knew that. It was up somewhere around Lake Wenatchee. Every other full moon, some group of hikers or a family in a cabin would get torn up.

We went up there month after month trying to track it down. No luck.

I had an idea but it wasn't a good one. It would take me out of pocket for a long time even if it worked. But it was the only idea I had.

You see, the Okano was also one of those areas where there were frequent Bigfoot sightings.

Sasquatch studiously avoided humans but they weren't invisible. People saw them from time to time and more often their signs. Lots of people studied them. Very few realized they were semi-intelligent with a definite language. The real problem was, nobody had a handle on the language.

So I requested some time off from the Nelsons to go hunt bigfoot and see if I could get them to communicate with me.

Making contact was going to be the hard part. All the yeti species were shy. But I had the records of Sir Edmund Hillary, the ones that were never publicly published, to guide me. Hillary had written the book on yeti. Some of that had to transfer over.

Yeti were addicted to a certain ginger candy made in Tibet.

There was a similar one made in China and even produced locally in Seattle. I filled up my pack with those as well as some other types of candy. I got a bunch of camping gear. I hadn't been camping since being in Uncle Sam's Misguided Children and civilian camping was different.

Then, in a wet and miserable spring rain, I parked Honeybear at a trail head, got out a massive pack filled with everything I should need for a couple of weeks in the mountains and started hiking up the trail into the Cascades. The Nelsons were going to come and pick up Honeybear when they got done with another vampire hunt.

I hiked for two days into those mountains, going up and up. I knew what sort of terrain and conditions I was looking for and found them near the head of the Little Wenatchee River. I kept in mind that there might be a werewolf in the area as well. I was armed with my old BDL, a .45 and both were loaded with silver.

I set up camp uphill from the river and started patrolling the countryside. I was looking for a certain sign and found it in a clearing on the slopes of Mount Howard. Early spring berries had been foraged and there was scat which, to the casual observer, would look like bear.

I pulled out some candy and placed it on bark stripped from an aspen tree, one candy per piece of bark. Some of it was the Chinese version of the ginger candy Sir Edmund recommended. I also had other candies, ginseng and lemon and even chocolate.

I left them there and went back to camp. I'd brought some books and I spent most of the time reading and doing the occasional patrol. But I stayed away from the candy.

I went back two days later and the candy was gone. Bear could have got it but most of the signs pointed to Sasquatch.

I put some closer to my camp. Less, I only had so much with me.

This time I heard them. They were quiet, but in the early morning "blue time," what's called Before Morning Nautical Twilight, I heard movement in the area I'd left the candy. I didn't react; I didn't want to startle them. But the Sasquatch were here. Then they left.

The third time, I put a bit more candy in the same place. This time I set up a hooch, a poncho held up with twine, and slept there. I woke up when I heard them approach and climbed out from under the hooch acting in the most nonthreatening manner I could. They were cautious but they could smell that mouthwatering candy and they wanted it.

I just sat there, cross-legged, and waited. Finally one of them, a younger one from the size, crept out from the trees. It looked at me with big, brown eyes and sidled to the candy. I just watched it.

Finally, it picked up one of the pieces of chocolate, an unwrapped Hershey's Kiss, and popped it in its mouth. When I didn't do anything, it grabbed a few more pieces and lumbered back into the trees.

I could hear low hooting from the assembled tribe. They weren't sure what to do.

The tones were so low it was hard to pick out any words, so I tried some North Chinese Yeti.

"Uh! Oomp! Oomp!" Friend! Good! Good!

That caused them all to pause.

"Guh! Guh!" one of them called. It didn't seem to be a threatening tone.

"Guh! Guh!" I replied. I wasn't sure what it meant but it was close in sound to "Uh!" friend in North Chinese Yeti, so I hoped it was the Sasquatch for "friend."

Which I later learned it was. Also their standard greeting and invitation to get closer, equivalent to the nearly universal Native American "How." Yes, it was a real word and, yes, it was one of the few nearly universal words in North American Native languages. It meant more or less "person who is not of your tribe who is not hostile wishes to speak with you."

Because the various yeti tribes in North America have gotten so spread out, there is no real universal but Guh! Guh! is still somewhat recognized by Louisiana and South Florida swamp-apes. The actual word in Louisiana Swamp-Ape is Yut! In South Florida, it is a very mellow Yoh! which I think might have created the slang term in English, by the way. The first time I heard someone go "Yo!" I swore to God they were speaking Everglades Swamp-Ape. The Laurentian yeti uses a more chopped Kuhk!

But if you're ever in the Everglades trying to make contact with swamp-apes, just let out a long, mellow "Yohhhh!" and they'd know what you're trying to say. They might not appear but they probably will leave you alone. Otherwise they tend to be the most hostile of the North American yeti species. Seriously territorial. Several reported "alligator attacks" in Florida were swamp-apes. Despite that, we generally leave them alone.

Two more Sasquatch, juvenile females, moved up to the candy and gathered it all up. They cast occasional looks my way. They were wary but accepted that I might not be hostile. I made sketches of them as they worked. Then they left.

Initial friendly contact made.

I won't do a full Jane Goodall but that's more or less what I did. I eventually found the clearing where they spent most of their time, at least at this time of year. There was a massive alpha male who never really liked me much but allowed me around. I called him Earl. There were seven adult females: Joan, Wanda, Brenda, Susan, Janet, Claudine and Marissa. There were nine adult or close-to-adult males. I won't bother with their names except for Herman, who was the one who had first made contact. He was a young adult male, human equivalent of probably sixteen. There were an additional ten mixed male and female juveniles.

I watched, I sketched and I listened. I also moved my camp closer to theirs. Slowly, I learned the very primitive language. Either they had linguistically devolved from the yeti, or Hillary had been overoptimistic on yeti. They only had about five hundred words in their language and half of them seemed to involve water in various forms. It was very polysynthetic and situational.

As the full moon came around, they got more and more nervous and a word started to crop up: Ch'kik! It was very different from most of their language and close to the Yeti for "tiger" Yek-tik! I wasn't sure if it meant "predator" or specifically "werewolf." But clearly they were as afraid of it as the locals who knew about the "frequent bear attacks" in the region.

I'd gotten closer to Joan and Herman than the rest. Herman saw me as some sort of threat. He recognized I was male and looked at me as a potential dominance threat. But he also loved chocolate.

They never tried to steal my candy. Just accepted it when offered. Sasquatch are more innately civilized than homo sapiens.

Herman's name in Sasquatch was Cho-cho-ka-ah. It's more of a nickname that means "Boy who made bad poop." He seemed to rise above it.

But one day as the moon was waxing, I sidled towards him.

"Cho-cho-ka-ah!" I said, not looking at him. "Guh! Guh!"

"Kuu-kuh-ah-ah!" he said, pulling at some weeds. "Guh!"

"Ch'kik! Mu! Mu!"

Mu translated as more or less "fear" or "bad thing." Kuu-kuh-ah-ah was my Sasquatch name that translated as "Broken one good food." They could tell, somehow, that I was sort of busted up.

"Ch'kik! Mu! Mu!" he agreed. "Ch'kik ulakula hakk!"

The werewolf/tiger/predator hunts/eats/preys upon our children.

"Kuu-kuh-ah-ah Ch'kik hakk!"

"Ch'kik hakk!" he exclaimed and backed up, fearfully.

I was afraid I'd mistranslated. I was just getting the hang of Sasquatch but time was getting short.

"Kuu-kuh-ah-ah Guh! Guh!" I said. I'm a friend. "Sushu Guh! Guh!" I'm a friend to the Sasquatch tribe of this region. I pulled out a Hershey's Kiss and laid it on the ground and backed away, being as beta as I could be.

The rest of the tribe had seen the interaction and wandered over, curious.

Herman retrieved the candy and went over to the tribe. There was a bit of conversation and social grooming. Even Earl got involved. The discussion got heated, then Earl reared up and charged.

I was afraid I was about to suffer death by Sasquatch as the massive male came lumbering over to me, gigantic arms swinging and teeth bared.

I maintained my beta position, head down, eyes turned away, but stood my ground.

He came up and poked me, rocking me back. I just held my ground. Two more pokes. They felt like being rammed with an iron rod. I didn't look up.

"Kuu-kuh-ah-ah hakk!" he bellowed.

You're a predator!

"Kuu-kuh-ah-ah Guh! Guh!" I said, definitely. "Kuu-kuh-ah-ah Ch'kik hakk! Ch'kik Mu! Mu! Kuu-kuh-ah-ah Mu! Hakk!"

I'm a friend. I hunt werewolves. I hunt bad things.

"Mu! Hakk!"

Bad thing! Hunter!

They'd probably been hunted by humans before.

He settled on his hindquarters and regarded me, huffing angrily.

I decided to drop the beta posture and look him right in the eye.

"Kuu-kuh-ah-ah Mu! Mu! Rahk hakk!"

I'm a great hunter of bad things.

He must have seen that despite the fact that I'd been just sort of hanging around being a nice guy, I was anything but.

"Kuu-kuh-ah-ah Shushu hakk!"

You're hunting Bigfoot.

This thing could rip me apart and I wasn't even carrying the Colt.

"Kuu-kuh-ah-ah Mu! Mu! Hakk!" I barked. "Shushu Guh! Guh!"

I hunt bad things. Bigfoot are good things.

He preferred the ginger candies. I pulled one out and unwrapped it and laid it on the ground on the wrapper.

He picked it up and continued to regard me. They may not have been strictly intelligent but they were smart at surviving. He popped it in his mouth and rolled it around.

"Ch'kik! Gah oh ooh."

The werewolf is not here/elsewhere.

"Ho, ho, Ch'kik? Kuu-kuh-ah-ah hakk Ch'kik!"

Where is it? I want to prey upon it.

"CHO-CHO-KA-AAH!" the big male bellowed.

Herman knew when his boss was in a foul mood. He came over at full beta, knuckle-walking and practically groveling.

"Kuu-kuh-ah-ah Ch'kik hakk," Earl growled. "Cho-cho-ka-aah ho-ho."

This human's hunting a werewolf. Show him where it lives.

Herman let out a very unhappy sound and wet himself a little.

Sasquatch are also not what you call brave.

There were two days to the full moon. Which didn't mean the werewolf couldn't change but I'd rather get to it during the other phase. So I'd need to move out.

I was about out of food. Good part, my pack was lighter. Bad part, I was about out of food. And for a mature werewolf I'd rather call the whole team. But Earl wanted me out of here, now.

I led Herman back to my camp and packed. I left most of the stuff like the pup tent. I was going to be travelling light. I took food, guns, water and ammo. I had a device for filtering water so I could drink from the local streams. That was a necessity.

When I was packed, I gave Herman one of my dwindling stock of Hershey's Kisses and said:

"Cho-cho-ka-aah ho-ho."

We were off on a werewolf hunt.

Herman was like a ghost in the wood and he had me on leg length and experience. And he wanted to get this over with as quick as possible. He constantly had to wait for me to catch up.

It took more than a day of travel to reach the werewolf's territory. I could tell when we were getting there by how Herman got more and more nervous. We bunked up for the night in a cave and I lit a fire. Herman didn't like fire. He stayed as far from it as possible. Since I'd put it near the entrance, he huddled at the back of the cave. But it was a good protection from animals in general and a werewolf doesn't regenerate from it very well.

When we came out in the morning, Herman was even more nervous. He hooted unhappily and pointed to some bushes near the cave. I sniffed them and smelled a strong, musky odor. The werewolf had found us and marked the spot. Now *it* was hunting *us*.

I'd checked my 700 BDL before leaving the cave and double-checked to make sure there was a round in the chamber. Then we set out.

We were on the east side of Mount Howard at this point in very broken terrain. The mountain reared up above us majestically, its summit still cloaked in snow and there was still snow in shadowed patches even where we were moving.

Herman was just about catatonic with fear. He kept stopping and hooting unhappily. He was clearly upset that his love of chocolate had gotten him into this predicament. I was unhappy to be hunting an experienced werewolf on its own terrain in nothing but my Marine issue cammies and armed with a bolt-action rifle and a 1911. One bite from the damned thing and I'd be eating Sasquatch babies on the full moon.

Babykiller indeed.

Just past noon Herman stopped and started looking around and smelling.

"M-m-m-Mu! Mu! Hakk!" he stuttered. I did not even know Sasquatch could stutter.

The werewolf burst from cover, charging the juvenile Sasquatch and ignoring me.

Herman let out a bellow of fear and tried to climb a tree. Sasquatch do not climb very well.

The werewolf sunk its teeth into his calf and ripped out a chunk the size of a good-sized sirloin.

Then I shot it with a .30-06 silver round right through its heart.

I worked the bolt and fired a second time as it turned towards me. It had felt the first one but in its battle fury, it could keep going for a few seconds without a heart. The second round took it just under the throat, to the left. That broke its right shoulder. It still launched itself at me. I dodged to the left, its wounded side, and butt-stroked it away with the BDL, keeping it from latching onto me as well.

I dropped the BDL and drew my 1911 from the holster. The damned thing had two silver rounds of .30-06 in it but it was still coming. Tough werewolf.

Seven rounds of .45 did it.

Poor Herman was leaning against the tree, moaning and crying and holding his badly wounded leg. I had no clue if Sasquatch could turn but I hoped not. Despite his fear, he'd shown me the route to the werewolf. Courage isn't being without fear. Courage is overcoming fear and Herman was the most courageous Sasquatch you'll ever meet. They're not big on courage. I got out my first aid kit and helped him as best as I could.

I'd checked with Dr. Lucius on what to do if I ended up killing the werewolf in the back country. His suggestion was "don't" but to get the PUFF, I had to have a tissue sample. So I took both ears. Herman didn't like that, either.

You ever have to help a Sasquatch with a wounded leg through twenty miles of broken terrain? I'm not going to quote the song. Brother or not, they are *very* heavy.

And the full moon was upon us.

The first night of the full moon I sat up all night in the cave, watching Herman sleep. I was out of food and worn to a frazzle but if he woke up and turned into a were-Sasquatch or something, I was going to be ready. It took a human a month to turn, but who knew with Sasquatch?

Apparently, despite being clearly related to humans, Sasquatch are immune to the curse.

The tribe found us; we didn't find them. By then Herman's wound was infected and I was worried about him surviving. Sasquatch live hand-to-mouth and they don't have access to advanced medical care.

But Joan was a wonder. She wandered off into the woods and came back chewing a whole wad of stuff. I don't know what was in it but it was way better than what I'd given him. Herman cheered right up and you could tell the infection didn't have a chance.

He'd been talking nonstop since we got back and the tribe all hooted along with his story as if repeating it. I couldn't keep up with most of it and I was tired enough I didn't really care. But Wanda came over with some berries which I accepted most graciously. The tribe really couldn't spare the food but I was that hungry. After Herman was done talking, Earl rose up and strode over to where I was leaning on a tree.

"Kuu-kuh-ah-ah Mu! Mu! Hakk," he grunted. "Kuu-kuh-ah-ah Mu! Mu! Rahk hakk."

You're a hunter of bad things. A great hunter of bad things.

And that's how I befriended the Mount Howard tribe of Sasquatch.

It took me nearly two days to get to the Ranger station on the banks of Lake Wenatchee even with the help of another of the young males, Snyder. I came in covered in scratches, exhausted and I'd been out of food for days. I also had both ears from an experienced werewolf with a body count. Nice PUFF.

I've been back to visit the Sasquatch frequently. Herman fully recovered. Bad scarring but full recovery. As Earl got older, it was Herman who stepped into the alpha male position easily. He got so much cred from going werewolf-hunting with "Broken human" that none of the other males even thought about vying for the position. Any time there's been a werewolf call around Mount Howard, I've contacted them and they've been able to lead me to it easily. And through them, I've made contact with most of the other Sasquatch in the region.

It was about six months after this that they did something extraordinary.

As usual, I had to be busted up to take a vacation. I'd broken my left arm, this time fighting an ogre (a story I won't bother with) and I decided it wasn't enough of an inconvenience to not visit my favorite tribe of Sasquatch. So, still in a cast, I headed to their late-summer foraging grounds close to where the Mount Howard werewolf had made his home.

When I got there, Joan chuffed and snorted over my broken arm. I told her it was all good. "Guh! Guh!" She didn't seem to think so.

That night she led me back to the banks of Lake Wenatchee and more or less told me to take off all my clothes and get in.

Look, Lake Wenatchee is an upland lake in freaking *Washington State.* There is no word in Sasquatch for "hypothermia" but there is one for "cold." Summer or not the water is very...

"Poo! Poo!" I snorted.

She was adamant. So I took off my clothes and, gritting my teeth, got in the water.

She started slapping the water and hooting—a low, long, call.

Nearby, the water rippled after a few moments and something emerged.

The best I can do is the *Creature from the Black Lagoon.* I recognized it immediately. It was a kappa, a Japanese version of nixie. The PUFF on one was extraordinary; the low end was fifty grand and they went as high as a half mil. They're considered one of the more dangerous sort of freshwater monsters, believed to be related to Deep Ones which are about as bad as it gets.

My balls couldn't have drawn up any more. But I trusted Joan the Sasquatch. I'd saved her tribe from a werewolf that had been eating their young, and she was a healer. She wasn't going to sacrifice me to a kappa.

They exchanged words. I didn't recognize the language and Joan clearly had problems with it. In the meantime, I was slowly dying of hypothermia.

Finally the kappa flipped over to me and started examining me from top to bottom. It made liquid sounds that I recognized as being unhappy. Unhappy about being around a human, certainly. But he also seemed less than thrilled about what the best human doctors money could buy had been doing with my bones.

I recalled that the kappa had the ability to heal bone injuries. But I wasn't sure it could work with plates and pins. And I was dying of hypothermia.

It seemed to recognize that and placed both webbed hands on my chest. Suddenly my body flooded with heat. I was back to being warm and toasty.

Then it forced me to submerge the plaster cast in the water and it started working.

The feeling was pleasant. Just warmth, no pain. Some areas would get warm and the kappa would suddenly emerge from the water and spit out a mouthful of metal. I realized they were the innumerable pins and plates I'd collected from the bombing.

It peeled the cast off as it softened until it could get to skin, then did the same thing there, laying its hands on my arm and licking it with its froglike tongue.

I went to sleep about the time it got to my thigh. That would be interesting.

I woke up with Joan dragging me out of the water. I'd started to get cold again. The kappa was gone.

I could tell that my bones were knitted back into shape again. The only one he'd apparently left alone was the right humerus, 'cause, like, there was no bone to work with.

I felt like a new man as I walked back to the Shushu. It felt great to have every freaking bone and joint be healed. I could tell I was going to have readjustment issues. I'd need about a week to get the muscles realigned. But it was like a miracle.

From a kappa of all things.

I spent a few days with the tribe, working on my dictionary of Sasquatch and taking notes on social aspects and other items to do a paper. I'd already decided Oxford needed a definitive paper on Sasquatch. I managed, with the limited language, to explain the general concept of monster hunting. They weren't particularly interested. All they cared about was where their next meal was coming from and whether there were predators that threatened their young.

According to legend, kappa love cucumbers. After I left the tribe, I went back down to the nearest town and just about bought the local supermarket out of cucumbers. That night I went back to the same spot Joan had taken me to—it was very near the Ranger station—and slapped the water and hooted in a similar fashion. Then I stuck some of my pins, no longer needed, into a few of the cucumbers and floated them out onto the lake. I wanted them to know who sent the cucumbers.

It was like watching fish hitting the surface and swallowing bread. In a few moments, all the cucumbers had disappeared. I waited, but the kappa—there had to be more than one of them—never showed themselves.

Because I didn't want anyone to get greedy about the PUFF, I never told them exactly where the kappa were. But there's a tribe of kappa in Lake Wenatchee. They're friendly. Don't kill them. But if you go down to the lake and slap the water like a beaver and hoot "Clo-clo! Clo-clo!" for a while, they might just surface and fix your broken bones.

Bring lots of cucumbers. And I've set a curse on anyone who kills one of them.

The curse is called Earl Harbinger.

CHAPTER 15

We were getting a lot of business right in the Seattle and Tacoma area. I'd stop by Saury most days I wasn't working. And about once a month there'd be some origami bird or flower with generally an address and thankfully some description. That's how we turned up the ogre that broke my arm. The werewolf spike had dwindled but there was always another vampire coven in town, various undead and monsters.

About once a week, I'd get some garbage and go to the rainwater outlet. Todd was another helpful source of information. As time went by, I learned the Gnoll terms for most of the city, and if there was something, I'd meet him closer to it the next day.

I got to know most of the city sewer maintenance people by name and my garbage collection contact didn't even bitch. The garbage was always gone in the morning and they didn't have to pay landfill fees so they were making money on the deal.

We'd gotten a replacement for Timmy named Roy Carroll. He came across as having the same issues as Timmy. He'd joined for revenge—his girlfriend had been killed by a death fiend—and for the PUFF money. But he was . . . excitable. Every hunt, he'd start chattering as we got closer to the monster and sound like he was about to run. But he always hung in there. I didn't give him a long life as a Monster Hunter but he always answered the page and we needed the body.

We were getting enough business from contacts that we had

trouble filling some of our out-of-town contracts. But then we got a call from the Perry County Sheriff's Office. They'd had a bad zombie outbreak in Renton, which was their county seat. And the call was from the only surviving deputy. The sheriff was, presumably, a zombie.

To describe Renton as "the middle of nowhere" is an understatement. The nearest town was Omak. Have you ever heard of Omak, Washington? Didn't think so. But that's where we flew to in a chartered Beaver with all our gear to go zombie hunting.

The area was sparse and dry, not like the Cascades. It was just about on the border with Canada. Middle of freaking nowhere.

We rented a U-Haul for most of our gear—there fortunately was a U-Haul outlet in Omak—and had to buy a couple of used pickup trucks to carry the team. Then we headed to Renton.

The State Patrol had established a roadblock in the pass over Renton. Dr. Lucius made contact with the surviving deputy there and got a more complete description of the situation. It wasn't just zombies. We'd gotten that. There were apparently some wights since some people had been paralyzed by "something big and gray and fast." They'd apparently attacked the local emergency station first, showing a degree of coordination that spoke volumes, then spread out and hit the whole town, concentrating the wights on leadership. The phone lines had also been cut.

"I got a radio call from the sheriff at his place," the deputy was saying. It was the tone of someone who'd repeated his story multiple times. "He told me to just get to Omak and call you guys. Gave me your number. I could hear the shots over the phone. And it cut off. I did what he told me."

"Which was the right call," Dr. Lucius said. "You did the right thing, son."

"He said it was zombies, and to call you. He was reading me the number when he started shooting. Said 'Call MHI!' and gave me your number. That was it. I called you, then I called State Police. They didn't believe me. I'm not sure if I believe me. But that's what the sheriff said. Do you think he made it, sir?"

"Sheriff Jackson's a tough old guy," Lucius said. "If anyone made it, he did."

"And you guys..." the deputy paused as I pulled the flamethrower out of the truck. We'd brought the kitchen sink. "You... handle this stuff?"

"All the time," Lucius said. "It's what we do."

MCB was already there. Some agents I didn't know. One of them walked up and I expected the usual harangue.

"We've established an overwatch position." The MCB agent was dressed in BDU pants and a polo shirt and had his cap on backwards. "We've spotted multiple shamblers and two wights. The wights seem to be being used as heavy hitters. The shamblers are also acting in controlled fashion. Some are randomly shambling, but large numbers are moving in coordinated groups. Some of the houses seem to be holding out. They're all surrounded. There is a large group by the school. They don't seem to be attacking, just standing there."

"Like they're on guard?" Dr. Joan asked. She'd kitted out and taken over so Lucius could get dressed.

"Appears that way. We'd had scattered reports of possible shambler activity in this area. But it makes no sense here."

"It sounds as if someone is trying to create an army," Dr. Joan said. "There've been other attempts. Bring about the apocalypse, 'cause the second coming, bring forth the Great Old Ones, whatever. Anyone who studies necromancy for any long period of time stands to suffer a psychotic break; at that point, direct logic—inductive or deductive—becomes moot, Special Agent."

She pumped her shotgun. "So we introduce the most direct logic possible," she added, smiling.

"This almost calls for SRT," the agent said. He sounded hesitant.

"If we can't deal with it, I agree, call your Special Response Team," Dr. Nelson said, loading another round. "But we can generally deal with it. I'm concerned about the school."

"So am I..." The agent's radio squawked.

"One of the houses failed," the other agent called. *"They're in."*

"We need to get moving," Dr. Joan said.

"Take a spare radio," the agent offered. "We may be able to spot threats you don't see."

That guy was going to go *nowhere* in MCB.

Ten minutes later I was in the back of a pickup truck, loaded for zombie and doing a rosary.

I'd started to write music. My mom had forced me to study violin before I got into total rebellion mode. But the truth was I liked music. I had even studied guitar on my own after I was out of the house. I'd recently heard some Christian rock and started to get into it. Totally Protestant stuff but I liked it. I was working on a few songs of my own. I was humming one as we approached the town.

"What are you humming?" Louis asked. "I've been trying to figure out where I've heard it."

"I'm writing it," I said. "All I've really got is the chorus."

I sang it for them.

"You are way too into this whole Holy Warrior kick, man," Jesse said, grinning.

My primary was my Uzi. If they weren't at extremely close range, it was better to fill wights full of silver. Going Mo No Ken was for when they were on top of you. Better to use .45 in most cases.

Or grenades. We had those. Or a rocket launcher. We had those. And if we got chased into a defensive position, we had claymores.

God helps him who helps himself. The God of Angel Armies might be on my side but so was a 1911 loaded with silver.

"Whom shall I fear?" I half hummed, half sung as I racked the charging handle. "I know who stands before me, I know who stands behind..."

"Shambler at the moment," Louis said. "You ready to pay attention to killing zombies?"

The sign for Renton was barely in sight. It was going to be a busy day.

"It's where I started," I said, getting up and looking over the cab. "Looking forward to it."

Jesse targeted the shambler with his BDL. There was a crack. "Shambler down."

"And it starts," Louis said, hefting a shotgun.

We rounded a curve and entered undead city.

There was a small park on our right and it had several shamblers in it. The truck stopped and we opened up. I used the Uzi. Not great for the range, but it would work. Jesse, frankly, got most of them, firing his BDL off-hand. Louis covered the other side of the truck and got a couple that tumbled down the hill.

As that cluster was cleared out, we moved on.

There were shamblers everywhere. It really did look like some movie about the zombie apocalypse. Shamblers weren't bothering me. I was worried about the wights. When the hordes got close, the Uzi came into play and proved its worth. While everyone else was reloading, I was still potting zombie brains. The one time that it looked like there might be too many, I dropped a bunch within feet of the truck and it was just *Pop, pop, pop, pop, pop, pop,* Zulu down with just about every round. And if I missed, I had more rounds to back that one up.

We were on a dirt road called Portland Street, headed to one of the houses the MCB said was surrounded, when we encountered the wights. And, Lord praise, we got a call in advance.

"MCB says wights inbound," Dr. Joan called from the cab. "From the west."

I ducked down and grabbed a LAW. Why not?

"You're going to use that back here?" Louis said.

"Backblast won't bother us," I said, opening the tube.

I oriented that way and was the first to spot them as they came out from around a house. I didn't even hesitate. I'd already spotted the range and let go. They were running right at us and I hit the one on the left square in the chest. It vanished in a dust cloud and a clap of thunder.

"THAT'S GOTTA HURT!" I shouted, then cackled madly.

When the dust cleared, it was apparent that one had more or less vanished—I'm sure its bits were somewhere—and the other one was not in great shape. It stumbled to its feet, missing an arm, and came trotting at us much slower than normal.

"Save the other rocket launcher," Dr. Lucius said as I bent down. "We might need it."

"Yes, sir," I said, targeting it with the Uzi.

All three of us in the back, as well as the team in the trailing truck, laid into it. The wight never even made it to the truck. Put enough destruction on them and they will lie down and be good dead.

Just to make sure, I got out, went over and tossed a Willie Pete grenade on it.

"We're going to have to find the *pieces* of the other one to get the PUFF, you realize," Dr. Joan said as I walked back to the truck.

"I'm sure there are some around somewhere," I said, grinning. "Pieces through superior firepower."

"That's just baaad," Jesse said. "Shamblers incoming."

A big crowd of them were headed our way from the direction

of Adams Street. That was the direction of the house that was under threat.

"Got that covered," Jesse said.

There were only about ten. My long range accuracy with the Uzi had improved. I think I got five. Not bad for head shots from fifty meters with a .45 subgun on moving targets. Jesse was more accurate but had to keep reloading. Louis was using an AR-15 but he really needed to spend more time at the range.

We followed the FBI directions to the house and knew which one it was when we saw the American flag being waved out a window.

A lot of the houses in town looked, frankly, worn. The area was definitely economically somewhat depressed. This was a newer house and very sturdily built. The walls were stone and the windows had had faux wood steel shutters that were functional. Some intelligent soul had closed them all. There was a new model pickup, jacked up, in the driveway.

We pulled into the driveway and the clearly reinforced front door opened. A man in his forties stepped out holding an M16 and looking around warily.

"All clear," Dr. Joan said, stepping out of the truck. "At least at the moment."

"Guess you're the cavalry?" the man said. He had the look I'd come to know when people encountered Joan in her work clothes. She was a slight, cute woman and just had that academic look. You expected her to be wearing peasant dresses and big glasses, not body armor and carrying a 12-gauge.

"Dr. Joan Nelson, sir, MHI." She extended a business card.

"Elmer Norton," the man said, taking the card then shaking her hand. He tucked the card in a pocket of his shooting jacket. "What the hell is happening, Doctor?"

"We were hoping you could shed some light. We got called in on a zombie outbreak but very little information got out. Do you have any?"

"I've seen 'em. But they ain't acting like real zombies. At least not like the ones in the movies. They're moving around in groups and there's a couple of fast, strong ones."

"Took care of those," Joan said.

"How?" the man said. "I shot 'em a couple of times and it don't faze 'em."

I reached down and picked up the expended LAW tube before Dr. Joan could reply and held it overhead in a victory pose.

"Ooor, oor, arrrrr!" I howled, imitating one of the Sand People from *Star Wars.*

"Okay!" the man said, laughing. "I like how you roll, young man!"

I could see there were people peeking out from behind him, including a cute little redhead holding a carbine. Probably a little young and given her probable dad . . . Need to be careful there.

"One thing you should know," Mr. Norton said. "I've seen 'em herding girls down towards the school."

"Girls?" Dr. Joan said.

"Yeah," Norton said. "Just girls. Looks like they've been turning everybody else or tearing 'em up. But girls like Sally here"—he gestured to his, yes probably, daughter—"they're not being turned. They're being taken towards the high school. Probably to it."

"That fits with the intel we've gotten," Dr. Joan said as there was a *crack* from the trail vehicle.

"One shambler down," Brad called on the radio. "How long we going to sit here?"

"We need to go," Joan said. "Other people to save."

"Want help?" the man asked.

"Probably better if you lock back up and protect your family," Joan said, walking back to the truck. "We've got this."

There were a bunch of dead shamblers around the house. We were going to be filing some PUFF on Mr. Norton's behalf.

"FBI says two more houses are surrounded," Lucius radioed.

"There's something going on at the school. We should stop that first, then clear the houses," Joan radioed.

"Concur," Lucius said.

The other two houses were about the same. They were both solidly built like Norton's house. Even the wights had had a hard time getting into them. Lots of shambler bodies. Those three houses had done a fair job of clearing out the town. They'd have to wait.

That left the school. This place was too small to have a school this size, but the other small towns probably fed into it. MCB overwatch reported there were still shamblers outside the school. They were concentrated by the gym.

We simply drove up, spread out and opened fire.

The shamblers just took it for a bit, then started shambling forward, dropping in twos and threes. There were about thirty of them, probably most of the remaining population of the small town, and they were all RIP before they got within thirty yards of the vehicles.

"So now to find out what's going on in that gym," Dr. Joan said. She'd unloaded from the vehicle and was standing by the open door.

"Permission to take point, ma'am," I asked. I'd reloaded the Uzi and reloaded my pouches from mags taken from my assault pack.

"Granted, Chad."

The gym had the normal double door system. The outer doors were glass. The inner were steel with reinforced glass windows. Most of the glass of the doors was shattered by stray rounds. There were a few bullet punches through the metal doors. No shamblers in the foyer.

I approached from the side and peeked in through the windows, getting a look around.

What had to be every girl in the town was sitting on a set of bleachers on the right side of the gym. They didn't look particularly happy. Most of them were crying.

There was a line of shamblers standing in front of the bleachers, apparently guarding the girls and keeping them from escaping.

At the back of the gym, a stage had been set up. On it was a big lounge chair and a table. A man I thought I vaguely recognized had a girl tied to the table and was cutting on her stomach.

"Necromancer on the far side," I whispered. "Girls on the right side. Ten shamblers guarding the girls. Sacrifice on an altar."

"I'll take the necromancer," Jesse said, hefting his BDL.

"Kill him and the shamblers go random," I said, hefting the Uzi. "Shamblers first."

"Agreed," Dr. Lucius said. "Try the doors."

"Watch your fire," Dr. Joan said. "Shout 'Get down, get down.'"

The doors were locked.

"Phil."

The doors opened outward. It was going to take one hell of a blast to open them. And that necromantic rite wasn't going to last forever.

Phil rigged the doors and we exited the building to blow them. It was a heavy charge.

There was a big *BOOM!* as the doors were breached.

"GET DOWN! GET DOWN!" I bellowed as I led the way in.

A couple of shamblers had gotten hit by the door. Big charge. None of the girls seemed injured but most of them were screaming and climbing up the bleachers trying to escape. Some of the shamblers were following them, others were headed our way.

Ten shamblers. Seven expert Hunters. They were down in seconds.

That left the necromancer. He'd hit the deck when the door went in and only stood up as we were finishing off the shamblers. I'd already started running for the sacrifice on the far side.

He didn't even try to finish the rite, whatever it was. He drew a pistol and started shooting.

Wrong move.

I skidded to a halt, dropped to a knee and put three rounds in his chest.

Then I kept going.

The girl was cut up bad. He had been writing something in a cryptic language on her stomach. Some sort of symbol that was ugly as hell. But she was alive. Crying but alive.

I let other people handle that and walked around the makeshift altar. Something about the necromancer was bothering me.

He was an ordinary-looking guy. Medium height, brown hair…

"Why, Reverend Donahue," I said, grinning and pointing the Uzi at his forehead. "How nice to make your acquaintance again."

"Who?" he said. "Help me…"

"You have got to be kidding me," I said, still grinning. "Elkins, West Virginia? Primitive Baptist tent revival? Ring a bell?"

"That was…you," he said, snarling.

"That was me. But that's not important, now. Done deal. Why the girls?"

"Fuck you," he spluttered. "Get me a doctor! I've got rights!"

"Doesn't work that way, not with necromancy," I said, switching to semi and putting a round in his knee. Then I stepped on it but didn't put pressure. "Why…the…girls?"

"Payment," he gasped. "Ten virgins for a…wight."

"To the lich in Seattle?" I asked.

"Who?" he said.

"To who?" I asked.

"No. Never."

I leaned on the knee as he screamed. There were some competing screams from his victims.

"Who?" I said, finally letting up pressure.

"The Dark... Masters..."

And that was about as much as his ravaged body could handle. He died.

Then his eyes flew open and he started to sit up.

And Mo No Ken took care of that little revenant problem.

We called in MCB to take care of the recently orphaned. The doctors warned them they'd be told to keep their mouths shut and to try to comfort each other. They noted that in mass attacks like this, group therapy worked quite well. Then we set out to fully clear the town.

There were a few shamblers still around. MCB had sent in school buses to get all the girls out. We ended up bunking with the families that had survived. We were clearing shamblers for three days.

On day three we declared the town clear and completed our count. This turned out to be a huge event. The MCB had their work cut out covering it up. I thought that had to be some sort of a record but it turned out the New York City blackout zombie outbreak had been three times our number. Total dead was higher. All the young children had been simply slaughtered. Some of them turned anyway but they were in pieces. Gruesome sight. I hate killing the young shamblers. That sort of thing shouldn't happen to children.

When the town was clear, we had a visitor.

We were putting away our gear outside the sheriff's office when a car pulled up and a tall man in his forties got out. He was wearing a revolver in a holster, one that had been used and seen some service, a shotgun vest loaded with cartridges and a Remington pump. Since the town was still under quarantine, we weren't supposed to have visitors. But at least he'd dressed appropriately.

I was closest, taking off my Kevlar pants, as he walked up.

"Garrett Terry," he said, holding out his hand. "Congressman for the Fourth District. Thank you for your service to our nation in resolving this terrible tragedy."

"Congressman," I said, shaking his hand. "Sorry for what happened to your constituents. We got here as fast as we could."

"I understand," he said, sitting down on the tailgate of the truck. "Okay, that's a lie. I forced the FBI agents to read me in. That took three calls to DC, with me increasingly steamed. Finally, I got a senior aide to force the issue. Now I almost wish I didn't know."

Dr. Lucius walked up to see what the hell was going on.

"Congressman Terry," I said. "This is my team co-lead, Dr. Lucius Nelson. Doc Lucius, Congressman Terry. This is his district."

"Congressman," Lucius said, shaking his hand. "I'm surprised MCB let you through."

"You wouldn't believe how much trouble I went through to get through, Dr. Nelson," Terry said, looking around at the empty streets. "I'm from Omak. I went to *school* here. This is *home*, Dr. Nelson. I'm damned furious at this. And even more damned furious that this sort of thing happens and nobody even *knows* about it! It's just made into myth! That's not the purpose of the Federal Government and a priori suppression of speech is a total violation of the Constitution signed by our Founding Fathers!"

I was starting to like this guy. But…

"I've read the secret letters of George Washington, Thomas Jefferson, John Hancock and Benjamin Franklin on the subject, sir," I said. "They were in agreement, though never in lockstep, on suppression of the truth of the supernatural. They were even negotiating with the British Parliament while the war was ongoing. The signed agreement of the Continental Congress to suppress the truth of the supernatural was one of the conditions the French required to come in on our side. It goes way back."

"You've read those letters?" Dr. Nelson said.

"Van Helsing had copies," I said.

"Like *Doctor* Van Helsing?" Terry asked. "As in *Dracula* Van Helsing?"

"The Institute named after him, sir," I said. "Congressman, be a bit cautious before you rock the boat on this one. We'll talk. But just keep your anger in check. MCB could possibly be a bit less heavy-handed."

"You think?" Dr. Nelson said, angrily.

"But these guys were actually helpful, which was the biggest surprise of this operation," I said. "You want to say something *good* about this? Compliment those agents up there. They actually helped. First time in my experience."

"It's extremely rare; put it that way," Dr. Nelson said.

"Emphasize the importance of keeping a lid on with your constituents. Help those poor girls who have lost their parents. And when you get to DC, try to get on the Oversight Committee so you can get fully read in."

"Hate to tell you this, but getting on a committee costs actual money," Terry said. "Campaign contributions to the party. And I just lost a major contributor in this massacre."

"Did you mention money?" I said. "Did they mention we get well paid for this? Like I said, let's talk. But later. There is lots to talk about."

I thought about what "Reverend Donahue" said the whole way back to Seattle. With my gear cleaned and put away, ready for another mission, I pulled out my rolodex and dialed a number in DC.

"Assistant Deputy Director Wilson's office. Who may I ask is calling?"

"Tell him it's Chad Gardenier," I said. "And I've got a lead on case number J-14458..."

The Dark Masters...Now who could *they* be...?

Denouement. Reverend Donahue was never officially identified to us. However, his depredations had been many. I'd reported to the incoming "professional" MCB agents that he was the same necromancer that had attacked in Elkins. Necromancers were paid out on a sliding scale depending on how powerful they were (he wasn't very powerful) and how many known attacks they'd been involved in (many).

We made a bundle off of Renton. I still wished it had never happened but that covers most of my career.

CHAPTER 16

This chapter's going to piss off Raymond III, Ray IV and Earl. But it has to be said.

We live in a representative republic. That's the technical term for our system of government. The way our system handles laws, regulations and so on and so forth is for the people (that's us) to choose elected representatives (Congress and Senate, state legislatures) to figure out all the messy "stuff" of government for us. That's what they are there for. Then the Executives, Presidents and Governors, set various "boro-crats" on the job of actually getting things done. Judges decide if they're doing so within the laws.

That's how it works. Civics 101.

What Civics 101 doesn't cover is the nitty-gritty. When you take the class they say "A bill will go through a committee..."

Okay, but how does Congressman Schmedlap get on such a committee? There are lots and lots of committees. How are congressmen and women chosen for them?

The Parties. There's a committee in each party specifically to choose which legislator from which party will serve on which committee. Not only do they choose who and what, they set the cost of each committee seat.

Cost? Yep. It's never discussed publicly but every committee seat costs money. The money is contributions to the party "in the name of" a particular legislator.

I'd heard about this way back when I was a kid. Remember, my mom was one of those politically active academics. We had congressmen and even a senator over to the house and I had big ears. Mom was always raising contributions for her favorite politicians. It was why she was so popular at UK. Because here's how it works.

Person A raises money for Congressman B. Congressman B then gets on a committee that affects the business, academic, scientific, whatever, of Person A. Congressman B then steers money to Person A's business. Person A sends some of it back to Congressman B. Lather, rinse, repeat.

Easiest example is the evil military industrial complex. Evil Defense Contractor is based in Congressman Schmedlap's district. EDC gives sixty thousand dollars to the Democratic party, via the congressman's aide. Said money is "contributed towards" the congressman getting on the Armed Services Committee. The congressman then ensures that EDC's primo weapon of choice gets pushed through whether the Marines want the AAV or not. Better competing systems be damned if they don't have the right congressmen and senators on the right committees.

Up to ninety percent of a politician's time is absorbed just doing fund-raising. That's how democracy works. Get over it.

Mom was a grant machine. She got on the grant committee in record time. Why? She knew congressmen and senators who were willing to steer grant money her way knowing that some of it would turn around and flow back into their sticky fingers.

You can call it bribery, you can call it a game, it's the way the system works.

Ray and Earl hate the system. They "refuse to play the game." When I started to play it on my own, I got an angry call from Ray. I told him, point-blank, he was a damned idiot. You see, we are *part of the game*!

We make ninety percent of our income from *governments*! The rest is contracts with various businesses. But most of our money comes from governments, especially the Federal Government in the form of PUFF checks.

Not playing the game was freaking insane. It was and is idiotic.

So here's my pro-tip—one that will piss off the bosses but they reluctantly accept with the words "It's your money; spend it how you like."

Find yourself a congresscritter whom you can stomach, somebody that matches your general political spectrum, whatever it might be.

And block out a certain amount of money from every PUFF bonus to that congresscritter. Ten percent, twenty percent, one percent, whatever.

The agreement is that he will use that money to get onto oversight committees for monster related activity and share information to the extent that he can legally.

If every Monster Hunter in the US did that, it would turn the tables on the MCB and monster rights groups. Because those guys decide how much money the MCB gets and how many grants monster rights advocates get. They control the purse. And money talks, bullshit walks.

About a month after the Renton Incident I sat down with Congressman Terry in a nice restaurant in Seattle. Just the congressman and myself. Dinner, Dutch, turned into drinks and a night out on the town. Man, that guy could drink. I didn't hand him a fat check. That's not how it works. We just talked. He'd been read in, wasn't on any of the committees, hadn't even known they existed, and wanted to know about monster hunting. I told stories. He told stories. He was former Army and a lawyer. He had some good stories. He explained some of the deep, dark secrets of how Congress actually worked. I told him I knew some of it. I talked about my bitch of a mother. He was aghast then laughed his ass off at the story about her visiting me at Bethesda.

I did not then and never did say "You need to increase the PUFF levels." It wasn't about that. But I did tell him that Monster Hunters—not MHI but the whole industry—needed a voice on the subcommittees. He couldn't even tell me how many there were or who had oversight over what.

I promised to come up with some money, my own and others. He had to spread it around. It had to go towards monster-related activities. He agreed. We shook hands over it at a bar right at last call.

The next week I sent his chief aide an envelope with checks worth over fifty grand from various members of my team.

Let me tell you, brother. For the rest of the time he was in Congress, Gary, as he prefers, took my calls. It was Gary and some other congresscritters and later senators who were snuffling in the Hunter trough that got us the contracts in Eastern Europe. And MHI made a packet on those. And when NY MCB got downright ornery—'cause it was NY and how could a bunch of yokels know how to manage monsters in NYC?—it was Gary, by then a party leader at least in part due to Hunter money, that smacked them the hell down and told them they'd fucked up the monster situation in NYC so they had a hell of a lot of nerve saying MHI couldn't handle it.

Which we did in our own inimitable style.

Over the subsequent years, I probably poured a million dollars of my own money into Gary's pocket and twice that much from other Hunters. Gary was Republican, so am I, but I sent checks to the Democratic party as well. Jesse, of all people, was a hardcore Democrat. Louis, surprisingly, was Republican. But I'd send money to the devil himself if it made my job easier. And Gary would pick out the *Democrat* who got it. Talk about bipartisan.

I ended up not only speaking before secret subcommittees but hanging out in the houses of congressmen and senators in DC. Generally when I was injured, yet again. And I'd tell them war stories. Few of them had ever met a Hunter. Not a damned one of them had ever fought a monster, face to face. Some had seen them; one of the members was from New Orleans. Some of them still had a hard time believing in monsters. They'd be showed videos of them or, in a few cases, live specimens collected by the MCB.

I found out about other groups, some of them really top-secret. I met President Reagan again. This time on business. He'd heard about me and asked to meet. We mostly talked about the philosophy of Hunter vs. police monster control. After the meeting I ended up taking dinner, en famille, with him and Miss Nancy. She wanted me to call her just "Nancy" and I couldn't. It was "Miss Nancy" and "Uncle Ron." He admitted he hadn't specifically remembered me from the bombing but he remembered meeting the airplane. I told him it had been the high point of my life to that point. I told them the troll story and Miss Nancy laughed so hard she spit out some of the veal. Even the Secret Service agents doubled over.

I ended up spending a weekend at the Western Whitehouse, their ranch in California. Again, while in recovery. Beautiful place and a great chance to talk. By then the GAO had been forced to do a cost benefit analysis of Hunters vs. FBI. Turned out that the FBI cost for one wight was *six times* the PUFF. Including the cost of PUFF administration which was nearly as much as the PUFF. Christ, the government burns money like it's coal or something.

And then I met my mother. Again.

At of all places a secret congressional subcommittee hearing.

Bitch was there representing Monster Rights Advocates.

Son of a . . . Yeah, that's what I am.

She sat there talking about how vampires were intelligent beings and deserved full rights under the Constitution. I'd gotten some of those sorts of questions from members of the committee before and now I knew who was writing the questions. I'd been asked by a staffer on "our" side to prepare some questions for a monster rights advocate and Gary just tore a strip off of her hide.

"Do vampires have souls?" Gary asked.

"I don't see why that question is germane," my bitch mother answered.

"I asked it. Answer it."

"There is very little way to determine if any being has a soul. This is Congress after all."

That caused some strained laughter from the very small audience. She had a few supporters. None from the committee—not even her supporters on it.

"Previous respondents have testified that when a vampire drinks, it drinks the soul power of the victim," Gary said. "Are you disputing that testimony, Doctor?"

"I am not an expert on the soul," she answered, bitchily. "But vampires are quite urbane individuals. Many of them are musicians, artists. Do they not deserve the right to life?"

"The only thing that may or may not deserve a right to life, madam, is something *alive*," Gary said. "You are advocating rights for something that rips the human throat open and drinks its blood. You are advocating a right to life for something that is dead and simply kept animated, and hungry, through the blackest sorcery. That only gains its sentience, its ability to think and reason, after taking the lives of human beings. A vampire may play music but show me the one that can *compose*! You are advocating allowing the continued spread of a curse and a disease! You might as well suggest we legalize the *Black Plague* or *Ebola*! Have you no shame? Have you no common decency?!"

He wasn't the only one that ripped her a new one. I was a major contributor to three of the members of the committee. Not only my money, other Hunters as well. One of them was a Democrat. All of her supporters were Dems so I was bipartisan. She wasn't.

After a long hour of back and forth it finally ended.

She hadn't seen me come in. I was the next to give testimony. She saw me when she got up and blanched.

"What the hell are *you* doing here?" she snarled. "Do you have to ruin *everything*?"

"I'm the next witness. You know, the pro 'stake 'em, cut off the head and cremate' side of the argument."

"Chairwoman!" my mother said, spinning in place and shrieking at the committee. "This . . . this . . . *This* cannot be allowed to speak! He is a warmonger! A babykiller! A . . . a . . . *He* is the monster! Here the monster *sits* before you!"

One of her supporters was the chairwoman but she banged her gavel with a pained expression.

"The testimony is complete and we will have order," the chairwoman said wearily. She might take my mother's money but I could tell she didn't like her.

When I sat down, I looked at my prepared remarks and set them aside.

"Madam Chairwoman, due to the outburst from the previous witness, I request permission to revise and extend on my introductory remarks so as to put it in some framework. I will try to keep it as brief as possible for I understand the time constraints of the Honorable Congressmen and Congresswomen on this committee."

She didn't want to give it but Gary chimed in. "Support the motion."

Two others chimed in as well including my loyal Democrat.

"Permission granted to revise and extend."

"The woman who just screamed at the honorable committee on the supernatural is my birth mother," I said, grinning. "I say birth mother because otherwise she was *my* personal vampire growing up . . ."

I didn't get into the whole intro to this book, but I did relate a few choice anecdotes about what it was like growing up with "that being" as my mother. And I related the Bethesda Incident.

By the time I got to *"Do the whole village!"* even the chairwoman was laughing in shocked hysteria.

"So please keep those facts in mind when considering the previous testimony," I concluded, "as well as the outburst on exit. That covers nothing of my original opening statement, but I considered it more important. I am now prepared for questions from the committee . . ."

The nice thing about Unearthly Forces testimony is that there's none of some congressman making a speech about the importance of making the bluebird the state bird of some state, then asking a koan. All of it is secret testimony so they stick to the subject.

Early on I was hit by a hardball from one of my mother's supporters on the subject of "vicious money-grubbing mercenaries killing anything that isn't human or on the endangered species list."

"Honorable Congresswoman," I said, nodding. "I am the author of the most definitive work on the Sasquatch of the Northwestern United States as well as the only dictionary of their polysynthetic agglutinative language. I have lived with them for weeks at a time, saved the young of their tribe from a werewolf which was hunting them and, when I arrived one time with a broken arm, they, in turn, introduced me to a kappa shaman healer. Not only did the kappa heal my broken arm, he healed almost all the wounds I sustained in the bombing in Beirut. I ended up with a pile of pins and plates the shaman removed by magic healing from my body. I can show this committee copies of my before-and-after X-rays should they need proof of this miracle.

"I should note that a single kappa is worth at the minimum fifty thousand dollars. A shaman would be probably twice that. They are considered extremely dangerous monsters, feared above almost all others in Japan—which they are when provoked. Not only I but my company, MHI, hold these kappa and Sasquatch sacrosanct. We will not even divulge to this committee, nor *anyone* else, their *location* . . . and will kill *humans* to protect them. So much for 'money grubbing mercenaries.'

"There are monsters which *are* harmless. There are monsters which are irredeemable. There are those which are in the middle. Bottom line, if they are not dangerous, MHI and any *credible* monster hunting organization ignores them. Live and let live. But *vampires*? Vicious, bloody, undead killing machines! You might as well argue for *zombie* rights! I know of not a single instance where they got their blood from blood banks. They get their blood from holding captives in disgusting conditions and feeding them the bloody *chunks* of those who perish from their draining. *Vampires*? Stake, chop and *cremate*! Unless you're very good with a sword, which I am, in which case you can skip 'stake.'

"When we don't aggressively hunt them, they breed like *mad*. Please stop reading Anne Rice, Honorable Congresswoman. Please," I finished, holding my hands in a praying motion. "If you try to interview a vampire, I assure you it will rip your throat out before you can ask its name," I added, chuckling. "That completes my response, Honorable Chairwoman."

I had a good quip for every single hostile question, I had every question nailed and I could answer them all in under two minutes. My mother had repeatedly asked to revise and extend and, with the chairwoman in her pocket, it had been allowed. My mother could be a very boring harridan.

But most testimony is for show, even with UF testimony. Where the real power lies is in knowing the staff behind the scenes and meeting in private. I couldn't spend all my time in DC. I had monsters to kill. I eventually found a medically retired Hunter—she lost her right leg to a luska—named Melanie Simmons who had picked up her law degree after retirement. She had a federal bar certificate and already worked for a lobbying firm in DC. I hired her to set up a lobbying firm for Hunter activities, to handle the background and explain that, no, Mr. Gardenier isn't available because he, you know, is out there saving people.

My mother was always available. Because she wasn't. That point also scored.

So did the fact that Hunters had money. Monster rights advocates had to have a hard time raising money. Where did they advertise? The back of a paranormal romance novel?

I later found out that most of their money came from grants from, you guessed it, the Federal Government, to "study" monsters and even to advocate for monster rights. And where did *that* money come from? The subcommittee I was testifying in front of.

What the fuck? Never mind. Democracy isn't the best system of government, just the best we've ever found.

In those private meetings, I stressed a few points over and over again. They weren't even about "Hunters are better than cops for this" or "we need more money."

The point was that those subcommittees were the most important job in Congress.

That point sort of caught most of the legislators and even staff off balance. "I don't think so" was the undercurrent. What about Ways and Means? Armed Services? Foreign Affairs?

"Think about the worst possible situation you can in the mundane world. Nuclear war? Nuclear war might blast us into a very bad decade. Would it wipe out civilization? No. There aren't enough bombs in both inventories. Most of the world would sit it out. And the US would have a very hard ten years, maybe longer. We'd be a third-world country for the next century. We might break up.

"If the Great Old Ones break through, if the Fey take over, human civilization will *end*. A few free humans might survive for a couple of generations, max. The Fallen would use us for sport until they get bored and then humanity will *end*. All the trees, all the bison, all the flowers will be smashed, burned, destroyed. The environment? Old Ones will destroy it. They would wipe out every bit of life on earth until the last rabbit is flayed alive and dies screaming.

"*None* of you will be spared. You won't be able to hide in the deepest bunkers or the furthest wastes. *Nothing* can protect you. Your *families* will not be spared. *Everyone* you love will die *screaming*. Eaten by vampires, turned into zombies, possessed by demons, devoured for a thousand years in the stomachs of shoggoths, their very souls stolen and denied Heaven and tortured for all eternity by the Old Ones. The skies will be black as night and the rivers will literally run with blood as the whole world screams for *decades* until there is no one *left* to scream.

"That is what these subcommittees consider every time they meet. How to save the God-damned *world* (senior staffer, congressman, senator.) *You* are the most important people in the world because it is, *every damned day*, in *your* hands.

"The Elder Things, the Old Ones, the Outer Powers, they only have to get it right *once*. You have to get it right *every single day*. And if you don't, every human, every animal, every plant on earth will perish in pain and fire.

"But no pressure," I'd add with a grin.

The argument even sunk home with some of the monster rights side of the table. Unfortunately, they preferred appeasement. "I'm sure we can negotiate with the Old Ones." Gah.

By the way, if you were a Monster Hunter or even a former Monster Hunter, do not bother to apply for any of those grants to study monsters. You are a vicious mercenary even if you do have two Masters from Oxford University. And later two PhDs.

Just to try to get my mom to stroke out, when I found out the address of her "secret" newsletter and "academic publishing house," I submitted my papers. They had, after all, been accepted by Oxford University Press.

I never even got a rejection letter.

Several times when I was in DC, I touched base with ADD Wilson. We even ended up going out for a drink to discuss the Dark Masters case. The depredations had continued. They'd gotten word from OrgCrime as well about a shadowy group looking for "virgins." Nobody could pin them down. They seemed to be working the whole US. And, with the exception of the Seattle job, none of the victims had ever turned up. There were probably more. Several of the girls in Seattle had been listed as "runaways." Most police departments list any teen who is a missing person as "runaway" whether there is any evidence for that or not.

I said I'd shake my trees and see if anything fell out.

It did, but not for a few years. And when it did, it again got personal.

Thornton, you really were a vicious prick but... Jesus. Ten virgins for a wight? Twenty thousand dollars for a virgin?

They really *were* as expensive as the vampire lady said.

"Got any idea how hard it is to find a virgin these days?" were practically my brother's last words.

CHAPTER 17

Enough about politics and my fucked up family. Back to monster hunting.

We'd just taken down an ogre magi and his "court" of three ogres and a satyr.

It was the sixth large-scale monster we'd taken down since the lich. Most of them, according to the gnolls who mostly gave me the tips, had moved in recently. We seemed to be in the midst of a monster migration. Good for business, bad for health. Doc Lucius was out for a significant period of time *before* the ogre magi courtesy of a necromancer with a big flesh golem; I had gotten seriously banged up by members of the ogre's court and Jesse was in traction. We were getting short on shooters at this rate.

Something was going on and it wasn't good. The problem being, we had no idea what. So I decided to shake a tree and went to Saury.

I ordered my usual, then, when the server came with the meal, I asked to see Naoki-sama.

Since I was a favored customer, and favored of the yakuza, the owner made his way over quickly.

"Assei-sama," Naoki said, bowing. "Is all well? The food is good?"

The food was always good. Because Saury was very traditional. I'd tried a couple of other bento places just to check and I couldn't believe what I'd seen. There was this new thing called a "California Roll." And some of the horrible geck that they put in them! Avocado! Can you believe they put *avocado* in a sushi roll? It was like using Mo No Ken to cut grass! Sacrilege!

"Excellent as always, Naoki-sama," I said, bowing back. "I would ask a favor. I have need to speak to a man of distinction. There are troubling winds and I would have his wisdom. I am aware that this may cause you issues. It is entirely your choice."

"It shall be as you desire, Assei-sama," Naoki said, bowing again. He had the perfect Japanese mien but I could tell he wasn't looking forward to calling the yakuza boss and telling him the gaijin wanted to chat.

"This is not a matter of haste or hostility," I clarified. "I truly need his wisdom."

About a week later, I'm in Saury again and using chopsticks left-handed courtesy of a particularly powerful kelpie. The damned thing had a kick like a mule. Just another in a long list of monsters that had been turning up. And Oshiro sits down next to me.

"You never call, you never write," Oshiro said. "This must be business."

"Do too. I sent you a birthday card."

"I thought the gray dust in it was a nice touch. What was it?"

"Vampire dust," I said. "But I knew it would look like fugu."

"Nice shiner," he said, handing over his order to the sweating server.

"Which is the business I would, yes, like to discuss," I said, juggling my roll. "I'm still not quite ambidextrous with chopsticks and my team is down to three hale people because we seem to be in the middle of a monster migration. Any clue why on your end?"

"The supernatural is your area."

"Had to ask," I said. "What am I going to owe for the honor of your presence?"

"Nothing," Oshiro said. "I'm not nearly that traditional. And this has been a very good business arrangement. But you seriously don't understand what is going on?"

"I wouldn't be taking up your time if I did. Do you?"

"I've got an educated guess. It seems simple to me. When you killed that lich, you created a power vacuum. Powerful entities have territories. Like Monster Hunters or government or my own humble self. You took out the big cheese in Seattle. Others, those without territories, are now trying to move in. And will continue to do so until a new entity takes this as its territory. And even after one has taken the territory, it will continue to have to defend it until others decide it is not worth the effort."

"So you think... every city or whatever has supernatural entities that control that territory?" I said, boggling.

"I think so," Oshiro said. "It seems like some large cities have several who respect each other's territories. Most are ones which are wise enough to stay off the radar. The recent immigrants would not have been so wise."

"Is there an answer?" I asked.

"Wait for one to move in that you can hold your nose for?" Oshiro said, shrugging.

"So far that hasn't been happening." The kelpie had seduced and drowned multiple women before we tracked it down. I think they were blaming the murders on "The Green River Killer." And the kelpie wasn't alone. It, too, had a group of hench-things.

"Find one that wants a territory and ally with it?" Oshiro said, gesturing at the bar. "It is not as if you don't occasionally make deals with the devil."

"Suggestions?"

"The supernatural is your area," Oshiro said, standing up. "I have other areas to manage. Good luck. Hope you survive. You've been helpful to my bottom line. The Fathers are pleased."

When Naoki-sama presented the check, he did so with trepidation. There was a "consulting charge" of ten thousand dollars on it.

I sighed and put it on the Gold Card. Not going to cost anything my ass. TANSTAAFL.

There Ain't No Such Thing As A Free Lunch.

I explained the conversation with the Doctors Nelson.

"I've never heard that theory before but it makes sense, I suppose," Doc Lucius said. "It doesn't surprise me that a criminal who thinks in terms of controlling turf would have a unique perspective on monster behavior."

"Theoretically, we could find something that could come to the Seattle area that we could work with," Dr. Joan said, biting her lip. "That is a very short list, both in terms of what we're willing to work with and what the MCB will allow. If we accept, say, a Major vampire, I'm fairly sure they would consider that 'conspiracy with outer powers' and *our* heads would be on the chopping block."

"So it would have to be anything that is either not on the PUFF table or for some reason PUFF exempt," I said, "but powerful enough and capable of using that power to bring order to the monsters in town. That has got to be a very short list."

"Assuming such an entity would come to Seattle," Dr. Lucius said.

"There has to be one looking for a territory," I said. "We need more information. I don't think the gnolls will be much use. They don't think much beyond 'Smells like teen urine.'"

"Talk to the elves?" Dr. Lucius asked.

"Oh, please, not those," Dr. Joan said.

By then I'd learned that elves were not the wise and noble creatures depicted in the *Lord of the Rings*. But I'd never dealt with them.

"I'll go," I said. "I've been sort of wanting to meet them, anyway."

"They won't talk to a human they don't know," Dr. Lucius said. "I'll go."

"Don't fall for their wiles, Chad," Dr. Joan said. "They can be dangerously seductive."

"I'm not worried," I said, grinning. "Me, too."

"That's what I'm worried about," Dr. Joan said, sighing.

"Hey, there," she said. "I'm Cheyenne. Hot car!"

The elf girl was about five foot nothing wearing purple hot pants, a red tube top and pink Candies. Red hair and deep blue eyes that were almost purple. She leaned in the window of Honeybear, arms crossed in such a way as to maximize the already noticeable cleavage of the tube top.

"Thanks." I gave her whole body a full peruse. Nice legs, great ass. Damn! I was going to *like* dealing with the elves. "I did all the work myself. I've got . . . great hands," I added, holding the left one up and wiggling the fingers suggestively.

Dr. Nelson wouldn't approve, but he was talking to the leader of the elf colony in the Spokane area. He'd suggested I wait in the car after lugging three cases of beer and five cartons of Marlboro Reds onto the porch of the beaten-down trailer.

"A nice sword," Cheyenne said. "Can I see it?"

I had Mo No Ken on the front seat.

"See it, yes," I said, picking up the sword. "I only let really close, personal friends touch my sword."

I drew Mo No Ken partially out of the scabbard and shifted it so she could peruse the steel.

"I just love big, *sharp* swords," Cheyenne said, batting her eyes.

"Are you a sword swallower?" I asked, putting Mo No Ken away.

"Depends on the sword," Cheyenne said, batting her eyes again. "I'd probably be willing to swallow yours. *All* the way down."

"Aggh," I said as Dr. Nelson came walking around the corner. "My boss is back. Maybe we can talk later? I could show you some sword tricks."

"I'd like that," Cheyenne said, leaning back. "Come any time. I'm always looking for somebody cute to come. Bye."

"Whoa, she was *hot*," I said as we left the trailer park.

"Check her age for God's sake, Chad," Dr. Nelson said. "Some of those park elf girls might look eighty or ninety but they're only forty or fifty. And that can kind of piss off their families. You don't want to do that."

"Anything?" I asked.

"No," Lucius said with a sigh. "The countess agreed with Oshiro's assessment. But she wasn't much help in terms of a solution. And another thing about trailer park elf girls, Chad."

"I gotcha. Wear a raincoat."

"More like bunker gear."

Back at my apartment, I thought about the problem while working out my right arm. It was getting better but still wasn't a hundred percent. And if I was going to take on an elf maiden, hah, I knew I was going to have to be in shape.

Not to mention whatever monster appeared next.

Finally, I picked up the phone and dialed a number in DC.

"Congressman Terry's office."

"Hi, it's Chad Gardenier. Is Bert around?"

Time to get some pay back for all that PUFF money I'd sent the congressman's way.

"There is only so much information I can give you, Chad," Bert said, grimacing over his caesar salad.

Bertram Gregory was Congressman Terry's senior aide. Heavyset, he was perpetually on a diet that never seemed to work. He'd been the congressman's campaign manager and was now the back-room dealer for the congressman. The man you handed the "campaign finance" checks to while the congressman shook hands.

Like the congressman, he shuttled between Washington state and DC. He had a house in Davenport, which was the "big town" of the congressman's fairly sparse district, but spent most of his time in either Spokane or Seattle.

"I just need a list of the types of powerful entities that aren't going to piss off MCB if we ignore them," I said. "There has to be such a list."

"The PUFF exempt list," Bert said, nodding. "Thing is, it lists them by name. And that list is closed. It's like WitSec. I don't even have access to it. But there are types that are off the PUFF list unless they put themselves on it, like elves."

"Not powerful enough," I said. "It's like saying 'what about a gnome momma?' I need something strong enough to hold down a *city*, that won't be sacrificing virgins to make wights, eating people or drowning women to suck out their souls."

"That pretty much boils down to some kinds of Fey," Bert said, grimacing. "I wish like hell you'd never gotten Gary into this. Like I don't have *enough* things to do? And all this PUFF stuff does exactly nothing for the district that anyone can see. It's like that stupid Afghanistan thing that Good-time Charlie Wilson is into!"

"Afghanistan?" I asked.

"Don't ask," Bert said. "Nothing to do with PUFF. The only thing I can think of is Fey."

"I don't exactly think a Baba Yaga is going to be an improvement over an ogre magi," I said.

"If I recall correctly, and I could be wrong, Baba Yaga is *one* type of Fey," Bert said. "Some are super powerful, but ambivalent about mankind. We don't put them on the PUFF list. They don't mess with us; we don't mess with them. But not a Fey Queen or a Hunt King. And you don't want a Hunt King. They tend to be . . . bad."

"Like the Horned One?" I asked.

"Yeah," Bert said, shuddering. "They're around but they generally keep a low profile. Know that story 'The Most Dangerous Game'?"

"Read it. Christ, is there anything out there that is fiction that *isn't* based on a real story?"

"*Old Man and the Sea?*" Bert said.

"Hemingway's boat captain told him the story."

"Then I guess not," Bert said. "But you could talk to a Faerie Queen if you dare. I don't suggest it. Most people who do deals with them don't end up well. And we've really appreciated the support."

I loved how similar that was to what Oshiro said to me. But I wasn't going to compare Congress to the yakuza. Not to his face.

"Yeah, but I need one who doesn't have a territory and preferably needs something. Something I can provide. Thoughts?"

"None that come to mind," Bert said. "Look, I'm back in DC next week. I'll talk to some contacts. See what I can come up with."

About a week and a half later Bert called. We'd cleared a nest of trolls and something that called himself a "Troll King." I didn't know trolls had kings. Tough son of a bitch but fortunately it was in an area we could use flamethrowers. He wasn't so tough running around in circles on fire. We'd added some powdered aluminum just in case.

"Guy's going to be visiting," Bert said. "He's from an agency that doesn't officially exist. You'll know who it is. Has a suggestion. He's the most dangerous man you'll ever meet. And I am *out* of this discussion."

"Assei-sama," the man said, sitting down next to me at Saury.

He was enormously tall, handsome, had thick dark hair, tan skin, and odd rose-colored, wire-rimmed glasses. I figured this was my government contact.

He was speaking Japanese so I played along.

"A mutual friend said you may be of assistance."

"Bert's a cog in a machine. He didn't find me. I found him. But, yeah, I can assist. First, my terms. No one, your employers included, can ever know we spoke. The Shacklefords don't approve of my agency, and they'd never approve this plan. They're shortsighted like that. The Nelsons want peace in Seattle enough they'll go along and not tattle, but when they ask how you got your information, make something up. This meeting never happened. Do you agree?"

"Fine."

"We have a deal. Don't fuck it up. I'll know if you don't keep your word." He didn't offer to shake on it. "You can call me Mr. Stricken."

"You have a suggestion on how to deal with the current dilemma in Seattle, Mr. Stricken?"

"Naw, I flew here from DC for shits and giggles," he said, filling out his order form. "Are you familiar with the stories of princesses trapped in towers?"

"They are all over various forms of mythological literature. Not only towers. Labyrinths, et cetera. So, yes."

"There's a princess of the Fey trapped in a tower in California," Stricken said. "She would probably be quite grateful to be rescued. She's been sentenced to be imprisoned there for twenty years. Not that long in Fey terms, but long enough to be rather bored. She would probably suit the need for a powerful entity to hold the Seattle territory."

"What's the catch?" I asked. I could tell Stricken was the kind of man who would always create a catch.

"She's sort of in a time-out. Her mother put her there. And this particular Fey Queen would be rather displeased if a mere mortal interfered with her daughter's punishment."

"What did she do to piss her mother off?"

"Besides being a teenage female with a powerful and dominating mother?" Stricken said. "There was something besides being, I warn you, a revolving pain in the ass. But, you'd have to ask her. I know, and find it as horrible and terrifying as her mother did, but I'll find it amusing when *you* find out. Nothing dire. Just... amusing. And horrible. And terrifying. But that is besides the point. She's potentially powerful enough, with a bit of mortal help, to hold Seattle. I'll call in a favor and make sure the MCB doesn't get in your way, and I'll ensure she's PUFF exempt."

I had never heard of this guy before. I'd never seen him in any of the subcommittee meetings, but if he could take beings off the PUFF list and boss around the MCB, he had some clout.

"So why are *you* helping?"

"If it works, I will, at some point, point out that she owes *me* a favor as well. I do such trade commonly. If it doesn't, no skin off my nose. With the Fey, it's all about the deal. A suggestion, if I may? I'll send over a file. Half of it will be redacted and the other half is guesswork. Do your homework, but with this particular Court, your musical background should prove handy."

"How'd you know about that?"

"I know everything. From what I've been told you're nearly as talented as I am, though I prefer the piano."

"Okay. So I'm supposed to rescue from a tower a fricking Fey princess who has been mystically bound there by a Faerie *Queen*, do a deal with a group which is notoriously tricky about deals, and then *somehow* survive a Fey Queen's wrath? That's all?"

"As I said," Stricken said, taking the sushi to go. "Amusing. Good luck. You'll need it."

"Just one more piece of information. Where is this tower?"

"San Fernando Valley. The rest you can figure out."

"We need to find a tower in the San Fernando Valley?" Dr. Lucius said. "That shouldn't be that hard."

"It is probably not a tower in a castle or something," Dr. Joan said, frowning. "It could be almost anything and anywhere."

"I'm going to have to take a road trip," I said. "This is the best bet we've got to stabilize Seattle and get this migration of bad things under control."

"There is more to it than that," Dr. Joan said, still frowning. "Even if you can find this faerie princess. Even if you can release her. There is the matter of her mother."

"I'm not sure you understand quite how powerful a Faerie Queen is, Chad," Dr. Lucius said.

"I've read the Oxford studies on them as well as Spenser, Doctor." And also the file from Stricken's secret agency, but I couldn't tell the doctors about that one. "Powerful magic doesn't begin to describe it. In their courts they consider ogres to be minor servants and have Fey knights who are so badass they make Lancelot look like a piker. I get how powerful the foe is, Doctors. But they *do* have vulnerabilities, else we'd be slaves to them. I plan to use their two major vulnerabilities against them."

"Which are?" Dr. Joan said.

"One is not so much a vulnerability as a strength. They are subject to their oaths. If they violate an oath it degrades them. They *are* bound by oaths."

"Which they are *notorious* about weasel-wording," Dr. Lucius said.

"Which is why I'm not going to make it a simple oath. I do have a plan on that one."

"What's the other major vulnerability?" Dr. Joan asked.

"Did I ever mention I studied violin?"

CHAPTER 18

I cordially detest L.A. I hate the complete lack of weather. The rain and fronts are one of the many things I liked about Seattle. I hate the smog. I really don't like most of the people. There are a lot of hot girls but I've never met one who had two brain cells to rub together. I mean, that's probably selection issues in the sampling data. But, seriously, town has more air in heads than in all the hot air balloons in the world.

"You sure about this?" Jesse asked.

There were several issues to this mission:

1. *Find* the faerie princess.
2. Release her.
3. Negotiate a contract with her to be the "big cheese" in Seattle that was as ironclad as possible.
4. While 2 and 3 were going on, keep her out of view of her nearly omniscient mom. Faerie Queens were *very* good at finding out information and would probably be even better at tracking family than the occasional human that pissed her off. Which we were about to do. In big bold letters.
5. Survive momma's wrath. Tricky that.

"Got a better idea?" I asked, looking out the window of the Beverley Hills Hilton. MHI, probably because it was based in Cazador, always seemed to end up in fleabag motels. We made enough money I preferred to travel first class. Besides, this was technically a "rogue op" so I wasn't putting it on the company card anyway. This was just me and Jesse potentially picking a fight with a powerful extradimensional being.

Some people would have thought the view was beautiful but it was, well, L.A. You could barely see the view through the smog. Gah.

"No," Jesse said. "First we gotta find her. Assuming your information is good."

I hadn't vouchsafed who I had my information from. I didn't trust the guy entirely, he smelled like CIA from a mile away, but I was pretty sure he wouldn't have sent us on a complete wild-goose chase.

"The info is good. Problem being, San Fernando Valley is a very big place. And we don't have any local contacts."

At the time MHI didn't even have a Southern California team. Six other little hunter companies covered the area and none of them were particularly friendly to MHI. We'd have to start by developing contacts. And trying to keep what we were looking for from getting to the Faerie Queen.

"This place has got to be crawling with trailer parks. I'll grab the phone book and start looking for the usual names."

"I'll go find a liquor store," Jesse said.

"Don't forget various types of smokes. Some of these elves like menthol."

Got any idea how many mobile home parks there are in *Pomona alone*?

Holy crap.

It took five days of searching through half the shitholes in L.A. And L.A. had *a lot* of shitholes. But afternoon of the fifth day, we finally found what we were looking for.

Mystical Vista Mobile Home Park was just another shithole in East Pomona. Ratty trailers, scraggly, barren yards, cars up on jacks. Truthfully, it was cleaner than most of the places we'd been looking in. We almost passed it by just because of that. There was an almost complete lack of real litter. That and there were a few definite non-elves in sight and elves usually didn't share their parks with humans.

But we caught a glimpse of some pointed ears on a mullet head working on a battered old Corvair.

"Think we found our spot," I said.

✧ ✧ ✧

It was hard to figure Asofodel's age. She had had so much cosmetic surgery she must have been half plastic. Bad fake boobs, fake lips, face lift, blonde wig, and I'd guess she had about monthly liposuction.

On the other hand, she was more doable than most elf queens.

"Most beautiful Queen Asofodel," I said, bowing as she made her way out onto the porch of the trailer.

"Queen?" She snorted. "There's only one elf queen. She's in Alabama. I moved out here to get away from her bossy ass. I'm a countess."

"We have brought fine gifts and seek your wisdom."

"I ain't doin' no more spells," she said. "Government says I can't. So what you got and what you want?"

"We seek information only, my lady most fair." I didn't think flattery based on vanity would work with most elves, but it was clear that wasn't the case with Asofodel.

"You really think I'm fair?" she said through lips that were barely able to move from all the work.

"As the dawn."

"Well, ain't you sweet," she said, preening. "What information?"

"I must first beg the Queen of the Morning's word that the nature of the questions are not revealed to others. I would not have the nature of the quest reach other ears."

"Depends on what the question is," Asofodel said.

"It involves Grand Fey."

"You don't want to get involved with them and neither do I. They're mean as shit. Ain't no amount of PBR would get me involved in their business. But you can ask the question. I won't say I'll answer but I won't tell nobody what you asked."

"There is a Fey princess trapped somewhere near here in a tower. I would know where the tower is and the nature of the entrapment."

"What the hell you want with that stuck-up bitch?" Asofodel asked. "I'll tell you you can't use her against her momma. If you tried to ransom her, her momma would *help* you drown that POS."

"We want nothing of the sort. Just where and how she is entrapped. Where is good enough."

"Hmm..." Asofodel said. "Like I said, I'm not getting involved for a few cases of PBR. Queen Keerla Rathiain Penelo Shalana is one right bitch if you cross her. She's a Taurus—holds a grudge for eternity. Knew one elf that crossed her years back. He's still mystically bound as a two-dimensional cartoon until the company stops using the logo. His name was Mickey if you get the drift."

"Damn, that's cruel," Jesse said.

"What will it take?" I asked.

She patted her curled wig and batted her eyes.

"You really think I'm pretty?" she asked, making a moue.

"Your eyes are the light of crystal suns."

A little later I came limping out of the trailer, favoring my still-healing right arm.

"Four hours?" Jesse said. "Four. I've been sitting here for *four hours.*"

"It felt longer," I said, wincing as I got in the car. "Damn. Good time, mind you. Just a bit painful."

"If sex is painful, you're doing it wrong," Jesse said.

"You clearly need your horizons expanded," I said, starting the car.

"I figured if the trailer was still rocking, I shouldn't come knocking."

"Good call," I said, pulling out of the trailer park. "Okay, this just got even more complicated."

"How?" Jesse asked.

"We're going to somehow get ahold of the plans for the Van Nuys Municipal Building and Courthouse. And then we're going to have to break in."

"This place was designed as a courthouse and jail," Jesse said, looking at the schematics. "It's designed to keep people from breaking in *and* breaking out."

The blueprints should have been impossible to get our hands on. They weren't just sitting around and if you walked into the courthouse and asked them for complete details of their layout, there were bound to be questions followed by police officers.

But, hey, there were yakuza in Los Angeles as well as Seattle. Money had changed hands. Voila! Blueprints. I even found a great bento place out of the deal.

"There's going to be a way," I said, flipping through the schematics. "She's up in that little spire thingy. Mystically bound by her mother to her normal Fey appearance as well as against any use of magic. And the hatch to the tower is locked. She gets fed by servants that come in through some sort of mystic portal."

"Wonder how long her hair has grown," Jesse said, grinning.

"Not that long. That spire thingy is way up there."

"That little spire thingy is a bell tower," Jesse said, pointing to it on the schematic.

"Must get fairly tiring to listen to . . . That's it."

"What's it?"

"Nobody ever checks workmen," I said. "And the bell has to be worked on, right? There's a mechanism. It has to be maintained."

"So?" Jesse said. "There's probably a regular company that does that."

"So we find out the company," I said, shrugging, "and impersonate a couple of their people."

"Here's a question. It probably, yeah, does require maintenance. So there would have been workmen up there."

"Probably."

"Why didn't they see her?"

"No real clue. Figure that out when we get there."

"I'd like to eliminate as many questions as possible before we get there," Jesse said.

"How many more false nails do you want to pull out of my ass?" I asked as I worked my shoulder. Something was definitely pulled there. Damn, that lady was strong.

"None," Jesse said, shuddering. "And we'd need to go get more Betadine. Another question. Assuming we can get up there undetected. Assuming we can release her. How the hell do we get her out? You said she was prevented from casting a glamour, right? What do Fey look like without their glamour?"

"Fey are like a dozen species, and some of those can change shape. They are generally described as being foxlike. Sometimes batlike. No real clue. Most of the pictures are pretty blurry woodcuts done by an artist based on descriptions from survivors."

"I don't like the word 'survivors,'" Jesse said. "But speaking of which, how do we keep her from being detected by her mom?"

"That's easy. She won't like it but the answer is iron. We'll line a fifty-five-gallon drum with something and put her in that. That way her mother won't be able to find her."

"And keep her in it?" Jesse said. "You're starting to sound

uncomfortably like a serial killer, Chad. I'm not sure I'm liking how your mind works."

"Get one of those big steel containers like the lich was keeping the girls in," I said. "Set up a little camp inside it. If we need to pull her out, back in the barrel. Trunk of the car? That's surrounded by steel."

"Seriously like a serial killer," Jesse said.

"Speaking of which," I said, looking at my watch. "I have an appointment to make. Keep looking it over. This will take a while."

"What appointment?" Jesse asked.

"Need to see a man about a horse."

"So you want an extremely detailed contract?" the lawyer said.

He was supposed to be one of the top corporate attorneys in L.A. He certainly had cost enough just to talk to.

"A really big one," I said, holding my hands up mimicking a pile of paper about a foot tall.

"Binding a Faerie Queen?" he said, clearly thinking I was mad.

"Yes," I said. "And a faerie princess."

"Faerie Queens don't exist," the lawyer said, his hand reaching under the table for what was clearly an alarm button.

"It's for a movie pitch."

"Oh," he said, pulling his hand back. There is nothing too stupid it hasn't been involved in a movie pitch and he knew it.

"The executive producer is going to read the whole thing, though. And he's a real anal asshole. So it's got to be even more anal. They have to actually *be* binding contracts that are *unbreakable.* Not just ironclad. Depleted-uranium-clad."

"Oh, we can do depleted uranium," he said, pulling out a notepad. "So, what are the terms...?"

"I thought you guys only came once a year," the security guard asked.

We'd found our objective and found the issues that we could determine. It wasn't the right time of year for the mission, anyway, so we dropped back to plan and organize.

One issue was the contract. After we had what looked like a "depleted-uranium-clad" contract I sent it to other lawyers in New York. They found wiggle room. We got rid of it. Then we sent it to lawyers familiar with PUFF. They cost even more than top-end regular attorneys. They found codicils and rulings that gave it some more wiggle room. We got rid of the wiggle room.

That took months. Most of the time, I was obsessively playing the violin. I was off duty for that. I couldn't afford to get an arm break.

It was the first time my metal humerus had ever given me real issues. Turned out, it slightly affected my play. But with enough practice that even got better. And so did I. I seriously doubted that my mother's intent when she forced me to learn violin was to allow me to bind a Fey Court. But that might be the outcome.

When I'd taken violin, I'd driven my teachers insane. I sort of liked it but I was a rebel from *before* potty training. So I'd forced them to listen to noises few regular students could wrench from a poor instrument. I'd found out you could do some really amazing things with a violin. Some of them were actually cool. At least if you were into heavy metal, which my teachers were not.

Occasionally, just to keep them guessing, I'd play something like Locatelli's Caprice in D major, Op. 3 No. 23, perfectly, just to keep them guessing.

Think of it as achieving a perfect C.

I had this one Russian defector teacher. Drove him nuts.

"How?" he would shout. "How can you play Paganini perfectly and the rest of the time it is nothing but *squeals?*"

Hey, Vladimir, try paying attention to modern music. Those "squeals" were the guitar solo from "Satch Boogie," man.

Which I could also play on guitar.

Took months to get back to that point. But I had months.

Finally, we had the contracts as ironclad as they could get and I was doing Liszt's Sonata in B minor for solo violin perfectly enough that the conductor for the Seattle symphony asked me why I wasn't a professional violinist and had I attended Julliard?

And we were ready. All we had to do was find this Fey princess and rescue her from her tower. How hard could it be?

"Turns out the primary lubricant we'd installed last time was the wrong type," I said, trying not to touch my fake moustache. "So we're having to go around to all our clients and replace it. Big screw-up. We've been to about sixty towns so far. All the same thing."

"As long as we don't have to pay for it," the guard grumped, looking at my fake ID.

More money had changed hands. For a considerable sum, the yakuza had come up with all the information and IDs we needed. In retrospect, that was the best head removal I'd ever done—the gift that kept on giving. As long as we had available cash.

We were both pulling dollies with fifty-five-gallon drums on them. Most of those had gone to the new blue plastic type. Finding actual steel oil drums had been the hardest part of the whole endeavor: two, because one was filled with oil; the other was empty. They were functionally identical. We'd simply put the princess in the empty one. It was lined with foam rubber and had discreet air holes, the better to keep our rescuee alive.

The one question I really had was if there was some sort of mystical tracker on the Fey. If there was, mom might notice right away when she dropped off the grid. That would be bad. I wasn't prepared to face Momma Fey, yet.

Yes, we were winging some of this.

"It's on the company."

"Okay," the guard said. "Go on through."

First hurdle crossed.

CHAPTER 19

We knew where the elevators were from the schematics and how to find our way to the small entrance to the bell tower.

Fortunately, there was a maintenance room under the tower. 'Cause this was one place where we had a hitch. There was no way to actually get the drum up into the tower.

The door under the tower was locked. The guard hadn't asked us if we needed the key. Presumably there was a maintenance supervisor somewhere with the key. In fact, we even had his name. No way we were going to bluff our way through that.

The empty drum also contained bolt cutters.

I climbed up the stairs, cut the bolt off and lifted the lid.

The interior of the bell tower was cramped. Most of it was taken up by a large set of bells. They were in a ring with a small space in the middle for the hatch. The actual mechanism was above the bells themselves. If we'd actually been here to change the oil, we'd have needed a very long line and a pump.

What I didn't see was a faerie princess.

"Cooee?" I said. "Anybody home?"

"See her?" Jesse asked.

"Does it *sound* like it?"

I climbed up and made my way between a couple of the smaller bells, looking around. No faerie princess.

"Gimme the sprayer," I said.

When we'd discussed the question of the missing princess

with the Nelsons, they'd suggested invisibility as a possible reason. It was possible the princess was bound to invisibility as long as anyone was up there. Throw in silence and immobility and she would be ignored by any workmen as well as unable to escape when the occasional maintenance crew went up there.

For which we had a solution. The Akkoran solution was supposed to reveal some kinds of invisible objects. It had required making a trip to Chinatown to get it prepared. And we were assuming that it was the actual Akkoran solution. It was just a bunch of herbs as far as I could tell.

I took the hand sprayer and started spritzing the area around the outside of the bells.

Sure enough, halfway around the circle I hit paydirt.

"Oh, crap," I said, blanching at the sight of the Fey princess.

Take a four-foot-tall bat. Take off the wings. Mottled, wrinkly, green-gray skin like a ghoul. Make the face uglier. Stretch out the snout till it was more of a proboscis. Give it really weird, tilted, insectile purple eyes. Long, skinny arms with ugly, taloned hands.

On top of being imprisoned, she was nude. You don't want to know what the body looked like. I seriously wanted to scratch my eyeballs out. I was open-minded but, God's left tooth, no! I started to understand the legend of the Gorgon which I'm pretty sure, now, must have just been a Fey.

There was no question in my mind that Fey were something alien to earth. The description above does not cover it. It was simply alien. I had the same reaction as most people's reactions to a spider. "That is just *wrong*!"

"You okay?" Jesse said.

"Found her. Trying not to retch. Fey are seriously ugly."

"She might be able to hear you."

"Fine. If she doesn't appreciate my opinion of her appearance, perhaps she'll appreciate getting out of here."

I tentatively touched one of the skinny arms. I really didn't want to, again it was like touching a spider, but we were here for a job. Pulling on her wrist showed that she could move. Pushing down on her head caused her to bend over. She was like a mannequin.

"We can do this," I said, picking up the feynequin and trying not to scream. This job really is a bit tough on the sanity. "Get ready to catch her. And try not to scream."

✧ ✧ ✧

Turned out there were containers that were already made up as living spaces. The one we had obtained had steel doors—the better to keep Momma's magic from finding the princess—and a nice interior. We'd added steel screens over all the air intakes and outlets. I wasn't sure if Fey magic could detect anything through there. Based on gnolls, we'd discussed waste issues. The waste receptacles could be hooked up to either a sewer system or a chemical waste system. We were planning on dumping those far from where we eventually put the trailer.

We'd gotten the drum into the trailer, gotten the feynequin out and set her up. But she was still a feynequin. I was worried about how long she could remain that way. She didn't seem to be breathing.

Finally, we just left the trailer. We'd set up a double door system, steel mesh, as a magic lock to keep Big Momma from noticing human entries and exits.

"What do we do now?" Jesse asked.

"Stay on plan. We take her back to Seattle. We'll figure out the feynequin..."

There was a banging on the wall of the container as I said that and we both started.

"Like, how did I get here?" a female voice shrieked from inside the trailer. At least I thought that was what she said. It was muffled. "This is, like, totally, like, bogus! What's your damage? If you think you can, like, kidnap a princess of the Fey you're, like, a total retard! Like, let me out of here! Like, now!"

"I think our feynequin is awake." The banging was coming through the walls of the trailer so she wasn't at the door. We could open up and finally speak to our rescued princess.

The moment I opened the door and stepped through, though, the banging stopped. And the solution had worn off so I couldn't even see her. Which was fine by me. There's ugly then there's Fey-ugly.

"Well," Jesse said. "That's a bit of a difficulty. Whenever someone comes into her presence, she must be enspelled to freeze and disappear. When we leave, she's mobile."

"Noticed," I said, frowning. "That's going to make negotiating difficult."

"You could say that. There is one good point."

"What?" I asked, frustrated. I knew there would be hitches,

but this one was unexpected. It's not the things you don't know in this business that get you; it's the things you don't know you don't know. I was having to wonder how many of those there were in this operation.

"She's not going to remember how you described her."

The answer was as simple as an intercom. It took a bit to install. Then we left. There was a mike on the exterior and it started squawking immediately.

"I, like, demand you let me go, like, *right now*!" Princess Shallala shouted. "When, like, my mother finds out about this, you are going to *totally*, like, be in trouble! I know you're, like, *listening*!"

"Calm down, Princess," I said, soothingly. "You're not being kidnapped. You're being rescued."

"Like, this totally doesn't look like being rescued!" She seemed to be calming down.

"Gimme a break. You've got a couch, a kitchen, a bathroom and a bed. That's got to be better than being stuck in a tower."

"Like, there's nothing to eat or drink in here!"

"There's a case of MREs."

"Like, what are *those*?" she said, disdainfully.

"Meals Ready to Eat," Jesse said.

"Like, in cans?" she asked, haughtily. "You expect *me* to, like, eat out of *cans*?"

"They're actually in plastic and foil packages. We can get you something to cook."

"Cook? You expect *me* to *cook*? Are you, like, totally out of your *mind*? A princess of the Fey does not, like, *cook*! That's like, like, totally saying I have to scrub, like, my own *back*!"

The pain in the ass bitch comment from Queen Cougar was starting to make sense.

"And there's, like, totally nothing to drink in here at all!" she continued to complain. "Like, what kind of a rescue, like, do you call this? What do you expect me to, like, do? Drink, like, tap water? I only drink Evian and, like, Dom Pérignon! Maybe, like, a totally awesome Napa vintage! And you'd totally better not be planning on feeding me, like, *McDonalds*! Grody! Like, *cook*? Like, food in *plastic*? Like, what's your *damage*? Are you, like, totally *mental*?"

"Oh, my God," Jesse said, turning off the speaker. "I, like, totally can't listen to it anymore."

"Like totally," I said, then blanched. "Gag me with a spoon. Oh, my God!"

"What?" Jesse said.

"My contact said she'd been imprisoned for twenty years for a severe infraction against her mother and 'all mothers everywhere,'" I said. I turned the speaker back on.

". . . and like, I totally, like, need some new clothes! Like, what's with all these, like, cheap T-shirts?"

"Princess," I said. "Princess? Shallala? You there?"

"Like, this is totally *bogus* . . ."

"Did the offense against your mother have anything to do with Valley Speak?"

"Oh my, God! I, like, totally invented Valley speak!" Shallala squealed, for the first time sounding happy. "It's, like, totally awesome isn't it? It's so *me*!" The last was a squeal of pure delight.

Jesse quickly shut off the intercom again.

"Chad," he said, seriously. "There are deals with the devil, and there are deals you don't make!"

"I know," I said, growling in frustration. "I know. But this is the only chance we've got to stabilize Seattle, Jesse. We have to do it."

"You want to, like, make a deal with the *inventor of Valley Speak*?" Jesse said. "Like, bring *that* thing to Seattle? Have you, like, lost your, like, ever-loving *mind*? Valley speak is, like, pernicious, like, infective and totally, like, practically on the PUFF list!"

"Jesse," I said, putting my hand on my best friend's shoulder and looking him in the eye. "Like, in this job, sometimes, like, sacrifices totally gotta be made, dude."

"Princess Shallala," I said as she continued to babble and complain. "Princess? Shallala? *Like totally shut up for a second!*"

"Are you, like, speaking to *me, mortal*?" she snapped.

"Do you want to know the plan or not? Because if you do, you're going to have to, like, shut up for a second!"

"Fine!" she snapped. "What-EVer!"

I could picture her with those long bat arms folded and her head to the side. The long and limber neck of the beast and its weird insect eyes made the whole Valley Girl head tilt make, like, so much more sense. She was, like, totally grody.

Oh, God. Pernicious. Infective . . .

I explained. I had to keep getting her back on track. I won't force you to read that. Anyone who has ever dealt with an ADHD Valley Girl off her meds knows what it's like. Jesse had to leave. I just figured I'd explain it to my father confessor and try to get it to count as a corporal work of mercy.

"So, like, you want me to go to, like, *Seattle*?" she said. "Oh, my God! Totally *puke* me, dork face! Seattle has like *no* malls! And it rains *all the time*! And there are like *no* hot clubs! Totally gag me!"

Gladly, I thought.

"Twenty years in a tower watching everyone else go to the mall," I said. "Or twenty years as the Princess of Seattle. Your call. All I've got to do is take you out of this container and run like hell. Your mom's people will be on you like a flash."

"And then she will totally rip out your soul and flay it for eternity, dork face," Shallala pointed out.

"I'll take that chance."

"She's, like, going to *anyway*, dumb butt. I can't, like, just be Princess of *Seattle*. The instant I, like, go out in public the Hunt will be on me in, like, a *second*. And then they'll, like, have your smell, and no mortal survives the *Huuunt*."

"Got that covered," I said.

"I'd like to hear *how*," she said.

So I told her.

"That's the stupidest plan, like, I've ever heard in, like, my *life*. And I've lived a *long* time, mortal. Totally stupid plan."

"Does she want you dead?" I said.

"Like, she totally wouldn't mind," Shallala said. "Bitch."

I was pretty sure that dealing with the inventor of ValSpeak would, like, totally drive the most stable mother totally insane.

"Well, we have one thing in common. We both totally hate our mothers. But seriously... is she going to be willing to let you die?"

"Like, duh," Shallala said. "No, she's not. I'm, like, her *heir*. No other *girls*, dork face. All she's had are boys. And only girls can, like, inherit from, like, their moms. We might hate each other, but like, she's not going to let me die. But she'll, like, know you won't go through with it."

"What do you mean?"

"She can, like, read *minds*, mortal," Shallala said. "Like dig right in. She'll know you're not willing to die."

"If that's the problem with the plan, it's not a problem."

"Like, it's *totally* a problem, dork face!"

"You're assuming I'm afraid of dying. And if it's a choice of dying or having my soul ripped from my body and tortured for eternity, I'm good. I'll take out you, her, the Hunt, me, everybody. I'm, like, totally into that samurai bushido stuff. Totally suicidal mental."

There was, for a change, a very long pause when she engaged what I suspected was an actually good mind.

"Then I totally don't like this plan," she said.

"Twenty years in that tower watching everybody else having fun, or we try to negotiate with your mom."

"You're, like, insane."

"It's been suggested," I said. "By professionals."

"This is a totally bogus plan."

"You don't like the clubs in Seattle? Build your own. That way you can have, like, your own court."

"Of mortals?"

"Mortals," I said, placatingly. "Fey you can attract to your court. You'll be like your own little queen of Seattle."

"That might be, like, okay," she said, thoughtfully. If it was possible for her to be thoughtful.

"You don't have to deal with your mother every day. You don't have to be stuck in a tower. You get to be the boss of everybody. Within limits."

"Like, *what* limits?" she asked.

"There's a contract. It's about six hundred pages. You can read it while we drive to Seattle."

"Like read a *six-hundred-page contract*?" she shrilled. God, that voice! That incessantly whining loathsome voice! It haunts my dreams to this day!

"You are such a total loser. Only a total loser would, like, read a six-hundred-page contract! I don't even like to, like, read the ingredients in, like, my *shampoo*! That's, like, what *servants* are for!"

"Okay," I said. "Then sign the signature pages. Basically boils down to you having to work mostly within human legal limits. No casting curses just because some human is a dork face. Stuff like that. And you have to remain as Princess of Seattle for the rest of your sentence. You're not stuck there, you can travel if you want, but you have to be the Grand Fey of Seattle for twenty years. If there's a serious threat of bodily harm, you can jump out, obviously, but you have to defend the territory to the best of your ability. My company, in turn, agrees to provide mundane human security support against outer realm forces to the best of our ability. There's a codicil that if you so desire, it is not required, you can provide members of your Court as combat support to members of my company. That way they can make money."

"Money?" she said. "How?"

"We get paid by the human government to take out supernatural things that harm humans," I said.

"So you're, like, a witch hunter?"

"Like that," I said. "More modern. But we get paid, and pretty well, to take out supernatural problems. Problem being, with the territory open in Seattle, there've been too many. Putting an outer faction entity in Seattle should balance that."

"I'd, like, need a real Court to, like, be able to hold the territory. Which, like, I don't *have*!"

"You don't think there are Fey who would like to join such a sweet and lovely princess?" I asked. Maybe flattery would get me somewhere.

"Well, duh," Shallala said. "I'm, like, totally popular!"

"Then you get your Court. And they can help you defend the territory. We'll help as well when we can. That's what the contract states. The rest is really boilerplate. But you can't go casting spells at any human just because they're a dork face or a dumb butt."

"That's totally bogus," Shallala said. "What am I supposed to do with them, then?"

"There are these things called 'bouncers,'" I said, sighing. This was going to take a while.

"Fine, fine, what-EVer!" she said. "There. Signed."

"Okay," I said. "There are five signature pages. Did you sign them all?"

"Like all the places where the little red thingies are? And, like, the initial places too. I was totally signing it while you were talking, like, forever! Now, there had better be decent food!"

"I know a good bento place," I said. "You like bento?"

"Oh, I could totally go for a California roll with avocado! I, like, totally invented that!"

The PUFF on a Grand Fey was astronomical. She never came closer to dying.

"Your wish is my command, Princess," I said. "I'll be back in a jiff."

CHAPTER 20

There was a gibbous moon under a sky of fleeting clouds on the kite hill of Warren G. Magnuson Park when the ground behind me opened up and vomited the Wild Hunt in all its horror and fury.

We'd gotten Princess Shallala up to Seattle, bitching the whole way. The Evian was the wrong kind of Evian. Why couldn't we get any good food on the road? What was this stuff? A burger? She didn't eat burgers! She was, like, vegetarian! Except, you know, steak. And chicken. And Dungeness crab. Could she, like, get Dungeness in Seattle? And, like, salmon. But only fresh-caught, none of this, like, sea-farmed for the Princess. Was it, like, totally all organic? Like, this is totally grody! Can we, like, stop by Napa? There's, like, this totally bomb winery up there...

I nearly strangled her half a dozen times. From time to time I'd get so tired of it, I'd get in the trailer and ride inside, just to get her to Shut... UP. When anyone was in her presence she was invisible, in stasis and had no concept of the passage of time. She also wasn't smart enough to read a clock. No skin off my nose. Besides, it was a comfortable place to ride. Technically illegal to ride in the back of a container but we'd kidnapped an underage Fey princess from her mother's time out. It doesn't get much more illegal than that.

The preparations had taken most of the day and much of Phil's ingenuity. He thought it was a very bad idea. So did I. It was just the best of a series of worse choices.

Then we rolled the barrel containing the fortunately quiescent princess up to the top of the hill, got her out, arranged the horrible feynequin body and Phil made the final preparations. Then everyone but me beat feet.

It only took the Hunt, zooming in on the location of their missing princess and heir, about ten minutes to disgorge from the crack in the ground through a portal. And they were there.

I was standing stock-still behind the feynequin of Shallala, holding a cocked .357 to her head. I was wearing finely wrought chainmail from head to toe. Not a single inch of skin was uncovered by steel. It was actually a Faraday suit like high-power lineman wear. Good luck getting Fey magic through *that*... I hoped.

"Make a move and the princess dies," I said. "This weapon is loaded with iron-cored ammunition. There are human technological traps near us that will kill you all, as well as myself and the princess. In front of me is a table. You will ride *well* around in a circle until you are *beyond* the table. If you come *closer* than that in *any* direction, we all die. When you are in front of me, we will negotiate."

"We do not negotiate with mortals," a voice hissed behind me.

The hiss sent shivers down my spine. It was a supremely visceral reaction. Pure animal. My instinct was to cut and run.

If I moved so much as a muscle, the whole hilltop was going to explode. There were wires attached to my body and laser trips all over the place. There were two hundred claymores pointed right at me, one strapped to Shallala's alien chest and another strapped to mine. If I was going to go out, I was going to go out with a bang.

"You can negotiate or we all die," I said, not looking around. "And, yes, the weapons that are pointed at you *will* kill you all. They are loaded with cold iron. And will kill myself and the princess."

"Mortals *fear* death," the voice hissed.

"I have been to the Green Lands," I said as calmly as I could. "The God of Angel Armies stands by my side. Whom shall I fear? Go wide around and come to the front of me. If you approach, you will trigger the traps. If you attack, you will trigger the traps. If you attempt to enspell me, you will trigger the traps. The only thing you can do to *not* trigger the traps is *face* me if you dare, Huntsman."

I heard more than the hissing behind me. A rattle of bridles. Snarls from their mounts. Shifting of riders.

The Hunt moved . . . well, around me. It was nearly silent, the "horses" of the Huntsmen padding on silent feet. Then they were in sight.

I nearly retched. If Shallala had been hideous, the Hunt was hideous and terrifying.

They were Fey without any sort of glamour. Massive compared to Shallala. Seven or eight feet tall at a guess. Thin, hideous and awful, alien and repugnant. Beneath their cloaks, their armor was in a riot of colors, all grays under the moon. If I had to take a guess at what it was made of, I'd say some sort of advanced polymer. It wasn't metal, that was for sure. They were armed with jagged black spears that rippled blue in the moonlight. I could tell they were charged with either some sort of Fey magic or, just as possible, electricity. There was no question in my mind those spears were nothing but pure pain at a single touch.

Their "horses" were anything but. Again, alien in the extreme. They had the general look of horses: long legs, long necks, straight bodies, long muzzles. But their genesis was something entirely different. They were nothing of Earth but if I were to pick earthly creatures, a hyena crossed with a weasel crossed with a greyhound crossed with a praying mantis. They had not skin but a sort of carapace. Their snouts were very insectile with underjaws that jutted out to catch prey. Their eyes glowed an eerie green in the darkness. They hissed and writhed at their riders' control, their eyes flaring and damping, passionate to rend the human limb from limb. They smelled of a carnal pit mixed with a toxic chemical dump.

I had never been more terrified in my life. Every instinct was telling me to run and run fast. That they were simply death. Not just death, my soul would be stripped from my body only after they had laughed for centuries as I begged to die.

I was a Marine. I had a job to do. I set aside the horror.

"We are come to the front of you, mortal," the Huntsman hissed. "Does our sight *please*?" he laughed and that was even worse.

I suddenly realized I might be talking to Shallala's father. Technically, if what Stricken's file said was correct, he had no legal control over her under Fey law. But he might have a vested interest in keeping her alive.

"I'm going to lower the weapon," I said. I decocked the .357 and holstered it. The pistol to the head was just insulting. "That was just to get you to pause. This is the real problem," I said, holding up the dead-man's switch in my left hand. "I drop this, I open my hand and this hilltop explodes. Do you understand?"

"I understand."

"I wish to negotiate with the Queen. I require a one-hour grace of no hostilities to myself, any other human or the princess. I in turn promise no hostilities save that we or any other group associated are attacked."

"The Queen does not *bow* to a human."

"The Queen has often *negotiated* with humans. I asked for no capitulation. It's that or we blow the hilltop. Princess dies. Hunt dies. You die. You cannot escape one hundred and fifty thousand steel musket balls going faster than any musket can fire. Would you have the entire Wild Hunt die as well as one of your rare princesses?"

He laughed again. "This is not the Wild Hunt. What you see before you is a shadow of the Horned King's might."

"My government would pay the cost of a thousand castles for this Hunt alone. I wouldn't collect, but friends would. Your call, Fey."

"This is a trap to kill my Queen," the Huntsman said, pulling his steed from side to side. He was as eager as his steed to kill me. No, rend me for a thousand years. *Yeah, that's a protective daddy reaction. Guess some things transcend species.*

"If I killed the Queen and managed to survive, mind you, my own government would flay me alive. The Queen is at peace with humans. She keeps the Fey such as yourself in check. She is a Very Important Person. I mean her no ill-will. In fact, I want to do her a favor. But, please, decide quickly. My hand is going to get tired at a certain point. You really don't want this," I said, holding up the dead-man's switch, "to slip from my weak mortal grasp."

The Huntsman was speaking into the mirror. He was speaking High Fey and assuming that no mere mortal could understand it. I'd studied everything I could about the Fey. I made out a couple of words, and even those hurt my brain. I was good at languages before, and I think Pete might have sent me back with the gift of tongues, but it had limits. I think he was telling her it was a trap, and not to come.

I couldn't catch the reply but it was querying.

I think the Huntsman didn't want his Queen to put herself in danger.

Definite tone. Orders. Long statement. You could tell who wore the pants in the relationship. And what exactly was the relationship with her husband? Never mind. Alien relationships do not equate to human.

"Human," the Huntsman said. "My Queen agrees to negotiate. One-hour grace on her word. We shall withdraw. She brings her Knights. If this is a trap, we have your smell. We know your people. We know your family. My Hunt shall be free to course upon them."

"Feel free to course upon my mother. But I get the picture. And it's why I don't want to injure the Queen. Not to save my friends and loved ones, but you wouldn't just course upon *them*, would you? I will not harm your Queen, Huntsman. You have my word as a Marine. If you are unaware, this is a knight of my lands. Our oath is 'Semper Fidelis.' We are always faithful to our oaths. Bring no harm to this place nor my friends and we will negotiate with honor. If the negotiations fail utterly, I assume you'll come for me. And then, Huntsman, we shall do battle."

"Farewell, Knight," the Huntsman said as the ground opened up at its feet. "We *shall* meet again." *Oooh, daddy was* pissssed!

"Really looking forward to *that*," I muttered.

I rotated my shoulders. I'd held swords for hours. But the horror of the Wild Hunt was one of those things that makes you want to open your hands to drop whatever you're carrying and run. I really didn't want to open my left hand.

Finally, I just put the pin in the dead-man's switch as I waited for the Queen to arrive.

The ground opened up again. There was a glimmer of purple light and first one, then another, then dozens of massive Fey in full battle armor erupted from it. They were covered from head to toe in the weird armor of their kind. It, too, looked alien but it was better than actually seeing them. Armor is, after all, armor.

The main difference between them and the Hunt, besides armor, was size. Most of them outmassed an ogre. But, based on how they were moving, they were also faster and more nimble.

Fighting one with anything short of a LAW would suck. Fighting the whole crew? You'd better be able to call in an arc light strike.

I pulled the pin again.

"Come no closer than the table," I shouted. "There are traps all about that will kill even you, Knights."

I wasn't sure if that was the truth. Depended on how robust that armor was. Claymores are powerful but they don't have much in the way of armor penetration. I think they'd have done for the Hunt, certainly the mounts, but maybe not the Knights.

The Knights formed a protective circle around the slit in the ground. Then the Faerie Queen came forth.

I don't know what I expected. Something that looked like Great Cthulhu, I guess. Maybe a giant beetle or like the queen in *Aliens*.

What I didn't expect was a forty-something woman, slender, in shape, red hair cut in a tight bob, in a designer business suit. I knew it was a glamour, but the fact that she was using a glamour and the nature of it was interesting.

"Absent this truly being in my favor, I assure you, you are going to suffer for longer than most mortal lifetimes," the Queen said calmly. "I will extend yours just to prolong the suffering."

"This is the primary detonation device," I said, holding up the dead-man's switch. "If I release it, absent putting it on what we call 'safe,' the entire hilltop explodes. There are others. If those are triggered, hilltop explodes. You will not escape. However, I do not wish you harm. I do not wish the princess harm. Do I have your oath that no hostilities will take place on your part for one hour?"

"You have my word," the Queen said.

"Why do I suspect you can weasel out of that?" I said. But I placed the dead-man's switch on safe and hooked it to my belt. Carefully.

"Because I can quite easily."

"There are various other traps and methods to prevent you from attacking me. Please let us not be silly in this regard. I do not fear death, but I have a duty to perform and dying now would not make that possible."

"I don't intend to be. You wished to negotiate."

"On the table are two documents. The first is a detailed

contract. Shallala has already signed it. The contract, broadly, states that Shallala will be given some rights as an adult and become the Fey Princess of this Principality. As Princess of this Principality, she shall have all rights and duties thereof including the collection of fees from all Fey entities which recognize your sovereign domain. There are details on who gets what and what course can be used for any redress. The primary course being suit in Federal Court, not Unseleighe battle. She, in turn, agrees to hold these demesnes as friendly to humankind. She shall work to ensure that no hostile Fey nor outer factions take residence thereof. In the event of a serious threat of bodily harm to her, you may respond as you see fit. But such threat must be real and present. Not 'she's out on a limb and you're worried about losing your heir.' Furthermore, I and my associates agree to also watch over her to prevent threats of bodily harm to her, to the extent we may, given our other duties. To enact this you must, of course, first remove from her all curses and bindings. Please don't do that right now 'cause if she so much as twitches, the whole hilltop goes up."

"Oh, that's all?"

"The second document is a letter of intent. You agree to have one week to analyze the contract and to return to this place after that week to sign it. I, in turn, agree upon that night to take the Harper's Challenge in expiation of having caused you mental grief and suffering in the removal of the princess from your imprisonment as well as this somewhat hostile negotiation. Should I pass the Harper's Challenge, you must sign the document. Should I not, you get me and Shallala back. I've already signed the letter of intent."

"Very thorough," the Queen said, making a face. "What's the catch?"

"None, really. We killed a lich and since then it's been a monster migration. We need something in Seattle to keep out other big baddies. Simply Shallala's presence will do that to an extent. Even if something is stupid enough to take on a princess of Faerie and her Court, *and* my company of human Monster Hunters backstopping her, *nobody* is stupid enough to take *you* on. The smart, powerful entities will avoid her principality and that is all I seek. The upside is *you* don't have to put up with her day after endless day. I've only been dealing with her for a week and I understand the desire to mystically bind her to just *shut her the hell up*!"

"We see eye to eye in that at least. You do realize why she was imprisoned. You would release my daughter once again upon this innocent world of unsuspecting humans?"

"Valley Speak is a trial," I said, "but we need someone to pin down Seattle."

"Valley Speak?" the Queen snapped. "Do you think that is *all*? That was simply the straw that *broke* me! Tie-dye! She invented those horrible tie-dye T-shirts!"

"Oh," I said, wincing. I hated those.

"Bell-bottom jeans!" the Queen shrieked, angrily. "The kind that get all *ratty* on the ends! Mood rings! My daughter invented *mood rings*! Would you have that monstrosity once again cast upon your unsuspecting mortal population?! *And* Birkenstock sandals! She even convinced the Germans, who should know better, to wear *ugly green socks* with them! She is insane!"

"I wasn't aware of those," I said. "I have to possibly agree..." No, stick to the path. Don't let her dissuade you. Fey were notoriously deceptive. "We need someone to pin down Seattle. Shallala can do that."

"Why the Harper's Challenge?" the Queen asked.

"Because Harpers are held in high esteem by the Fey," I said. "Right now you've been, in the human terminology, disrespected. I stole your daughter. I've forced you to come to this place to negotiate. Even if there is an upside, and I think there will be several, you still need to save face. I will put my life and soul on the line by the Harper's Challenge. If I succeed, other Fey will see that you were up against not just any human, but a Bard. That allows you to save face. Bards have always been the bane of the Fey."

"And you think you are good enough?"

"We shall see."

"Are you aware of the full details of the Harper's Challenge?" the Queen asked.

"I must play the whole of the night without stop or let, and note-perfect."

"*And* songs I have never heard before," the Queen noted. "And I listen to *everything*. I even sort of like Jimi Hendrix, speaking of Seattle. Heart I can live without."

"Oh?" I squeaked. "Uhm . . . entirely new songs?"

"Yes," the Queen purred in a decidedly catlike tone. "Entirely new songs."

"Oh," I said, carefully pulling at the mail by my throat.

"And for three nights consecutively!" the Queen said.

"*Three* nights? I thought it was only *one*!"

"Hah!" she laughed merrily, the sound having timbres so alien I again wanted to turn tail and run. "Three! I *may* allow my wayward princess to infest your pathetic city, human. Let Seattle bear the brunt of her insanity. It deserves it. But when you fail in the Harper's Challenge, your body and your soul will be *mine*! And now *you* are bound to perform for *me*."

She bent down, scrawled her name in burning letters on the letter of intent, picked up the thick contract and disappeared. The knights disappeared into the hole which snapped shut—and they were gone.

"Phil!" I yelled into the darkness. "You, you know, want to call EOD and have them start getting me out of this stuff?"

Christ, that took a long time. You ever watched EOD guys sweat? Nobody sweats like EOD. I *hated* the one guy whose hands kept trembling.

CHAPTER 21

A week later, as the salmon sun set behind Seattle's omnipresent clouds, the preparations were complete. The field was freshly mowed, the last of the caterers had fled, the team was gone and once again it was just the feynequin princess and myself up on the kite field awaiting the arrival of the Faerie Queen and what I suspected this time would be her whole Court.

Caterers?

I had studied every record I could find of a survivor of the Harper's Challenge. I knew damned well it had to be new music. I knew damned well that it was for three nights, not one. I also knew, from the sparse records of survivors, that there was more to it than that. The Fey were awful, ugly, scary at an evolved, primal level. Playing note-perfect was easy for many musicians. Playing it surrounded by monsters? Without a single muscle trembling so much as once?

But the Fey had a weakness. "True" Fey were susceptible to being bound by music. This was where Stricken's hint to do my homework came in handy. Every description of survivors was the same. It wasn't that you couldn't rest at all. But when they were in the presence of music, they were charmed, held, captured. All of them from the Queen on down. The only ones who were not were their servitor races. That used to be elves, I guessed, before they got left behind.

And it wasn't that you could take no break nor breath. When you stopped playing, they took a short time to throw off the spell of the music. You could take an occasional breath, a sup of wine—if you had some with you. And if, in that locked state, they were exposed to sunlight, they became permanently bound absent powerful magics. They "tunt stun at dawn litte." They "Putaḷē jhālē." They "égine agálmata." All the records were the same. You could bind them all night, then turn them to stone at morning's light.

I suspected it was not "stone" but into feynequins. I wasn't, however, planning on testing it. I was just going to play this straight down the middle.

The other issue was "ne'er sup of the faerie." Don't eat their food, or drink their wine. A pretty good and what appeared accurate description was by a contemporary of Thomas the Rhymer in the Oxford Secure Vault. In it the Harper, one Gadal Thane, wrote of avoiding the trap of Fey food by drinking from his iron flagon of ale. He had apparently taken the Harper's Challenge *three* times and in one had used the "liquor of the Irish monks" to get the Court drunk. But he "ne'er supped of the faerie" and knew of others who had failed that particular test.

So instead of supping of the Faerie, I had *brought* sup.

Specifically, a number of high-end Seattle restaurants had been approached. A very reclusive foreign noble, wealthy, was resettling in Seattle or would at least be here frequently. She often dined out and had a very large entourage. Were they willing to provide some samples? We'd defray the cost but not pay full.

A surprising number answered, "Sure." Part of that was due to quiet assurances from various movers and shakers that the "noble" was the real deal.

There were tents set up covering tables filled with all sorts of goodies. Everything from donuts to haute cuisine. And, yes, Saury was there. There was forty thousand dollars in just alcohol. No servants. I assumed the Queen would be bringing her own.

I hadn't worn the Faraday suit. I had worn it the last time assuming, it looked like correctly, that it would prevent the Queen from reading my mind. This time, I really didn't care if she did or not. Better that she see the determination.

I had a steel cooler full of holy water and sacramental wine on a steel table with a bunch of steel cups to drink from in case

I lost one. Steel chairs in case my feet got tired. And a steel barrel of bows and two spare violins. It's easier to change weapons than reload or restring if one broke in combat. And this was combat, make no mistake.

The park had been cleared of all visitors and was surrounded by MCB.

I'd had months to prepare and called in a lot of favors for this.

It appeared that the MCB didn't want to be here. My argument was that if it worked, Seattle would be a "safe zone" from major monsters. We'd stop having to burn Troll Kings at King Street Station—'cause it was "King Street" and he was a Troll King—with flamethrowers and leave *them* with the difficult task of explaining. A recent battle on Laurelhurst Park with some sort of entity called "Mayhem" was another example. They were still trying to explain all the damage, and the insurance companies were angry.

The MCB thought I was nuts. They'd brought in SRT. I was pretty sure their Special Response Team was going to be pissing in the wind if the Queen got a bee in her bonnet. If it had been up to the MCB agents, they probably would have just shot me in the face and written a suicide note, but whoever Stricken was, he'd kept his part of the bargain.

We weren't going to be disturbed, that was for sure.

This had been scheduled, planned and prepared for months. It was two nights before Litha, the shortest night of the year. So not only was I not having to play as long as, say, at midwinter, each night would be shorter than the last. Not by much, but when you have to fill three nights with entirely new music, anything helped.

As the last bit of sun dropped below the horizon, a large slit began to open in the ground at the summit of the hill. And the Hunt exploded forth.

For just one moment I was sure it was on, that the Queen had gotten so ticked off by being in check from a human that she was going to war. The Hunt burst forth and spread out, their mounts questing for threats, keening at the moon. The noise was unearthly, scary, alien. The sound had to carry as far as the UD. What the non-MCB agents and marshals on the outer perimeter of the event must be thinking, I had no clue. They'd been told they were providing security for a foreign VIP.

Very foreign. Not of this world.

But the Hunt didn't attack. They simply scouted, checking out the venue and the surroundings. They didn't even approach the officers at the base of the hill. I could tell they scented them, spotted them, were aware of them. But they didn't approach close enough to be spotted.

Finally, the Huntsmen went back to the portal and entered for a moment. Then the rest of the Court began to arrive.

First, again, the Knights. The light hadn't entirely faded from the sky and tiki torches had been set up to illuminate the scene. I wish we hadn't done that last bit. They were more clear in the torchlight. Massive, alien, scary, their armor was made in a scale pattern that seemed to replicate dragonskin. Their weapons were axes, swords, hammers, all sorts of medieval armament again playing violet-and-blue fire over their edges. This time they too were on mounts. Similar, again, to those of the Hunt but more massive. Their paws left divots on the manicured lawn of the kite hill. Those were up to MCB to explain.

Then wave after wave of every sort of Fey creature. Trolls, including massive ones such as the Troll King. Ogres by the score. Brownies and a dozen other different types of small beings. Kelpies and boggles. Lions and tigers and bears, oh, my.

There must have been a billion dollars in PUFF on that hilltop. I wondered if MCB had a B-52 in orbit. Probably. And some MCB Senior Agent watching through a night-vision scope *had* to be thinking "One call. All I gotta make is *one call*..."

The various monsters had at first come over to play "scare the Harper." I ignored them and lightly bowed the strings in various well-known and easily played violin pieces. Then they smelled the food and booze. That got their attention but none of them touched it. They just circled around, talking, waiting. Some of the ogres were drooling and nobody drools like an ogre.

Finally, Queen Keerla Rathiain Penelo Shalana appeared, this time on a sedan chair borne by six enormous ogre magi. She was not in glamour this time. And it appeared that Fey Queens must continue to grow as they aged. She was massive and Fey-ugly. Her face was much more dragonlike than Shallala's and her body seemed more solid and armored as if her skin had hardened over the years.

The sedan chair held a large comfortable sleeper sofa that looked very much like it had been made by Broyhill. The Queen knew she was going to be more or less in stasis for hours and intended to be comfortable.

There were five tents on the hilltop. Most of the food was under cover in two. Two others with booze. And the largest set up in the center where I was stationed along with the feynequin Shallala. The sedan chair was brought into that tent and set on the ground. The massive ogre magi took up station around the Queen protectively.

"Well, Harper, we are come," the Queen said.

"Would you and your court take sup of the foods here presented, Queen Shalana?" I asked, strumming lightly through Bach's Sonata No. 1 in G minor.

"I see you are not taking sup of ours," the Queen said, looking around. "You cannot avoid the Challenge by offering us tempting morsels."

"I'm not avoiding it, but it's going to be a long three days for all of us. I'm fine. Already ate and I'm ready to play. But a lot of caterers went to a lot of trouble to put all this out. Feast, Queen of the Fey. Let your Court enjoy the viands of this fine land. When you are prepared, I shall be more than happy to fill your soul, what you have of one, with music such as you have never heard."

"As I have said, I have heard many tunes, Harper," she replied.

"Have you ever heard tunes not made for violin *on* violin? You said something of being a fan of Hendrix."

I brutally switched from the light Bach piece into the solo from Hendrix's "Voodoo Child." I could see the Queen settle into stillness which seemed to spread out through the whole Court. Every troll, ogre, and boggle of the night slowly stopped moving around and turned into what were virtually feynequins.

Then the True Fey among them began to dance. Even the Hunt, which had dismounted, began to dance. Knights swung and bounced, the Hunt went through wild leaps and bounds, noncombatant Fey were leaping among them. Trolls made the most spastic sort of dances. They were worse than junior high nerds. Ogres just thumped their massive feet and pounded their hands together. Even the mounts of the Hunt and the Knights were rocking back and forth on their leads, their horrible bodies writhing to the music.

Servitors danced through the mix, bringing food and drink to the Queen, who could not take it from them.

I wound to the end of the piece and paused.

"Truly, Queen," I said. "We've gone to a lot of trouble to make you and your people happy at this party. Eat, drink, be merry. I will play, lightly and known pieces, whilst you enjoy yourself. Then, when you are ready for the Challenge, tell me. I have more than enough to satisfy you through a thousand nights, much less three."

"I did some digging into you, Harper," the Queen said, clearly unhappy. "I probably should have *before* accepting this challenge. But you are known as a warrior, not a minstrel."

"Eh," I said, doing a quick riff from "Jungle Love." "I'm a man of many parts."

"We shall partake of sup," the Queen said, lying back on the couch. "As the Harper said, 'Eat, drink, be merry.' When midnight comes, we shall engage in Challenge."

Trolls have the worst table manners you've ever seen. The rest of the Fey were not much better. It's like they were still stuck in "throw the leftovers on the ground. The dogs will finish them off."

Which the mounts were doing.

I'd been okay with the Fey. I'd faced monsters before. Once I'd seen them, I was pretty much over it.

Fey eating was like Fey-ugly. Not something anyone with a queasy stomach should observe. Cleanup was going to be a bitch.

"Why are you doing this, Harper?" the Queen said, downing a large crab cake in one bite.

"I like a challenge," I replied, still lightly bowing the violin. "We truly do need something to stabilize the supernatural in Seattle. I could not figure out a way to do it that wouldn't get me on your bad side and I'm trying to get off of it. Fey, from what records exist, both fear and respect Harpers above all other humans. This way I might be able to get back on your better side and not have to be looking over my shoulder the rest of my life."

"Given the contract you presented me, it would be tough for me to take action against you . . . or your company or anyone you've ever known or so much as met."

"I considered leaving my mother and brother off the list, but you'd like them too much."

"I think not," the Queen said. "Your mother I've met. I rather loathe bootlickers. Your brother is of another faction and, even for a human, despicable. So, no."

That my brother Thornton was "of another faction" was interesting. I made a note to look Thornton up and find out what he'd gotten himself into. I wasn't sure, then, whether that was to see if I could get him out of it or see if he'd made himself PUFF applicable.

"Play, Harper," the Queen said, finally. "Let us see what you have that is truly new. Mere modifications will not suffice."

"Very well, Queen," I said, working my neck. "Prepare to enjoy yourself."

Here's the thing. Back in the old days, there were very few people who had the time and resources to play, practice and study music. Everyone was working day in and day out just to survive. That went from the greatest king, trying to hold onto his kingdom, to the lowliest field hand trying to fill his rice bowl.

The Industrial Revolution changed that by introducing other forms of work into the equation and increasing capital across the board. There started to be this thing called "leisure time" which had never existed before. And still doesn't in most cultures.

In 1187 A.D., there were no such things as large-scale marching bands.

In 1987, every small town had one.

In 1187, one in ten thousand people had been trained in music and populations were sparse.

In 1987, there were *millions* of people in the United States *alone* trained in music, and hundreds of thousands who loved it and wanted to write it and have the music in their heads be heard. Thousands who went through the actual process of writing it down and submitting it to various groups, hoping to get it publicly performed.

Of those thousands of songs written and copyrighted every year, a bare handful were ever publicly produced and performed. And some of the stuff that was written and ended up on a shelf was a hell of a lot better than what actually made it on the radio.

For a nominal fee, I was sent thousands of violin pieces submitted over the years by various musicians. I read through all of them and picked out a few hundred that stood out. For another nominal fee, I was granted rights to perform six hundred pieces that had never seen the light of day. This would be the only time they would ever be publicly performed for more than the composer's few friends. Virtually guaranteed that the Queen had never heard any of them. And if she had, I had plenty more where those came from. I had my own pieces if nothing else because, yeah, I wrote music too when I had a chance and even if it wasn't written down, I had dozens of songs in my head to perform. I was holding those for an emergency.

Playing music, really playing it, is hard to explain to someone who has never played or never seriously played. It is an absorbing process. My mind works on dozens of different tracks. Even when I'm having sex, I've got my mind on half a dozen things. Is she enjoying herself? Should I try a different technique? Am I enjoying myself? Can I sneak out in the morning? Where does she keep the coffee?

About the only times when my mind settles on just one thing is in the middle of combat or when I'm seriously involved in a musical piece. It is transporting, electrifying. Combat and music are, for me, better than sex. And I like sex a lot, obviously.

Avoiding music, just to piss my mother off, had been the tough part. The last few months had been intensely enjoyable as I reentered that world and absorbed myself in it.

Now all I had to do was play. Something I loved.

The Queen was hosed.

As I played, most of the Court began to dance. Music would not stop a troll or an ogre from attacking you in most cases, but they were clumping along to the tune and just as enspelled as the True Fey. Sirens were possibly either created by the Fey as entertainers or, just as possibly, were from the same universe as the Fey and evolved their innate musical abilities as protection against the Fey.

The theory on this was that the Queen was actually projecting the effect, that it was, in part, protection for her. Stricken's file had said that Fey Queens controlled their Courts of unruly subjects through many means. Control of resources, internecine manipulation, but at least one way was through direct mental control. When she became ensnared by music, that ensnarement translated down through the link to the rest of the Court. This might be a side effect or intentional. Some of the Court must have been tired of being eternal servants. If they were left to their own devices while she was ensnared, they might take matters into their own hands.

Whatever the reason, the vast majority of the Court was caught by the music. Most danced. The Fey were extremely graceful in their dance. Trolls and ogres not so much. Boggles mostly bounced around like little hairy ping-pong balls. Most of them, whatever the melody, formed a mosh pit and slammed into each other. The ogres followed their lead and there went the beer tent.

I wasn't just sitting on my ass. I enjoyed dancing as much as any in-shape, graceful guy, and I was dancing among them. I was also testing the limits of the brief pauses between pieces. How long it took the Court to break from the spell seemed to depend on what type. The smaller ones quickly. Then the stronger and stronger types until only the True Fey were left in stasis and they shook it off. The difference wasn't great; the True Fey broke from the spell after about twenty seconds, but it was noticeable.

I nearly got eaten by a troll playing with it, so I made sure to keep the breaks short after that.

After hours of playing, with some short breaks to take quick drinks of water and wine, the alarm clock went off. I had no interest in turning the Court to stone and I knew I could get so into music I wouldn't notice the calling of birds at daybreak.

I really didn't feel tired. I felt as if I could keep playing all day. I knew better than to push it, though.

I lowered my bow and worked my shoulders as the Court came out of their frenzy. The birds were singing in the distant trees. It was time for the Court to leave.

The Queen finally shook herself from her trance.

"You need to depart before the sun catches you, Queen," I said, taking sips of water and wine.

"All night without break nor let nor false note," the Queen said.

In truth, I'd had all three. The Fey weren't as perfect at that sort of thing as they believed. I'd let her keep her illusions.

"Is the sun going to hurt the princess?"

"No," the Queen said. "Not as long as . . . No."

Not as long as I am not enspelled I suspect she was going to say.

"Can you do it again tomorrow night?" she asked.

"I could keep going now," I said, gesturing at her daughter. "But one Fey statue is all I can handle. Be back tonight to find out."

The hole in the hill opened once again and in moments the Court was gone.

A few seconds later the sun peeped its way over the flanks of Mount Rainier.

✧ ✧ ✧

"Well, this is a hell of a mess!" Agent Garrison said.

"Fey manners are like Fey-ugly," I said, shrugging. My hands weren't even cramped thanks to countless hours of practice over the last few months.

Agent Franks was there in armor followed by an SRT foursome. They were examining the tracks. If the mess bothered him it wasn't obvious. He was ignoring me and I decided to do the same.

"We have people prepared to handle cleanup," I added.

"We got some view from the distance," Garrison said. "Was that a *Hunt*?"

"I'm pretty sure the Huntsman is her dad," I added, gesturing with my chin.

"You're playing with fire here," Garrison said. "Fey are entirely unpredictable."

"Not when it comes to music. They're always curious and entirely at the mercy of it. Look, I gotta do this again tonight. Feel free to stay and analyze or pick up a trash bag and clean up. But I gotta go get some rest."

The truth was I was still too jazzed up, pardon the pun.

I went home and played the rest of the day.

CHAPTER 22

"You appear tired, Harper," the Queen said.

The second night started much the same as the first. Same eruption of the Hunt as scouts, then the rest of the Court. Some of them looked the worse for wear. Dancing all night can take it out of you.

"I played all day," I said. "I just was enjoying myself too much not to."

"And you think you can still play all night? This night we will not sup. You will play from nightfall."

"Okay," I said, and immediately started the first song on the planned list.

The Court immediately stilled as the Queen sunk into the charm of song, then began to dance.

The only difference was that I was tired. I spent more time sitting down and less dancing. And there were a few more false notes. Not that the Fey noticed. They were out of it.

When the buzzer went off, I stopped playing and let them get their head space and timing back.

"One more night, Queen," I said. "Then you must sign the contract without addition or addendum. Tomorrow night I request that you release the princess from her enchantment before the music begins. And I will stop a short time earlier to give you time to sign."

"If you can manage a third night," she said menacingly. But I could tell her heart wasn't in it.

"I'll explain why it is not just possible but easy tonight," I said. "But the sun is rising. I would suggest you flee, Fey." I raised the bow again. "I could keep playing if you'd prefer."

And the Court was gone.

The only real change this time was a large bonfire in honor of Litha. The Parks Department had nearly put its foot down on that one. Fires were *not* allowed in the parks. They'd had the argument before with the local pagan community.

They'd never tried to have the argument with MCB.

The other change was under the tent. On a wooden table in the middle of the tent was the full contract and the required five signature sheets. All the signatures and initials were complete except for those of the Queen. Beside the document was a pen.

I'd slept this time. Gotten up nicely rested. Shit, shower, shave. Good meal. I'd replaced bows and strings. Tested everything out. All my weapons were ready to rock.

"Will you release your daughter now or in the morn?" I asked when the Queen was in position on her sedan couch.

This time *she* was looking the worse for wear and distinctly displeased. I was pretty sure she knew she was beaten . . . and had probably been dealing with crap all day from members of her Court. I suspect her Huntsman consort was arguing to just kill me.

Me, I was fresh as a daisy. The Doctors Nelson had been handling MCB. Worse luck for them but this was working so far. Now if MCB would just stay out. I had some serious assurances on that from the political side, but MCB sometimes thought it was a law unto itself.

"Not till the dawning, Harper," she said, harshly.

"Then release her when I stop playing, Queen. For on the morrow, do you not sign the documents, I shall simply *continue* to play. You and your Court will become new statues for this fine garden. And that," I said, pointing at Shallala, "shall ascend as the Queen of the Western Realms. Let's just say that neither of us wants *that* to happen."

"If you can play flawlessly through one more night," the Queen snapped.

I began to play.

I could tell this time she was trying to fight the spell. She was paying as careful attention to my playing as she could through the charm of the music. There were a few false notes. Once when a string broke, I snatched up a new violin and kept playing. She had tried to rouse but was unable before I started playing again. And the rest really didn't seem to care.

I played like a banshee all night. I ran through rock and roll riffs. I ran through music designed for violin ranging from classical European through pieces by Japanese, Chinese and Indian, drawing from all three cultures. I did riffs on African music. I emulated a popular song from Afghanistan that is a bawdy ballad about a farmer's hard-luck life. I played songs designed for the didgeridoo, which is tough, and Peruvian flute, which isn't. I covered the whole world in one short night.

I'd set the alarm for five minutes before sunrise. I knew the Queen was going to be a bitch about signing the contract.

When it went off, I stopped playing and worked my shoulders again—but I kept my bow on the strings. This was the tough part.

"The dawn is about to break, Queen. Sign the contract."

"The music was not flawless," the Queen said.

"It was flawless enough to hold you and your Court." I began to play again and she went back to being hypnotized by the music. I stopped after a minute. "Three minutes, Queen, and you're a statue for children to climb on!"

"You ask me to put my only heir out in the wilds, Harper!" the Queen snapped, rising from her chair to her full height.

There was more than enough light to see real Fey-ugly. And, damn, she was ugly. There are double baggers and then there are "can we just put her in a body bag?" ugly.

I put the bow to the strings again and played for a few moments.

"Sign!" I shouted as she struggled from the enchantment.

"This document practically makes me an *ally* of your stupid company of bravos!" she shouted.

"You *took* the Challenge!" I replied. "I have *met* the Challenge. You are *pledged* to sign! SIGN!"

"I shall not!" she shrieked.

I began to play—one of my own compositions—and sing.

As the last note trailed off, I looked at her, reared up in all her alien Fey horror and glory.

"The God of Angel Armies is by my side," I said, calmly. "Shall I fear a mere *Fey*? Sign the document, Queen. Your daughter shall be safe by my word and my 'company of bravos.' Or be a statue. I care not. You are not of this world. You are nothing to my God. Shall I continue to play and bind all of your Court? Then I shall be the most famous, and by far the wealthiest, Hunter in the world. No bombs nor guns nor mines nor flamethrowers. All by the use of one or two violins. My mother would be so proud. Sign, Fey!"

She signed, then snapped her fingers at the feynequin statue.

Shallala came to life and immediately glamoured as a skinny blonde in a bright pink dress.

"Did it work?" she asked.

"It worked," I said.

"Be happy, daughter," Queen Shalana snarled. "You are free of your imprisonment."

"Oh my God!" Shallala screamed and started dancing around in a circle. *"That is so totally awesome! Yay, me! I'm so me! Go me!"*

"This is your fault, Harper," Shalana said, shaking her head. She, too, had glamoured back into the business suit. She picked up her copies of the papers and waved them at me. "I can't believe you made me sign a *six-hundred-page contract*!"

"I can't believe your daughter signed it without reading it," I said.

"Like I'm going to waste my time, like, *reading*!" Shallala said. "Like, where's the nearest *mall*? I totally need a *shoe store*! Like *right now*!"

"Daughter, dearest," the Queen said, snapping her fingers to get her attention. "That document you signed? It means *I* no longer have to keep you. You have to find your own food and your own clothing. Which means you have to find your own *money*. No more coming to mommy for gold."

"What?" Shallala said. "Like seriously?"

"Like seriously," I said.

"That is so totally bogus!" Shallala screamed. "Like no *shoe shopping*?"

"Not unless you find a source of income," the Queen said. "And it also means I no longer have to put up with you! Court! We are gone from this place!"

Leaving just me and Shallala the Faerie Princess on the hilltop.

"You mean... I'm *poor*?" she asked, stunned.

"Gimme a break. Any idea how many ways you can earn money?"

"Several come to mind!" the Queen shouted from the hole in the ground, which then snapped shut.

"Not *that* way!" I said. "First of all, you guys live approximately forever, right?"

"More or less," Shallala said, still stunned.

"Have you ever heard of the human magic called 'compound interest'? Oh, and, by the way, those Court members you're going to be getting? Any of them, say, Knights or Hunt? 'Cause there's this thing called the PUFF..."

And thus ends the story of how Seattle got its own fairy princess. Much to the chagrin of various club managers, the Seattle City Council, and the MCB, but much to the cheering of various shoe stores, clothing shops and high-end restaurants.

'Cause, yeah, there turned out to be a lot of ways a Fey princess can earn money. And, no, not that way. Shudder. Fey-ugly.

CHAPTER 23

Might as well finish the story I started with. I don't want to. I don't want to return to that spider-haunted dark.

But the story has to be told. Just like we've got to go in, nothing says we're going to come out.

The story has to be told.

When I'd first joined the Warthogs, we'd worked the Portland area frequently. About a year after I joined, there was a special election for sheriff. Sheriff Greene had been in a car wreck, off duty, and got really busted up. He decided it was time to retire even if he was in the middle of his term of office. So there was an election. And a guy named Robert Schmidt was elected.

Robert Schmidt had a good resume. He'd been with LAPD for years, risen to the rank of captain, then moved to Portland when his wife's father became ill and didn't want to leave the area. Nice family touch there, Bob. He also had contacts to do the fund-raising. (That again.)

Bottom line, Sheriff Bob Schmidt got elected and immediately started cleaning house. One of his election platforms was "efficient service for the taxpayers." Efficient meant cutting costs. One of the costs was going over all the contracts the Sheriff's department had with various companies. He'd brought up a sycophant from L.A., Kenneth Jones, who was promoted on the spot to lieutenant and had the job of negotiating all new contracts and cutting corners.

When Lieutenant Jones contacted MHI and spoke to Dr. Lucius, Lucius' first question was "Are you read in on UF?" The lieutenant was not read in on UF. Thus Lucius had a very hard time explaining why the Multnomah County Sheriff's Department was paying us a thousand dollars a month for "twenty-four-hour emergency response."

I'm going to do an "it sort of went like this" story from someone else's perspective. Bear with me.

Captain Israel Lyons was the head of the UF department of the Multnomah County Sheriff's Office. Portland is in Multnomah County although the "greater Portland area" stretches outside the county.

Lyons had no official staff. He had some sergeants and lieutenants he knew on various shifts who had encountered enough weird-ass shit in their time that when something came up—frequently, it being Portland—he'd call one of them to go handle it until he got there.

Despite having no staff and no department and, apparently, no real job, his official title was "Special Actions Assistant to the Sheriff" and he had a choice, big office right by the sheriff's. Because the way it worked back then was this: When a new sheriff was elected he'd get all sorts of briefings. One of them was always from some nice fellow from the FBI who would talk about jurisdiction and cooperation. At the end of the meeting, the nice fellow would mention that another department would be calling and would need to talk.

Then someone from the MCB would call and say something like: "At some point in your county there may be something that happens which is extremely unusual. When it does, call us."

Newly elected sheriffs would ask what "extremely unusual" meant and joke about little green men.

"You'll know it when you see it."

The sheriffs would tend to forget the conversation until they saw it.

Sheriff Greene had only had to deal with one "unusual event" before he delegated that job to then-Lieutenant Israel Lyons, second in command of Multnomah SWAT, in exchange for promotion to captain.

Israel Lyons had a beeper. It always seemed to go off at three in the God-damned morning. He rued the day he'd let Sheriff

Greene talk him into taking the fucking job. He also had a wife who had suffered through his job for ten damned years. That fucking beeper, those three A.M. phone calls, all the incredible horror he'd had to visit and especially the fucking MCB were *not* worth a choice office and a captain's salary. But Israel Lyons also had a strong sense of duty. The reason that Sheriff Greene had chosen him. So he suffered through it.

Then the sheriff was T-boned by a drunk driver and took early retirement. And that fucker Schmidt took over.

As one of his first cost-cutting moves, Schmidt tried to fire Lyons. He had a budget and an office but no real job as such. Schmidt didn't even ask Lyons to explain what "Special Actions" were. It was clearly a cynosure for the ex-sheriff's buddy. But Lyons was two years from retirement. That was hard.

So Schmidt transferred Lyons to head of the Parking Department, in charge of all the meter maids. It was in the basement of the sheriff's office. It hadn't had a captain, for which it was slated, in twenty years. It was usually run by a politically unpopular lieutenant.

And that brown-nosing fuck Kenneth Jones got Lyons' office.

He could have it. Maybe he'd get that fucking beeper too. Serve him right.

Captain Lyons moved about half the stuff from his old, bigger office down to Parking, took the rest of it home, moved into his cubicle of an office, put his feet up and took a deep, relieved sigh. In his first few weeks he got reacquainted with his family, his grandkids, the game of golf and fishing, which back before fucking UF had been a passion. He arrived at eight A.M. after a full night's sleep, went home at five on the dot every damned day. He only worked Monday through Friday. His fucking phone never went off at three A.M. There were zero emergencies in fucking parking at three A.M. The meter maids all went home at five when the meters went to "No need to pay."

He had a captain's salary, no real work to speak of and he had fucking UF off his plate. Not to mention some of the meter maids were cute and *none* of them had heard his stories from his SWAT days. They ate those up. He couldn't tell the UF stories, obviously.

It was fucking *heaven*!

So now we transfer to Sheriff Schmidt's perspective.

✧ ✧ ✧

Sheriff Bob Schmidt ("Vote Schmidt, he's the Shit!" was a rejected campaign slogan) was peacefully sleeping at three A.M. a week after he'd taken office when his home phone rang. Sheriff Schmidt did not have a beeper. They were for lesser individuals.

"Sheriff, we appear to have a UF incident."

"A what?" Sheriff Schmidt said.

Sheriff Bob Schmidt had worked the beat in LAPD for a while, then passed the detective exam. If there was a UF while he was on beat, he was one of the guys on the perimeter who were being lied to assiduously. He did stolen cars, normal for intro to detective, not a place where you run into the supernatural, then a time in Narc, also not a big supernatural area.

While in Narc he'd burned a supervisor for diverting some of the recovered cash into his own pocket. Give Schmidt props for honesty. Personally, I think he just wasn't being offered a cut. But it made him unpopular with the regular Joes. So he wangled a transfer to Internal Affairs.

IA is an important department. *Quis custodiet ipsos custodes* is actually an important question, one I'd posed to Congressmen about MCB and other groups several times. Cops are human and subject to a lot of pressures that normal civilians aren't. Bribery, intimidation, all sorts of excesses happen. They do. Cops are important and special. But they're not superheroes, any more than Monster Hunters are. We get watched like a hawk by MCB, trust me. IA is one of those sad, sorry necessities.

But IA is not a well-liked department. And, very importantly in this case, it is very, very rare that anyone in IA encounters anything supernatural-related. They're internal affairs. Unless some narc cop turns out to be a werewolf they're not going to get involved. (Happened once. Omaha. Seriously violated the rights of a guy who was pushing to young teens. Like, tore him into shreds then, unfortunately, tore into all the other narc cops present, the pusher's family, et cetera. If it had been just the pusher, hey, more power. As it was, MHI had to chase him down and terminate with prejudice.)

If he'd been Homicide, it was guaranteed. Even missing persons it was likely. Narcotics and IA are the two departments least likely to encounter the supernatural. Although Narc sometimes does in gnomes.

Bottom line, he'd never heard of Unearthly Forces, did not believe in Unearthly Forces and had a very hard time adjusting.

At the insistence of the lieutenant, then the precinct captain of Portland PD, who knew about UF but not my jurisdiction, thank you, not my plate, don't want it on it, this is your job, he went out to the scene at oh-dark-thirty on a rainy night. MCB was already there. A house had been torn apart and almost the entire family was dead. A twenty-something son was missing. His torn clothing was on the floor in his room. There were massive slash marks on the inside of the door and it was busted outwards.

"Who's your Hunter company?" was practically the first thing out of the MCB agent's mouth.

"My *what*?"

The more experienced agent's question was more on point.

"Where's Captain Lyons? Doesn't he handle werewolves anymore?"

"Handle *what*?" was the new sheriff's response.

At that point it started to sink in that maybe there was a reason for Lyons having a choice office other than being the previous sheriff's buddy.

So he had dispatch call Lyons.

Dispatch called back and told him that Captain Lyons' reply had been to laugh, tell them he didn't do that anymore and hang up the phone. They didn't add "hysterically" to the laugh comment. Dispatch knew all about UF, why Lyons had the job, why he'd been demoted and were trying not to laugh hysterically as well. They'd had three positions cut. The new broom was not particularly popular anywhere in the department.

Lyons, though, had a sense of duty. So he called a lieutenant he knew was off duty and had her shit together, Kay Shaw.

Kay had broken through all the barriers. She was the first female lieutenant in the Multnomah Sheriff's Department, she was one of their premier homicide dicks, and she'd already been one of Lyons' go-to people. So at three A.M. on a night off, she put on her rain slicker and went to the scene.

She arrived on scene and found the sheriff on the front porch trying to explain to a Monster Control Bureau agent that werewolves were something from a bad horror movie.

"Morning, Sheriff," Shaw said.

"And you are . . . ?" he said, then remembered his premier and only female homicide detective. "Good to see you, Lieutenant Shaw. Uh . . . were you just driving by?"

"Agent Flores," she said, nodding at the MCB agent. "What do we got?"

"Probable lycanthrope," the agent said, appreciating that someone with their head in the game had turned up. "Probably the son. No survivors."

"Well, the good news is you don't have to shoot them, then," Shaw said. "We got any other calls?"

"Looks like he took off," Flores said. "No other reports we've picked up."

"I'll clue in Dispatch to keep an eye out for Code W," she said. "Sheriff, we need to talk."

"Of course, Lieutenant," the sheriff said. His butt buddy had been summoned and immediately followed.

"Without Lieutenant Ass-boy," Shaw said, pointedly.

"Excuse me?" Lieutenant Jones said. "What did you call me?"

"Sorry, make that Lieutenant Brown-nose," Shaw said. "This conversation is between you and me, Sheriff, or I can let you go back to trying to figure this out yourself."

"Jones, give us a minute," the sheriff said.

Kay led him around to the side of the wrap porch and looked through the windows into the house. It was a shambles.

"Did the MCB cover that everything you've ever seen in a horror movie exists?" she asked.

"This can't be happening," Schmidt insisted. "I was in L.A. for fifteen years! And this did not happen! Is this a Portland thing?"

"You were IA," Shaw said, distastefully. "Why would IA handle this crap? Any homicide detective runs into it eventually. To be immediately told to leave the premises, this is a Federal matter, and you didn't see anything, this never happened. But you know about it. Ever have a potential 'excessive force' charge, probably resulting in the death of a suspect, mysteriously pulled by the FBI?"

"A couple," Schmidt said. "You mean . . . ?"

"Some cop ran into a monster," Shaw said. "A real one. Not a metaphor. So get your fucking head in the game, or say you never should have run for sheriff and resign. I don't give a shit which. But you either pull it out of the sand or your ass or wherever it is, fast, or I'll go back to bed and forget we had this conversation."

"I'm the sheriff. Remember you work for *me*, lady."

"And if you try to fire me over this conversation, I'll hit you with a screaming EEOC suit," Shaw said, walking away. "Because it never happened. Good night. Have fun!"

Sheriff Schmidt thought about it for a second then let her walk.

"Jones!" he barked.

"Yes, sir!"

"You're now in charge of... UF," Schmidt said. "Apparently we're supposed to use a contractor company. Who is our contractor for this?"

"I don't think we have one, sir," Jones said.

"Find one," Schmidt said. "Give me a report in the morning..."

For the next two nights, Portland was terrorized by the Gresham Serial Killer and then the attacks abruptly stopped... when the full moon passed.

The next month, the Gresham Serial Killer was *back*. But it wasn't just in Gresham anymore. There were at least four different killers. They were copycats, obviously, but it was like they were *breeding*!

Jones had by that time gotten enough information, pulling hen's teeth, that he'd found a Monster Hunter company.

Troutdale Supernatural Issues was willing to guarantee 24/7/365 response, no more than three hours on site, for the measly price of five thousand dollars a month. Remember, we'd been getting a grand. And they deployed immediately to take care of the Gresham Werewolf.

They managed to track two down without any casualties. The third one ate them a new asshole. And Troutdale Supernatural Issues went out of business when the owner and founder got a silver bullet through his head in the hospital, courtesy of MCB. He sort of let himself get bit.

MHI? That was about the time that we had more business than we could handle in Seattle. But we offered to send in a team before the next full moon. Since it was from out of town and "weren't you the one who canceled the previous contract?" all expenses had to be paid up-front. Jones didn't like that. He kept making calls.

I think they went through four companies, two of which went out of business, in as many months before they'd gotten that one werewolf and its "offspring" under control. I think at one point they had seven werewolves running around, which I thought was seriously bad until I worked New Orleans. But by that time Portland had developed a vampire problem as bad as Seattle's. Portland was still a major wood processing town and I swear they started running out of stakes.

Look, MHI is the best for a reason. We only take people who have dealt proactively with supernatural outbreaks, we train the hell out of them and we support them aggressively. We only take the best, we expect the best and we get the best. There are always fly-by-night companies looking for that fat PUFF check. And there's a reason those bounties are so high. This isn't a business for amateurs.

There are other groups that are as good as we are overseas and nearly as good as we are in the US. But they are *all* busy. So just because your particular town or county is getting overrun with werewolves, vampires, zombies, or whatever, an emergency on your part does not constitute an emergency on ours. Point being that *everybody* has emergencies. Constantly. That's why we've been in business for damned near a hundred years. If you wanted us to respond like lightning bolts, you shouldn't have cancelled the contract.

Then MCB had had it. Vamps were out of control, and there was a werewolf surge going. That's when they got permission to call in SRT. And the sheriff got read the riot act by the agent in charge and got punched through a window by Agent Franks when he "responded hotly."

The sheriff, sporting a newly broken nose and two black eyes, formed a Monster Control Squad. There were lots of volunteers. At first.

There were six funerals of sheriff's deputies in the next two months. And no good excuses for why. Half of them were killed in one "drug bust gone bad."

Even the bravest can freeze the first time they see a real, no-shit vampire or kappa or gangrenous slime. People who haven't seen the supernatural and lived through it, fought through it, should not be Hunters. SRT members generally spend some time as regular MCB and the rumor is they're trained on captured monsters.

These guys were SWAT wannabes. Not bad people but most of them probably only sort-of believed in the briefing. And from reports, most of them freaked out when every horror movie turned out to understate the danger.

Then an entire bum camp disappeared. Just flat up and disappeared.

And we had to respond. It was time.

Again, I have to put it briefly from the perspective of the Multnomah County Sheriff's Office.

Sheriff Schmidt walked through the scattered bedding and small shelters with his hand over his nose and mouth. Partially it was from the smell. Bums don't regularly shower. Partially it was the natural human reaction to seeing every sign of a total massacre.

Except the blood.

"Why isn't there any blood?" Sheriff Schmidt asked.

The encampment was in one of those underground open areas that exist under any city. This one was a turning area for vehicles attached to a corridor that these days led to nothing that was in use. It was abandoned, empty and dry. The bums had just sort of occupied the empty and unused space.

"I don't know, sir," Lieutenant Jones said.

"Then what do you know, you idiot?"

"Spiders," Agent Duncan said. He was just about sick and tired of dealing with this idiot. "Species probably Arachnida Gigantus Sassus. That's the most common species in this region. You can see the remnant silk."

"What?" Schmidt said. "Silk?"

"Giant spider silk?" Duncan said, as if speaking to a candidate for the Special Olympics. He held some up. "This stuff? Left behind by giant spiders after they paralyze and bind their victims?"

"So you're saying some *spiders* did this?" Jones said, laughing.

"You know you sound like a hyena when you laugh, Lieutenant?" Duncan said. "Sheriff, if MCB has to call in the SRT again, the Attorney General will remove you from office for complete and utter incompetence. There had to be other disappearances before this. This wasn't one spider. This was a *nest*. And even if we were authorized to handle this, which we are not, it would *take* a full SRT. I've got a couple agents in Portland, and could not even *dream* of handling a Sassus nest by ourselves. We're talking about fifty to two hundred spiders the size of horses. And it almost assuredly means a spider mother. Think tarantula the size of a *mammoth*. Sheriff, are you *ever going to figure out that this is important, you fucking idiot?*"

"Special Agent," his partner said.

"No!" Duncan said, swearing. "You blithering God-damned idiot and your laughing hyena butt-fuck-buddy have caused the unnecessary deaths of *dozens* which *we have had to cover up!* If you don't figure out how to deal with this shit, I will personally put a *bullet* in your head and deal with the paperwork later! Do you understand me? I am absolutely serious! *Fix this! Now!*"

The Special Agent stormed out.

So Sheriff Schmidt went back to his office, picked up the phone and politely asked Captain Lyons, Parking, if he had a moment to spare.

"Heard about the giant spider attack," Lyons said, shuddering as he sat down without being invited. "A full nest? Just one is nasty as hell. Never had to deal with a freaking nest. Sucks to be you. Cleanup is going to be a *bitch*."

"You dealt with this for..."

"Ten horrible years," Lyons said. "Don't ask. You can't make me and the answer is no. It's not worth the nice office and I'm already a captain. I even like Parking. No stress."

"I can order you," Schmidt said, darkening. He did not like to be crossed. "Failure to obey a direct order would constitute grounds for termination without retirement, *Captain*."

"Ah, but you'd have to explain to a county review board what the order *was*," Lyons said, holding up a finger. "Which you cannot because UF is secret-squirrel."

"So you're just going to let people die?"

"Is that a recognition on your part that you are completely out of your depth?" Lyons asked. "Before you kill yourself admitting that, be aware that it's become obvious to everyone with a clue about UF in the county. People who *don't* have a clue are wondering why the death rate is through the roof and why we lost several very good deputies to random accidents. So just go ahead and say yes."

"Yes," Schmidt ground out.

"Good," Lyons said. "That's the first step of twelve, admitting you have a problem. I gave you the answer to your problem the first night but you rejected it."

"Lieutenant Shaw?" Schmidt asked, frowning.

"Shaw is sharp, ambitious and has a strong gut so UF doesn't throw her," Lyons said. "She also has no life except work, which is something you're going to want. So you're talking to the wrong person. But you won't like working with her. You won't like working with anyone who is good at UF. Because the sort of people who can look at the kind of mess vampires and werewolves leave behind, and still keep it secret, are not going to sugarcoat it. And you'll have to deal with them regularly; they'll have to live in your hip pocket, because at the best of times, this is constant. Not as bad as lately but constant. And there's constant cover-up, funerals, contacts that have to be managed. So you'll have to get used to someone who you deal with on a daily basis who is not going to kiss your ass. But that is the only bone I'm going to throw you, Sheriff. Now, Traffic doesn't run itself so don't call me again and I won't call you."

And he left.

So then the sheriff called in Lieutenant Shaw.

"Kay," the sheriff said, escorting her into his office and gesturing to a seat. "I think we got off on the wrong foot."

"Even if he is read in now," she said, gesturing to Jones, "we're not going to have this conversation, or any other conversation about UF, with him present."

"Who are you to tell the *sheriff* what to do?" Jones snapped.

"We wouldn't be having this conversation if you weren't desperate, not after our first one. And I'm not going to have your butt-boy interjaculating all over it."

"That is an obscene thing to say to the sheriff!" Jones snarled. "And I take offense at your insinuation that—"

"Jonesy," Schmidt said, holding up a hand. "Why don't you step out?"

"Sheriff," Jones said. He could see that choice office slipping out of his fingers.

"We'll discuss it later, Lieutenant," the sheriff said.

When Jones had left, Shaw just waited.

"I'm considering you for the Special Actions position," the sheriff said, uncomfortably.

"I don't care about the choice office," Shaw said. "I don't like you, you don't like me, I'd rather not be that noticeable, anyway. If it's necessary, it's necessary. But unless it really is, Jonesy can keep his office. But it's a captain position."

"The budget..."

"Nice talking to you, Sheriff," Shaw said, standing up.

"Wait," Schmidt said, letting out an angry breath. "Just tell me one thing. Why *you*?"

"I know what to do and how to do it, Sheriff," Shaw said, sitting down. "I know who to call. I know the people and *don't* have a bad relationship with them. You have, frankly, pissed in every *single* well. I haven't. Give me the budget and the authority and you can stop being woken up at three A.M. every damned night. But that means *I* will be. And I'll have to be able to take charge of any scene, order *anyone* around including Lieutenant Jones since he's handling so much of your administrative trivia. That means *Captain* in big, bold letters on my door in the basement. I'm fine with the basement. But the door says 'Captain Shaw' or I can go back to chasing human homicidal maniacs. Much safer and waaay less stress."

"We've got a serious giant spider problem," Schmidt said.

"Heard," Shaw said. "Worse than you probably realize."

"What do you mean?" the sheriff said.

She'd talked to Lyons about the issue the day before and just repeated the briefing. He'd gone through this once before and the Hunters had given him the details. "If they need that much meat, she must be breeding. Once they've digested all those homeless, takes a day or two—which has already passed—she'll be laying eggs. Those take four weeks to mature. Then the babies, each about the size of tarantulas, burst out. She grabs as many of the females as she can for snacks. Shelobs don't like competition.

"The males stick around and grow. They'll have to be fed. They take about six months to mature. Given the number of homeless that were taken, we're looking at, currently, one hundred to two hundred spiders. In six months, if we don't kill the nest, we're looking at double that number. And any females that escape will start to grow. Takes about six years for a shelob to mature to breeding size. So we've got time on that one. But when four hundred spiders have to be fed, they're not going to be satisfied with dogs, cats and rats. In about ten to twelve weeks we'll start losing people at a rate even MCB won't be able to cover up. And all over the county. Breaking through from toilets, into basements, into homes... Welcome to Arachnid Apocalypse, Portland. MCB will cover it up with some hokey horror movie if they can. But we'll be looking at hundreds dead. And that is not an exaggeration, Sheriff. That's why MCB went off on you. And, yeah, I heard about that."

"I hadn't realized..." the sheriff gulped.

"You see why I don't really want this job? I have to worry about shit like that so you don't have to."

The sheriff actually stopped and did something he didn't enjoy. He thought. Shaw let him.

"We have a giant spider problem," the sheriff said, then held up his hand to forestall a reply. "There are others but that is the big one right now."

"Understood," Shaw said.

"Take care of that," the sheriff said. "And I'll make you a captain and you can choose your office."

"Lieutenant Jones is not involved in any way, shape or form."

"The lieutenant is..."

"Not involved or I'm not involved," Shaw said. "His real position in meetings is interjecting comments to throw people off. This is not something open to debate or playing games. When I need to talk to you, I need to talk to *you*. Not him. Because I need you to tell someone something. From you. Not him. And if I'm talking to you and he keeps talking crap, I'm eventually going to punch him through a wall and go find a job with a Monster Hunter company. Pay's much better, anyway. He takes orders from me, yes. When I have to call to get something that absolutely doesn't have to come from you but Jones can handle, I'll call *him* at three A.M. so I don't have to call *you*. But he understands that he's subordinate and he does *not* get between us. No Jonesy or no me."

"No Jones," the sheriff said.

"Same budget as Israel."

"Agreed."

"And I am neither going to blow smoke nor waste your time," Shaw said. "You might have noticed I don't kiss ass."

"Which is why you're probably right for the job," Schmidt said, smiling as broadly as he could manage.

"Agreed," Shaw said. "Fuck me on it and anyone who *could* do this job competently will tell you to piss up a tree."

"Understood."

✧ ✧ ✧

Shaw didn't currently have a UF office at all, so she went back to her substation and her cubicle to think. Then she picked up the phone.

"I got the job," she said.

"I knew you would," Lyons said.

"What the fuck do I do *now*?" she asked.

"You let me make some calls," Lyons said. "Then when you've saved Portland and Multnomah from giant spiders, you come pick up my rolodex so you can make them next time."

CHAPTER 24

Doctors Nelson were taking a well-deserved joint vacation. We'd been working our asses off and they weren't getting any younger. Naturally, it was to a seminar but everyone vacations in their own way.

But Brad was in the office when the phone rang.

"MHI, Brad speaking," Brad said.

"Brad, Captain Lyons, Multnomah."

"They give you your job back?" Brad asked.

"Better, they gave it to a protégé, who has no life anyway. Me, I'm learning to fish for salmon again. I think the most fun is having the time to slowly go through catalogs looking at new rods and lures. At my office on taxpayer time. Good times."

"Sounds good, sir."

"Please tell me you'll pick up a job for an old and trusted customer," Lyons said. "We've got a nest of Sassus and probably a shelob."

"Shit," Brad said, scratching his head.

I was watching this interplay from the jig so I turned it off and raised an eyebrow.

"Nest of Sassus," Brad said, turning on the speaker. "And probably a shelob."

"Wow," I said. We'd handled a few individual giant spiders. Nasty fuckers but easy to kill in small groups. A nest, though... "How big of a nest?"

"Hundred to two hundred," Captain Lyons said. "We're missing a shitload of bums. Who's that?"

"Chad," Brad said.

"Hey, Chad," Lyons said.

"Hey, Cap," I said. "You get your job back?"

"Won't take it in a million years," he said. "Turned it over to a protégé. And if you come on to Kay Shaw, she'll rip your balls out through your throat, Romeo."

"I'll keep my comments to myself," I said, grinning. "Is she cute?"

"Hot redhead," Lyons said. "Real va-va-voom body. Dead shot, kicks ass with the best of them."

"I'm already in love!" I yelled.

"I will seriously fucking kill you, Romeo," Lyons said. "Brad, do an old friend a favor. I know Portland is on your shit list . . ."

"We're not going to let giant spiders take over Portland," Brad said, rubbing his head. "But the Docs are out of town and our newbie is in recovery. We've only got five guys. And if she's taken a whole bunch of homeless, she's breeding so we've got to step on this nest, fast."

"With you there, buddy," Lyons said.

"We're going to need more support than normal," Brad said. "And it's probably going to get exciting. We're going to have to use a shitload of flame and explosives."

"Underground chemical fire caused by a build-up of methane gas," Lyons said.

"You working for MCB now?" I asked, grinning.

"Bite your tongue, Romeo, but I've been doing this for a while. Will you take it?"

"We'll take it," Brad said, frowning. "Good money. Assuming any of us survive."

"That's the spirit," Lyons said.

"Time to summon the clans," I said. "It's gonna be a hot time in Portland. Probably *tomorrow* night at this rate."

"Oh," I said. "Va-va-voom *indeed*!"

Lieutenant Shaw was classic bodacious Irish redhead. I was instantly even more in love.

"*I* will kill you," Brad said. "Don't fuck this up. We can use Portland back on our list of contracts."

"I am always a gentleman," I said. "Well, generally."

As we unloaded from the team van, Brad introduced us to Multnomah's new UF manager.

"Lieutenant," I said, taking her hand in both of mine, "may I just say what a *pleasure* it is to meet one of Multnomah's *finest*?" Strong emphasis on "finest." It was clear I was referring to her beauty, not her position as a law enforcement professional.

"You must be Romeo," Shaw said, dryly. "Israel warned me about you."

"Why don't we get to business here," Brad said, frowning.

"Yeah, where's the nest?" Jesse asked.

"After we lost seven officers to four vamps, nobody will touch anything UF," Shaw said. "So we don't know."

"Bug hunt," I said, all business. "Rig up, boss?" I added in a distinct southern accent.

"Rig up," Brad said.

I was careful to not even look at Lieutenant Shaw as we rigged.

"We're not going to take on the nest until the heavy stuff gets here," Brad said as we were donning our gear. "The U-Haul couldn't keep up."

Jesse was in the process of loading his vest with grenades as he said that.

"What do you call this?" she asked as I racked the Uzi.

"Our light stuff," I said.

"I'm sort of looking forward to seeing your heavy stuff," Shaw admitted.

Be still, my beating heart. A gun and boom nut with a size 36F chest. I might just have to quit my philandering ways.

Nah.

"If you're extra special nice to me," I said, winking and slinging the Uzi, "I might let you play with my Barrett."

"Is that what you call it?" Jesse asked. "Man, that's sick. Get a life."

Looking around the encampment made me want to puke. There was not a trace of real horror. It was the lack. Food, what there was of it, was still in dishes. A coat that was in the middle of being darned. A stuffed rabbit. There'd been kids.

"Ah, Jesus," I said, shaking my head. "These poor people. Please, Lord, let it have been quick."

"You actually care?" Shaw asked.

"Am I a lounge lizard SOB?" I said. "Guilty as charged. Am I a mercenary? Yep. Do I do this purely for the money? I've got a sky-high IQ and could have gone to Harvard business and be making a phone number in investment banking or something. This is for me, literally, a mission from God. I got sent *back* from Heaven, by choice, to fight monsters. 'Cause, yes, Lieutenant, I give a shit."

"You're serious?" she asked.

"He's serious," Brad said. "Trail leads down this sewer. Lieutenant, why don't you go back to the clear air. If we're not out in . . . four hours, tell MCB to call SRT. Because if we can't handle it, nobody else can."

"I can go with you," Shaw said.

"Lieutenant," I said. "One, we're experienced at this. Two, we're armed and rigged for this. Three, you're *way* too pretty to get paralyzed, strung up in a web, then later injected with an enzyme that turns you into a gooey substance to be sucked up through a feeding proboscis."

"I'll head up top," Shaw said.

The trail went through the sewers for about a really disgusting mile then went up into a large, round tube that was up near the top of the sewer tunnel.

"New guy gets to check out the tunnel," I said.

"Oh, hell, no," Roy said, backing up. "I'm not going in there!"

"I think the biggest pain in the ass gets to check out the tunnel," Brad said, dyspeptically.

"You've got to be kidding me," I said. "I can barely fit in there!"

"You're also our smallest guy," Louis pointed out, enjoying my discomfort.

"Oh, fuck me . . . Help me get out of my gear."

When I was divested of all my gear, I pulled out a rosary and said a quick prayer.

"Saint Michael, Patron of Warriors, give me the courage and the strength," I said, holding the rosary in my clenched hands. "Let me bring a light to the darkness. Amen. I'm gonna need a boost."

I carried my 1911, same one I'd carried in Elkins, and a Maglite with really fresh batteries. And that was it.

When Jesse and Brad had boosted me up, I poked the flashlight into the tunnel and then reached back.

"Louis, hand me my Uzi."

"You'll never fit it in there," Brad said. "And you're heavy. Quit stalling."

"I'm not stalling," I said, taking the Uzi. I pointed it into the tunnel, leaned to the side and fired off a mag on full-auto. None of the rounds ricocheted but I could hear them travelling quite a way up the tunnel. "I'm using suppressing fire."

I handed the Uzi back and clambered into the tunnel.

It was one of the worst experiences of my life. There was barely room to move. Brad had tied a long rope to my boots so they could pull me out. That was how little room there was.

The air was close and foul. I wasn't even sure there was enough to breathe.

But I started wiggling down the tunnel, looking for giant spiders. I had to wonder how the spiders had managed to get through there, especially towing human prey. I had to wonder how much chance I'd have if one of them came down the tunnel searching for fresh prey.

Not damned much, that was my chance.

The damned tunnel seemed to go on forever. We ran out of rope. I had to sit there while somebody went back to the surface for more. Just sit there in the fetid dark. Finally they shouted they had more rope. I had to hope they'd tied them together with really strong knots.

It wasn't straight. It curved after a while. I was really nervous going around that curve. And it was sloped down. It was getting deeper. But there was air. A slight cross-current. There was an end to it. I just hoped like hell it wasn't actually in the nest. That would be bad. I only had eight rounds in my pistol.

I committed to saving the last round for myself. I knew suicide was a sin. I was pretty sure that Pete would intercede on that one. I was not going to be sitting in a cocoon, waking up from time to time in agony, waiting to be spider chow.

I wasn't going out that way.

Finally, I saw not a light at the end of the tunnel—despite what it shows in movies, sewer tunnels are never lit—but an opening at the end of the tunnel. That was nervous-making. I shut off the light and listened. Any skittering? Not a bit. Not even rats.

That was a bad sign. There were always rats in tunnels unless there was a super-efficient rat predator. Like, say, hundreds or thousands of giant spiders.

The opening was another tunnel. A big one. A huge one. I briefly considered just going out that way. Then I thought better about it. Giant spiders. Let the team haul me out.

There was a number on the far wall. Very faint. The paint was old as was the brick.

"57."

Shit. No. Not that damned number again!

Make that "157." One fifty-seven. Better or worse, I wasn't sure. But it might give us a clue where I was at.

I jerked my feet up as hard as I could a couple of times. Time to pull me out.

The number lingered in my memory on the long slide back to my teammates.

"Given the description of the tunnel and the number, it has to be support tunnel 157 for the old PHG cistern."

Portland's chief city engineer wasn't sure why he was being grilled by a lieutenant from the sheriff's office, three FBI agents and some overarmed civilians that looked like a militia—a very smelly militia.

"PHG?" Louis asked.

"Powell-Hurst-Gilbert," Shaw said. "Local area."

"Roger."

"Can we access the tunnel?" Brad asked.

"You can practically drive a tractor-trailer down it," the engineer said, flipping through maps. "The entrance is here. Main entrance is welded shut, though. We haven't used the cistern in sixty years."

"You can either handle opening it or we'll do it," Phil said. "I've got three hundred pounds of C4 just *itching* to be used."

The U-Haul had arrived.

"Uh, we'll open it," the city engineer said, clearly not sure if Phil was serious.

"Probably the better choice," Brad said, blandly.

Once the massive double doors had surrendered to cutting torches and some judicious use of hammers and levers, no C4 to Phil's disgust, the tunnel was as advertised. It was twelve feet high, seventeen feet wide, brick-walled and cobblestoned. It was also in very bad repair. Bricks had fallen in at several points including bits of the ceiling.

"Well, this is fun," Phil said. "No way we're going to be able to do this without heavy firepower and if we use heavy firepower, it looks like the ceiling is going to cave in."

"We'll figure it out," Brad said, thoughtfully. "We always do. Louis, go get the van."

"Yessa, Boss," he said, trotting back to the team van.

"We're going to drive the van down till we find definite sign," Brad said when he was back. "Louis, you're going to have to back it. Iron Hand, Jesse, in the back with flamethrowers. Phil, behind them with an Uzi. Hand, keep an eye out for where you came out. When we get to that point, firemen unload and walk it. Keep an eye out for when you get to solid web. But with the flamethrowers you can keep the bugs off till you get in the van. If we get hit by a wave we jump in the van and drive like hell. Got the plan? Questions?"

"Flame suits?" I asked.

"Yeah," Jesse said. Since Ray III got barbequed, any time we used flamethrowers, we tended to put on silver suits.

"Up to you."

Ten minutes later, Jesse and I were in the back of the Ford Econoline, feet dangling from the back, as Louis backed slowly into the tenebrous tunnel...

Our silver-suit helmets had fairly powerful lights on them and Phil was shining a million candle spotlight between us. But it was still hard to spot where the tunnel had come out. There were a bunch of little tunnels entering the cavernous one.

It was the spider silk that we spotted first. And Phil that spotted it.

"Hold up. I got silk."

Brad bailed out as we clambered down, unbalanced by the weight of both flamethrower tanks and air tanks. The silver suits were hermetically sealed so we had to carry air tanks to breathe. The design was specially made for us with the air tanks down and sideways on our waists rather than vertical. 'Cause our flamethrower tanks were right on our backs where the air tank would normally be. The air tank was inside the silver suit, the flamethrower tank outside.

Brad examined the silk, then backed up and looked at the openings.

"Iron Hand," he said from up forward of the van. "This look familiar?"

I walked back—there was enough room between the van and the right wall to fully open a door—and checked it out. There was an opening. About the right size, maybe. It looked even smaller than I remembered and I remembered it small.

But on the far wall was a barely visible "157." It had been stenciled on the wall who knew how long ago and was harder to read from where we stood than when I'd been in the tube.

And there was a definite trail of silk bits from the tube.

"This is it," I said.

"Start walking."

I took the left and Jesse took the right. I was paying as much attention to my air gauge as the possible spider infestation. Run out of air in the middle of a firefight and we'd be screwed. I was going to change when we were down to about a quarter tank. My breathing in the suit sounded like Darth Vader, and the visor kept fogging up. From time to time I'd have to let go of the flamethrower with my left hand, pull it out of the sleeve and glove, and wipe the visor to clear it. I realized we should have trained more with these things.

Pro-tip: Understand *fully* any piece of equipment your life *might* depend upon. Train with everything you *might* use and be fully prepared. We hadn't trained with silver suits. We'd gotten a company to familiarize us with them. There's a difference. Train, train, train.

Second pro-tip: Turns out the answer is to keep a roll of paper towels under your arm. There's a spot they stay pretty well even if you're moving "vigorously."

The tunnel continued onwards in a straight line, but we could see there was a bend to the right coming up.

Walking in it was a pain. It was hard to see down with the silver suits on and watch your feet. There were bricks and other debris scattered on the floor everywhere. I'd stumble and catch myself every ten feet or so. I kept that in mind in terms of making it back to the bus if we had to run. Again, another "issue" of silver suits that we'd have discovered if we'd properly trained.

We approached the bend carefully. It was wide. The van and

even the U-Haul could make it easily. but we didn't know what was on the other side. Jesse angled left, getting away from the wall, and I moved almost to the left wall, creeping forward cautiously, pilot light aflame. We were ready to rock and cook at the slightest sign of movement.

Around the bend we found what we were looking for.

Various places on Earth, there are things called "funnel web" spiders. They are various different species, even genuses, but they all make webs like a funnel.

The entire God-damned massive tunnel was one giant funnel. About ten feet from the bend, the web started and from there the web was side-to-side across the tunnel. By the time it was fifty feet in, it was covering all the walls and the ceiling in a solid web that looked like the van could drive up it. We couldn't even see exactly where it led. There was just a hole leading to who-knew-what horrors.

"Think we got web," Jesse radioed. "What's the call, Boss?"

"Torch it," Brad radioed in a satisfied tone.

"Right. Charbroiled it is," I said, not bothering to key the radio. I just hit the second trigger on the flamethrower and let it play.

The web burned quickly and efficiently, torching like a pine tree. The heat was so high I could feel it through my silver suit. But the flamethrowers could only reach a few dozen feet. We had to move forward.

"We've got movement up," Phil radioed. "There are more of those small tunnels up by the roof. I just saw a leg stick out of one."

I looked up, saw what he was looking at and blanched. There were an unknown number of small tubes, spaced about thirty feet apart, up by the ceiling on my side. Overflow for the cistern or something. But any of them could pour spiders out at any moment.

"Put a burst into each one as you pass," Brad radioed. "Phil, unass, get up top and keep an eye on them. Roy, get in the back and keep an eye on our boys. We're going to back up till we have this configured."

I put a blast into the nearest tube, then the next one; there was one behind me at that point, as I backed out of the tunnel.

The web was burnt to the point it no longer ramped to the floor of the tunnel. It was sheared off about waist height as if cut by a laser. Interesting effect. And I could now see that the webs were nearly as solid underneath it as the top. That was a lot of spider silk. And some of it was really thick individual strands. Really thick.

"Brad," I radioed. "Can't point specifically. But you see some of this silk? Most of it is about the thickness of a hair. I'm seeing some that's closer to a pinkie."

"I can't see it exactly," Brad radioed. Despite a flow of air, the tunnel was choked with smoke and fire. "But if it's that thick we've definitely got a shelob. Big one, too."

"Shit," I muttered. One aspect of being in the silver suit was a feeling of being totally alone. It was weird. Intellectually, I knew the team was there. But there was no "feel" of a team.

The instructor, an old fireman, had noted that fire teams regularly made physical contact. Now I knew why. It was scary, feeling this alone when you were facing a spider horde.

We backed up to the tunnel and talked by radio as Jesse and I kept an eye on the funnel.

"We need to see where that funnel leads," Brad said. "The plans say there's a large double door to the cistern up ahead. Probably where the funnel terminates. We need to see if it's fully open."

"At least one of those tubes is open to the spiders," Phil argued. "I know I'm the only one who saw it and it might have been a trick of the eyes but I swear I saw a leg."

"Agreed," Brad said. "Plans show those. I missed them when I was reviewing the diagram. But, yeah, those lead right to the cistern. So assuming that's where the nest is, they can drop on somebody from there any time."

"We need some fire up in there that'll hold them," Jesse said. "Something that'll keep burning. Or a way to block them."

"They can only get out one at a time," I said. "Keep the van back. Either I or Jesse will cover the holes and our backs. As we go forward, the 'tube' guy will fire up each tube. The forward guy will work the web. When we get to the door, we lay down suppressing fire and back up. If any spiders come down from a tube where the fire's gone out, the tube guy suppresses and burns and we back out. Before we do this, we change air packs and refill the napalm. We'll do that one at a time and the other will cover."

"That sounds like a plan," Louis said.

"Says you," Jesse said. "I'm already feeling freaked out for some reason. This suit is giving me the heebie-jeebies."

"I felt that, too," I said. "There's a real feeling of being totally alone. And we're going to have to do a lot of coordination. We'll have to stay in contact. Hard with both hands working the flamethrower. Which do you want, tubes or forward?"

"Forward," Jesse said.

"I'll have your back," I said. "Before you step forward, release with your left hand and put it on my arm. Firmly, like the instructor said. Then pull me along with you as you step forward. Then resume burning. If you get low on napalm, we'll switch and you cover back. When you get to half a tank, we switch. Sound good?"

"Sounds right," Jesse said. "You're right. It's the feeling of being cut off. Sorry to freak like that but it's weird. Feels wrong. My gut was screaming something was off."

"We should have trained more with this stuff," Brad said.

"My thoughts exactly, as we were coming in," I said. "Also, the ground is littered with rubble. We might want to stop to clear the path as we walk. If we have to hoof it, that way we won't stumble . . . as much. This stuff is not exactly made for mobility."

But that's how we did it. The tubes terminated before the bend so the rest of the team got in position to give covering fire. We didn't even have our body armor on under the silver suits, no room with everything else, so it had better be accurate covering fire.

As we'd reconfigured, reloaded and re-aired, there had been a couple of peekers from the tubes. The spiders were definitely in them. And who knew which direction they could come from? Sassus were not known for tactical genius but shelobs were poorly understood and were rumored to be somewhat intelligent, which was why Roy was in front of the van, checking six.

Finally, we were ready. I flamed the nearest tube, Jesse put his hand firmly on my right arm and pulled me forward, sideways from my perspective.

"You have the tubes forward," I noted. "Flame up to them as we move. I'll keep an eye up, left and behind us."

"Got it," Jesse said, squirting a tube.

I just trusted Jesse to tell me if anything was amiss on his vector and concentrated on mine. That was the benefit of having a buddy you knew you could trust. With his occasional hand on my arm, and being frequently in contact along the side and back, that horrible feeling of aloneness dwindled. I could concentrate on my vector.

As we passed each tube, I would turn off the pilot light, fire some unlit napalm up into the tube then torch it. Sometimes it burst back on me, full tubes or something. But even then it just hit the silver suit. Benefit of using them.

"Okay," Jesse said after what seemed an eternity. "Web's clear in the passage. I can see the door and kind of into the cistern. More web but it clears out and . . . Motherfucker!"

I didn't even look. I could hear and feel Jesse continuously flaming but my focus was on the tubes. Then one of the first ones down the tunnel disgorged a spider, then another. The flames in that one had burnt out.

"Back up," Brad said, calmly. "Jesse, keep flaming and back slowly. They're not getting past your flame. Hand, we've got these. Check Jesse's tank."

I released my hand from the trigger and reached back to Jesse's tank. I found the bottom and lifted it and shook.

"Down to half," I said, based on weight.

Jesse bumped into me, clearly backing, and I backed. Phil had moved forward and was carefully plugging the exiting spiders with his Uzi on semi. He was careful to get the shots into their bodies since a ricochet could hit the flame team. I put a flame into a tube, no messing around, to keep more from pouring out.

"Jesse, Hand, prepare to rotate," Brad said. "Hand, you'll take the tunnel; Jesse, tubes. Prepare to rotate . . . Rotate."

We flubbed it at first, Jesse turned left and I turned right. I quickly turned in a full spin on one heel, nearly lost my balance and was looking down the tunnel towards the cistern.

There was a wall of burning napalm that stopped about ten feet from the large, open doors. They were as high as the tunnel, arched like it, opened into the cistern. And behind the flame, circling the door on the floor, walls and ceiling, were more spiders than I ever wanted to see in my life. You could see the flickers of their eyes inside the cistern, climbing on webs, looking through the door, hungrily trying to reach the evil intruders that threatened their nest and their queen.

Jesse grabbed my arm and pulled me and we backed. I kept up a nearly continuous flame. Fortunately, the short bursts I'd been using before hadn't used up much of my fuel.

"Jesse," I said, taking a hand off to key the radio. "How's your fuel?"

"Feeling awful light," Jesse said. "But we're nearly there."

The spiders had moved forward, though. And we were passing more tubes. I turned and squirted a jet into one. It was still burning from Jesse's shot but better safe than sorry.

The wall of flame and smoke was the only thing holding the spiders back from our team, though. When it burned out, when we ran out of fuel, it was going to get ugly.

And I didn't have a pistol to save the last round.

"We're nearly to the van," Jesse said. "Last tube is on your left."

"Still holding them," I said, backing.

"We're to the van," Jesse said.

The spiders had advanced as the tunnel cleared of fire. They didn't like the heat but they were bound and determined to get us.

"Everybody else is in the van," Brad radioed, calmly. The guy was infuriatingly calm at times like this. "Hand, keep up the flame and keep backing. Jesse, lead him to the van. Just get in the back, sit down and keep up the flame. When Hand's in, Jesse, get in next to him."

I let Jesse lead me back until my knees collided with the door frame. I sort of jumped up and into the van, sitting down. I was still playing the rapidly dwindling flamethrower back and forth.

"Roy, hold onto Jesse and Hand—tight! Phil, you ready?"

"Ready," Phil said.

They weren't in the flame suits, could talk and had been planning something.

"Louis, get ready to step on it. Roy, do *not* let them fall out of the back of the van."

"Got it," Roy said, nervously.

I could feel his trembling hand holding onto my tank. Not the most reassuring thing in the world. I knew his hands were wet with sweat.

"I'm getting low," I said. You burn through an amazing amount of napalm with these things.

"Throw it, Phil," Brad said. "Stop flaming. Louis, get us the hell out of here."

As the van pulled out, Roy yanked us both back into the van as something flew past our heads.

The next thing I knew I was on my back, halfway into the team van, and the doors were shut.

"Doors shut," Roy called.

"Punch it, Louis," Brad called.

We were flying down the tunnel, bouncing over the occasional rubble.

"Can I ask what 'it' was?" Jesse asked.

"Thirty pounds of white phosphorus and thermite and a brick of C4," Phil radioed, then cackled madly. "Thirty-second delay. Assuming all the fire doesn't set it off."

I sat up and looked through the back windows. There was very little light but it was clear the spiders were following us. You could barely see them in the light from the van's taillights and the remaining flickers of flame. They were coming on but we were outrunning them. I'd hate to think what it would have been like to try to outrun them on foot. Probably like those poor bums.

Then there was plenty of light. Too much. It looked like God had sent down a God strike, like a flaming angel's sword from heaven.

I put my arm over my face to shield it from the blazing white light.

"That right there is a bee-yootiful sight," Phil said.

"Uh, Apache," Jesse radioed in a formal voice. "We are feet wet."

Feet wet was the call sign in Vietnam that an aircraft, like search and rescue or a Navy fighter-bomber, had left potentially hostile airspace and was out of danger.

I looked down at the smoking ejector of my flamethrower.

The van's floor carpet was melted in a six-inch circle around it.

Feet wet.

"There is no way we can survive penetrating directly into the cistern," Brad said, pointing out the cistern on the map. It was laid out on a table in the "crisis management" tent set up by city engineering.

The city engineer had been briefed in when the MCB realized it was that serious. So had the fire chief. They were still grappling with Portland being overrun with giant spiders but trying manfully to ignore it. Shaw told me, later, that the fire chief had pulled her aside and tried to get her to admit this was all some sort of cockamamie drill. She'd taken him down to the bum encampment, shown him some of the spider silk and asked him where she could get some more.

"Well, we can't just blow it up," the city engineer said. "It's nearly a football field in length and width. That would make one hell of a big cavern in the city. And there are houses on it."

"We can evacuate them if we have to," Special Agent Elbert Mathis said. "We *will* have to. Shaw, get Portland PD on that if you will."

"Got it," Shaw said, making a note. "Buildup of potentially toxic gases detected by city engineering in an abandoned cistern? Possibility of explosion. Some fires have already occurred. Probably nothing but we're evacuating you for your own safety."

The spiders had broken off pursuit after Phil's little present. But that didn't mean they were done. I was of the opinion all those homes should have been evacuated two days ago. The spiders were going to be looking for new victims soon.

"You bucking for a promotion to MCB?" I asked, grinning.

"Bite your tongue," she said. "No offense, Special Agent."

"MCB is the worst job in the government," Mathis said. "Probably the worst in the world. And when you get briefed in on everything? You never get another wink of sleep and realize that, yeah, it's one of the most important in the world. The shit that's out there makes this look like *Disneyland*. Not getting the job done? So if not into the cistern . . . what?"

"We're going to have to drive them out," Brad said. "Set up a trap in the tunnel and drive them all into it."

"Got a ton of pesticide around?" Jesse said, then looked at the scale of the map. "Twenty tons?"

"This is bad enough I'm thinking of calling for a ton of VX gas," Mathis said.

"Not in my county," Shaw said.

"Spiders don't react to standard pesticides," I said. "They're fairly resistant to organo-phosphates, period. So VX would hurt us more than them. They'd die, don't get me wrong, but they're more resistant."

"You know this how?" Mathis asked.

"I'm a fund of sometimes useful knowledge," I said. "Fire chief?"

"Yes, sir?" the chief said. He was still sort of boggling.

"Know if there's an *ethanol* plant in town?" I asked. "Or a transfer station? Somewhere we can get a tanker car full of ethanol?"

"You planning on getting ripped, Chad?" Shaw asked.

"After the day I've had?" I said. "What spiders don't like is any form of alcohol. Anything with an OOH chain, chemically.

Methanol or isopropyl would work but they're also poisonous to humans. Ethanol is but to a much lesser degree. If there's somewhere we can pump ethanol into the cistern, that will drive them out or kill them. And if there are any surviving b . . . transients they might survive. Not that I'd want to after a Sassus bite. But that's a possibility."

"There's an ethanol plant over on 148th Avenue," the fire chief said. Anything as flammable and potentially dangerous as ethanol, a fire chief would know where it was made and stored.

"There's a water test pipe," the city engineer said. "Somewhere. Has to be with a cistern . . ." He flipped through the sheets. They were really old diagrams. Thank God for bureaucrats who were pack rats for information. "There. But that's . . ." He pulled out another map and considered the two. "I think it's buried in some homeowner's backyard. Somewhere."

The cistern had once been in open country. Then Portland had expanded.

"Get a metal detector," Mathis said. "Find it."

"But if you drive them out, you still have to kill them," the fire chief said.

"Obviously," Brad said.

"How?" the chief asked.

"We've got an M2 fifty-caliber machine gun, two hundred claymores, three hundred pounds of C4 and more ammo than an army division in the U-Haul," I said.

"I really want in your U-Haul," Shaw said.

"Glad to give you a personal guided tour," I said. "Very personal."

"What I thought," the chief said, ignoring the byplay. "You realize that ethanol is flammable."

"I've set enough curtains on fire pretending to be a dragon," Jesse said. "Yeah."

"And in a confined space it will, let me make this very clear, *explode*," the chief said.

"The force of such an explosion is a function of the amount of accelerant and the area of confinement," Phil said. "I'll calculate the maximum amount of ethanol to pump in to prevent structural collapse."

"You can do that?" the chief said.

"I can do that," Phil said.

"He can do that," Brad added. "The question is if it's enough to get the spiders out."

"They really don't like ethanol," I said. "It's like tear gas for them. Fucks up their book lungs."

"You probably rock at Trivial Pursuit, don't you?" Shaw said.

"Not the only place I rock, honey."

"Would you two get a room?" Louis asked.

"Call me 'honey' again and it'll be the morgue," Shaw said.

"Chief, if you would arrange for the tanker of ethanol," Brad said, still looking at the maps. "Engineer, find the inlet pipe or whatever. Shaw, FBI, if you would coordinate on clearing all the potentially affected neighborhoods. Despite my assurance and Phil's, these structures are old and creaky. So, yes, we might just end up with the Portland Crater. That's a chance we're going to have to take. I'll point out that my team is going to be right in the center of it and just as likely to be buried. We'd appreciate a rescue plan being in place. One that assumes all the spiders are terminated.

"While those arrangements are being made, we're going back in. We'll recon to see if the spiders have cleared and start setting up an ambush. That will take time during which you have to get your end ready. We'll pay for the ethanol. Someone else, probably fire personnel, will have to do the pumping. You probably want to have the actual ethanol tanker and whoever is going to be using it beyond the edge of the cistern."

Those were the most words in one breath I'd ever heard Brad say.

"That sounds like a plan," Mathis said. "A risky one but the best we're going to get."

"The 'underground toxic chemical buildup' is ethanol," I added. "Due to a rare form of yeast that has been breeding in the old cistern. That will explain any smell. Might want to keep the ethanol sign off the truck when you bring it in. If it all goes to hell and we get buried, you can tearfully talk about a specialty company that was brought in to handle the hazardous emergency and lost their lives when the ethanol detonated while being cleared."

"I'll get started on the press release immediately," Mathis said. "Just in case."

"Just hoping is more like," I said, grinning.

"We got gear to move," Brad said, straightening up.

"Why?" I asked. "Let's just back the U-Haul down. We can even set up the Ma Deuce in the back and use it for cover."

"And I have to go clear neighborhoods," Shaw said, sniffling theatrically. "I wanna shoot the Ma Deuce!"

"Maybe later," I said. "But you gotta be *really* nice to me... honey."

We backed the U-Haul down. It was tighter than the van, but it fit.

Louis was in the back manning the Ma Deuce. Why Louis? We drew straws and he won, lucky bastard. Roy was the assistant gunner, feeding ammo. Why Roy? Nobody trusted him anywhere else. Phil and Brad were in the back working on gear as we rolled. Jesse drove.

Aware that the small tubes on the walls of the maintenance tunnel could be used by the spiders, I'd drawn the really short straw and was up on top of the cab of the truck, prone, Uzi in hand and back in armor, watching for infiltrators. So far so good.

We were finally back to the tube I'd crawled through. It was about two hundred yards from the bend. Far enough back to set in a serious mechanical ambush.

That was the technical term for what we were planning. Most of the firepower was going to be mines and explosives, thus the "mechanical."

We started at the far end of the ambush, backing the truck down to save on walking and as a means of rapid exit if necessary. Jesse moved to the front, by the driver's door, to keep an eye on infiltrators from that direction. Louis, Roy and Brad, most of the time, were in the back watching the main avenue of approach.

That left Phil and me laying in most of the explosives. Which suited me just fine.

I'd been trained in laying in claymores in the Marines. The main difference was those were assumed to be blown by an individual Marine infantryman using a clacker. What?

Ahem.

The M18A1 is a directional antipersonnel (or anti-spider in this case) mine. In form it is a small, green, curved plastic box with four folding spikes on the bottom, two on either side, for feet, a "knife" sight on top along with two "detonator wells" with screw-in detonator points and a notice on the front, molded into the plastic, that says "Front Towards Enemy"—spiders in this case.

Inside the mine there is, from back to front, the exterior plastic box wall, a thin metal plate, a slightly thicker layer of explosive, then 750 ball bearings about the size of a .25 caliber round, then the front of the box.

It comes packed in a green cloth bag with a strap, twelve to a case. In the bag is a reel of heavy copper insulated wire—very useful for repairing electrical systems at home, by the way—attached to a detonator (safety tip: you want to detach that if you're going to use it for home electric repair). There's a rubber doohickey—also something to remove for home electric but not a safety tip—with two prongs extending in a rubber cover. This is designed to connect to the M57 firing device or, in the parlance, "clacker." The M57 firing device is a small box, sized to fit in the average hand, with a spring lever on top, some lights (won't get into those) and a metal doohickey that's the "safety."

To use it, normally, you go to where you want to set it up, unfold the feet, press them into the ground, sight it using the stupid and useless sight, connect the detonator by unscrewing one of the two plastic plugs, slipping the wire into the slot on the side of the plug, pulling the detonator back until it is snug, screwing it back in, unreeling the wire back to your hole then connecting the M57 firing device with metal wire safety doodad firmly in place.

To detonate, remove metal wire safety doodad, hold it with your fingers underneath and your palm on the lever and depress the lever. Three times is what you have to do to pass the test you get repeatedly as a Marine infantryman.

That's about the only step that didn't change in my truncated Marine career. They were constantly changing how you were supposed to lay the damned thing in.

That is the basic "This is what we teach you grunts" way to lay in a claymore. We were not using that way.

The only thing I was doing was laying in claymores. All the rest of the shit was staying in the bags. And mostly I wasn't even unfolding the feet. I was using bricks to prop them up slightly to point at the overhead. That way, when they detonated, the metal plates would be less likely to come flying back and hit us. The ball bearings were going to ricochet all over this tunnel. With all the claymores we were laying in, anything in the tunnel was going to get shredded.

Where we had something solid to brace them on, I was putting them facing forward down the tunnel. And some of the ones pointing up were pointed at the walls. We knew the Sassus were going to come pouring down on every surface.

We just didn't know how many we were going to face.

In the meantime, Phil was laying in a daisy chain.

In my unnecessarily long description above, I mentioned two detonator plugs. And there's this thing called "detonation cord."

Det cord is made by, somehow, filling a long, thin tube of plastic with pure RDX. I don't know how they do it but I'm pretty sure that magic is involved. Fortunately, I've never gotten called in when the magic goes awry at an explosives plant. That would suck.

Bottom line, when you detonate the RDX, the cord blows up all along its length. Sort of explosive... cord. Or detonation cord. You get the picture.

What Phil was doing was coming along behind me, connecting det cord and detonators to the claymores. He'd run a line of det cord, with a detonator on the end, into the detonator well on one side of the claymore, then det cord back out. The second one didn't need a detonator. It was going to blow up. That line would be connected to another claymore and so on and so forth. He even had places where the det cord crossed over and was tied, to make sure that the explosion would, in the parlance, "propagate." Once the first explosion went off, all the claymores, occasional not-quite-random bits of C4 and det cord *were* going to blow up. Once it started.

Once we laid out every claymore we had, although not all the C4 since we wanted to survive the encounter, and they were all daisy-chained together, Phil had me go back to the van, which was now parked a hundred meters behind the last claymore, and he set up the detonation circuit. We'd really prepared for that. We'd gotten several hundred yards of conduit and while I was laying out claymores, Brad had "wire-fished" it in two separate sections with, in one section, det cord and, in the other section, a pretty standard household electric wire. The conduit had been laid down on both sides of the tunnel at the base of the wall, right up against the wall, and staked down at intervals with big staples—another one of my jobs and, let me tell you, hammering in metal staples to cobblestones is not a treat.

When all was said and done, Phil carefully connected the det cord on one side and the wire on the other to separate detonators. He left the wire detonator for last because that was the most unstable. The conduit led to within a few feet of the pile of C4 that would be the "initiator."

"As long as both lines don't get cut, we're golden," Phil said, prophetically.

"What happens if they both get cut?" Roy asked.

"We're fucked," Louis said curtly, still peering over the sight of the M2.

"We'll handle it," Brad said. "We're still going to have enough firepower to kill a dragon. Now, let's get it all out of the truck."

There was a lot. We'd all brought, if not everything in our personal arsenal, then most. It's easier to change weapons than magazines if you're in a fixed position. We'd even gotten some sandbags and set them up as mini-bunkers. We were set.

The last thing we unloaded was the Ma Deuce. We had to break it down and we didn't want to do that until we were fully set. It was sort of like a security blanket. We were all nervous as hell and, with the exception of Roy, trying not to show it.

"Are we sure it's going to stop the shelob?" Roy asked as he was unloading .50 ammo. "Shouldn't we have the flamethrowers, just in case?"

"That's a lot of C4," Phil said. "It'll stop an elephant. And if we use the flamethrowers, the fire will burn the connections and the trap won't blow."

"But what if..." Roy said.

"Roy," I finally said. "Will you just shut your yob? Please? We all know the risks. We all know what can go wrong. Better than you. We can get killed by one of the claymore plates. We can get killed by ricochets. We can get killed by one or our grenades going off on our vest. We can get wrapped up and turned into spider Kool-Aid. There's a thousand ways to die in this business, none of them good. If you weren't up for that, you shouldn't have raised your hand."

"Roy, if you're not up for this, you can go," Brad said, placidly. "No problem, no issues. No hard feelings even. But decide. And if you're staying then, yeah, shut your yob. You're not helping."

Roy shut his yob, for a while at least.

"So what's the PUFF on a shelob, anyway?" Phil asked.

"Based on fang length," Brad said. "Minimum I've ever seen was two-fifty. And that was for a baby."

"Two hundred and fifty dollars? For a spider queen?"

"Two hundred and fifty *thousand*, Roy."

"Quarter mil," Phil said in a satisfied tone.

"Ooooh."

Finally we were done getting everything in place.

"Hand, take the truck back," Brad said. He could tell I was on my last nerve with Roy. "Get a hardline. No radios from now on. It can set off the electrical circuit. Drive it out, walk back."

We weren't going to leave the truck there. It still had about two hundred and ninety pounds of C4 in the back.

"What about the flamethrowers?" I asked.

"Leave one," Brad said, shrugging. "No silver suits, though. And make sure it's full and replace the pressure tank."

The napalm was driven out under pressure by a nitrogen pressure tank. Nitrogen was a nonflammable, mostly inert gas.

We prepped the flamethrower and I drove the truck back out. I was in for a long walk in the spider-haunted darkness. Wasn't looking forward to that.

"We're going to need a phone," I said when I found the city engineer. "How's it going up here?"

"We're still getting people out of their houses," he said. "We've got phones that will reach. You'll have to carry a long wire spool."

"Yep," I said.

"I'll get somebody on it."

Lieutenant Shaw was out managing the clearance of the innocents. Which really sucked. I'd have liked to have, you know, said hello and good-bye sort of thing.

When the phone and wire turned up, I headed back into the spider-haunted darkness.

The spiders were coming off the ceiling in a shit-brown waterfall.

The ethanol had worked. Too well.

We were overrun. MCB was going to have to handle this. Portland was going to be overrun. The mechanical ambush had failed.

Maybe.

Military explosives are very stable. You can set them on fire. You can stomp them, knock them and shoot them. Even det cord is surprisingly stable.

Generally. Mostly. In the main.

Detonators, not so much. Detonators ride on the knife edge between "a bit unstable" and "stable enough." Every explosive expert knows to be careful with detonators.

Hit one with a .50 caliber round and it's going to blow up. Take the claymore with it? Maybe. And then the daisy chain would start and that led all the way to the C4 the shelob was still occupying.

The problem being a detonator is a little tube of metal about the length of a woman's pinky and the thickness of a pencil. One of those gimmicky narrow pencils. And the nearest one was nearly a hundred yards away. Even for a Marine, this was going to be a tough shot, with spiders already on our position and fangs inches from my body.

It's one of those times when the words "Don't panic" go through your head. You have to do a series of steps very carefully and very quickly or you're going to die. Take a prone position. Get a good butt-to-cheek-to-shoulder weld. Place finger on trigger. Let breath settle. Take careful aim. Adjust for distance. No wind in a tunnel. Ignore the screams as Roy turns and runs, dropping his shotgun, the fucking coward. Ignore the legs of the spiders in the way, they don't matter. Focus on the target. Will the round to...

The sear let go without me even thinking about it. Then the world fell in.

I'd known it was going to be a big boom. It was like a string of God's own firecrackers. In the enclosed space it was positively painful. All the spiders on the ceiling and bulkheads, even the ones that were past the last claymore, fell off. The compression wave stunned most of them, even the ones that got to our position.

I didn't notice. I was back on my feet in an instant, laying in with my Uzi. I could not reload fast enough. There was smoke and dust everywhere. The tunnel had partially collapsed to the right of our position. Freaking spiders were still twitching in every direction.

I laid in with .45, standard hollow-point expanding rounds—full-auto as I'd been taught—when the ambush triggered and the air was filled with dust, mag empty, reload without thinking, thousands of hours of practice making the moves fluid.

The last spiders were down. The wave was gone. My smoking Uzi was out of rounds and I was out of mags in my pouches.

I drew my 1911 and walked over to one of the spasming monstrosities. It was on its back and thrashing its horrible legs.

I pumped a full magazine into it and reloaded. It was still quivering, the fucker. I was pretty sure it was dead. Not sure enough. I shot it twice more.

"Shit!" I screamed, holstering the .45 with shaking hands. "Shit, shit, shit..."

"Anybody hit?" Brad called. "Anybody hurt?"

"Jesse's down!" Phil screamed.

One of the last spiders had gotten a bite in up and under his body armor. Right in the abdomen.

"Oh, fuck no," I said, slumping to the floor. My friend, my best friend, was shivering as the poison worked through his veins.

"Ch... Cha..." he said, trying to reach for me.

"I know, buddy," I knew what he was asking. We all knew the deal with spider bites.

I thought about the kappa. Too far, and they were bone doctors. Joan the Sasquatch. But I knew the truth. There was no mystical cure. There was no miracle this time. Doctors would try, so hard, to save him. The miracles of modern medicine would keep him alive in screaming agony for days, weeks, maybe a month. With the hit where it was, more like weeks. And that would be all she wrote. Weeks of agony for nothing.

I pulled Jesse's head and shoulders onto my lap and drew my .45.

"It's the most beautiful place you can imagine, buddy," I said, tears making it hard to see. "*So* green. Every day is stalking that perfect buck. That one you know is too wily to catch. And right at dusk, when you've finally given up, he walks into your sights... You can go hunting with your dad again. He'll like that. It's *so* much better than this hellhole..."

And I blew my best friend's head off.

Nothing says "I love you" like double-aught to the face.

As I laid Jesse down on the floor, the smoke was starting to clear.

The tunnel was littered with bits and pieces of spider bodies. Sections had partially collapsed. Every claymore and bit of C4 had detonated.

The shelob trap, though, had detonated behind the massive arachnid. And the shelob, leaking fluids from every side, most of its legs blown off, peppered by claymore pellets, blind from having its eyes blown out, was still crawling down the tunnel.

"What does it take to *kill* that thing?" Phil asked, stunned.

"Hand, ammo for the fifty," Brad said.

I didn't hear him. I just stood up and started striding down the corridor towards the shelob.

"Ah, hell," Louis said. "Target's kind of blocked."

"Let him get his mad out," Brad said. "Phil, provide him some cover fire. Some of them are bound to still be alive."

I didn't hear any of it. I didn't hear the order. I couldn't have heard the explosion again. I couldn't see or think. My world was red rage.

When I was halfway to the wounded shelob, Mo No Ken came whispering out of the sheath. And I started running.

"ASSSSSSEI!"

The main neural junction on a spider is on the forepart of its abdomen. That is the "sweet spot" for killing a spider. The head just has sensory and food organs on it. And the fangs, of course. No real brain per se.

I knew that. I didn't care. I was going to get to the central neural processor by blending the head into the floor of the tunnel.

At the first slash of the blade, the shelob reared up, trying to bite. First one fang, then the other hit the floor. The poison sack burst down my blade as I stabbed upwards. I slashed across and the head was cut in half. The shelob writhed in agony, trying to back up, trying to escape the pain.

I cut and cut in a fury that was primal. This thing had killed my friend. The shelob might not have touched him but it was her fault. She was going to pay. She was going to die in pain.

I cut until Mo No Ken was starting to, unbelievably, blunt. And I kept cutting. I literally cut myself halfway through a shelob. I chopped that bitch to pieces. I was covered in spider ichor. I was standing in spider guts.

None of it brought Jesse back.

Brad finally came up behind me and gently put his hands on

me as I was futilely swinging Mo No Ken, trying to get some of the spider ichor and guts and whatever the hell else off the blade.

"Chad," Brad said. "We've got stuff to do. We need you back here."

"Roger, sir," I said, automatically.

"I sent Louis back for the truck," he said. "We need to break down the fifty and start preparing to pull out the gear for clearance and cleanup."

"Aye, aye, sir," I said, turning away from the shelob.

"Let me take the sword," Brad said.

"Sir..."

"Chad," Brad said, placing his hand gently on the hand that still held Mo No Ken. "I've been around katanas for years. I'll clean it. You go break down the fifty, Marine."

"Aye, aye, sir," I said, releasing Sword of Mourning.

Mo No Ken. Sword of Mourning. The irony burned like the enzymes splattered on my face.

Louis had found Roy halfway back to the surface, sitting against the wall with his chrome-plated .45 in hand, sobbing. Louis had carefully led him back to the surface, then gotten the truck.

Phil and I had everything ready to pack up by the time he got there. Including Jesse. We'd brought body bags just in case.

Brad made me wash some of the goo off. The enzymes from the burst poison sack really did burn. We had a cream for that. We packed up. I rode out in the back of the truck, door up, with my buddy.

Clearing the shelob carcass was a pain. Clearing all the carcasses was a pain. MCB finally allowed a handful of firefighters to get read in. They came in with hooks and pulled out the carcasses. We provided security. It took a tow truck to pull out the shelob and the body kept falling apart.

One hundred and eighty-three Sassus males. Maybe some more up in the tubes we never recovered. One mature Sassus female. The PUFF for our five-man team cleared three-quarters of a million dollars. And, yes, Roy got part of that as his severance bonus.

Still didn't bring Jesse back. His mom had already lost her husband. Now we were going to send his remains home in an urn with some bullshit cover story and a check.

Didn't seem fair.

There were only three of us left to clear the cistern. We went back in with air packs sans silver suits and with flamethrowers. We fired them up at the bend, just in case. Then got blown on our ass when the ethanol exploded in the most gentle explosion of all time. No injuries. Jesse would have laughed his ass off. None of us laughed.

All of the spiders had been in the assault. We found not one in the cistern. Nor did we find any survivors. Lots of web. Big pile of bodies, not only human. Rat, dog, cat, even a few deer and rabbits.

I didn't find that out then. Found it out later. Didn't really care, then. No human survivors. Jesse's still dead. What'd you say again? I was thinking about something else.

The Doctors Nelson showed up at some point, having cut their vacation short. They shouldn't have. We had this.

They should have. They needed to. We didn't have this, it had us. We were all shell-shocked. Not just about Jesse. Even tough, stoic Brad was in a daze. We were working on muscle memory and could barely form a coherent sentence. And it was just us three left. But we had this. We'd hold the line or die trying. We hold the line! *Hold this line*, Marine! Stand your ground! Not one step back, Marine! Do you understand me? Chad! Chad! You there, Chad?

What do you mean, we already won?

We were all still in the spider-haunted darkness.

The Nelsons took over working with MCB and the locals. Amazingly enough, Special Agent Mathis was not being a prick when we came out of the tunnels. He could see the horror in our eyes. He also knew we were both necessary and crunch toast. So he called MHI and they called the Nelsons and the Nelsons got on a chartered jet, courtesy of MHI, and flew back in champagne class.

Even they couldn't get through to us. We didn't have to worry about nightmares for the rest of our lives. We had an abundance. We were walking in them.

It was two and a half days after Jesse died when I woke up in a woman's boudoir.

It wasn't the first time in my life I'd woken up in a woman's bedroom by any stretch. And what with some occasional overindulgences in the demon drink, it wasn't even the first time I'd woken up in one not remembering how I got there. But it was the first time after an op. And I was still covered in dried spider goop, which was messing up the sheets.

I looked around trying to ascertain some clue about where I was, how I'd gotten there. There was a picture on the bedside table. A tall man was standing next to a redheaded girl of about nine at a guess. She was holding up a salmon and grinning ear to ear. The man was holding a rod and also grinning.

"My dad," Lieutenant Shaw said from the doorway.

"Looks like you had a better relationship with him than I did with mine. Mine never took me fishing. He did take me to a strip club when I was about that age. He used me as a prop to pick up a stripper."

"Yours still alive?" Shaw asked. "That was the summer I was ten. The following fall he was coming home late from work one night and a junkie killed him for five dollars."

"I'm sorry. Back story of why you're such a dedicated policewoman explained. Mind if I use your shower?"

"Please," she said. "That spider crap's starting to rot. It's going to be hell to get the smell out of the bed."

She climbed into the shower while I was soaping my hair.

"I have shampoo, you know."

She really did have a spectacular body.

"Marine habit," I said, rinsing out the soap. "Saves time and effort."

"You do my back, I'll do yours," she said.

"Why? I'm good with any answer including sympathy."

"That," she said, "and I don't know a better way to help with mourning. And . . . I don't have any relationships 'cause I don't want them. Workaholic. Relationships get in the way. So having somebody on the side who feels the same way is doable."

"Well, I'm all about doable."

"And you promised to let me play with your Barrett," she said.

"If you play your cards right."

And that's the last of the Seattle stories. It's not that there weren't other hunts or other stories. I was in Seattle for five months after the Portland Shelob. But it was the last spectacular or unusual or important one.

So now on to the assignment that put the Portland Shelob in perspective.

One last note. I later had to leave Seattle courtesy of Cheyenne, the trailer park elf girl. Long story for the next memoir. But shortly before that little issue came up, I was in Saury, per usual. I filled out my form and handed it to the server. A new guy.

"You want California roll?" he asked in broken Engrish. "We got riff avocado!"

For all the good I have done in my life as a Hunter, I still feel deep and abiding guilt for two things: I infected Seattle with California rolls and ValSpeak and that bitch later met a down-and-out guitar player called Kurt who'd spent months living in the company of gnolls.

Remember my comment "Smells like teen urine"? The record company balked at the word "urine."

Yeah. I'm ultimately responsible for Grunge. I sincerely apologize.